Best Tales of Texas Ghosts

Docia Schultz Williams

REPUBLIC OF TEXAS PRESS
Lanham • Boulder • New York • Toronto • Oxford

Library of Congress Cataloging-in-Publication Data

Williams, Docia Schultz.
    Best tales of Texas ghosts / Docia Schultz Williams.
        p. cm.
    Includes index.
    ISBN 1-55622-569-5 (pbk.)
    1. Ghosts—Texas. I. Title.
    BF1472.U6W552   1998   98-13263
    133.1'09764—dc21   CIP

Published by Republic of Texas Press
An imprint of The Rowman & Littlefield Publishing Group, Inc.
4501 Forbes Boulevard, Suite 200
Lanham, MD 20706

Distributed by NATIONAL BOOK NETWORK

ISBN 1-55622-569-5

Contents

Dedication

This book is dedicated with love and gratitude to my husband, Roy Williams. His support and assistance has been invaluable.

Acknowledgments

Many people have contributed to my efforts in recording Texas' ghost stories over the course of the last six years. I am grateful to all these people who have shared their personal experiences with me. Each story is special to me and has its own unique message, which I have tried to convey to my readers.

I am especially indebted to Sam Nesmith and Robert Theige, both gifted psychics, who have never turned me down when I have called upon them for assistance. They have shared their insight with me as I have delved into the realms of the supernatural, trying to find reasons for certain occurrences when none seem to exist.

My "Spirits of San Antonio" tours, which have attracted a loyal following of dedicated participants (many people have gone on the tour over and over again!), would not have been possible without the cooperation of Marcia Larsen at the Alamo Street Dinner Theatre, Ernesto Malacara at the Menger Hotel, and homeowners Victor and Diane Smilgin at the Terrell Castle Bed and Breakfast Inn.

To my editors, Mary Elizabeth Sue Goldman and Dianne Stultz, and to publicist Ginnie Bivona, all of Republic of Texas Press, whose confidence in me has never wavered, what else can I say but "thank you."

Most of all, I must thank my husband, Roy Williams, who has accompanied me all over the state as I have searched for stories and interviewed people and who took many of the photographs which appear with the stories. He spent countless hours at the computer, correcting and perfecting my manuscripts. Without his invaluable assistance, there would have been no books! Thank you, Roy.

GHOSTS
Docia Williams

Ghosts fly high ... and ghosts fly low ...
Where they come from we don't know ...
Ghost take off in roaring flight,
Most often in the dead of night.
They're often felt in spots of cold,
You feel their presence, we've been told.
Some are large, and some are small,
Some, merely shadows on the wall.
Some are friendly, some are bad ...
Some are playful, others sad.
They're often heard, on creaking floors,
Opening windows, slamming doors!
Wails and moans they sometimes make,
Making us poor mortals quake!
They like all kinds of dreary places,
Houses, churches, and open spaces ....
Sometimes they dwell in mist and fog,
They're heard, we're told, in howls of dogs ....
Some, balls of fire seen in the night,
All in black, or dressed in white;
Some show a glimpse of shadowy faces,
Then, they're gone. They leave no traces
To ever let us mortals know
Where they come from ... or where they go ....

Introduction

This book is the result of the bringing together of the best stories from the four books I have written in the past five years, plus a section of selected stories from Central and Northeast Texas that form the nucleus for a book that is yet to be completed! I have found that "ghostwriting" is like that! There is always one more good story to track down, research, and report. It is a never ending challenge that is both time consuming and fascinating. With such a hobby, life is never boring!

For now, within this book you will find some of the best stories from our spirit-filled state of Texas. I hope you will enjoy reading them as much as I have enjoyed assembling the collection.

Whether or not one believes in ghosts or spirits (they are really one and the same whatever nomenclature is used), their stories are interesting, even if taken with a grain of salt by the nonbeliever. However, I have to say, after studying the subject of ghosts and hauntings for a number of years, personally witnessing numerous supernatural manifestations, and interviewing literally hundreds of intelligent, well-educated people who have shared their experiences with me, I have concluded that without a shadow of a doubt, there are things happening all around us that can only be labeled as "supernatural." These strange, unexplained things have led me on a quest to gather stories from people all over the state, and in so doing, my own beliefs, beginning with an experience I had as a young woman living in a haunted manor house in England, have strengthened a hundred fold.

Ghosts, which are the spirits, or souls, of people who have passed on but are either earth-bound because they cannot move on towards the Light, or who simply remain on this side of eternity out of personal choice, are what this book is all about. What these entities can do, and where they can appear, is amazing! The energy they generate can turn lights on and off at will, open and close windows and doors, turn television sets and radios on and off, cause curtains to flutter and unoccupied rocking chairs to go into motion! Their footsteps can often be heard on stairways and hardwood floors. While sometimes they are only heard, often they can be seen as well. Some appear as shadowy, misty apparitions. Others are so powerful they can manifest into forms that look as human as you and I.

These spirits can inhabit public buildings, old hotels and inns, restaurants, schools, university dormitories, theatres, and churches. In the course of my searches I found them on windswept Texas coastal beaches and on the dusty high plains of far West Texas. They are with us, all around and about us. Because we are still alive and not of their dimension, we can only speculate about why they are at these places and why they do what they do. That is what makes the unknown realms of those who seem to exist in limbo, neither in life nor quite yet in death, so fascinating.

Whatever your personal beliefs, I believe you will find these stories provocative and intriguing. I have not recorded them with the object in mind of converting my readers into "believers." I am only a storyteller, a chronicler of experiences related to me by those who have lived them. My intention is to enlighten and, hopefully, to entertain.

Many writers over the years have sought to explain the phenomena of hauntings. Back in 1778 the great English writer Samuel Johnson penned these words: "It is undecided whether or not there has ever been an instance of the spirit appearing after death. All argument is against it, but all belief is for it."

Personally, I believe it.

Section I

Dallas to East Texas

The Land Where the Tall Pines Sway

This section takes us on a ghostly tour of Northeast Texas, with its beginnings in the metropolis of Dallas, then moving eastward and southward, taking in that part of the state that is the most like the Deep South associated with *Gone With the Wind*. Steeped in tradition, the old plantations of East Texas thrived when Cotton was King. It was a rich and prosperous era, at least for the plantation owners, when gracious hospitality was the common denominator of every estate. There, tree-shaded avenues led to stately old mansions often built by slave labor prior to the Civil War.

Then, there are the swamps and bayous and the forests green with stately pines and hardwood trees. The forest floors are carpeted with needles from the tall giants that still are a source of Texas timber, and wild orchids and ferns nestle in the shady undergrowth. Every March, wood violets sprout along woodland streams, and the forests are etched with the lacy accents of the pristine white dogwood blossoms that come as spring's first harbingers. The wisteria vines, heavy with purple grape-like clusters of blossoms lend their heady fragrance to the air as they wind about the trees and trellises on every estate. It's a beautiful land, green and fertile and rich in its traditions, close in family ties.

And, I have discovered, it's a haunting land, too. Spirits of long departed souls return to old towns, old plantations, and old hotels. They were not ready to leave when they were called on to enter into eternity, and many of them keep returning to their old haunts in this lovely land of the whispering pines.

1

FROM THE WHISPERING PINES
Docia Schultz Williams

When the swaying pine trees whisper
 And the night birds rest from flight
The moonlight shines like silver
 In the darkening of the night;
That's when a footstep echoes
 As the night grows deathly still,
And a cozy living chamber
 Turns cold; a sudden chill...
Then you know those souls are wandering
 In the place they once called home
Back to familiar places, where
 They feel compelled to roam.
If you stop and listen closely,
 As the breezes softly sigh;
You might hear the plaintive echo
 Of a lost soul's mournful cry.
They come to old plantations
 And to tiny towns as well.
Their spirits often linger,
 Where, alive, they used to dwell
You'll find them in East Texas
 There, where the pine trees sway,
They're the wandering, lonely spirits
 That are there, content to stay.

Dallas County Hosts a Plethora of Spirits

Sometimes one hears a little here, a little there, but never quite enough to substantiate a story. It's always just a "hearsay" situation, and many of Dallas' stories are like this. They almost fall into the category of being legends. They've been around a long time and are most often repeated each year when Halloween rolls around, just to tantalize and fascinate the younger generation by adding a special "treat" to their night of trick-or-treating. Several of these little tales have been told in more than one version, which definitely leaves one to speculate if there is anything to them, other than they just might be the product of some lively imaginations. At any rate, I would like to share some of these mini-ghost tales with you!

For instance, they say over in Pleasant Valley Cemetery at Cedar Hill, there's a Ghost Mountain. The story goes that a group of teenagers, seven in all, once visited the cemetery just for a lark. There they disturbed some devil-worshipers, who put a curse on them for invading their privacy. The teens left the cemetery, but the car in which they were riding collided with another vehicle, and four of the teens were killed. Their spirits are said to still haunt the place.

In Oak Lawn, an area where I once lived as a child, there's the oft-told tale of a young man who caught his sweetheart with another young man. He was so distraught he hung himself in his apartment. He's said to still come back to his old neighborhood, where he visits the bars and nightclubs, orders drinks, and visits with people as he goes about searching for his long lost love.

There are two stories about the same place, which makes one doubt whether either one of them is true. Since they have both been around a long time, I will certainly let you be the judge, to believe them, or not. The first version goes this way: Back in the 1950s, gangs from two rival high schools used to meet at an old abandoned wooden bridge that spanned the Trinity River. This was supposed to be somewhere on the Arlington-Bedford Road. One night the usual playful taunting between the rival groups suddenly became heated. Ugly dares were shouted back and forth across the river. Finally they decided a football star from each school would start driving toward one another on the bridge, a version of the "chicken game" some of the dumber kids used to play. This was considered a real proof of manhood. As the rival cars approached one another, the weight was said to have been too much for the rickety old bridge, and it collapsed. Today, they say fishermen out on that part of the river late at night hear the dying screams of the boys.

That story was bad enough. Now here's the other version. This story concerns four Arlington high school girls who were killed when their car ran off a bridge spanning the Trinity on the Arlington-Bedford Road. People driving in that area at night say they can still see the headlights of the car shining as it plunges into the river. And, they say the screams of the four dying girls are often heard in that vicinity.

Both versions of this story state that the bridge is known as "The Screaming Bridge."

Since the 1980s, the story has been told about a condominium on University Boulevard in University Park, where two sisters once lived. Evidently their spirits come back to chase off any tenants they don't like. They also flash lights on and off and cause all sorts of mischief, according to Arthur Ingels, a Dallas psychic and ordained minister, who was quoted in the *Dallas Times Herald*, October 29, 1987 edition.

The Dallas Magazine, October 1987 edition, also had a lot of good little fright tales. It made mention, for instance, of the "Doll House," a place in the wealthy Bluffview area. The house is always dark at night except for just one light in an upstairs window. Sometimes it's said you can see a little blonde-haired doll swinging slowly, hanged by its neck with a noose. The story is that a little girl who lived there was brutally killed by an intruder, and her poor mother, who has grieved continuously, was almost driven out of her mind. The poor woman is said to come back now, and on certain nights she hangs her little daughter's favorite doll in the window.

Gear Park, in the University Park neighborhood, is said to be haunted by two ghosts. These are the spirits of teenaged sweethearts who met on the banks of the little pond in the park one evening. The next morning they were found, drowned, their hands still tightly clasped together. Some people think they may have made some sort of love pact because their parents did not approve of their romance. They decided they would rather die together than live apart. They say, at night, if you sit very quietly, the girl's voice is still heard to whisper, "I'll love you, forever."

Some people claim to have seen the phantom crew of the ill-fated Delta Flight 191, which crashed back in the early eighties. The crew is seen on an Airtrans car, and they all wear their Delta uniforms. They circle around and around the airport as if they are looking for something. Could this ghostly crew be searching for their plane?

Everybody knows they stage great rodeos over in the community of Mesquite. But have you ever heard of Hotshot, the great outlaw Brahman bull? Seems nobody could ride this animal, but one night one cowboy finally did, staying on for the full twenty-second count. Humiliated because he couldn't throw the young man, old Hotshot crashed out of the gates and disappeared into the night. They say that the cowboy who rode him for the countdown was found trampled to death in the front yard of his home the next morning. And to this day, many a bull rider will say they've been awakened in the middle of the night by a strange sound—the sound of a bull-like snort, followed by a pawing sound on the ground, and then the hoofbeats, as the strange phantom bull runs off into the darkness!

In the community of Carrollton, there's a story that has been around a long time. It concerns a strange new family that moved into the town sometime around the turn of the century when Carrollton was still a small town. They were a very serious family, and the children never laughed or played with the neighbor children. Then, one day the whole family just disappeared and was never seen in those parts again. Months later a peddler came into town. He was white as a sheet and badly shaken. He said he was walking on the north side of Carollton when he heard a little child crying. When he turned around suddenly three children appeared to him. But as soon as he started walking towards them, the trio disappeared! It is said that people claim to this day, when they are walking in that area around dusk, they can hear children, who aren't there, crying out in the fading twilight.

Snuffer's Bar and Grill on Lower Greenville Avenue was the site of a speakeasy during the Prohibition area. Employees at the popular grill think the spirits of some of the inhabitants from that era still hang around. An unidentified ghost has been seen by guests and employees in the restaurant. Workers say they are often the objects of pranks played by the unseen spirit or spirits. Long after customers have left their tables, cigarettes move from one ashtray to another, doors unexpectedly swing open and shut, and on at least one occasion it's said that red, glowing eyes peered out from under table number seven!

Then there is the tale that's been around a while that ought to make all teenagers stay home at night! It's said a boy and his girlfriend were parked around Trinity River Basin when they heard on the car radio that a dangerous criminal had escaped from the jail. The description of the fugitive included the fact he had a silver hook in place of his left hand, and he was described as extremely dangerous. The young couple decided they'd better call it a night and so they left their trysting place. The boy drove his girlfriend home. Once there, he walked around to open the car door for her, and to his astonishment, there, shining in the moonlight, was a silver hook dangling from the door handle! I'm sure the couple had sweet dreams that night!

The Ghostly Dallas Doctor

This interesting story came to me by way of my Forth Worth friend Terry Smith. He and Mark Jean have an unusual hobby. They call themselves "Ghost Stalkers," which is different from "Ghost Busters." They have, with permission and varying degrees of success, probed a lot of the poltergeist stories in Tarrant County and throughout the state of Texas. Terry heard about my writing and has had me as his guest on his public television network show, on which he talks with writers and reviews their books.

A number of stories that were featured in my book *Phantoms of the Plains* were gained through leads given to me by Terry. And the story about a former osteopathic hospital at the corner of Colorado Boulevard and Hampton Road in Dallas is one of Terry's favorites. A man who was a medic at the now-closed hospital recalled that the nurses there talked a lot about a ghost who stalked the second floor. It was supposed to be the specter of a physician at the hospital who had committed suicide.

The medic said he saw the ghost one night during the summer of 1983. He had been called out on a routine call with several other E.M.S. technicians. They arrived at a scene of a self-inflicted shooting. A man had shot himself in the cheek with a small handgun. The bullet had exited around the right crown at the back of his head, removing a large portion of the back of the man's skull. The man appeared dead except for "antagonal reflexes," and once they transported him to the hospital, he was placed on a mechanized respirator called a "thumper." After several minutes on the machine the physician on duty told the medic to "call the time," which meant he was to pronounce the man dead.

A little later the medic went to the break room upstairs, where he drank a coke. Jo Ann, one of the nurses, came in, saying she had seen the ghost-doctor. The medic turned and looked through the glass window of the break room, and he saw a doctor with a stethoscope around his neck. He was wearing a white physician's coat and was walking from the ICU unit, accompanying a man. He had his arm around the man's shoulders, as if he were trying to console him. The startled medic recognized the man with the phantom doctor as the suicide case they had just pronounced dead a few minutes before!

The medic, who couldn't quite believe what he was seeing, came out of the break room and followed the two figures towards a doorway leading to a stairwell. They were too wide to make it through the doorway walking side-by-side, yet somehow they just passed through and then turned to go up the stairwell.

Later on the medic and nurses and others who had seen the ghostly doctor realized there was a connection between the phantom-physician and the newly dead patient. Both men had been distraught over family and money problems. Both had shot themselves in the head, with handguns, in their offices. They were kindred spirits, no doubt!

Spirits at Olla Podrida

Back in the 1970s when I frequently visited my late parents, who lived in Garland, one of the favorite "to do" things we enjoyed together were little excursions over to Olla Podrida, in nearby Dallas. This quaint, folksy, mini-mall was made up of a labyrinth of up-scale, unusual boutiques, gift shops, ethnic shops of all kinds, and a few interesting eating-places. There you were sure to find the unusual, and it was seldom that we came home empty-handed. I recall especially a little Egyptian shop that was run by two gentlemen from the land of the pyramids and the Sphinx. They had such a fascinating collection of scarabs, burial beads, unusual scents, and incense from that faraway land! My parents were especially taken with them and always dropped into their shop for a visit.

I was saddened to learn the little mall had closed. This took place, I believe, in July of 1996. It had been in operation about twenty-four years.

Knowing my fondness for the place and my interest in ghosts, a friend in Garland, Sue Watkins, sent me an article from the July 15, 1996 edition of the *Dallas Morning News*. It was written by columnist Larry Powell, who said that Olla Podrida was the home of several supernatural residents, and some of the shopkeepers had become sufficiently attached to them that they hated to go off and leave them when the mall closed.

Roger and Vickie Francis, who operated a candles and carvings shop called the "Front Porch," had several experiences with the Olla Podrida ghosts. They consisted of a trio of ladies, one man, and one small child. They used to walk through the mall, occasionally passing the candle shop. The three ladies wore old-fashioned clothing, very much like those worn in the late 1800s; long skirts, white shirtwaist blouses, and they wore their hair piled high on their heads. The distinguishing quality about the male ghost was he was a cigar smoker. Although some of the shopkeepers at Olla Podrida saw the man, Vickie never did, but she frequently smelled his cigar smoke. It was a strong scent, which only lasted a minute and then totally disappeared. Unlike real cigar smoke, nothing was ever seen, but the smell was unmistakable!

The little child ghost, who was mischievous, was often blamed for alarms going off in the shops that were closed up even though no prowlers were about. Also, merchandise was said to fly around some of the shops, and tools were often misplaced.

One of the female ghosts was credited with turning the water on in the ladies' restroom and politely opening the door for women entering the powder room.

According to the Francis couple, the ghosts all looked like real people. They weren't shadowy or transparent as some spirits are known to be. These entities passed by the shops, and when shopkeepers dashed out to see them better they always managed to do a disappearing act!

On October 29, 1987, an article ran in the now defunct *Dallas Times Herald*. This article mentioned the old Gaslight Playhouse in the Olla Podrida Center and told about the ghost there. It is a different spirit from the strollers seen by the shopkeepers. Numerous actors attested to having seen a sad-looking woman in a black dress, who sat in the back row of the theatre. Anytime she was approached, she disappeared. There were also frequent noises and unexplained drafts and cold spots.

Robin McGee, a former actor at the Gaslight, kept a record of the spirit's appearances. He said she was dressed in late nineteenth-century style of clothing.

There were also stories about strange, unexplained lights in the popular playhouse. An actress saw a white haze hanging over the empty seats in the theatre. The owner, Joe Andaloro, and a bartender had just closed the place up and turned out all of the lights when a bright, blinding blue light lit up the hallway. It was very intense and was accompanied by a high-pitched ringing in their ears. They got out of there fast and were never able to explain the strange blue light!

The most generally accepted reason for the Olla Podrida area, located on Coit Road, just north of Forest Lane, for being haunted, lies in the frequently told story that the small mall was built atop a long forgotten pioneer cemetery. Then, other people brought forth the theory that the little mall was made up of all sorts of antique wooden parts, and perhaps the spirits had arrived with the woodwork!

Whatever the reason, the area was haunted at one time. Whether the spirits are still hanging around the now boarded-up area, or have taken up their residence elsewhere, is anybody's guess!

The Haunted Mansion

Every year, around Halloween time, newspapers print ghost stories to work up a few goose bumps among their readers. The *Dallas Morning News* ran one such story on October 31, 1982, which was of special interest to me. This was because I recall having seen the house when I was a young woman living in Garland, a suburb of Dallas. I also recall recognizing the woman who was the real subject of the story.

While I did not know Bert DeWinter personally, I knew who she was. She was one of Dallas' most fashionably dressed ladies in a city where women were known for being well dressed. When I was in college I was often in the original downtown Dallas Neiman Marcus. There I attended "walking classes," conducted by the store's staff of glamorous high-fashion models. We were taught to walk, pivot, pose, and otherwise show off the clothes we might be called upon to model. Those in the class who "walked" well and were considered attractive enough, were singled out to model in Neiman's fashion shows and to serve on their prestigious college board. This was back in the late forties and early fifties. I learned to model at Neimans and subsequently was selected to appear in a number of their back-to-college fashion shows. From this training, plus a degree in merchandising, I enjoyed a career in modeling, commentating, and fashion coordinating that lasted for many years!

At Neiman-Marcus, the millinery department was presided over by the immaculately coifed and exquisitely attired Mrs. Bert DeWinter. Today most department stores scarcely have a millinery department at all, but in those days, beautiful hats were a must for every well-dressed woman, and Mrs. DeWinter knew just what to select for every woman who came into her boutique!

All of the young ladies in the walking classes knew who Bert DeWinter was, and we were all in awe of her. And, we always wondered why she worked. Everybody knew she was very wealthy. She lived in a gorgeous big brick house with a beautiful flower garden out on Amherst in the prestigious University Park section of Dallas. She was often featured in the society section of the newspapers as having entertained the rich and famous who visited Dallas and often found their way to the doors of the elegant fourteen-room DeWinter mansion. Why, even the Duke and Duchess of Windsor had enjoyed the famous DeWinter hospitality. The fashionable milliner was known to be a generous and lavish hostess, and her invitations were coveted. In fact, Laura Goldman, the arbiter of couture at Neiman's when Mrs. DeWinter was director of the millinery department, said DeWinter lived extravagantly. She had the best of everything and did everything with great flare and perfect taste. In fact, Goldman described DeWinter's lifestyle as resembling that of a princess! She also added that she was the most chic woman she had ever known. Mrs. Goldman was an elegant lady in her own right, so this was high praise, indeed.

In 1973 Don and Dian Malouf moved into Mrs. DeWinter's former home. This was a year after the fashionable Mrs. DeWinter passed away. From what Dian Malouf told me, Mrs. DeWinter had

The former DeWinter Home

not had a long illness. She died in the hospital after a short stay, and it was rumored she may have been given the wrong medication which precipitated her demise. Malouf added, in view of what later happened, she certainly believed that Mrs. DeWinter had not been ready to go.

It wasn't long before Malouf, a prominent tax attorney, and his wife were to realize that their new family home was occupied by an unseen presence. From the offset, they believed the spirit was Bert DeWinter.

DeWinter loved the home she lived in and decorated so lavishly. Many of her antique pieces were left in the house when the Maloufs purchased it. It had stood vacant for over a year after her death, and according to Mrs. Malouf it was in pretty run-down condition. Dian Malouf, a professional photographer, writer, and jewelry designer, said the house required a lot of restoration, and she made numerous changes to the place as well. For instance, she said she had to use a pick-ax to dig up the black slate floor in the room that DeWinter had called her "Peppermint Twist Lounge." This room had been decorated with red and white striped chintz wall covering to resemble the lounge with the same name in New York City.

As the Maloufs went about restoring and remodeling the house, they became more and more cognizant of something, like a strong presence, being there with them. The whole house took to creaking loudly, and in the middle of the night they often heard footsteps crossing back and forth across the dining room floor. The sounds were like the flip! flop! flip! flop! noise of an open-heeled mule or house-slipper, as the steps crossed back and forth over the hardwood floor. A recent telephone conversation with Dian Malouf revealed that soon after she began to hear the footsteps in her dining room she went on a trip to New York City. During her visit she had lunch with a woman who had been a friend of Bert DeWinter. When Dian told her luncheon companion about the flip-flop sounds she had heard, the woman replied, "Why, that has to be Bert!" She went on to explain that Mrs. DeWinter always wore mules, or "springala-tors," as the heeless shoes then in fashion were called. Dian said the cold chills ran up her spine at that revelation.

Malouf said from the first week the family moved in, the curtains in the master bedroom would often stand straight out, and their four children often screamed and cried in their rooms, which were similarly affected. Mrs. Malouf said they were all just terrified. They knew the spirit was Mrs. DeWinter and that she probably wouldn't or couldn't harm them, but it was upsetting nevertheless.

These strange nocturnal disturbances continued for the better part of a year. The Malouf family finally became more or less accustomed to them. The whole time they lived there, Mrs. Malouf said, she was convinced that even though she was only there in spirit form, Mrs. DeWinter still wanted to be "in charge" of things. While setting the table for a formal dinner party, Ms. Malouf actually saw a manifestation of Mrs. DeWinter. She was swathed in a French Porthault sheet (the most costly kind!). She was not wearing a hat, which rather surprised Mrs. Malouf. After all, Bert DeWinter had modeled and sold hats for over thirty years!

Dian Malouf said that whenever she was getting ready for a special dinner party she always felt the presence of the former mistress of the house. Although she never felt any particular hostility, she always sensed that whatever she did just did not measure up to the elegant Mrs. DeWinter's standards.

The house, with its imported Italian marble fireplace and walls covered in pink damasks and silks, was long a gathering place for international society leaders. While it was a beautiful house, the Maloufs never felt like it was their home. It seemed like it still belonged to Bert DeWinter! Blake Malouf, the Malouf's oldest child, was ten years old when they moved into the house. She said she never liked it. In fact, the youngster was quoted in the *Dallas Morning News* as having said she hated it from the onset because it didn't seem like a home, but more like a museum. She added it was more "her" house than "our" house. Things of DeWinter's kept turning up quite mysteriously, as well. It was as if she was leaving little messages around. One evening during a black tie dinner dance at the house a guest of the Maloufs noticed a piece of jewelry just lying out on a table and commented about it to Dian Malouf. She told him that pieces of Bert's jewelry showed up all the time, most often at odd times, in odd places.

Tiring of their spirit-filled life in the house, the Maloufs finally consulted a professor of history at Southern Methodist University who was a former Jesuit priest. They wanted to know what they might do to get the spirit to move on. He suggested an exorcism. They were afraid this might anger or harm the spirit, and so they didn't take his advice. However, a friend had told them about an old folk ritual that just might work and advised them to go home and try it that very night. There was a thunderstorm going on outside that night. All the lights went out in the house. They decided this was as good a time as any to see if they could get Mrs. DeWinter's spirit to move on. They lit a twelve-candle candelabra that was made of wrought iron and had little angels in the design. While the candles flickered, they sprinkled salt in every corner of every room in the house. For whatever reason, the footsteps and other manifestations just gradually faded away after that night!

The Haunted House on Prairie Avenue

Leo Furrh, a Dallas air-conditioning service man, no longer owns the old gray house on Prairie Avenue in Dallas, which is the subject of this story. He had such great plans for the place when he bought it! In fact, he'd planned to convert the sizable dwelling into a duplex, where he would live on one side and rent the other for additional income. Unfortunately, his plans never quite materialized.

As soon as Furrh bought the house and began to remodel and renovate it, strange things started to happen. Once, when his son Neil was on the outside of the house standing on a ladder, he glanced into a window. There was a face looking out at him! He thought at first it was one of his family members; then, remembering that none of them was around, he hastened inside the house and made a thorough search, upstairs and down, and found no one there at all.

Furrh's son-in-law, Winford Richardson, was with him once when both men heard someone running up the stairs. Then they heard a lot of footsteps walking back and forth upstairs and then onto the stairs, coming down again. When the spirit, or whatever it was, got to the bottom of the stairs it made a little jumping noise as if it had missed the bottom step. These sounds continued off and on for quite some time.

One night Richardson, who had begun to read books and articles about psychic phenomena, came to spend the night in the empty house with his father-in-law. Richardson brought a pistol along "just in case." That night both men heard somebody coming down the stairs, but a careful search revealed there was no one in the house with them.

Furrh said once, during another all night sleep-in at the unoccupied house, he woke up and plainly saw a dark-haired woman about thirty-five years old, just looking at him. She disappeared, then suddenly reappeared near the doorway a few minutes later!

A family finally moved into one side of the duplex after Furrh got the remodeling done. They didn't stay long! Their seventeen-year-old son saw the dark-haired woman. The family also heard mysterious footsteps and finally had double locks put on all the doors. They should have known that locks don't deter ghosts at all! The family, who was Hispanic and devoutly Catholic, made crosses and mounted them over all the doorways. And they kept the lights on twenty-four hours a day. Furrh said the electricity bill was horrendous! The tenant family finally tore away some of the wall paneling because they thought maybe someone had been murdered and then stuffed between the walls! Finally, this family moved out. They'd had enough.

Furrh said the man from whom he purchased the place never had mentioned it might be haunted, but when Furrh confronted him with what he had experienced, the man didn't seem at all surprised. Furrh is convinced the man knew all about the hauntings before he sold the house!

The White Rock Lady

When I was a youngster growing up in Garland back in the 1940s we used to hear a lot of "White Rock Lady" ghost stories. When we drove from Garland to Dallas we always passed a small portion of the lake that fronted on Garland Road, near the overflow spillway. It never looked particularly spooky to me, but I saw it mostly in daylight hours. The lake was a popular recreation spot for picnickers and for swimming parties. There was a lovely man-made beach, bathhouse, and grounds surrounding a roped-off swimming area in those days. Today the old bathhouse has been converted into a cultural center, and no swimming is allowed in the lake.

We had a lot of church and Camp Fire Girls' parties at the lake when I was of middle school age (except we didn't have a middle school in Garland back then; it was still a small town of around 2,500 people).

I recall how we'd sit around and listen to the older kids talking about the White Rock Lady ghost, and we'd all shiver in fright, at the same time wishing we COULD see her and yet terrified we WOULD! There are a number of versions to the story that has been around over fifty years to my certain knowledge. I think our mothers used to mention the possibility of her appearance should we venture too near the lake at night. The tree-shaded drive-outs were favorite parking places for teenaged couples to go "parking." I was pretty much of a bookworm in those days, and turned down what few opportunities arose to go roaming around the lake area at night with boys. So I never saw her. And I don't know anybody else who ever did. But there are all sorts of versions of the appearances of the White Rock ghost in my files. In every sense of the word, this is a Dallas legend.

In his book *Ghost Stories of Texas,* the late writer Ed Syers mentions "the Lady of the Lake." He quoted a Mark J. McCarthy of

Kermit who seemed to know all about the ghost. Back in the 1920s there was an excursion boat that operated on the placid lake. The flat-bottomed boat had a dance band, and refreshments were served. It was a favorite place to party on hot, humid summer nights. There was no air-conditioning in those days, so the cool breezes wafting across the lake must have afforded the partygoers a wonderful opportunity to cool off.

According to McCarthy, a Dallas couple went out on the boat to a special party. Everyone was dressed in formal attire. During the evening the couple argued, and the evening ended on a sour note. The young lady bounded off the boat as soon as it docked and jumped into her escort's big, powerful automobile and drove off. (The account I read didn't say if the couple was married or not.)

The young woman was obviously distraught. She may have been drinking as well. The twisting road around the lake was dark and narrow and not very well maintained back then. She supposedly lost control of the car as she approached the area where Lawther Drive runs into Garland Road, and the car plunged off the road into the deep waters of the lake. She died in the accident.

It is said that the spirit of the young lady returns to the scene of her death at certain times. She has manifested many times in many ways. Usually she appears as a hitchhiker; a pretty girl in a soaking wet white evening dress. When a sympathetic motorist stops to offer her a ride, she gets in the back seat and gives an address in an area which was one of Dallas' most prestigious neighborhoods back in the 1920s, out on Gaston Avenue. But soon she disappears, and the startled motorist is left with only a wet seat to attest to her having been in the car. Several people have said she leaves a wrap in the car that bears a 1920s era Neiman Marcus label!

Other people say she has gone to the front doors of some of the big houses that face the lake on Garland Road. She asks to use the telephone. Then she disappears. According to Syers' book, Mr. McCarthy had some friends who actually saw the apparition, but recognizing her as the phantom of the lake, they did not stop and offer her a ride.

According to *Dallas Morning News* columnist John Anders, who wrote a story in the October 27, 1995 edition of that paper, there's still another version of the story. Anders quoted the late Frank X. Tolbert, who was a longtime *News* columnist, as describing one of her appearances. The Tolbert version has a married couple driving around the lake late at night when they see a pale young woman in a long gown standing forlornly by the roadside. They stop to pick her up and notice she is soaking wet. She says she has gotten separated from her boyfriend and is looking for him. Shivering with cold, she gets in the back seat of the car and gives the couple a Gaston Avenue address. When they get there, they glance into the back seat and the young lady has totally vanished. But the seat is wet from her clothing! The story doesn't end there. The stunned couple goes to the door of the house and rings the doorbell. A man listens to their story and tells them that years ago, on that very date, his beautiful daughter, wearing a white evening gown, drowned in the lake. Every year on the anniversary of her death she appears and asks some motorist to drive her home.

White Rock Lake, Dallas

I read in Dennis William Hauck's book *The National Directory of Haunted Places*, that the ghost often has appeared to couples in their parked cars. He also noted that one man who lived near the lake, named Dale Berry, reported in September of 1962 that he answered his doorbell only to find no one there. On the third ring, when he again went to the door, he saw a screaming apparition, who promptly disappeared, leaving only a puddle of water on the porch.

On October 29, 1987, *Dallas Times Herald* columnist Lorraine Iannello wrote a special Halloween story about Dallas' most famous ghosts. She mentioned one Phyllis Thompson of Dallas, and her daughter, Sue Ann Ashman of Mesquite, as saying they had actually seen the White Rock Lady. But the ghost they saw was in the water! The mother and daughter were sitting on one of the boat docks at night when they saw something white floating towards them in the water.

Mrs. Thompson said she heard a blood-curdling scream, and at the same time whatever it was in the water rolled over on its back and stared at them with big, vacant, hollow sockets where the eyes should have been. Then the terrible thing just disappeared. I would imagine that Phyllis and Sue Ann did their own disappearing act from the dock soon after that episode!

I wonder. Have any of you readers ever seen her? Is she still out there, a poor lost soul wandering around the lake trying to find her way back home? Surely by now her parents are dead and gone. Maybe they've all become reunited in eternity, and there's no longer any need for her to come back and wander the dark roads around the lake. Let's hope so.

The Haunted Catfish Plantation

The small city of Waxahachie seems to have a lot of resident spirits, and the Catfish Plantation Restaurant at 814 Water Street has achieved fame not only for having the best Cajun cuisine west of Louisiana, and certainly the finest catfish to be found anywhere, but also for its trio of ghosts who have made the place their permanent address. The establishment even hands out special information brochures to their guests, telling all about their well-known spirits!

The owners, Tom and Melissa Baker, opened their business in 1984. The restaurant is situated in an old terra cotta painted Victorian house, complete with gingerbread trim and green and cream colored accents. The house, which is surrounded by a cream-colored picket fence, was built in 1895, so it is over a century old. It was the birthplace of the great professional baseball player Paul Richards.

Catfish Plantation, Waxahachie   (photo by Tom Baker)

Richards was a former manager of the Baltimore Orioles and Chicago White Sox and he played for the New York Yankees.

The attractive building that houses the restaurant fits right into the ambiance of Waxahachie, site of the largest number of historic registered homes in Texas. It is often referred to as the "Gingerbread Town."

The Bakers hadn't been in the business too long before they realized they just might have something strange going on in the building. The very first thing that happened to make them wonder was the morning that Melissa opened up to discover clean coffee cups were neatly stacked inside the huge tea urn, and it had been placed, for some mysterious reason, on the floor. Then a few weeks later, upon arriving, Melissa found a freshly brewed pot of coffee waiting to welcome her!

Then the employees started reporting all sorts of strange things happening to them. There were so many unusual occurrences in such rapid-fire order that the Bakers almost wondered what kind of weird employees they had hired to help run their business. The couple didn't really believe in ghosts and certainly had never had any prior experience with them, so they didn't recognize the strange happenings as being symptomatic of spirit occupation at first. These "symptoms" included: breaking glasses, toilets flushing when no one was around, toilet seats flying up by themselves, opening and closing of doors, doors locking and unlocking by themselves, the strong floral fragrance of roses, the stereo being turned on and off by itself at all hours, sudden strong breezes and wind felt throughout the house, the sound of a piano playing an unidentifiable melody, sudden cold spots felt all over the building, restaurant silverware and place mats, set the night before, all crumpled and jumbled up the next morning, nonworking clocks chiming nevertheless, knockings on the walls, flying coffee cups, dishes and pots flying around the kitchen, alarms going off for no apparent reason, floating dollar bills, sudden cold chills in the ladies' restroom, glowing blue lights seen through the windows at night, "possessed" wine glasses flying through the air, radio changing stations by itself, etc. If all that wasn't enough, one fry cook had to dodge pieces of cheese and bottles of chives as they were tossed about the kitchen by invisible hands. Another cook watched in astonishment while he was making French fries, as a fry basket rose up and floated in the air next to him.

Rane Burress, a former employee, said she is absolutely convinced the place is haunted. She used to open up in the morning and often found the silverware and place mats all jumbled on the table tops that the staff had very carefully set the night before just prior to closing up the restaurant. And once, when her husband, Sean, picked Rane and another waitress up after work, as they started to drive away, one of the women remarked that she thought she saw something in one of the bay windows. Sean stopped the car and backed up, got out and walked up the little path towards the porch. He had just walked a few feet when he saw it. There was the white, glowing figure of a woman floating about a foot off the ground. Rane said "There's no doubt that what we saw was not a living being. It's beyond explanation," she stated.

Catfish Plantation owner Melissa Baker

I usually ask people who think they may have a haunting to describe what has happened to leave this impression. Usually two or three of the symptoms are evidence that a haunting exists. But the Catfish Plantation has, as we say here in Texas, "the whole enchilada." There's absolutely no doubt the place is haunted!

At first, the Bakers tried to keep the mention of all these events under wraps. They were afraid it might be bad for business. But all the help was experiencing these things, too, and there was no way that the word would not get out that something was very strange over at the new restaurant. Finally, one morning in 1987 when Melissa was listening to a radio talk show on Dallas station KLIF, the discussion that particular day centered on supernatural happenings. Melissa called the talk show. A parapsychologist called into the show with a reply for her, and he suggested she have a professional come out and check out the place.

Two weeks later a parapsychologist named Dwanna Paul called the Bakers, and after asking what type of activity was going on, told Melissa that they had every symptom of a full-scale haunting. (Parapsychology is the study concerned with investigations of evidence of paranormal, or supernatural, phenomena.)

A date was set with the Bakers, and they had the restaurant tested at no charge, strictly for the research information obtained. The investigation took place after closing hours, and a whole crew of people came with sensitive sound equipment, laser light beams, thermometer gauges, infrared cameras, etc. Engineers, scientists, and psychics were in the group, along with photographers and two representatives from the University of Texas. The crew came for five different investigations, spending many hours going over the place, checking out every nook and cranny. Finally the psychics all agreed that the restaurant was inhabited by three spirits: two females and a male entity.

Later on, *D Magazine* wanted to do an investigation. This took place in August of 1988. Their psychics determined the spirits were probably all involved with the house at one time or another. One was identifiable as Elizabeth, a young woman who tragically died on her wedding day, strangled to death in the dining room of the house. This was around 1920. Psychics seem to think she was murdered by an ex-boyfriend, who crashed the wedding party. Then, there's Will, a Depression-era farmer, who mostly just sits by the fireplace and doesn't do much of anything. Caroline, or Carrie, who is the most active of the three, is a matronly type, according to all the psychics, who isn't very pleased with the presence of mortals living in her domain. It is she who is more than likely responsible for things being thrown about, or objects disappearing.

Melissa says the ghostly activity has calmed down a lot in recent years. The Bakers have talked to the ghosts and made them aware that they are known and accepted. They don't need to throw things and make noise anymore. It is almost as if they've more or less become friends with the mortal occupants of "their" house.

The Bakers have a guest book where they ask their patrons to jot down anything that might have happened that was "different" while they were dining at the Plantation. Some of these candid statements are included here:

One man wrote, "I have placed a two-dollar tip on the table and the bills rose, hovered, and then fell to the floor."

One guest stated, "I had a free dinner coupon folded in half. It was inside my shirt pocket. Suddenly the coupon flew from my pocket and landed on my left hand."

Another statement was, "While sitting and reading to my son about the ghosts, my purse turned upside down and dumped everything, even from the side pocket, too, on the floor."

One guest observed, "We had just sat down, when a spoon on the table just jumped sideways and hit against the wall."

One lady wrote, "The metal part of my sandal literally flipped apart. I felt a cold chill at the time of this experience."

"The coffee maker kept making coffee all evening by itself. It just wouldn't stop," was another observation.

A young woman penned, "I was sitting in Dining Room B when something reached up and grabbed my knee and snatched my napkin off my lap. I thought it was my father-in-law trying to spook me, but he had his hands on the table, holding his iced tea."

Another entry in the book reported "High singing sounds around the table several times. Lemon on plate flipped over. Page in book flipped. Ice cold air around. Chair moved away from the table."

According to a fine feature article that ran in the Sunday, October 30, 1994 edition of the *Dallas Morning News,* which was written by an acquaintance of mine, Michael Precker, one couple literally bolted from the restaurant, not even finishing their meal. This was when their baby's name suddenly materialized on the surface of a misted-over window. And another client was absolutely dumbfounded when his old driver's license, which he believed he had lost in Vietnam, materialized while he was dining in the restaurant!

At the time he wrote the article, Precker interviewed a well-known Dallas psychic, Bertie Catchings, who says spirits are just a part of life. She advises people that they should not be afraid. She says if you have a spirit in your home who isn't hurting anything, you should feel lucky. You should feel honored that an entity has chosen your home because it feels happy there. She also refutes the idea that spirits only hang around old, dreary, dismal, damp dwellings. Not so! If mortals wouldn't want to be in a depressing, dilapidated building, why should a ghost? And of course, the Catfish Plantation is not at all dilapidated. It is charmingly furnished in antiques and warm colors, a perfect background for delicious food and warm fellowship.

The famous restaurant has been featured in many newspaper and magazine articles, such as the *Fort Worth Star Telegram*, the *Dallas Morning News*, and *D Magazine*. Arthur Myer's fine book *A Ghosthunter's Guide to Haunted Parks, Churches, Historical Landmarks and Other Public Places* has a lengthy chapter devoted to the restaurant. Another book, *The National Directory of Haunted Places*, by Dennis Hauck also has a feature article about the Plantation.

The restaurant has also received publicity in *USA Today, Texas Monthly*, and *Southern Living*. In addition, they've been featured on CBS, NBC, and ABC affiliates, *Current Affair, Fox Network*, and *Telemundo*. Not only has their wonderful catfish made headlines, but the very existence of the ghosts that Tom and Melissa Baker tried to keep secret for a long time has brought them all sorts of business and publicity! Could it be that Elizabeth, Caroline, and Will are saying "thank you" for the tolerance and acceptance that the Bakers have shown them all these years? I think it just might be!

Rose of Sharon

When Sharon Shawn first saw the old house at 205 Bryson in Waxahachie, it was deserted and forlorn. Somehow she saw beyond the rundown facade to the heart which still beat within. She loved the house on sight, and her intuition coupled with her shrewd realtor's mind told her it was well built and could once more be the charming home it must have been when it was all shiny and new back in 1892.

The first owner, F.P. Powell, a lawyer, had the house built for his new bride. The couple had two daughters, both of whom were born in the house. They lived there until 1912 when the attorney was offered a job he couldn't turn down in Austin, and so the family moved away from Waxahachie, selling their beloved home.

After the departure of the Powell family, the stately old house had a succession of owners, none of whom took particularly good care of the place. The house had wrap-around porches, both upstairs and down, which formed shady recesses to rest and enjoy life away from the hot summer sunshine. Evidently one of the owners placed avarice ahead of aesthetics and sealed the porches in, making several little rooms out of each one. Thus the house was turned into an apartment house. Only a small portion of the porch was left at the front entry. It was in this state that Sharon first viewed the house. The front was partially covered with dead wisteria vines. It was truly a forlorn and neglected place. Still, for some reason she can't even yet explain, she wanted it. She had a builder come and inspect the foundation, and the verdict was the house was in sound condition. It just badly needed some cosmetic touches and tender loving care!

And so it was that Sharon Shawn purchased her "new" old home!

Right after she bought it, before any work had been done on the house, which she planned to restore to its 1892 appearance, Sharon went over to the house just before the workers set to their tasks. It was still all cut up into small apartments. Sharon walked through the large front parlor through a tiny little doorway into what was, and now once more is, the formal dining room. She left her purse, which was quite heavy, on the floor in the little doorway and proceeded to walk back into the rear portion of the house. As she walked, she tried to imagine all the things that had to be done to make it become what she wanted it to be. When she came to the room farthest back, she found the floor was strewn with stacks of old magazines and newspapers. She said she just flopped down on the floor and sat there, among all the bits and pieces, and started thumbing through some of the magazines that must have been there for years and years. She was fascinated with the fashions and articles and didn't realize how the time was passing. Finally, she realized she had been in the house much longer than she had planned to stay, and she retraced her way back to the spot where she had dropped her handbag on the floor. It was still there, but so was something else! About a foot or two from the purse lay a pair of fourteen carat gold hoop earrings, a pair she had especially loved and treasured, and had lost over a year before! She had searched high and low and had not found them, and now here, in a house she hadn't even owned a year ago, was her treasured pair of lost earrings! She said she was, and remains to this day, completely baffled by their sudden appearance in the old house she had just purchased.

As we talked about this, we discussed the reason for the appearance of the lost jewelry, and we agreed that the spirit of a former owner, probably Mrs. Powell, was glad someone who would love the house and take care of it again had purchased it. She produced the lost earrings as a way of welcoming Sharon to her old home, which was to be Sharon's new residence! Of course, we don't know how it happened, but then ghosts can do all sorts of things we don't always understand!

In 1991 Sharon decided to let other people enjoy the home she has so lovingly restored. She opened it as a bed and breakfast inn and calls it the "Rose of Sharon Inn." She has enjoyed having people from all over the country as her guests since that time, and they all have enjoyed her warm hospitality and bountiful country gourmet breakfasts!

There is one room that Sharon named after her granddaughter. She calls it Kathleen's Room. It is a large upstairs bedroom, which Sharon believes was once the master bedroom. Often when she enters the room she suddenly feels a presence, as if she isn't alone. It is not at all spooky or frightening. In fact, when I questioned her, Sharon said it remains very warm and welcoming. (Some rooms, when haunted, become extremely cold.) She has frequently glimpsed the shapes of a little family, transparent, yet visible, shades from the past. There is a man who wears a top hat, a woman wearing a long dress in the style of the late 1800s, and two little children who appear to be little girls. The children are the least visible because they always have their backs to Sharon, as they stand in front of their parents. She believes it is the Powell family, judging from the style of their dress, and she does know that they had two little girls. She believes they are well pleased with all the careful restorations that she has made to insure the home is as lovely as it was when first built.

Rose of Sharon Inn, Waxahachie

Sometimes the friendly innkeeper has heard music, too. She can't tell exactly where it comes from, but the sounds are of stringed instruments, violins more than likely, and the music sounds like waltz music. She also sometimes hears footsteps in empty hallways and on the stairs leading to the second floor, causing the old wood to creak, as old wood does. But never is Sharon afraid. She knows the little spirit family, which hasn't been seen now in a couple of years, was friendly and just happy for her to be in their old residence.

I was very pleased that Sharon was willing to share her experiences with me. She told me she hadn't told many people, because she was afraid they wouldn't believe her. I told her I had heard many stories, and many were much stranger than hers.

I asked Sharon about the Inn. She describes the Rose of Sharon as a cozy and homey place, filled with antiques and treasured mementos. She says some of her guests have likened it to going to "grandma's house" to visit! Sharon is a local guide in Waxahachie, too, so she can tell her guests all about the history of the charming small city at the same time she showers them with Southern hospitality and a bountiful breakfast! For reservations and information, call Sharon at (972) 938-8833.

The Ghost at the Bonny Nook Inn

Vaughn and Bonnie Franks are the proprietors of the Bonny Nook Inn, located at 414 West Main Street in Waxahachie. The gingerbread-trimmed Victorian house with its inviting guest rooms filled with antiques has an interesting history and a definite aura of mystery, which all add up to giving visitors to Waxahachie a comfortable, charming place to spend the night!

Bonny Nook Inn, Waxahachie

To begin with, Nathan Brown, a Waxahachie merchant, bought the lot on Main Street and two other lots for the sum of $1,000 in 1887 from the R.P. Sweatt family. Between the time he bought the land and 1894, he built a large Queen Anne Victorian house on the property. He later sold the house and lot to W.T. Hunt. Hunt kept it only a year, and then sold it to Dr. W.F. West around 1896. West moved into the house with his wife, Gertrude, their baby son, and Gertrude's spinster sister. Soon after the Wests settled into their new home, they built a new kitchen onto the house and equipped it with a new wood burning stove. This resulted in a terrible tragedy, for the new stove blew up, and so badly was Mrs. West injured that she died from her injuries.

Just a few months after his wife's tragic death, Dr. West married her sister, who had been residing with the couple. At first, being of a suspicious turn of mind, I thought, my! my! A freak accident with a new stove. A single sister living in the house with the couple. A romance going on between the doctor and the sister, and a need for removing the wife! And then, I decided I have been reading too many romance-mystery novels! The obvious reason in those "proper Victorian" days would have been, Dr. West, a respected physician, could not have coexisted in his home with a single young lady. And if he was of a practical turn of mind, he probably badly needed her help in rearing his motherless little son.

For whatever reason that Dr. West married his sister-in-law, they lived on in the house until 1914, when the residence was sold to Mary Wyatt. Mrs. Wyatt was the grandmother of Mrs. O.K. Smith. The house remained in the family for sixty-five years until Pete Smith sold the house in 1979. Finally, the Franks came into possession of the home in 1983, having decided they would buy it, restore it, and open it as a bed and breakfast inn.

My husband and I were warmly welcomed when we dropped in on a recent visit, and the Franks proudly showed us around the large house, which is beautifully furnished with period pieces, all done up in excellent taste, and of course, kept immaculately clean as well. Each of the bedrooms has a private bath, some with Jacuzzis! All of the rooms have names, from their own families, and one, the Murrow room, was named for family friend Stan Murrow.

The Franks told us the Murrow room was in deplorable shape when they bought the house. It had been abandoned because of a bad roof leak and the ceiling had collapsed in places. New beams had to be added and the ceiling put back to its original height. This room features a beautiful antique sleigh bed. For some reason, this is the room that seems to be haunted. A woman's presence has often been sensed here, and Bonnie believes it might be the spirit of Mrs. Gertrude West, who got to live for only a short time in her lovely home. If it is not Mrs. West, it could be any number of other former homeowners, since it is a very old house and has changed hands numerous times.

The spirit has appeared at the foot of the sleigh bed, checking on, and also frightening, numerous guests. One woman reported the wraith was clad in a long white gown. She has been known to shove suitcases off furniture, and she once turned a pet parakeet loose in the house! In 1996 something new started happening in the room. Whenever the room is unoccupied, a small skull appears on the headboard of the bed. It is white, and plainly visible. The Franks showed it to my husband and me.

Bonnie said a number of their guests, who have professed to be psychic, have told them that they have both seen and heard the spirit. They say she is benevolent and harmless, just a lonely little soul who can't quite give up her home.

Several guests did not mention anything about the ghost to the Franks, but they left little notes in the guest book saying they saw and heard some "strange things" during their stay at the inn.

Footsteps are often heard in the upstairs rooms when they are downstairs, and they know no one is upstairs. Various things seem to move around the house quite often as well. Bonnie told us the strange manifestations began in 1984 and continue to this day.

Frankly, I'd have to say that the Franks have created such a comfortable inn for their visitors, that any ghost would have to be reluctant to leave. This spirit probably knows a good thing when she sees it! The Inn is so beautifully and tastefully appointed that *Bon Appetite Magazine* named it one of the ten top bed and breakfast inns in the country! It has been featured in *Texas Highways Magazine* and *Forbes Magazine*. A full old-fashioned breakfast is a part of the stay at the Inn, and a well-stocked tea and coffee bar is available to guests at all times. If you are planning a visit to Waxahachie, a city noted for its gingerbread-trimmed Victorian homes, you might like to call the Franks for information and reservations. Call the hospitable hosts at (972) 928-7207.

The Rafael House

Ennis is a bustling small city of some 15,000 people located about thirty-five miles south of Dallas. The city was founded in 1872 as the northern terminus of the Houston and Texas Central Railway. It was named for the director of the railway, Cornelius Ennis. The first settlers who came there were largely Czechoslovakian families who had immigrated to Texas to get a fresh start. Local surnames, businesses, favorite foods, and seasonal festivals all reflect this ethnicity. Cotton fields surrounded the community, and the economy prospered from the very beginning.

There are many beautiful old homes in the city. One of the most elegant and charming is known as the Rafael House. Until recently it was a bed and breakfast inn. The former owners, Danna Cody Wolf and her husband Bryan Wolf, recently added a new baby to the family, and they have sold the large house to Harriett Adams, an interior designer from Dallas. Prior to the closure of the business, the inn was ranked among the top thirty bed and breakfast inns in the nation by the prestigious Innovations Bed and Breakfast Association in Cranford, New Jersey.

The Rafael House was the subject of a feature article in the February 1993 issue of *Texas Highways Magazine*. There is an interesting history along with a haunting bit of mystery attached to the old mansion. It seems some of its former occupants haven't been able to let go of the latchstring as yet!

The house, a spacious white frame neoclassic structure with pillared porches and a red brick foundation trim, is situated on a large shady lot at 500 West Ennis Street. Quite large, with over 5,200 square feet of living space, the house was built in 1905-06 by Edmond Rafael, who came to Ennis by way of Corsicana. After the Jewish businessman came to Ennis he met the daughter of a respected family of merchants, Fannie Jolesch. The Jolesch family had come to Ennis from Alsace-Lorraine, a section of France bordering on Germany, from where many early Texas settlers came. In fact, the town of Castroville west of San Antonio was founded by a whole colony of Alsatians led by Henri Castro in 1844.

Fannie Jolesch's father owned the most successful business in Ennis at that time, the Jolesch Dry Goods Store. It wasn't too long before the young couple married, and in fairly rapid succession they produced four children: Ernest, Raymond, Wilhelmina, and Allyne.

In 1903 Rafael bought the large town lot on West Ennis Street. He began construction of his house in 1905. The building project was completed in 1906, and the couple moved into their lovely new home. They were accompanied by Fannie's newly widowed mother, Julia Chaska Jolesch, who had helped the young couple finance the building of their home. Unfortunately, she didn't get to enjoy the new house for long, as she died there in 1907. Soon after her death, the couple welcomed one more child into the family circle. They named little Julia Chaska Rafael in honor of her late maternal grandmother.

The Rafael House, Ennis

The Rafaels were one of the few Jewish families in Ennis. Since there was no synagogue in the town, they had to drive, by carriage, to Corsicana or some other city to attend services. When Julia was but a small girl, about seven or eight years old, she recalled being the target of taunts by anti-Semitic hecklers. They threw tomatoes at the Rafael's carriage and yelled oaths at the Jewish family. This made a great impression on the little girl who always felt she was "different." And later on, she stated that right then and there she had decided she would do whatever she wanted to do, and she wouldn't care what anybody in that little town thought of her. Apparently that was exactly her attitude for the rest of her life!

Because Julia was the youngest child she was spoiled by her siblings and her parents. She also was not as highly intelligent as her sisters and brothers, and recognizing this, her parents felt that she might meet some man as she grew up who would take advantage of her lack of business acumen. Therefore, Edmond and Fannie made what in this day and age would be considered an outlandish request of their youngest daughter. They stipulated that upon their deaths Julia was to inherit everything they had. This was to include the house and its contents, stocks and bonds, real estate, and whatever cash they might have at the time of their deaths. But there was one condition. Julia was never to marry. If she did, the inheritance was to be divided among her siblings. This wasn't as strange as one might think. It was a fairly common practice in those days to appoint a sort of guardian-caretaker to aging parents and their property, and usually the task was assigned to the youngest child. Danna told me it was her understanding that the Rafaels didn't particularly want any of their children to marry. They were very strict adherents to the Jewish faith, and there were so few Jews in that part of the state they were afraid that one of their children might stray and marry outside the faith.

When Edmond Rafael died in 1927 he left a little book of instructions for Julia. He told her how to handle her financial affairs, including instructions to save all receipts and never throw anything away. Danna said at the time she bought the house there were receipts for every newspaper bill ever paid, every check Julia had written since 1927, all the old utility bills, grocery store receipts, and even sacks and sacks of old Wonder bread wrappers cluttering up the house. Danna had to work through all these things before she could start living in the house. Julia had certainly taken Edmond's instructions literally!

Fannie Rafael survived her husband by about twenty years. She shared the house with Julia and her brother Ernest, who at that time had not married. According to Danna, Julia's two brothers had very different personalities and interests. Raymond, who never married, became a successful banker in Dallas. He still made frequent trips back to Ennis to help look after his mother and sisters. When something needed repairing in the house he saw that it was fixed, and he took great pride in the garden, which was quite lovely in its heyday. Ernest, a geologist, looked after the family's financial affairs since neither Julia nor Fannie had much of a head for business. When Edmond Rafael died he left a lot of unpaid debts, and Ernest, who was the oldest of the children, paid them all.

After Fannie died, Ernest married, late in life, in 1953. He brought his wife, Polly, to live in the house with him and Julia. Danna told me that Julia and Ernest had always played a lot of bridge and were formidable partners. Evidently Julia became very jealous of Polly, who soon became Ernest's regular bridge partner. When Ernest suffered a heart attack and passed away in 1957, Julia promptly evicted Polly from her house!

As soon as Polly, a prim and proper widow, packed up and departed, Julia invited her boyfriend, Jamie Haynes, a man at least ten years younger than she was, to move in with her! Can you imagine what a flutter that must have caused in the conservative little community of Ennis? Here was a spinster, fifty years old, from one of the most influential families in town, a pillar of the community, living in SIN with her much younger lover! Julia could not marry Jamie because she would have to forfeit all of her property. And so it was that the couple lived happily, albeit sinfully, together for about sixteen years until Jamie died in 1973. Julia was so grief stricken by the loss of her companion that for more than a year she drove over thirty miles to Kaufman every single day to visit his grave.

By then Julia was sixty-six years old. She was not in good health. Always a large-framed woman, she had become extremely obese. In fact, she was unable to negotiate the stairs to her upstairs bedroom, and the last year she occupied her house she slept in the library, which she had converted to sleeping quarters. There was no full bathroom downstairs, so she resorted to sponge baths in the downstairs half bath. The poor woman weighed over four hundred pounds and, unable to tend to personal hygiene, was not the most pleasant of companions. Even her most faithful bridge playing friends quit coming around, and her hairdresser even gave up on making house calls to shampoo and style Julia's hair. She finally had to move into a nursing home, not because she was all that ill, but because she needed help to tend to her personal needs, somebody to lift and place her in a bathtub, someone to help her dress, etc. She also seemed to like to have people waiting on her. It is said she still occasionally drove her car on shopping trips to Dallas, so she was apparently not really sick.

However, the woman, who made no effort to lose weight, decided not to move back into her house. It was closed up and left just as it was the day she walked out to go into the nursing care center. For the first seven years she was in the care center she didn't let anyone go near her house. Donna Kucholtz, who resided in Ennis during the time Miss Rafael was in the nursing home, recalls the house well. She said it was slowly deteriorating, as houses do when they are long neglected. Some of the police officers who checked the place from time to time told Donna that dust was all over the furniture and cobwebs hung festooned on the walls and in the doorways, giving the appearance of a macabre movie set to the deserted house. Everything had been left exactly as it was when Julia left. Even her breakfast dishes were still on the table!

Later on, Julia allowed an old friend of hers, a man named Roger Haynes (he was not related to Jamie), to go and look after the place. She trusted him, and he did not let her down. But Haynes died in 1983, and by then Julia was about out of cash and decided to sell the house she had treasured so long. The aging spinster had refused to sell any of the furnishings although she had many offers.

Finally, the place was put up for sale, and some of her siblings and their offspring showed it to prospective buyers. At this time much of the furniture was sold, and some had apparently been stolen. It was evident that long neglect had taken its toll on the once proud mansion.

Danna Cody was an Ennis girl who had gone away to college and had then taken up residence in Austin where she was pursuing a career as a buyer in a department store. She came home for a visit, and she and her mother decided to go see the old Rafael house, which was up for sale. The two women just went out of curiosity, but Danna fell in love with the place immediately. She could see beyond the chipped paint and fading carpets to what could be done. She thought the place would make the perfect bed and breakfast inn. Finally, after doing some research and deciding she was up to doing all the work that had to be done, the young woman decided to buy the house. She spent months scrubbing, sorting, cleaning, and restoring. Contractors had to be called in to redo the electric wiring and the plumbing. Lots of time and money had to be spent in reviving the tired old mansion. There were books, linens, dishes, and boxes and boxes of receipts and all the other things Julia never threw away. All of this had to be sorted out. Some of the Rafael furniture was still in the house. Danna was able to track down other pieces that had been sold, and she was able to buy them back. The pieces were all turn of the century, and made in America, which was considered prestigious at that time. Most of the bedroom furnishings, several chairs, a china cabinet, and a buffet all found their way back into the house. Danna used impeccable taste in bringing life back into the old building, and numerous people in Ennis got behind her efforts to restore the house. Some of them even gave her family heirloom furniture, dishes, and linens, to help lend the proper period look to the place. Estate sales netted such treasures as an 1863 John Broadwood and Sons rosewood baby grand piano, which Danna placed in the wide front entry hall.

Soon after Danna purchased the house, Julia Rafael passed away. Some members of the Rafael family tried to tell Danna the house was haunted, but Danna didn't believe in ghosts, and if she had, she really didn't care. She wanted the house badly enough that she said if she had to put up with a few ghosts it really wouldn't matter to her.

I first learned about the hauntings by reading an article by *Dallas Morning News* writer Steve Blow, which ran on October 31, 1993 (what better time than Halloween?) after he and his wife visited the inn. It seems the first "ghost incident" occurred on an afternoon when a thunderstorm was approaching and Danna attempted to close an upstairs window that had been left open to air out the room. The difficult window is located in Raymond Rafael's old bedroom. After straining to close the window, which absolutely would not budge, and fearful of the damage the oncoming storm might do to the interior, Danna laughingly said, "Ok, Raymond, won't you cooperate and help me close this window?" To her absolute amazement, the window came down with just a gentle pull with one hand!

Then another time, a contractor working in the house had a window that had been stuck suddenly slam down right beside where he stood. And Rosemary Garcia, a housekeeper, said when she made the beds, as soon as she got them made, something or somebody sat down on them, leaving a definite imprint on the coverlets. There were also the sounds of footsteps going back and forth, back and forth, in the upstairs area. Although these rooms were all carpeted, the sounds that were heard were footfalls on bare hardwood floors. Although Danna was puzzled by all of this, she never once was frightened.

Danna thinks that Raymond was the "original" ghost in the house. She mentioned that when she bought the house she had all the old flowerbeds dug up and the old plants discarded. The grounds and flowerbeds were in a sorry state, and it was a very big job. For some strange and mysterious reason, bulbs that Danna said she knew had been removed sprang up, with blossoms blooming in places where she knows nothing was planted, and no bulbs or plants were left there. These are all "old-fashioned" plants, such as spider and day lilies, apostle lilies, narcissus, and petunias, all plants she was told that Raymond had planted and lovingly tended.

A strange thing, for which there is no explanation, took place soon after Danna moved into the house. Several members of the Rafael family, including Katy and Edmund Pelt (Edmund is Wilhelmina's son) and Miriam Jolesch, were visiting her. They were about to leave, and as she stood at the front door talking to them, her pearl earring fell off. She heard it hit the floor. She and her visitors searched everywhere, but they could not find it anywhere. The next day when she sat down at her desk and opened the drawer, there, right in front of her, was the earring she had lost the day before! She also told me that the family members had told her to ask Raymond to help her find it. Frankly, I believe that Julia's spirit would have been more likely to hide the earring, since it was a woman's piece of jewelry.

Danna Cody lived alone in the big house for four years, enjoying the company of her frequent bed and breakfast guests, and drop-in Ennis friends and family members. In 1993 a young man named Bryan Wolf arrived as a guest at the inn. The two were very compatible, and it wasn't long until wedding bells rang out in Ennis! Soon after Bryan moved into the house with his new bride, all the "Raymond activities" ceased. Raymond had long looked after his mother and sisters and then apparently had come back to watch over Danna, another lone woman living in the big house. He must have felt she was being properly loved and protected by her new husband, who specializes in the restoration and renovation of old properties.

The couple now has two youngsters, a toddler son of three and a brand new infant. They decided the bed and breakfast business was just too much for them at this time in their lives, and so they recently sold the Rafael house.

A final word. Julia Rafael was born in the Rafael house. She lived and loved in that house. Probably her happiest days were during the time when she lived with her lover, Jamie Haynes. In order to retain the ownership of the house, she was prohibited from marriage and having children. Probably during the time Jamie shared the house with her, the couple lost the respect of many local citizens of Ennis. In some ways, the house might have been considered as a symbol of sacrifice for Julia Rafael. It doesn't surprise me that her spirit might be a little possessive, coming around to roam the spacious rooms she loved so well, until she was unable to remain. Her spirit should be well pleased with the loving attention that Danna lavished on her beautiful old home, bringing it back to its former life and luster.

The Keever House

When Donna and John Kucholtz moved to Ennis in 1980, they had no idea that they would soon be cohabiting with the former mistress of the household! The couple decided to leave the Dallas metroplex in search of a calmer, quieter place in which to bring up their young son, Kevin. They looked at several places in the small city of Ennis, but one house on Knox Street really caught their fancy. It was one of the larger homes in the community, located about thirty-five miles south of Dallas and nineteen miles north of Corsicana on IH 45. The beautiful house, a two-story frame Georgian style dwelling, was painted gray with white trim and forest green shutters. It was situated on a large, nicely landscaped lot.

The place had stood vacant for a couple of years, but it had been well maintained by the real estate company that was offering it for sale. The Kucholtzes looked at the place a couple of times before deciding to make an offer. After each visit, after she had been in the house for a while, Donna became terribly nauseated and upset for no particular reason. She later learned nearly everyone who had looked at the house had more or less the same experience.

It was strange, but at the time the couple just chalked it up to "small town behavior," that the real estate agent who showed them the place would not go inside the house with them while they looked around. He stood outside or waited in his car, telling the couple to just take their time looking around; he would be glad to wait for them. Usually, having had experience with numerous realtors, Donna and John knew that real estate agents were quick to accompany prospects as they viewed a house, pointing out all the outstanding details of a place to help cinch a sale. They found their salesman's behavior a bit strange, but thought no more about it.

The more they thought about the house, the more they wanted it. Donna said it was a lovely home, built in 1920 by master

The former Keever House, Ennis

carpenters. Every detail was custom made. The cabinets, doors, and trim were all made "right in the front yard," according to Donna. The wood was the finest money could buy. The cabinetry was outstanding, mostly all of cherry wood. All this was done at the orders of the first owner, Mr. J.E. Keever, a respected businessman who owned the mortuary and funeral home in Ennis. He built the large house for his wife, her parents, and his parents, as well as the two Keever sons. It's hard to imagine living with my own parents and in-laws all under one roof, but apparently it was quite a satisfactory arrangement for the Keever family. There were three large bedrooms upstairs, plus a glassed-in sleeping porch, which the Keever boys occupied. The downstairs area was composed of a huge living room, formal dining room, library, and a tremendous kitchen, which was actually a combination kitchen, breakfast room, sun room, laundry, and walk-in pantry. Donna said it was very large and absolutely wonderful for cooking and entertaining. There was also a small half bath and a storage room tucked in under the staircase.

At the time he built his own house, Keever also built two other houses, one on each side of his residence. One, he sold right away to the First Baptist Church in Ennis to be used as a parsonage. The other he kept to use as rental property. Later on, the Keevers gave that house to their son Sam, when he got out of the Army and brought a lovely young bride, a Savannah, Georgia, Southern belle, back home to Ennis.

Right after the Kucholtzes signed the papers finalizing the sale, the realtor said to them, "Well, welcome to Amityville." That movie had just been released about the time they purchased the house. Donna said, "What on earth are you talking about?" The realtor's reply was "You'll soon find out." Then the salesman agreed to walk into the house with them for the first time. After a few minutes of standing in the big living room he made another strange remark. He told Donna, "I believe she likes you." Donna said, "Who is she?" The realtor's reply again was a very cryptic "You'll find out." He went on to tell the new owners that his wife and a lot of other people wouldn't go into the house, but he believed that the Kucholtzes were going to be acceptable to "her."

And almost from the first, things happened to cause them to believe that the house was indeed occupied by a spirit. They talked to numerous townspeople and were convinced that the caretaker spirit was the possessive and proud Mrs. J.E. Keever, former mistress of the house. She had loved to entertain and show off her fine Georgian style home. It had been the scene of frequent open houses and social functions. Donna says she thinks Mrs. Keever just wanted to make sure the new owners would take care of the house. A previous owner had painted many of the beautiful cherry wood cabinets and woodwork with ugly yellow latex paint. The Kucholtzes undertook the arduous task of removing the old paint and taking the wood back to its original luster. The solid rose-brass carriage lamps with leaded glass windows at the front entrance had been covered with black spray paint. Donna and her husband painstakingly removed this paint and had the brass refinished to again gleam at the front door. Donna said they felt they were almost being "led" to do certain things to the house to help restore it to its original state.

The couple bought a big couch that converted to a bed for houseguests. Donna said the downstairs area was quieter and made a nice guest retreat when the sleeper sofa was put to use. The library was close at hand, the little half bath was readily accessible, and the adjacent kitchen always had a well-stocked refrigerator for late night snacking.

But it was strange. Whenever this guest area was in use, Mrs. Keever seemed to make her presence known. The houseguests often became aware of an almost overwhelming fragrance of roses. Mrs. Keever loved her rose garden; they were her favorite flowers. And according to people who knew her, she always wore tea rose perfume. The fragrance would sometimes linger for quite some time, and often guests asked Donna if she had used rose-scented room spray. Donna said no, in fact she hated room spray! Often guests asked Donna if she had come downstairs and walked around while they were sleeping, or had she gone and checked all the doors to see if they were locked. They told her they had seen the dark shadow of someone roaming about and had heard footsteps of someone moving in the room. They also heard the sounds of the doorknobs jiggling as if someone was checking them to see if the doors were securely locked. She said her guests were usually startled when she told them she had not been downstairs at all, but they had probably been visited by "old Mrs. Keever," whom she also referred to privately as "the hostess with the mostest."

Kevin was the only Kucholtz family member to whom Mrs. Keever made herself visible. The youngster first saw her when he was four years old, the year the family moved into the house. He told his mother a "lady in a white dress" had come into his room to see him. At first Donna and John chalked this talk up to a little boy's vivid imagination. But as the years rolled by and the boy continued to see the figure from time to time, they began to believe him. Fortunately, the apparition did not seem to frighten Kevin. To me, it is not all that strange that Mrs. Keever singled Kevin out to visit. She was the mother of two sons. She was used to little boys and probably was happy to have a little boy back in the house.

Donna said all through the years there were sounds of footsteps and numerous cold spots in the house. These things didn't really bother the family. But there was one area in the house that was very disturbing to Donna. This was the area beneath the stairs, which was divided between the small half bath and a little storage room. The storage room always smelled musty and moldy—an unpleasant odor. She just couldn't force herself to go into the storeroom, and the few times she did, she always became nauseated. She had the feeling she was "trespassing." There were boxes of things shoved back into the room, and she said she never did try to find out what was in them. They kept the door to the room locked, but it would often fly open by itself. They even taped it shut with duct tape and placed bricks in front of the door, but nothing seemed to work. If the door decided to open, it just did!

Most of the activity connected with the spirit seemed to take place when the family had overnight visitors occupying the sleeper-sofa. That's when the rose smell would permeate the living room and the footsteps would be heard all around the house. One such visit stands out above all others with Donna. She had become friendly with a young woman named Rebecca Lange, who was going into the ministry. Rev. Lange was doing work on her master's degree in theology at Texas Christian University's seminary in Fort Worth. Part of her work towards the degree was to serve a pastorate each weekend. And so she came to the First Christian Church in Ennis to preach each Sunday morning. Donna suggested to her that she stay in her home in order to save motel expenses. In fact, she even gave Rebecca a key to the house so she could come and go.

The first night the young pastor was there, she had just settled down on the comfortable sleeper-sofa and was about to doze off. She was startled to hear a bloodcurdling scream! The Kucholtzes, in their bedroom upstairs, heard it as well. They dashed downstairs to see if something had happened to their guest. She was sitting upright in bed, obviously terrified. She said, "I didn't scream. Did you?" It only happened that one time, but it certainly made an impression on them all! Then, later that same night the apparition of a woman appeared to Rev. Lange, and she heard footsteps all night, walking back and forth across the room. She smelled the strong fragrance of roses, which was almost stifling in its intensity. She was a nervous wreck by dawn. She called the church where she was supposed to preach and told them she was sick and asked them to find a replacement to fill the pulpit that morning. Then she did a rather strange thing. She asked her hosts if she might go to the Episcopal Church with them.

As soon as the service was over, Rev. Lange asked the Kucholtz' priest, Reverend Dennis Smart, if his church still performed "house blessings." She told him of her terror-filled night. Reverend Smart said he had heard about the presence of a spirit at the old Keever house for years, but didn't think it was anything serious. It didn't take long for Rev. Lange to convince him it was! The clergyman got his holy water, incense, and stole and drove to the house right after church to bless the house and, hopefully, to release the spirit to go on to the Light. He performed the ceremony, and Donna said they had very little contact with Mrs. Keever after that. She could finally go into the little storage room in the stairwell without being frightened or repelled by the musty smell, which could no longer be detected.

However, Donna said that her young son, Kevin, told her while Mrs. Keever sort of settled down, she hadn't gone away. She still visited his room several times after the house blessing took place.

In 1988 the Kucholtzes moved back to the Dallas area. I asked Donna if the spirit of Mrs. Keever finally drove them off, and she assured me this was not the case. They left because they missed their friends in Dallas, and they also missed a lot of the cultural activities and events that they had always enjoyed there. Donna said that she guessed they just weren't cut out to be "small town folks" after all. City life was really more their cup of tea!

Donna said she was never particularly frightened by Mrs. Keever's presence in the house. They felt while she was obviously possessive of the house she had loved, she was also protective and benevolent to its occupants. Donna laughed when she told me that while some folks had watchdogs, they always felt as if they had a "watch ghost" to take care of things for them!

As our conversation drew to a close, Donna said, although she loved being back enjoying her friends and all the activities of a metropolis, she really missed the beautiful home they had shared with Mrs. Keever for those years in Ennis. She added, "Sometimes we even miss Mrs. Keever."

HAUNTED HALLWAYS
Docia Williams

Hotels, like houses, can haunted be...
By ghosts one can both hear and see.
In inns and charming dining places
Spirits dwell in the hidden spaces.
At one, there's a wraith that walks the hall
And one, there's banging on the wall.
In one, a shadow, dark and scary
Enough to make a traveler wary!
Candles move, and lights go out,
When 'ere the spirits are about.
So when you stop to spend the night,
Perhaps you'd best leave on the light!

The Excelsior House...
is it Haunted?

Jefferson, Texas, was once the most prosperous city in East Texas, one of the largest cities in the state, and certainly the largest inland port. In the days just following the Civil War, the population swelled to around 35,000. A natural barrier in the Red River caused water to back into Cypress Bayou and made river navigation possible as far as Jefferson, which became a bustling river port as early as 1845. Steamboats came from New Orleans and from points on the Ohio and Mississippi Rivers. From the early 1860s through the late 1870s the city was a budding metropolis as thousands of bales of cotton found their way into the holds of the big river steamers which held up to 6,000 bales in their storage areas. Passengers traveled in the steamboats as well, and many were elegantly appointed with fine staterooms, good dining facilities, and excellent entertainment. In those days just about all the cotton raised in Louisiana, southwestern Arkansas, and North Texas was shipped by wagon to Jefferson and often stacked up for six or seven miles waiting to be weighed. Over 100,000 bales were shipped from the port of Jefferson annually!

With so many people arriving and departing by steamboat, there was obviously the need for a good hotel in the community. Captain William Perry bought a piece of property not too far from the waterfront about 1858. He built a small hotel there, which was first known as the Irving House. Today it forms the northwest portion of the Excelsior House. Another wing to the southwest was added sometime between the close of the Civil War and 1872. After Captain Perry died, the hotel changed hands numerous times. Known briefly as the Exchange Hotel, then the Commercial Hotel, it finally acquired the name by which it is known today, the Excelsior House, when Mrs. Kate Wood purchased it in 1877. The brick portion of the old section was added that year. In the 1870s when the population had soared to its peak of 35,000, the hotel, lavish for its day, was the scene of many of the famed "Queen Mab" balls. These balls were a part of Jefferson's own Mardi Gras, which was comparable to that of New Orleans with its parades, floats, bands, and parties.

During this heyday period, Jefferson was one of Texas' leading cities. A lot of this population growth was due to the port facilities being there. However, unfortunately for the city, the U.S. government decided the huge dam of logs on the Red River which had dammed up Cypress Bayou, making the water deep enough for a port, should be blown up. When the logjam was released, the Big Cypress Bayou became unnavigatable. By 1890 the population began to dwindle away as people who had been associated with the shipping business in one way or another went elsewhere to seek employment. The once prosperous little port dried up fast, becoming a sleepy little East Texas town on a shallow river, now completely devoid of river traffic. Only a little timbering and farming seemed to keep the community alive.

During those drying-up days, Mrs. Wood and her daughter, Mrs. Amelia Wood McNeeley, operated the Excelsior until 1902. From 1902 until 1920 Mrs. McNeeley managed the property. Upon her death, it was revealed that McNeeley had bequeathed her hotel to George S. Neidermeir. He and his family operated the hotel until 1954 when it was purchased by Mrs. James I. Peters.

Mrs. Peters began to do a lot of restoration to the almost century old hotel. She brought in the beautiful fountain to enhance the lovely courtyard. She added fine light fixtures and furniture. Her restorations added extra charm to an already lovely building.

Finally, in August of 1961 the Jessie Allen Wise Garden Club purchased the hotel from Mrs. Peters' heirs. The club set about doing a lot of major restorations to the building, but it remained open throughout the restoration period. It was furnished with some very fine pieces: spool beds, four-posters, marble topped dressers, sleigh beds, fine pieces in cherry, maple, and mahogany.

The inn, which has seen so much Jefferson history pass by and through its doors, has played host to many famous personages. Its register bears the names of Presidents Ulysses S. Grant, Rutherford B. Hayes, and Lyndon Baines Johnson. Jacob Astor, W.H. Vanderbilt,

Oscar Wilde, and Jay Gould were also guests of the hotel. The latter, angered that Jefferson would not sell him a railroad right-of-way through town, penned "the end of Jefferson" beneath his signature. He assured the citizenry that grass would soon grow in the streets and bats would roost in the church belfries!

Down through the years, a number of ghost stories have surfaced concerning the old hotel. This isn't uncommon. Many hotels are known to be haunted, and it only adds a certain measure of charm and mystique to a venerable old building. My files, collected over the years, are fairly bulging with accounts from well-known journalists and respected publications. Not wanting to merely parrot what has been reported by others, I called the hotel in hopes of gaining some new information. The lady who answered, a representative of the Jessie Allen Wise Garden Club, which manages the hotel, was adamant that there were NO ghost stories connected to the Excelsior Hotel and furthermore the Garden Club management did not want to be associated with any such stories! There was an icy tone of hostility in her voice! So that was that...but....

I honestly believe I would be terribly remiss if I were to deny my readers what other writers, who obviously found the management at the times they made their reports more cooperative than I did, have reported through the years. After all, the first I ever heard about Jefferson, when it was to me an unknown East Texas community, were ghost stories told to me in the 1970s by some native Jeffersonians about the old Excelsior Hotel!

You might take note of this information gleaned from my files and then make your own conclusions, perhaps even including an overnight stay in the beautiful old hotel.

The *Texas Parade Magazine,* November 1971 edition, mentions that a woman from Shreveport wrote to the late journalist Frank X. Tolbert that she had a strange experience when she spent the night at the Excelsior in the Rutherford B. Hayes Room. The woman said the covers were suddenly yanked off her bed. There was no one in the room but her. Then, the covers were flung across the room, landing near the fireplace. Then she heard a light tap on her door. When she went to answer it, no one was there. The woman asked Tolbert to go to the Excelsior and spend the night, which he later did. He had no supernatural experience. However, he did speak with one of the hotel maids, and she told him she occasionally saw a headless man strolling around the Jay Gould Room on the second floor. She didn't seem terribly upset about these appearances; at least she hadn't quit her job!

An article entitled "The Ghosts of the Caddo Lake Country" by the late Frank X. Tolbert ran in the October 1980 issue of *Texas Homes*. Later, the information formed a chapter in Tolbert's fine book *Tolbert's Texas*, which was released in 1983:

In Jefferson, Texas, just up the Big Cypress Bayou from Caddo Lake, there is an old hotel in New Orleans architectural style called the Excelsior. The big rooms are graced with antique furniture and paintings, some of these originals from the 1850s version of the inn. Cissie McCampbell, the longtime resident night manager, was nationally famous for the delicious country style breakfasts she cooked.

Some sensitive persons, including Ruby Britton, for years a maid and now one of the cooks, claim that the lovely hotel has ghosts in residence. The spooks are usually described as friendly.

One of the more frightened persons ever to spend a part of a night at the Excelsior was Steven Spielberg. He is the director of numerous motion pictures such as *E.T.*, *Raiders of the Lost Ark*, and *Close Encounters of the Third Kind*. Mr. Spielberg said he had an inmate encounter of some kind with one or more of the Excelsior ghosts.

Spielberg told columnist John Anders of the *Dallas Morning News*: "There's an old hotel, the Excelsior, in Jefferson, which really freaked me out. We pulled in there one night during the filming in Texas of *Sugarland Express*. And we dragged ourselves upstairs after a rough day. I swear my room was haunted. "I made everybody wake up, pack up, and get back in the cars at about two o'clock in the morning. We had to drive twenty miles to the nearest Holiday Inn and everybody was hot at me.

"I should add that I am not normally superstitious."

Spielberg was upstairs in the east wing of the Excelsior. A number of guests who've spent nights in this, the oldest continuously operated hotel in Texas, have also complained of spooks. And Ruby Britton, when she was a maid, refused to go upstairs alone in the east wing because of what she described as a "headless man" in the room occupied for one night in 1878 by Jay Gould, the railroad builder and "robber baron." Gould signed the hotel register with a good likeness of a jaybird drawn at the end of his signature. He skipped without paying his hotel bill. He had been angry because the Jefferson citizens wouldn't pay a bonus in money and land for running his trains through town. He said that unless he got the "bribe" he wouldn't put machine shops in Jefferson.

A Dallas man who has four university degrees and is a hypnotist claims he has a "sixth sense" for detecting the presence of disembodied human spirits. This fellow will be called "the Ghost Detective" from now on, for he makes his living as a dentist, and he doesn't want his patients to know that hunting spooks is his "hobby."

He said he has seen "only twenty-five apparitions" in his lifetime but he has heard and "smelled" other persons from the spirit world. Some time ago he said he spent the night in the north wing of the Excelsior and he complained: "A hard-breathing yet unseen-even-by-me presence worried me all night."

On Sunday, October 29, 1995, *The Dallas Morning News* ran an article by columnist Kent Biffle, who specializes in Texana. The writer mentioned the same Steven Spielberg incident that Frank X. Tolbert had mentioned earlier. But then he went on to mention retired ABC newsman Lyndon (Dave) Adams of Garland and his wife, Carol, who had a most unusual night in the Excelsior. The night they spent in the hostelry was September 5, 1995. After reading over the old hotel register and "soaking up some history" they went to their room. For some unexplainable reason, Adams said, the tune of the *Gold and Silver Waltz* by Franz Lehar kept going through his head as he unlocked the tall door to the high ceilinged room. Following are quotes from Biffle's article:

> Inside were two double beds with big wooden headboards, and antique chairs, one of them a rocker. The bathroom had an old, footed tub.
>
> We sat on the pleasant veranda, which overlooks a brick courtyard, in its center a huge iron fountain. And we had a fabulous dinner a couple of doors down from the hotel at a place called the Galley Restaurant.
>
> Afterward, bedded down, they fell asleep watching TV.
>
> Mr. Adams recalled, "I awoke because I had to go to the bathroom. I turned the TV off, then shuffled sleepily to the bathroom. "I noticed that the door was starting to open slowly. I shut it, and it latched firmly. Later, when I returned to the door, I found I couldn't turn the knob.
>
> "Something or someone was apparently gripping the knob on the other side, tightly. I said, 'Come on, Carol ... very funny.' The pressure let up. The knob turned easily.
>
> "I flicked off the light as I opened the door. Across the room, standing beside the bed was the figure of a woman dressed all in black, with a black veil. For one split second, It thought it was Carol, but she was in bed, wearing a white nightie. The apparition vanished.
>
> "I became aware of the scent of perfume in the room. I stood for a moment, slightly shaken, but then got into bed and lay there wondering.
>
> "I thought of waking Carol, but thought better of it. She would be frightened and want to leave.... I drifted off to sleep.
>
> "I awoke to the odor of cigar smoke. I heard what sounded like someone riffling newspaper pages. I sat up, but didn't see anything. The sound stopped."

Next came a "knocking sound from the headboard near my head. Then I heard fingernails being dragged across the headboard, right above my head.

"My hand touched Carol, sound asleep. About 4 A.M. she woke up and asked if I was having trouble sleeping.

"I did go back to sleep. I had a vivid dream, a woman in black, seated at a grand piano was playing *The Gold and Silver Waltz*. Returning from dinner, we'd peeked into the huge parlor off the main lobby and noticed a black grand piano.

"I once again awoke, to noises in the bathroom. I even heard the toilet flush. I reached over. Carol was still beside me.

"The knocking resumed, this time quite persistent. I really thought I was beginning to lose my marbles. I drifted off to sleep again.

"I awoke to bright sunshine streaming through the windows. I went into the bathroom, looked at myself in the mirror, and thought, 'Nah. It couldn't have happened."

Carol awoke. He told her his experiences. She recalled the knocking.

"The desk clerk was an attractive white-haired lady named Mary Jo Brantley, who said she'd been with the hotel for twenty years. I told her what had happened. She turned to another employee and said, "These folks had visitors in the Gould Room last night."

"She went on to say that her son, who had worked at the desk, had once heard a guest's report of a woman in black rocking in the rocking chair with a baby. Mary Jo said her son accompanied the man to the room, and he also witnessed the apparition for a moment.

"Her son told her that when the figure vanished, the chair continued its ghostly rocking for a few seconds."

Whether or not the ghostly manifestations still continue is anybody's guess. Maybe the spirits of former owners, employees, or guests who once haunted the place have moved on. Perhaps the spirits have happily settled down to peace and rest. Just as peaceful as you might find a night spent at the lovely Excelsior House!

The Doll in the Window

Jefferson physician Dr. Donald Ray Whitaker and his wife purchased the old F.A. Schluter mansion on South Line Street, a stately
home of some 11,000 square feet and four stories, including the attic
and the basement, a couple of years ago. They are slowly, painstakingly, and lovingly restoring the house to its former grandeur. Their
target date for the completion of this gargantuan project is January of
1999, when they hope to move in and live in their restored home. In
the interim, the Whitakers have, from time to time, welcomed
groups of people who are interested in the processes involved in restoration to come and visit the century-and-a-half-old home.
Eventually, they plan to open the historic building for tours and have
even thought of the possibility of making the mansion into a bed and
breakfast inn someday!

I first learned of the Schluter property from an acquaintance in
Jefferson, historian Bill Savio. It was he who put me in touch with Dr.
Whitaker. The good doctor was most helpful and cooperative, going
out of his way to do some historic research on the house, which he
said he had not heretofore done, mainly because, between his medical practice and the restoration of the house, he had not had that
much time. He sent me some wonderful information about the
house, one of Jefferson's finest, and I would like to share it with you
before we get into the "ghost part" of the narrative.

The property on South Line Street was once a part of what was
known as the Alley Addition. Mr. D.N. Alley purchased the land from
Stephen Smith in 1845. Alley sold the land to F.A. and Ann T.
Schluter in 1847. The deed was not filed until 1850, when the couple
began construction of their home, but the completion date is not
known to Dr. Whitaker. He believes it was finished sometime around
1856, so it predates the Civil War. It was built in the style of many of
the old Deep South plantation homes, with spacious halls, tall

columns, and wide galleries. Situated as it is on a corner lot, it is visible from several vantage points.

In years past the house was on numerous home pilgrimages when visitors came from all over to visit the fine old mansions for which the city of Jefferson is well known. The home shows some definite indications of having been built by slave labor; however, there is no proof as yet that F.A. Schluter owned slaves or employed them in the construction of his home. Records showed that one Noah Stephens, a black man, helped to carry brick for the basement, but he failed to say whether he was a slave or free man when he was questioned about his work on the property. He did say the Schluter house was only the second house to be built on Line Street, the first one being the Oppenheim home.

In 1857 Mr. and Mrs. Schluter bought some lots adjacent to their home in order to expand their property. They had a number of outbuildings, including stables, on this land.

Schluter House, circa 1890, Jefferson
(photo courtesy of Dr. David Ray Whitaker)

Between the years of 1859 and 1863 the Schluters lost four of their children, who were buried in the family lot in the city cemetery. So there must have been several deaths in the house during those years.

According to Dr. Whitaker's information, the first mention of the house was made in the county records in 1860 when F.A. and Ann T. Schluter made a deed of gift to W.P. (Walter) Schluter, a son, for all the community property. There were four heirs to the family estate: W.P., Louis, Gus, and Virgie. This deed of gift stated that all records of ownership of the house had been destroyed by fire. Schluter, a wealthy dry-goods merchant, reserved the right to use all the property during his lifetime. Ann T. relinquished any right to the property. F.A. evidently did not join the army, because during the Civil War years there are numerous accounts of business transactions he made in Jefferson. In 1864 Ann died, and there is no information as to who ran the household or who took care of the heirs.

Schluter died in Tennessee in 1882. He left another estate to his second wife, listed as M.G. Schluter, and the surviving four children from his first marriage.

In 1882 W.P. Schluter gained control of the house. He was married to Annie Laurie Hale and they had one child, a son, born in 1884. The youngster was named F.A. for his paternal grandfather. I learned, from a small booklet entitled *A History of Jefferson, Marion County, Texas*, written by Mesdames Arch McKay and H.A. Spellings in 1944 as a project for the Women's Auxiliary, Christ Episcopal Church, that the W.P. Schluters honored little F.A., who died on August 8, 1892, at Hughes Springs at the age of eight years, by donating an organ to the Jefferson Methodist Church South, of which the family were active members. They added to savings the youngster had kept over the years and gave the organ for use by the Sunday school in his memory. This gift was made shortly after his death, in either 1892 or 1893.

The W.P. Schluters did not have any more children, but they helped to raise several children who were related to the family, including Rena Belle Hale and Garwood Schluter. They were related to both W.P. and his wife Annie, because they were actually cousins (not unusual in that time for cousins to marry).

In 1897 W.P. and Annie Laurie moved to Waco, but sadly she died only a month after they made the move. It is not known exactly how long W.P. stayed away from Jefferson, but it is known during this time the house was occupied by various family members, including a Mrs. Hale, who took in boarders. Dr. Whitaker said one interesting highlight was just before the family had moved to Waco, Garwood Schluter and several others had done some extensive digging on the property, believing it to be the hiding place of some of F.A.'s accumulated wealth!

W.P. Schluter remarried in 1900. The new bride was a widow, Eugenia R. Stump, who had one child, Willella. That wife brought David Rowell into the home to reside with them. He was somehow related to both sides of the family also.

W.P. Schluter died in 1925. His will stated: "I request that my home never be sold to anyone out of the connection." However, it did eventually leave the Schluter family, first going to Eugenia, W.P.'s second wife, then to her daughter, who was Mrs. G.N. Campbell. She continued the family tradition of raising a child there that was not her own. She died in 1946, and her husband, G.N. Campbell, inherited the place. He sold it to G.E. Blain in 1948, who owned it for many years and did much restoration and repair work.

Now, Dr. and Mrs. Whitaker, also outside "the connection," own the house. Maybe that isn't the way W.P. wanted it, but I believe he would be happy to know that they are going all out to restore it and are giving the home a lot of tender loving care!

When I questioned Dr. Whitaker about the ghost history of the place, he confessed he didn't know much about that, but he was so fascinated, he would try to find out something about any turbulence that might have taken place around the house. Good as his word, he soon sent back the information that a notorious carpetbagger of the post Civil War period was killed just a few yards from the house. He also found out that in 1869 the house figured in a stirring military court trial, with F.A. Schluter appearing as a witness. On October 4, 1868, an angry mob murdered a white man in the city jail, which was located just across Line Street from the Schluter home. The mob

then marched two black men off in the direction of the Schluter stable. One of the men, Anderson Wright, escaped the mob and
disappeared through the Schluter premises. Nothing was ever
proved in the trial, but the military contended that Anderson Wright
was caught and hanged from a beam in the Schluter stable. Mr.
Schluter recalled there may have been a temporary beam there at
the time, and he also stated that the board fence had been torn down
and rebuilt since October 4, 1868.

Doctor Whitaker also told me about the famous bell, which hangs
in the belfry of the Methodist Church and which is directly connected to the Schluter family. The story goes that in 1858 the famous
Menelley Bell Foundry of Troy, New York, was contracted to cast a
bell for the church. Mr. F.A. Schluter gave 1500 Mexican silver
pesos, to insure a silvery tone, and had a trusted manservant deliver
the silver to New Orleans, from whence it was shipped to the foundry. The finished bell was brought by riverboat down the Ohio and
Mississippi Rivers to New Orleans, and then back up the Mississippi
and Red Rivers to Shreveport and through Caddo Lake and the
Cypress Bayou to Jefferson, a long and tedious journey in those
days. F.A. Schluter was never a man to indulge in frivolous social
activities, but he was a staunch supporter of the church.

Dr. Whitaker did well in establishing some turbulence, at least,
which had been attached to the old house. Four little Schluter children may have passed away in the house, then there was a
carpetbagger killed and a black man hanged on the premises. So far,
so good! Then, I told the doctor a little of the story I had heard from
Bill Savio about the "doll in the window." Savio said there had been a
fire in the middle of the night in the big house in its early days. The
family was unable to reach one infant who was in its crib in a smoke-
filled room, and the baby perished that night. The infant's spirit supposedly returned to its old nursery and was heard to cry in the night.
His mother is said to have hung a little doll in the window of the
room in order to keep the baby spirit company. After that, the cries
ceased.

Dr. Whitaker had not heard about any fire. However, some of the
historic information that he gave me indicated that, in 1860 when
F.A. made a deed of gift for his property to his son, W.P., "all records

of ownership of the house have been destroyed by fire." This might indicate a fire in the house, since where else would he have kept his papers? And the records also stated that between the years of 1859 and 1863 the Schluters had buried four of their children. Could one possibly have been an infant, its life cut short by a fire?

Although the doctor knew nothing of the fire story, he did know about the "doll story " He had heard that a Mrs. Mouton had once owned the house, and it was she, after hearing the cries of an infant, who had hung a little doll in the window. Dr. Whitaker didn't know much more than that about the doll in the window. But, he did tell me that when he and his wife bought the place, there was a faded, dusty, dirty, tattered little doll hanging in an upstairs bedroom window. When they removed it, the little toy completely fell apart, its limbs asunder. They had no idea how long it had hung there, but there was indeed a doll in the window at the old Schluter house!

As Dr. and Mrs. Whitaker have gone about the tedious task of restoring the old house, they have seen, heard, or felt nothing to indicate a haunting. However, Dr. Whitaker did say they had not yet spent the night in their lovely mansion. It might be a good idea, just "in case," if the Whitakers would buy a nice, new, shiny little doll to hang in that upstairs bedroom window before they spend that first night in the old Schluter house!

Ghosts Galore at the Jefferson Hotel

The famous inland steamboat port of Jefferson near the Louisiana border abounds in historic buildings. One of the oldest is the Jefferson Hotel. Originally constructed in 1861 as a cotton warehouse, when thousands of bales were being shipped out of Jefferson each year, the old building has had a colorful past.

The back of the hotel was once used as the front entrance of the structure. The great iron doorframes are still visible where large arched doors of the 1870s era hotel faced the busy bayou and Dallas Street. Today the front is located on West Austin Street. It has a long shady porch that runs the length of the building. The architectural style reminds one of many old buildings seen in New Orleans' famous French Quarter.

The Jefferson Hotel (taken during a classic car show)
(photo courtesy of Carol Meissner)

The cotton warehouse closed down when the steamboat port closed. The building has since been used for many purposes in its long history. I am very grateful to the current owners of the Jefferson Hotel, Carol and Ron Meissner, for sharing this history with me. The hotel manager, Jody Breckenridge, spent hours in assembling information, about both the history and the hauntings at the fine old hotel. Ms. Breckenridge did such a fine job of compiling the information, I am going to quote much of her correspondence just as she sent it to me:

As the years passed, the hotel lived a colorful life. In one deed of sale, a business upstairs was listed as a "school for girls," although everyone knew it was actually a bordello. A Chinese laundry was downstairs in the back of the building. Then, sometime after World War I during the flapper era of the Roaring Twenties, it was reopened as a respectable hotel, one of the finest in town. Big dances were held downstairs on Saturday nights. In the '20s the Jefferson Hotel was the place to go. One owner used to hold gambling parties in a back room.

During World War II a couple named Mr. and Mrs. Mosley owned the hotel. They served a popular family style dinner for just twenty-five cents! The clientele sat at one of the long tables and black ladies brought in bowls of chicken and dumplings, vegetables, biscuits and cornbread.

Then hard times came to the old hotel. Business started falling until there were just a few old folks living in the rooms. Some of the old men drank too much. The clientele continued to slip until most people considered the place just a "flop house." The hotel kitchen was run by a man named "Red." He took care of the old drunks and made sure they had hot coffee and breakfast every day. Few people could resist Red's gumbo, or his version of red beans and rice. His retainer, a scrawny little black woman named Aida, who smoked big cigars, served the food.

The hotel changed hands numerous times through the years. Today the restored Jefferson caters to the many tourists who visit the historic city. Walking through the front door, one feels an aura of timelessness. The atmosphere fairly vibrates with the past! Late at night the worn wooden boards creak, and the walls sigh with the whispers and memories of long ago. Some people believe the hotel is haunted. And still others say they KNOW it is haunted!

Have you ever felt that you are not alone when you know without a doubt you are by yourself? Anyone who has ever worked at the hotel can tell you firsthand about the many strange occurrences there. You can hear footsteps going down the halls. Doors open and close and there is knocking on the walls. Rooms that have been prepared for the arrival of guests will be found in disarray only minutes after the maid has left the room.

The hotel consists of a large lobby and dining area and twenty-four guestrooms. (There is no room number thirteen!) There are certain rooms that have become popular as the rooms most likely to have unusual activity. The main one is room nineteen, a corner room at the end of a wide hallway upstairs. The room, which has thirteen-foot-high ceilings, is furnished in country Victorian antique decor. Many guests have said that they are awakened in the night by someone sitting down on the side of the bed, and they have seen a shadowed figure hovering in the corner of the room. Some people simply state that they feel very uncomfortable in the room and request they be moved to another room. One hotel employee went in to change a light bulb, and as she walked around the end of the bed, it felt as if she had walked into an icebox, with a definite thirty-degree difference in room temperature. It caused the hair to rise at the back of her neck and goose bumps prickled her arms. Reassuring herself that she was just letting her imagination run wild, she turned to exit the room when the scent of clover or allspice filled the room.

A guest who recently stayed in number nineteen told of waking up in the night to sounds of popping and clicking and what sounded like knocking on the walls behind the headboard of the bed, only to find that there is not an adjoining room where the noise could have been coming from, only a twenty-four-inch-thick wall to the outside. After getting up to use the restroom and turning off the light, she lay back down and had the feeling of being watched from the end of the bed. Still fully awake, she turned to face her husband's side of the bed, where she saw a lady with long wavy hair reaching towards her. She actually touched her arm. She pulled away and yelled for her husband. After she turned on the light, there was no one in the room.

Guests in room twenty talk of the water in the bathroom sink coming on full force in the middle of the night. After turning it off and getting almost back to sleep, guests hear the old faucets squeak and squawk and the water comes on again. Guests in rooms five and eleven often tell of the knocking that is heard in the walls. People try to rationalize that the noises are water pipes knocking.

Carol Meissner, the new owner of the hotel, heard the knocking one night and thought it was her son at the front or back door. But she found by calling that he was at home, fast asleep. Every ten or fifteen minutes it is possible to hear the repetitive knocking. This happens even when no guests are in the hotel, and therefore no water has been turned on or used.

Brian Morrow, a carpenter working at the hotel, is now a true believer in the hauntings. He had never before paid any attention to the tales. Nor did he think a place could be haunted. But one evening around 8 P.M., just after the hotel had been purchased by the Meissners, he did have an unnerving experience. He and two other workers who had been working late were alone in the hotel. He was going back upstairs to leave his tool belt in room six for use the following day. Upon reaching the top step he got an eerie feeling. His intuition told him he was not alone. Continuing down the long corridor, he walked into a cold spot. The hairs on his arms and head were literally electrified! He dropped his tool belt in the middle of the floor and turned around, expecting to see someone staring back at him. He saw only an empty hallway. He made it in record time back to the bottom of the stairs.

The local police have made numerous "wild ghost chases." One officer, now retired, has admitted to being a believer after having a tug-of-war with a door in an empty room! In late March 1993, Jefferson Police Department Officer Allen Teer was working security at the hotel when he walked upstairs to turn off the heat in rooms that were not occupied. He unlocked the door to room two, stepped in, and had walked halfway across the room when the door slammed shut behind him. Since it was a windy night and the old hotel is pretty drafty, he didn't think much about it. He turned off the heater and switched off the light and came out of the room. He reached for the door to pull it shut and lock it. But something, some unseen force, from inside the room kept pulling at the door. He would get it almost shut, and whatever was inside would pull the door back open about three or four inches, with Teer leaning back and pulling against it as hard as he could to close it. The tug-of-war lasted several minutes before the officer got thoroughly upset and pulled with all his strength, finally slamming the door shut. He started to walk away when something, from inside the room, threw something at the door! Whatever it was hit the door with a real loud crash! Teer said he didn't waste much time getting downstairs! Teer was quoted at the time of the occurrence as having said, "I didn't believe this spirit stuff until I started working at the hotel. I'm a certified police officer, graduated from the Lufkin Police Academy in 1983, and in my business I encounter a lot of strange stuff, but when that happened, when something hit the back of that door when I knew there was nothing in the room, I'm not going to lie about it, it scared the living daylights out of me!"

And a former manager of the hotel, Donie Chappell, had some strange incidents during the time she was there. In 1993 a couple confided to her they had experienced a "haunt." They had been to the hotel the previous year and stayed in room twelve. They requested that same room during their next stay. It seems they had experienced seeing a smoky, wispy image, not a total form, in their room. They could tell it was a female entity, and the feeling they got was it was very gentle, very feminine. She came into their room and stayed quite a long time. They said they were not frightened at all. It was as if it had a warm, loving feeling about it. Also they sensed the wraith was lonely and wanted to be acknowledged. The man said the spirit actually touched him in a gentle manner. He could feel being touched on the face and caressed a little on the cheek. There was no threatening feeling whatsoever, and the couple wanted to come back to the same room to see "her" again. They were terribly disappointed, when, on their second visit to that same room in the hotel, they had no nocturnal visitor. They even stayed an extra night, hopeful she would come. Chappell said they really wanted to have another experience with the spirit.

Just about everyone connected with the hotel has his own story to tell. Most people say they never get used to the various occurrences. However, they have learned to accept these things as just being a part of the hotel. No one can explain why footsteps and voices are heard or why shadowy figures are seen going into rooms only to find the rooms are vacant. They can't explain who the female apparition is who has been seen in rooms twelve and nineteen.

There has never been a feeling of fear with an encounter. The only fear is of the unknown. It's more of a feeling that something, or someone, is there to help look after things and they want you to acknowledge that they are there.

If you ever want to journey back to a slower pace of life and experience the old world charm of a stay in a historic hotel with a touch of the unexplained added for good measure, come visit the Jefferson Hotel at 124 West Austin Street in Jefferson, Texas. Hosts Carol and Ron Meissner and manager Jody Breckenridge and their unseen staff of spirits will be there to welcome you!

For reservations call (903) 665-2631 or the Breckenridge Reservation Service at (903) 665-2633.

Ghosts at the Grove

The Grove is the name that was given one of Jefferson's finest restaurants, because of the numerous native pecan trees that surround the historic old home-turned-restaurant. The bill of fare sounds like a gourmet's delight, and the surroundings must indeed be beautiful!

The site, on West Moseley Street in historic Jefferson, was first owned by Amos Morrill, lawyer and friend to Robert Potter, who was Secretary of the Navy during the days of the Republic of Texas. Morrill was the first federal judge for Texas, too. (The first federal court was actually held in Jefferson.)

Morrill sold the site to Caleb Ragin in 1855, so the house on the property was built after that date, probably around 1861. There were several owners down through the years until finally in 1885 it was bought by Mr. C.J. "Charlie" Young and his wife, "Miss Daphine." The house remained in the Young family until the death of their daughter, Miss Louise Young, in 1983. Miss Young was a longtime Jefferson educator and benefactress to local churches and schools. The Jefferson School District has an annual Louise Young Memorial Scholarship for a deserving student, thus honoring the former teacher.

I received a lengthy letter from current owner Patrick Hopkins, after having a very enlightening telephone conversation with him. The letter he sent is so interesting that I am printing it almost verbatim, for after all, who can tell a better ghost story than the person to whom the ghost has become attached? I think you will enjoy what Hopkins had to say to me:

I guess the best place to begin is at the beginning. I am Patrick Hopkins, the chef and co-owner of a Jefferson restaurant called The Grove. My business partner is my sister, Mary Hopkins Callas.

One day in 1989 I received a call from Jefferson to my office at La Camarilla Resort, Scottsdale, Arizona, asking what it would take to bring me back to East Texas. Mary mentioned an idea we had both expressed back in 1976 on opening an old-house restaurant, hopefully in Jefferson (our parents were married there in 1939, but moved shortly thereafter to Hughes Springs, twenty-five miles distant). We were familiar with the town and its history, often driving over for weekends and pilgrimages.

I flew back from Arizona, while Mary and her family remained in Abilene waiting to make their move to the Longview area. I scouted the Jefferson and East Texas small towns looking for that "just right' house (of course, always with price, condition, and location in mind). We had just about decided to make a bid on an old home in Atlanta, when I decided to make one more trip to Jefferson just to make sure I hadn't missed some house or perhaps another had come on the market.

After making the usual circuit and seeing nothing new (I thought I knew all of the old houses of Jefferson), I decided to return home, and seeing Highway 59 in the distance, thinking this street, Moseley, would lead right into it, I started down the street. Halfway down Moseley, I heard what sounded like a man's voice hollering "Hey!" and turning my head to the right, I saw a beautiful Greek Revival home almost covered with vines and underbrush, with a "For Sale" sign on it!

Stopping my car to get a better look, and copying down the telephone number of the realtor, I saw a huge old home and a vast lot with at least a half dozen very large old native pecan trees. I called the realtor right away. The price was just right, and I made my second call to my sister, Mary, in Abilene. I remarked, "I've even got the name for it. Let's call it "The Grove."

After Mary's arrival, we went to the realtor's office, and as he brought out the papers on the property, he remarked,

"Oh yes, let's see, this house is now owned by a Mr. and Mrs. Grove!"

The first few months we owned the place were devoted to removing the undergrowth, removing accumulated trash, taking estimates and bids on the restoration, plus learning some of the history of the property. The Groves had purchased the property a few years prior and had started the initial cleanup, but sickness in the family had caused a halt to the project and they decided to put the home back on the market.

Prior to their ownership it had belonged to Louise Young, a "maiden lady" school teacher, who had lived in her home from 1887 until her death in 1983. Her father, "Mr. Charlie" Young, Jefferson's "gentlemen's barber," had purchased it in 1885. This we know, but the house was obviously older than this. The most important matter now was just getting the house in shape.

We finally found our contractor. He was Mr. Billy Ford, from Marshall. He assured us he was familiar with working on old houses, saying, "The last one I worked on was the Fox Plantation in Marshall."

The renovations began, and continued with too many strange and eerie happenings to note. At this point, I must admit, Mrs. Grove did tell me, "Before we sign the final papers, I think I must tell you something about the house ...." I interrupted, saying, "I think I know what you're going to say. All I want to know is, have you seen anything?" Replying, "Yes. I brought my Bible (her husband was a minister) one night with the intention of praying for them, but I fell asleep. When I awoke, all I ... saw was a black swirling mass."

This conversation I kept to myself, not even telling my sister Mary! So, I was surprised when Mike, the other contractor, quit, but not when Billy Ford said, "Mike kept having bad dreams and waking up at 3 A.M. and not falling back to sleep until dawn." The same phenomenon was happening to me, my sisters, and my nephew. But still I remained silent.

Finally one day, at our lunch break, Billy asked, "Patrick, is this house haunted?"

I said, "Why do you ask?"

"Well, right before Mike quit, we were working on the staircase and I sent him out the front door to find a tool in the truck, while I kept working. After awhile I heard footsteps coming from the back, and I wondered why he was coming from that way. I was still working. The footsteps came to the front where I was working and then stopped. After a while I wondered why Mike was just standing there watching me. I turned to ask him, and it wasn't Mike!"

"Well, what was it?" I asked.

"All I could say was it was like a gray, moving fog, and as it was registering to me what it was it just disappeared!"

After finishing the major work, Billy left, and the family continued with the plaster work, paint removal, sanding, painting, wallpapering, etc. which left a little time for me to look up the property records in the Marion County Courthouse (Jefferson) and Cass County Courthouse (Linden). Marion County was a part of Cass County until around 1860.

What I found was that it was originally part of the Stephen Smith land grant, to Daniel and Lucy Alley, one of the co-founders of Jefferson. Then it went to Amos Morrill, Texas' first federal judge and lawyer, to Harriet Potter, the widow of slain Secretary of the Republic of Texas Navy, Robert Potter, then to Caleb Ragin and his wife Sarah Wilson Ragin. She was the daughter of former Arkansas representative Colonel John "Mule Eared" Wilson, who had to G.T.T. (Go to Texas!) after killing the Arkansas Speaker of the House over hunting rights in the state of Arkansas. Then the house went to W. Frank Stilley and his wife, Minerva Fox, from Marshall (of the Fox Plantation that Billy Ford had mentioned!), and unlike most property cases at that time, this property was in her name, not her husband's, even though he was a successful cotton broker, with his own offices and warehouses. These washed away in the great flood of 1866, but he was back in business by 1875, even though the U.S. Census of 1870 listed his status as a clerk. They had two sons named John R. and Frank. (It is interesting to me that my oldest brother's name is Frank and he has two sons named, in order, John R. and Frank!) Also, it is unusual for the times that Mrs. Stilley's will was made out to her sons, with her husband as executor.

A tragedy occurred along Moseley Street in 1868, during the Reconstruction era. A Northern carpetbagger arrived in Jefferson and with the help of newly enfranchised blacks was elected local state representative. During one of his speeches he remarked to his audience, mostly ex-slaves, that they would never be free until Jefferson burnt. Shortly after this, much of the town did burn, and threats were made. The occupying Union troops placed this gentleman and four of his black aides in protective custody in the city jail at the east end of Moseley. The Yankee captain lived in the end house on the west end of Moseley.

Several months later a group of two hundred men surrounded the jail and disarmed the Union troops. They entered the jail and took the carpetbagger out and shot him, then they took the four black men and either shot or hanged them, all along Moseley Street. (Note: This incident is also mentioned in the Schluter house story.)

The Union forces reacted, sending reinforcements. They built a stockade two hundred yards south of The Grove. They imprisoned and tried suspects. A map drawn up by the military court lists one of the witness sites as "Mr. Stilley's House." What is interesting, shortly before finding this information, my niece was having her "Sweet Sixteen" birthday party here. After the party and while they were waiting for their parents to come take them to the local mall, they took a walk down Moseley Street. Shortly, we heard screams and the eight girls ran back saying they had seen a black man lying in the road, and as they got closer to see if he needed help, he completely disappeared! This was before we knew anything about the carpetbagger and his black aides being killed on Moseley Street!

Also, shortly after we bought the place, a black lady named Ruby B. Critton stopped by for a visit. She said it was a beautiful house, but didn't we know it was cursed? A black man was hanged on the back porch, and he died cursing the place.

Apparently Mrs. Stilley died around 1879, for her husband was selling the house from Weatherford. A family by the name of Burks bought it for $175! Then six months later, they wanted their money back! The house then went to bridge builder D.C. Rock, his wife, Amanda, and a live-in employee of the Rocks named O'Toole. (A physic from Dallas once asked me who the young dark-haired and bearded young man in a waistcoat was. "He lived here but he did not own the house.")

Finally, in 1885 Mr. Charlie Young bought the place and raised two daughters and a son here.

Now, for my own personal experience with the "lady in white." Friday, July 26, 1991 . . . it was 4:45 P.M. just fifteen minutes before we open. Just my sister and I were in the house, she to wait tables. She was wearing a white blouse and black slacks. As I passed through the hall I noticed the old trunk in the hallway needed dusting. It was Louise Young's and has her name painted on the side. Her father gave it to her in 1906 when she went to college. I got the cloth and oil and got down on one knee to dust. I heard and felt footsteps coming from the kitchen and thought it was Mary. Then the footsteps stopped in the Blue Room and crossed the hall. I looked up and saw a woman in a long white dress with puffed sleeves, and when she neared me she pulled her skirts aside, exposing high buttoned shoes. She passed me and went into the ladies' powder room, which had been an old bedroom. I was stunned and thought, "That's sure not Mary!" I got up and went into the powder room, and there was no one there! The young woman I saw was not foggy or misty and did not float. It was a very real solid person! My next reaction was to locate my sister, and the first words out of my mouth were, "Did you just walk past me?" knowing full well she didn't. When she said, "No, why?" two customers were coming up the walk!

The second appearance was two years later, in May 1993. We were doing a dinner theatre production of *Angel Street*, a murder mystery done in period dress. During the dress rehearsal, the light technician, Jennifer, was on the front porch with some equipment looking through the window, watching the action, and doing some light cues. She felt someone staring at her and looked to her right. There, standing on the east side of the house by the porch was a lady in white! When Jennifer saw her, the lady started walking behind the east side of the house. Jennifer ran down the steps and turned the corner and the lady was gone. Jennifer said either she ran (the house is eighty feet long) or was there a door on the east side? In fact, there was a door there, which led into the Blue Room. Meanwhile inside the house rehearsals were still going on. Molly Gold, the actress portraying the heroine, was coming down the stairs, and when she reached the landing she looked into the ladies' powder room, spoke to some cast members, then reached the bottom step and looked to her right and saw someone "in costume" standing in the corner. She thought it was a cast member, but when she spoke the "lady" disappeared!

Seven months later during the Candlelight Tour, a couple from the Dallas area took a picture of the Christmas lights on the neighbor's house to the east of The Grove. The next Friday they called me to say, "We're sending you a picture." Indeed, they got their photo of the Christmas lights, but in the foreground, surrounded by a "smoke ring" is a lady in a high-collared, puff sleeved white dress!

The most recent occurrence was when a neighbor lady living a block behind us said, "Let me tell you what my sister and I have seen recently. My sister was standing on our porch one night around 9 o'clock when she called me out to see a glowing white figure across the street. She looked like she was inspecting the renovation of an old building."

When I asked the woman what it was, she said she didn't know. When I asked her where it came from, she said it came from the east side of The Grove! The lady said she and her sister had witnessed this several nights in a row, and in parting, she said, "You know, a lot of people think you're pulling their leg about that house, but we grew up right here, right behind it, and we've always known about that house!"

(photo courtesy of Patrick Hopkins)

I am certainly appreciative of Patrick's taking the time to tell us all about this "lady in white" who has become quite a fixture at the beautiful restaurant known as The Grove. The description of the house on the menu, which he sent me, depicts it as of Greek Revival style with twin double parlors on either side divided by a central hall. In 1870 a dining room was added to connect with the formerly detached kitchen, which still fulfills its original purpose. During restoration, Civil War era newspapers as well as newsletters of the local Episcopal Church were discovered lining the walls. The house is built of oak and cypress wood. Several of the rooms still retain heart pine flooring and tongue and groove wooden ceilings and other interesting architectural curiosities.

The menu certainly lists a lot of wonderful delicacies, including a dessert called Jefferson's original pecan praline cheesecake! If ghosts have taste buds, no wonder they hang around The Grove!

Jefferson's Haunted
Little Theatre

Marcia and Donald "Tator" Thomas live at 112 Vale Street, in
Jefferson, in a former commercial building they remodeled into a
delightful townhouse. A French-Quarter styled early Victorian building of handmade clay brick, it was designed by David C. Russell in
1869. Many businesses have been located in the building at one time
or another, including the *Jefferson Jimblecute* (a newspaper, believe it
or not!), The Old National Bank, an antique shop, a used furniture
store, a gambling and domino parlor, a tax collector's office, and a
reputed "bawdy house." For thirty years it was used as a motor supply shop. Then the Thomases, who were both brought up in
Jefferson and were high school sweethearts, took over the building,
which had been in family ownership for over fifty years, and converted it into their comfortable residence in 1983.

The building received a Texas Historical Medallion in 1965 as a
Texas Landmark Building and was entered into the National Register of Historic Buildings in 1971.

Marcia McCasland Thomas is a fascinating and multitalented
woman. Born and raised in Jefferson, she attended high school there
for two years and then traveled to London, England, where she lived
and studied drama, dance, and voice, graduating from the American
High School at Bushy Park, England, where she was named "most
talented." While in England she did semiprofessional and community
theatre work. She told me she had always been "on stage," having
performed since the age of three when her mother entered her in a
local talent contest as "Mae West." Thomas says she started off as a
singer who liked to do a little acting. Now she is an actress who does
a little singing!

The talented Thomas has had a lot of careers: She has managed a
dress shop, was manager and secretary for Marion County Chamber

of Commerce, has served as a free-lance writer, newspaper columnist, banker, newspaper ad writer, etc. Now, she owns, manages, and stars in her own little theatre!

Soon after the conversion job on the house was completed, Marcia decided to establish the lower floor living room, which is quite spacious, into a little theatre where she could present one-woman theatrical productions. She calls it her "Living Room Theatre," and it seats an audience of thirty. She presents one-woman dramatic dialogues about interesting "Texian Women," most of which she has written. She is currently doing the story of Harriet Potter Ames, who was the wife of Robert Potter, Secretary of the Republic of Texas Navy. The first monologue that Marcia did in Jefferson, that launched her popular little theatre, was *The Belle of Amherst*, by William Luce, which is the story of the life and works of poetess Emily Dickinson.

Soon after Marcia and Tator settled into their new-old townhouse, they started to notice some strange things about the place. First off, their cat and their little French poodle seemed to always be on the alert. The cat stared for long stretches of time in the direction of the staircase, obviously observing something the Thomases were unable to see. The dog frequently sat and stared up the stairs as if he was seeing some invisible being. The cat's hair often stood up on end, indicating extreme agitation.

Because both animals were housebroken, when the Taylors left the house for short periods of time to run errands, they just left their pets inside. They began to notice that the throw pillows, which Marcia arranged a certain way on the bed in the master bedroom, were always rearranged while they were away from the house. Thinking the animals might have jumped on the bed and caused the rearrangement, they decided to check up on this, so they put their pets outside the next time they left home, and Marcia took careful note of just how she had placed her pillows. This time when the couple returned, the pillows were all neatly stacked, one on top of the other. The house had been locked. Nothing else was disturbed. The animals were outside. The pillows were definitely NOT as Marcia had left them. The Thomases began to wonder.

Next, the couple began to hear footsteps pacing back and forth up in the attic. It sounded like a child's footsteps, rather rapid, light footfalls. At first only Marcia heard them, and her husband told her she was just imagining things. Then, one night he heard them too. He also began to believe.

Marcia found out that the site on which the building was built in 1869 was previously occupied by a house, which was torn down. It had been a rather small dwelling. The property was traded off, and included in the property trade was "a little twelve-year-old 'yellow' slave girl (probably a mulatto) named Mary." Perhaps the child-like footsteps that Marcia and Tator heard are those of the little slave going about her evening chores!

Marcia told me of another strange and rather unsettling experience she had in the house. She is a collector of vintage clothing and often stages fashion shows called "Fashions with a Past." She also uses old clothing in her dramatic monologues. She said she had driven to Austin where she has located several good shops that specialize in vintage clothing. She found an interesting dress, from about the 1930s era, a green silk crepe topped by an ostrich feather trimmed cape. Although she noted it had seen better days, it still looked quite good, and best of all, it fit her! After her Austin trip, she drove up to Dallas where she did a performance. When she finished her show it was quite late. She told the man who helped her load her car to be careful and not put anything heavy on top of the costume that she had purchased in Austin, because the feather-trimmed cape was rather delicate. Then she drove back home to Jefferson.

It was midnight by the time Marcia reached home. Tator was out of town. She was so tired she decided not to unload the trunk, but just go on in the house and go to bed. She was exhausted, and it wasn't too long until she was sound asleep. Then, suddenly, she was wide awake and sat upright in bed! She saw, very plainly, standing at the foot of her bed, the figure of a young woman, dressed in a chemise over which she wore a short length kimona styled dressing gown. She was just off the floor, not standing on it! She was an attractive young woman, but she was crying. Marcia decided to speak to her, even though she was quite sure she was observing a ghostly visitation. Marcia said, "Why are you crying?" There was no answer. Then, suddenly the name "Faye" came to Marcia. She said, "Is your name Faye?" and the figure nodded. Then Marcia realized that maybe the 1930s clothing she had in the car might have belonged to the young spirit. "It's the clothes, isn't it?" Marcia said. She said she instinctively knew the clothes locked in the trunk of the car were connected to the figure which stood crying in her room in the middle of the night! Fully awake, Marcia turned on her bedside lamp, and when she did the figure disappeared. Immediately, although it was dark outside, Marcia ran out to her car and found the green silk gown, which she had instructed the porter to place on top of everything else, lying under a lot of heavier items. She removed the gown from the car trunk and carefully hung it and its matching cape in the closet before she again retired.

The phantom figure never returned.

Marcia said her late grandmother had once owned the building where she and Tator now live. It was a rental property that had been made into some small apartments. Marcia recalled one day she drove her grandmother down to the building to collect the rent from the tenants who occupied the building. At that time, which was back in the 1950s, a man "kept" several young women there. They were employed in the oldest profession! Marcia, who was younger, was quite cognizant of what was going on but didn't say anything to her grandmother, whom she is sure knew nothing of what the man and "those nice young ladies" might have been up to. Later, Marcia laughed, thinking her grandmother, a strict and proper lady, was actually a "madam" of sorts since she owned the building where the women were employed!

If you are contemplating a visit to Jefferson and might possibly be there on a Saturday night (the only evenings that Marcia performs), you might like to drop in at the Living Room Theatre. For reservations and information, call Marcia Thomas at (903) 665-2310.

Magical, Mysterious Liendo

Near the small town of Hempstead, about thirty-five miles northwest of Houston, there is a lovely old plantation home called "Liendo." I was fortunate enough to visit the house when my husband and I were guests on a familiarization tour of that part of East Texas hosted by the East Texas Tourism Association.

Although it has been several years since that visit, I recall well our leaving the main road, turning into a quiet country lane of red dirt that wound its way past green fields in which sleek, well-fed cattle grazed. The tall grasses grew around magnificent old Spanish live oak trees. We came through a gate into the grounds of the charming two-story plantation house, where we were greeted by Will Detering, the owner. There had been a big storm just a few days before our visit, and the evidence was still there. Numerous splintered big limbs lay scattered about the yard, and one lay dangerously close to the house itself.

However, it was the pastoral tranquillity of the place that most impressed me. As we were told the history of the house, I could understand what great love all of its owners must have had for it.

One of Texas' earliest cotton plantations, the place was named for the original holder of a Spanish land grant. His name was Jose Justo Liendo. The grant was for 67,000 acres! At least eleven leagues of that property (a league is three miles) were being farmed by the year 1833. In 1849 Colonel Leonard Groce bought the property. He was the son of one of Texas' most respected landowners, Jared Groce, who had sustained Sam Houston's little army of volunteers prior to their march to San Jacinto in April of 1836. There were around three hundred slaves on the property, and they made all the bricks for the foundation of the house that Groce built for his family in 1853. The house itself was built of the finest Georgia longleaf pine. Groce had it freighted in from Houston. And there were six fireplaces with magnificent marble mantels. The outbuildings were made of handmade brick as well. The columned front porches, one above the other, formed shady places to rest on warm spring and summer days. It was, and is, a fine example of antebellum plantation architecture.

The great house that Leonard Groce built, with its formal parlors, music room, dining room, and guest quarters, was the scene of much lavish entertainment in the days just prior to the outbreak of the Civil War. The larder was always full; the welcome mat was always out. In fact, the place was often described as having been the center of social life in all of Texas, having received and entertained the leading dignitaries and notables of that era.

Like so many Southern plantation owners, Groce was hard hit by the Civil War. There were no longer any slaves to till the soil and plant the crops. There was no money coming in and not much to eat. It was to this place that George Custer came, commandeering Liendo as a Union prison camp for Confederate soldiers. The Groce family was as kind and hospitable as they could be under the very trying circumstances. Their kindness to their uninvited guests served them well. General and Mrs. Custer were so impressed with the Groce's and their lovely home he gave special orders after the war that no harm was to come to the place, as a token of his appreciation. Many plantations in the area were put to the torch, but lovely Liendo was spared that fate.

But Leonard Groce was broke. He could no longer keep up his beautiful estate. And so the plantation fell into the hands of numerous owners, until finally in 1873 it was purchased by a fascinating and eccentric couple. When the world-renowned German sculptress Elisabet Ney and her husband, Dr. Edmund Duncan Montgomery, arrived to look over the place, the famous artist is said to have walked out on the balcony, where she threw her arms open wide and said, "This is where I will live and die!"

Although the couple had come to this country a number of years before, they had never found a place where they felt truly at home until they purchased Liendo. Elisabet was what one might call a "liberated woman" long before Woman's Lib existed. She did not choose to use her husband's name. In fact, the strange pair did not even profess their marital status to most people, preferring to refer to one another as "best friends." Montgomery, in his own right, famous as a philosopher and biologist in his native Scotland, referred to his talented wife as "Miss Ney." Since the couple had two little boys, just infants when they moved to Liendo, you can imagine the stir this must have created in the little community of Hempstead, which was often referred to as "six-shooter junction." The lifestyle of the pair was considered totally out of sync with the rest of the inhabitants. They were more or less given the cold shoulder in what passed for "society" in the community.

Elisabet adopted an unusual style of dress, going about her estate clad in Grecian togas, Turkish bloomers, and wrapped turbans. She often rode horseback while wearing this outlandish garb, sometimes armed with two six-shooters and a dirk as well! The sculptress, widely acclaimed in Europe where she had sculpted some of the most famous men of her time, was considered "odd" to say the least.

Ney turned her back on her art, content to spend her time at the "art of molding flesh and blood," referring to the couple's two sons, Arthur and Lorne. Unfortunately, two-year-old Arthur, the eldest child, contracted diphtheria in an epidemic that was sweeping the South Texas woodlands area. Little was known of the disease, and no real treatments were available. Dr. Montgomery and his eccentric wife barred all comers from their estate, to block the spread of the disease. They treated the toddler as best they could, but they could not save the little boy. And so young Arthur died. Although no real documentation has been found to verify what happened next, it is said that Miss Ney sequestered herself in a room with the little boy's body and for a time refused to turn his body over to anyone. Then, she made a death mask of the child. After that, it is commonly accepted as fact that she and her husband took the little body of their son and placed him in the fireplace in the front parlor, which was to serve as a crematorium for his remains. Finally, the ashes that were rendered there were placed in an urn which long adorned the mantel in that room. How often the parents of that child must have gazed on that urn and recalled his last gasps for breath as the life in his disease-ravaged body slowly slipped away. The couple reasoned that cremation was the only way to kill the deadly germs of the disease. Of course, this unusual conduct was just one more reason for the people of the community to think the couple was exceedingly strange!

For the next eighteen or so years, Ney turned all of her attention to raising her younger son, Lorne. The scholarly Dr. Montgomery knew nothing at all about running a plantation, so the place became pretty run down. It is said that Miss Ney was no housekeeper. The house was kept in a ruinous state. The couple was said to have existed with sparse, primitive type furnishings, and the place was a far cry from its former antebellum days when Liendo was a place of great elegance and charm.

When Lorne was a young man, he became quite a rebel. When he was a child his mother had made him wear the same type of strange clothing she wore; turbans, togas, and bloomers. Finally, when he was about twenty, he married a local girl whom Elisabet did not like and became completely estranged from his parents. Elisabet opened a studio, which she had built in Austin. She named it "Formosa" after the first studio she had when she and Dr. Montgomery were newlyweds. This first studio had been on the island of Madiera, and the name, "Formosa," meant "beautiful" in Portuguese. After a long sabbatical from her art, Ney was back! And she was prodigious in her production, including the statues of Stephen F. Austin and Sam Houston that are in the state capitol, and the recumbent likeness of General Albert Sidney Johnston that can be seen in Austin's state cemetery. The studio, in a wooded area where Elisabet felt a certain tranquillity, provided the proper place for her once dormant art talent to flourish, and she became very famous. While Dr. Montgomery stayed at Liendo most of the time, there was a small study provided for him at Formosa.

Ney died in Austin in 1907 at the age of seventy-four. Dr. Montgomery lived four more years. Both of them are buried, along with the ashes of little Arthur, in a small cemetery at the foot of the little hill on which the plantation house stands. The sculptress had even carved her own tombstone in anticipation of her death!

But has the family ever really left? It is said that at the long, white guesthouse on the estate, come darkness, the little toddler

Arthur comes. A tiny, gasping cry has been heard there many times. A foreman on the estate named Dick Gannaway, who was questioned in 1981 for an article that appeared in the *Houston Chronicle*, said help is hard to come by at Liendo. He sort of smiled when asked of the plantation's "visitors," but he admitted numerous other people had sensed or heard them. One former cowhand on the place, who requested not to be named, said he had heard it...the sad mournful cry of a little boy lost. It came from down at the little cemetery surrounded by the tall oak trees, filling the darkness with a sound that put chills down the back of the tough old cowboy. It was enough. Enough to cause him to move on. The folks there accepted his excuses. They knew why he left. He didn't have to tell them.

Some guests at the plantation have even claimed to have seen the apparition of the little boy, down in what they call the "sacred grove" near the cemetery west of the house. Sometimes he has also been seen on the front porch. And present owner, Will Detering, who bought the place in 1960 and has completely restored it, says that in 1993 two ladies were visiting, when one of the guests said a lady came into her room. At first she thought it was her friend. Then she felt something get into the bed with her, which she found very odd. When she turned over, there was nobody there at all! At that point she became frightened.

Detering said another guest told him the room suddenly turned cold. At the same time, this visitor said she felt very peaceful. And then a strange woman appeared and said, "I know you are a guest here." The guest thought the woman was Will Detering's mother. She wasn't.

The plantation house, beautiful Liendo, is open for tours on the first Saturday of each month. Also, it can be opened at other times, for special groups, by appointment only. The telephone number of owner Will Detering is (409) 826-3126.

The Haunted Taylor Mansion

The small town of Karnack is a short distance from Marshall. It's also fairly close to Jefferson and the little town with the unusual name of Uncertain that sits on the banks of Caddo Lake. Claudia Taylor, better known as "Lady Bird," the widow of former President Lyndon Baines Johnson, was brought up in Karnack. The former first lady lived in a big house called the Taylor Mansion, where she was born in one of the upstairs bedrooms.

Lady Bird's brother, Tony Taylor, told a story to the late Frank X. Tolbert, which appeared in one of his *Tolbert's Texas* newspaper columns back on July 10, 1966. Lady Bird's father, Thomas Jefferson Taylor, bought the mansion, which is now over one hundred and fifty years old, back in the early 1900s. It was built in 1843 by the first county clerk of Harrison County, C.K. Andrews, on a six-hundred-acre plantation. He employed George W. Taloo as the builder. The columned front facade is formally balanced with a gabled portico, a balcony, and thirty-foot-high brick columns. It is still a very elegant Southern mansion.

Mr. Tolbert's article stated that Tony Taylor had told him the place was supposed to be haunted by the spirit of a young lady, possibly the daughter of the builder. The story goes that she was seated by the fireplace in what is known as the "East Room" when a bolt of lightning came down the chimney and struck her, killing her instantly.

Taylor said he didn't blame the girl's spirit for being angry and confused. Here she was, just sitting by a cozy fireplace, during a stormy night. She doubtless was feeling all snugly safe and sound, and then the next minute the poor girl was gone! Taylor told Frank Tolbert that he had never seen the spirit, but people who had seen her said she was very beautiful. Taylor did say he had heard various sounds at night that made the hair stand up on the back of his neck. The sounds were described as "lady-like sobs."

Tolbert also talked to Mrs. Pauline Ellison, who was the sister of Mrs. Ruth Taylor. Mrs. Taylor was the second wife of Thomas Jefferson Taylor, Lady Bird's father. Mrs. Ellison said she had spent the night in the room where the young woman had been struck by the lightning bolt, and while she never saw or heard a ghost, she did have one strange experience in that room. One night, when all the windows were closed, the curtains started to move as if someone was walking around pulling at them. She could find no explanation for this.

According to Mrs. Ellison, Taylor had bought the big house from a medical doctor who had an eccentric hobby. He collected hickory nuts. When Taylor bought the house he found one room was almost entirely filled with nuts. This didn't bother Taylor all that much. His wife had died soon after little Lady Bird was born, and he lived as a widower in the house for a long time. He wasn't much of a housekeeper. In fact, for a time he stored hay in the living room, and hens made nests and laid their eggs all around the house! At one time, according to Pauline Ellison, cows even walked into the mansion!

When the eccentric widower married Ruth she changed everything around. She had the place all cleaned up and restored, making it into one of the handsomest houses around in a portion of the state that boasts a lot of grand old nineteenth-century mansions.

Today a state historical marker designates the house on the Karnack Highway as the birthplace of the gracious former first lady, Claudia Taylor "Lady Bird" Johnson.

Henderson's
Howard-Dickinson House

Henderson is a small, dynamic city located on Highway 259 about thirty miles north of Nacogdoches. It is filled with lovely old homes and quiet, tree-lined streets. The city is proud of its heritage, as is evident in the work done by the Rusk County Heritage Association and the Renaissance Club. The Heritage Association was founded, in fact, in order to save one of Henderson's beautiful old homes from destruction. And therein lies a very interesting story.

I first heard about the Howard-Dickinson House, at 501 South Main Street, during a familiarization tour of East Texas that my husband and I took with hosts Howard and Kathy Rosser, founders of the East Texas Tourism Association. It was mentioned at that time the house might have a ghost story attached to it.

When the possibility of doing an East Texas book arose, I got in touch with Dr. Woodrow Behannon, president of the Heritage Association, who is in charge of the restored house, and with Wanda Sparks, a former docent at the property. Both were helpful in providing information about a fascinating part of the Henderson community. I also spoke at length with the vice president of the Heritage Association, poet-writer Mary Craig, who is a retired schoolteacher.

The story of the old house is extremely fascinating. In 1855 two brothers, David and Logan Howard, came to Henderson from their native Virginia. The brothers were builders and brick masons. Soon after their arrival in the community they bought a piece of property on which to construct a house. The brick was made there on the property, fired in a kiln constructed expressly for that purpose.

The house was a showplace for its day. The pillared porch is accented with a galleried balcony, and there is a portico with pillars as well. There are six fireplaces, built right into the brick walls.

Floor-to-ceiling windows afforded maximum ventilation in the days prior to air-conditioning.

Few East Texas homes had basements, but the Howards, accustomed as they were to colder Virginia winters, designed their home to include a basement which was three-quarters underground. The original house was built of red brick that was painted yellow on the outside and plastered on the interior. There were six large finished rooms, two on each level, including the basement.

When the Howard brothers built the house, David brought his wife Martha to live there. They had ten children as well. Logan, a bachelor, also resided with the family. In fact, he outlived David and remained in the house with his brother's widow and the children until his death in 1905. At that time Martha Howard sold the place to a Mrs. Katherine Dickinson. In 1905, when the house was nearly sixty years old, Dickinson had a frame addition added on to the building. There are only two floors in this portion, as no addition was made to the basement, which is kept as it was originally. A back bedroom on the ground floor has since been converted to a kitchen.

Dr. Behannon said Mrs. Dickinson enlarged the house in order to make it into a boardinghouse to help support herself and her two children, Katherine and Brad. When the widow died she left the house to Katherine, a spinster, stipulating the house would belong to her only as long as she remained single. If she did marry, the property was to pass on to Brad, who was married and had a daughter.

Katherine never married. She finally just closed up the house and left it in 1950. No one knows where she went. All sorts of theories were projected at the time. Did she elope? Was she just tired of taking care of the old house? Was she frightened living alone, or what? For whatever reason, the house, which was in pretty bad condition, was soon sold. A local businessman purchased it, planning to tear it down to utilize the land on which it stood to expand the downtown business zone of Henderson. He had the property zoned for business. However, for some reason he changed his mind and decided not to tear it down.

From 1950 to 1965, the century-old house was left vacant and forlorn, slowly deteriorating. The building had been condemned. Finally it was rescued by the Rusk County Heritage Association, which had been organized by a group of dedicated historians and civic leaders to save it. They bought the old derelict building, which during its vacant years had been referred to by local youngsters as "the old haunted house" where Halloween parties were held on the porch to "scare the girls." It was by then in deplorable condition, but the price was right! The Association purchased the house for the sum of $1.00 with the stipulation it must be restored. Today those efforts have been rewarded as it is now listed on the Texas Historical Register.

The house is also the venue for the monthly meetings of the Heritage Association. Tours may be arranged to see the house, and it is the frequent location for receptions, weddings, catered luncheons and dinners, and other social functions. The Association also stages annual candlelight tours during December, when the lovely old mansion is decorated with fresh greenery native to its East Texas locale, such as pine, cedar, and holly. The decorations are tastefully done in the Victorian style of the house itself.

Often during such events, the old pump organ in the parlor, which belonged to the Howard family and still works, is put to good use. It was one of the first organs in East Texas and for many years belonged to Stephen F. Austin University in Nacogdoches, who graciously returned it to its original location when the house was restored.

There have been stories over the years that the house is haunted, and from what several people have told me, there is basis in fact to these stories.

Dr. Behannon told me that at least one tragedy took place in the house during the time the Howard family occupied it. It seems one afternoon, two of the sons, young men by that time, were downstairs in one of the basement rooms. There is speculation to this day whether or not the brothers might have been drinking. At any rate, a shot reverberated through the house. One of the young men, visiting from Houston, was mortally wounded. It is said the brothers were cleaning their guns when one of them accidentally discharged.

The victim was barely able to struggle upstairs to his mother's bedroom where he collapsed and died from loss of blood. He left behind a young widow, two fatherless little children, and a brokenhearted mother. Although the death was ruled accidental, there has always been some doubt as to the exact cause of the tragedy. Dr. Behannon told me there are still bloodstains visible on the floor of the room where the young man died, too young, too soon.

Wanda Sparks, once a docent at the house for over a year, says when she used to come to the house to open up, a light was always burning in the basement, although she knew she had turned it off the evening before. She also knew she was the last person to leave the house and the first to return to open it up. She could never find an explanation for this.

Wanda told me another woman, a member of the Heritage Association, once saw the figure of a woman in a white dress. She entered the house through the front door and climbed the stairs to the second floor. The society member said she also noticed the figure wore a wide gold bracelet on her wrist. When she went upstairs to see who the strange woman in white was, she found no one there. She was quite alone in the house! A talk with a granddaughter of Mrs. Howard's verified that the gold bracelet was a family piece that had been lost for a long time and was never found! Some people theorize the figure was that of Mrs. Howard returning to the room where her son had died.

A century ago, table etiquette demanded that the dessert fork always be placed with the table setting, never on the dessert plate. Mary Craig told me that often, when events are catered in the old house, the forks have been placed on the dessert plates, with the cake or pie or whatever is being served, to facilitate service. When this is done, invariably, the forks fall to the floor when the servers are bringing in the dessert course. It is quite evident that Mrs. Howard or Mrs. Dickinson (one can't be sure which lady was the stickler for proper procedures of her day) is displeased with such a breach of etiquette, and causing the forks to fall off the plates is a gentle reminder of how she wants the serving to be done!

Mrs. Craig also told me that one time a police officer was passing the Howard-Dickinson house when he chanced to spy a woman standing on the upper floor balcony. She was frantically trying to get his attention, waving him to stop. When he stopped and came into the house, no one was anywhere to be seen. Who the woman was remains another mystery. Could it have been the spirit of Mrs. Howard trying to summon help for her son who lay bleeding to death in her bedroom? A replay of that scene, traumatic as it must have been, would certainly not be uncommon.

The enthusiasm of Dr. Behannon, Wanda Sparks, and Mary Craig is quite evident. They, and others like them, are very proud of the old house and the fact that their association brought it back to life, re-creating the ambiance it once had as a beautiful house of the antebellum period. Dr. Behannon said he and his wife, who is a Henderson native, were living at one time in Arkansas, but they came back to Henderson for his in-laws' fiftieth-anniversary party, which was held in the Howard-Dickinson house. They moved back to Henderson a short time later to help look after Mrs. Behannon's mother after her husband died. Recently the Behannons celebrated their own fiftieth anniversary in the restored house.

Mary Craig added another bit of intriguing trivia to the history of the house. She said General Sam Houston and Martha Howard were cousins, and the famous Texas leader was often a visitor to the house. He and Logan Howard were close friends as well. One of the antiques in the house is an old campaign trunk that belonged to Houston. Just prior to the Battle of San Jacinto he left his trunk and belongings at a plantation home with some friends. He was wounded at the battle and unable to return for his trunk. Later on, the woman who owned the plantation, whose husband was killed at the Battle of San Jacinto, was able to return the trunk to Houston's relatives, the Howards, there in Henderson. It is said the woman was so taken with Henderson and its friendly people she decided to sell her plantation and stay in Henderson, where she eventually remarried.

Today, visitors may tour the famous old house, which is furnished with period pieces, many of which were donated to the house by a Howard family granddaughter, who acted as an advisor during the restoration. For information and touring hours, please call the president of the Heritage Association, Dr. Woodrow Behannon, at (903) 657-7140.

The Phantom Train

When I wrote the story about the Howard Dickinson House in Henderson, I spoke with one of the docents, Mary Craig. In chatting about ghosts and how many types there are and why they do what they do, she also volunteered an interesting bit of "ghost talk," as she called it, to me.

Mary had heard about a funeral that had taken place in Mineola several years ago. She didn't know all the details, but she said a friend had told her that the deceased was an elderly retired railroad man. He had been a devotee of trains and the railroad he had served all of his life. His family had selected a burial plot in the cemetery that was close to the railroad tracks.

The graveside ceremonies had just come to a close, and the man was about to be buried in his final resting place. Just then, a train came into view. It was moving very, very slowly. It hardly made a sound, just a gentle "clickety click" as is ran along the tracks just outside the cemetery. The relatives of the dead man were impressed and pleased with this. They thanked the undertaker for arranging to have the services at just the time when a train would be running past the cemetery, as they felt this was a fitting tribute to their departed loved one who had lived with and loved trains all of his adult life.

Can you imagine their stunned surprise when they found that not only was no train scheduled to run on those tracks that day, but no train *had* run that day!

A phantom train passing by in final salute to an old railroad man. How's that for a good shiver or two?

The Moore House in Marshall

There is an attractive, century-old frame house in Marshall, often described as a "Victorian cottage." Located at 1006 East Bowie Street, it was purchased by Richard J. Moore in 1989. He has done quite a bit of restoration work on the lovely dwelling, which, at 4,100 square feet, is really quite a bit more than a "cottage."

The house was built in 1893-94 by Mr. Edwin B. Gregg Jr. He was the nephew of George Gorman Gregg, who has often been referred to as Marshall's leading nineteenth-century financier. Mrs. Gregg was the daughter of Dr. Granville M. Phillips, the owner of Fry-Hodge Drug Company and the Capitol Hotel. The wealthy Dr. Phillips gave the large lot on which the house is located to his daughter, Ophelia, who was often referred to as "Peachy," as a wedding gift. The young couple built what they described as a "conservative Queen Anne cottage" on the property.

Ophelia "Peachy" Gregg lived in the twelve-room house until her death in 1956. Then there were several owners until Tanya and Neeley Plumb of Marshall bought the house, and after extensive restoration they opened it as a bed and breakfast inn in 1986.

In 1989 the Plumbs decided they wanted to sell the house. Moore, who was then residing in California, although he was brought up in Marshall, was home for a visit, which coincided with his thirty-fifth high school class reunion. This was in June of 1989. Moore was just driving around his old hometown, trying to locate a house he had lived in when he was a small child, when he accidentally stumbled upon the "cottage" as he made a wrong turn!

Seeing the place was up for sale, Moore decided, almost on the spur of the moment, he wanted to buy that house! The bachelor had recently retired, and although he had many interests and a host of friends in California, he had no real reasons to remain there any longer. And besides that, Marshall is not noted for its earthquakes!

Moore had been a data processor for thirty-three years when he retired in 1988. He also had a sort of "second career" in the film and entertainment business, having always been fascinated by movies and film personalities. In fact, Moore has an extensive collection of movie memorabilia, which he houses in a room he had especially designed for that purpose in his new home. For a time he served as the entertainment chairman for the San Francisco Press Club and also served a term as vice president of the National Film Society. I am sure the Californians hated to see a person of such talent move to Texas!

It would seem the cosmopolitan Moore has been able to adjust quite well to the slower paced life of an East Texas city, although by his own admission he says he really doesn't like to have much company and is pretty much of a loner. He told me he thinks the house would like to have more visitors around but he really likes being by himself. In his own words he says he is an "outgoing recluse." Frankly, I found him fascinating!

Moore seems to think the spirit that he is sure resides in his home is probably that of the original mistress of the household, whom he refers to as "Miss Peachy." Moore believes she would like to see more social life in her lovely former home. Or maybe the varied decor of the rooms, a French dining room, an Oriental living room, and an English library, all reflections of Moore's eclectic taste, his travels and interests, are not to the taste of a prim and proper Victorian housewife.

The first time Moore felt there might be a spirit or ghost in his house, was in the middle of December 1994. However, previous owners had numerous experiences that they had spoken about to Moore. These included the usual ghostly manifestations, symptomatic of a haunting, such as doors opening and closing and lights going on and off at will. There were cold spots all over the house, the television set was continually going on and off all hours of the night, and sounds of a piano playing were heard in the house from time to time. No one could identify the melody. A former maid who worked at the house in the 1970s also reported she saw the apparition of a woman in the house during the time she worked there. In addition, Moore, as well as previous owners, has experienced things being moved about or hidden, and he has heard footsteps upstairs in the attic area. Moore has also frequently detected the presence of a strong floral fragrance, perhaps a favorite perfume worn by "Miss Peachy." Moore certainly knows it isn't the aroma of his favorite after-shave lotion!

Richard told me that after Peachy Gregg died in 1956, there was one owner who is said to have poisoned her little baby and then tried to kill her husband during the time she lived in the house. The woman also set fire to the place, but fortunately not much damage was done. Since he believes the woman may still be living, we didn't really delve into this part of the house's history.

Moore's mother, Edith Moore, who lived in Marshall, died shortly after her son moved back there. He had to sort through her belongings, and now some of her former possessions are in his house. One of these things is an old Victorian candleholder. Just before Christmas of 1994 Richard had the antique in his hand. He was getting ready to put a votive candle in it and had just opened the pantry door to get a candle off the shelf when something hit him in the face. As he recoiled from the blow, he saw a ball of mist, head high, sort of moving in a circle inside the large pantry. At the same time, he observed a pool of water had formed on the pantry floor. The incident is totally unexplainable.

One of the strangest incidents Richard can recall occurred on a day when he had invited some ladies to come over to see the house. He had gotten up quite early to tidy up the house, and he made his morning coffee. Finished with cleaning, about 9:30 he put a cup of coffee, now cold, into the microwave oven to heat. Then he ran upstairs to change clothes. He didn't hear the beeper sound, so he came downstairs to get his hot coffee. But something was really wrong! The mug wasn't in the oven where he had left it. He turned around, and there it was, sitting on the breakfast table. And it was piping hot!

The same day of the coffee incident, Moore noted the door leading into the attic area was ajar, about six inches, although he was sure he had closed it tightly, because he didn't want his cat or his dogs wandering around up there. Periodically, this door seems to have a mind of its own and opens all by itself. He has finally come to the conclusion that Miss Peachy likes the attic, and this is where she usually hangs out. He even discussed this with Tanya Plumb, the previous owner, and she told him anytime they had a strange experience with the spirit, the attic door was always found ajar soon afterwards!

Moore kept reciting all sorts of odd incidents. Once, when he sat alone in his kitchen, he first heard a horrible grinding sound, then a loud crash, then a deep growl. He thought it might be one of his four dogs, but a quick look around revealed they were all right there in the kitchen with him, looking just as startled as he, as if they too were puzzled by the noises. Richard got up to look around and discovered that a votive candle holder he had lit at the little Buddhist shrine he has in his living room was broken in half. One half, which looked like it had been sawed in two, had flown across the room and lay on the floor. It is fortunate Richard heard the noise when he did. The candle was still burning.

I asked Richard to tell me more about the Buddha shrine. He said it is about two feet square, in a small, carved carrying box, and he has it set up in the living room. It is several centuries old and was just one of those things he had to have, when he saw it at an antiques sale! He said he had to pay a lot for it, but he likes it and it is pretty and gives him pleasure. It fits into the Oriental decor of his living room and goes well with his other belongings.

Once Richard heard the Buddha actually rattling around in its case. Upon careful examination he saw it had just been split apart by some unseen force. And another time, he said he was hit, with a hard blow to the head, by an eight-pound brass hand of Buddha, an Oriental art object he keeps on a shelf up over the little Buddha shrine. He said the hand had to have been hurled at him, because had it just fallen off its shelf it could not possibly have hit him where he was standing!

Moore is convinced that Miss Peachy doesn't like anything Oriental. Moore has a number of Oriental art objects in his home. (He lived in San Francisco, remember?) Peachy doesn't seem to care for votive candles, either, and Moore says they are just one of his "things." He says he has always enjoyed having them scattered around the place.

Although sometimes the spirit can be irritating, and in the case of the hand of Buddha thrown at Richard's head, downright dangerous, Richard is still not afraid of it. He has talked to his live-in unseen guest and has told her he plans to stay there and is taking very good care of her old home. She is welcome there, too, but he makes it clear he wants her to calm down, because he's not planning to leave! Proof of this: the last time I spoke with Richard Moore he had recently purchased several houses on his street and the house just behind his, as well. He said if you want to be sure your neighborhood is kept up well, the best thing to do is just go out and buy the neighborhood! He is restoring houses, making a couple of them into upscale small apartment dwellings, and he has some great, innovative ideas including the making of a neighborhood park for all the people around there to enjoy. For an avowed "recluse" this man is something else!

They make peach-scented candles these days. Maybe if Richard were to buy a few of these and tell Miss Peachy they were there in her honor, she just might start to like them!

THEY ARE THERE

If you look for them, you'll find them
In the darkening of the night
If you listen, you will hear them,
Even though they're out of sight.
If you stand still, you will feel them
For they bring forth a sudden chill.
In all their poignant stories
You can feel their presence still.

Docia Williams

A Haunted House in Gilmer

A letter I received from Gilmer homeowner Yvonne Ray indicated she might have some ghosts attached to her house. The
residence was built in 1932. The first owners were a brother and
sister, Margie and John Edwards. Mrs. Ray thinks they are the resident spirits.

The Edwards siblings both died in the house. John's funeral was
actually conducted there as well. Yvonne cannot recall the exact
years, although she said she did recall hearing about their deaths.

I would have to say, in view of other haunted places I have written about and many people I have interviewed, that the Ray's house
has enough symptoms to indicate there might be a spirit around, trying to make contact in a mild, rather cautious manner.

For example, back in 1972 Yvonne said the blender came on at
3:30 A.M. Both she and her husband, Horace, were asleep, but the
noise woke her up. She could find no explanation for this occurrence.

Then, once, their small grandson saw a figure of a man in the
front hallway. Although Yvonne did not see him, the child was so
positive he had, that she believed him. My husband, a retired state
law enforcement officer, says children make excellent witnesses.
They just say what they see. Period.

Yvonne Ray says the upstairs lights have turned on when they
have not been upstairs and are positive all the lights were turned off.

And one time, Yvonne said, there was the most awful wailing,
crying, or sobbing sound, that seemed to be coming from the point of
where the breakfast room wall meets the ceiling. Every time Yvonne
entered the breakfast room the sound stopped, and then when she
stepped out of the room the sounds would start up again. She was
quite frightened and extremely puzzled by these strange unexplainable noises and finally left her house, not daring to enter the house

again until she saw her husband drive up in the driveway in his truck.

Mrs. Ray told me that before they installed central heat and air conditioning in the house, it was very cold and they could never seem to get it warm. In searching for the source of the cold air on one particularly frigid day, she found an upstairs window open in the dead of winter, and she *knew* it had been closed. She could never explain this.

She sent me a letter in which she stated that just this past year a door had slammed in the house, and there were no windows or doors open to create a draft. She said when she is alone in the house she keeps all the doors locked. And the windows are all nailed shut! Therefore, there was no breeze to cause a door to slam, and slam it did, hard! She called her husband to come home and check the house. Horace came home and dutifully checked every closet, under the beds, and anyplace an intruder could possibly hide. There was no one there.

Yvonne added that she and her husband spend most of their time at their lake house now, and while they are away they don't know what goes on at their town house. I told her I believe nothing does! Based on interviews I have had with people who own haunted houses and talks I have had with gifted psychics, I think most ghosts are fairly sociable by nature and probably make an appearance, a noise, or some gesture to indicate their presence when there is someone around. They do these things in order to be noticed.

My guess is the former owners, Margie and John Edwards, just miss their old home, since they spent so much time there, and both of them actually died there. They come back on occasion just to check up on things. Based on what Mrs. Ray was able to tell me of the brother and sister, whom she refers to as "Mr. John," and "Miss Margie," I believe they are friendly and can be considered benevolent, watchful guardian spirits.

A Ghost Named Chester

The Stephen F. Austin University in Nacogdoches is situated on a beautiful tree-studded campus. One of the buildings, the Fine Arts Theatre, is said to be haunted by a ghost named "Chester," who made his first appearance in 1967.

The first time the ghost appeared was when a young professor was working alone in the Turner Fine Arts auditorium in the wee hours of the morning. He was up on the stage doing some work on a set when he suddenly felt an ice-cold draft of air hit the stage. Simultaneously, a heavy door blew open and then loudly slammed shut. The professor thought maybe an intruder was trying to frighten him, but after he thoroughly searched the building he was convinced no one was there. He was quite alone in the auditorium!

He returned to his work. Again, the strange blast of cold air came. And now he heard footsteps coming towards him, but there was no one there, no one at all. The echoing steps passed right by him and faded as they reached the side of the stage. He knew he was alone, but there was something very strange that he could not understand going on. He decided it best to call it a night and go home.

That was only the first in a long list of supernatural happenings that have occurred in the theatre in the past thirty years. There have been so many, in fact, one professor, Dr. William Waters, professor of theatre, gave the spirit the nickname of "Chester."

In the same year of Chester's debut, the drama department presented Shakespeare's *MacBeth*, which includes ghosts in the plot. In Act IV there appear eight ghostly actors, portraying the ghosts of the eight kings of Banquo. But on the stage that night, the audience saw a ninth ghostly king. The drama professor in charge hurried backstage in order to catch the prankster who had appeared with the cast on stage during that act. But as the eight characters came backstage, they all appeared to be terrified. They too had seen the ninth ghost, and they realized the real ghost of the auditorium had made a cameo appearance that night!

There have been many tales of lights going on and off in the building, footsteps on the catwalks high above the stage, weird flickering lights in empty rooms, strange whistling noises. The stories keep adding up!

During the 1967 production of *The Ghost and Tiny Alice,* a play written by student LaGene Lacy Dykes, a photo was taken of the set. An apparition of a human form in a cowled hood, like a monk would wear, was seen in the developed film. The photo and its negative were sent to Eastman Kodak to determine whether or not the film had been tampered with. The experts said no, absolutely not. The vaporous image was undoubtedly a ghost!

During another production, which was called *A Flea in her Ear,* staged in 1987, a graduate student named Janet E. Walker was standing behind the curtain waiting for a curtain call when she looked up and saw a distorted face. She had no explanation except "It must be Chester." In 1985 a senior student named Mark Seigell was in the theatre alone up on the catwalk, where he was trying to focus the lights for an upcoming opera production, when he suddenly heard footsteps on the empty stage below him. He looked down and saw a long shadow of a person in the corner of the auditorium. He called out, "Who's there?" When there was no answer he climbed down and investigated the building, but no one was there. He climbed back up on the catwalk and completed his work on the lights as fast as he could, because the strange footsteps were once more echoing on the empty floor of the stage!

Another student, Jana Means, the daughter of Mr. George Means, a faculty member, reported having an experience during the time *Tiny Alice* was in production. She was sitting in the auditorium studying after an evening rehearsal. She thought she was alone. Suddenly she heard footsteps on the stage. She first called out, but when no one answered she got up and went to the stage, pulling the curtain open. She plainly heard footsteps leaving the stage, going down the stage steps into the aisle and out the door. The door opened and closed, and then it opened and closed again. The footsteps came back

into the auditorium and passed her. She felt a cool breeze as the footsteps went by, and then she saw a light in the shape of a human body
materialize. There was a face, but no features were in evidence. It
was blank and expressionless. The figure departed, then returned,
then began to rapidly move about the auditorium. Jana also heard
what she later described as an unintelligible monologue coming from
the strange unearthly figure. At that point, she decided to leave,
extremely puzzled over what she had seen and heard. Strangely
enough, she said she was not at all frightened.

Some people think there are actually two spirits at the auditorium. The one referred to as Chester is friendly and benevolent. The
other one is hostile and malevolent.

One drama professor, who asked not to be named, thinks the
spirit has gone home with him several times. A friend of the professor, Dan Delaney, from Houston, once came over to visit and spend
the night in the trailer house where the professor lives. Delaney
slept on the couch in the living room. The apparition of a ghost
appeared to him in the night which seemed to question his being
there. It moved between the living room and the bedroom where the
professor slept. It did this twice and then just disappeared.

Delaney, a Catholic novitiate, had obtained the priest's cassock
and a crucifix for use in a play. When the production was over, the
items were returned to him at his apartment in Houston. The night
the items were returned, Delaney had a vivid, disturbing dream in
which his friend, the drama professor at Stephen F. Austin, was
fatally injured with the blow of a hammer. When Delaney awoke, he
saw the cassock and crucifix on the foot of his bed. He got up and
placed them in his closet. Then he went back to sleep. The dream
came back to him even more vividly than before. When he awoke he
went into the adjoining room. Everything was out of place. The room
was a wreck! And the cassock he had hung in his closet now lay all
crumpled beneath a chair. Wrapped in its folds was a hammer that
Delaney knew was always kept in his garage!

Disturbed by all of this, Delaney called his friend, the professor,
and warned him of the dream he had and told him to stay away from
the sets. The professor ignored the warning and continued to work
in the theatre until a heavy hammer fell from out of nowhere (there

was no one up on the catwalks or scaffolds!) and landed where he had stood only seconds before!

In November of 1986 a student named Andy Long had a strange experience with the ghost. He recalled a time when he was alone in the auditorium. He started across the stage and a huge spotlight picked up on him and followed him across. The board was not programmed to do anything like that, and he knew no one was in the auditorium at the time. He decided it was time for him to leave!

Periodically, numerous newspapers and publications relate a new Chester experience, but when asked, no one seems to know who the strange spirit that has attached itself to the theatre might be. Some people say it is the architect who designed the building. Others attribute it to the spirit of a construction worker who supposedly fell to his death during the construction of the building. It is said that neither the architect nor a worker died during the time the theatre was being built. However, it is known for a fact that a foreman on the job did die of a heart attack during the construction.

For some strange reason, theatres seem to attract ghosts. There are many such stories in my files. The old theatre in El Paso, the theatre at Texas Wesleyan University in Fort Worth that has a ghost named Gussie, the San Pedro Playhouse, the Harlequin Dinner Theatre, and the Alamo Street Dinner Theatre in San Antonio are all haunted. Perhaps it's the sense of the dramatic, all that energy and excitement that clings to theatres that makes them the likely habitat for spirits.

And it looks like the Turner Fine Arts Theatre at Stephen F. Austin has a long-term resident, for sure. It doesn't look like Chester plans to move on anytime soon.

Tyler's Haunted Fire Station

The old firehouse is gone. They tore it down in 1955. Built in 1886, the two-story fire station at the corner of College and Locust Streets in Tyler had been a city landmark for years. Where it used to stand there's a drive-in bank and a big parking lot. But there's a good story about the old building and the men who served their city while it was the fire department headquarters. And of course, there is a ghost story attached to it as well!

According to an article written by Deborah Wilkins that appeared in the October 30, 1988 edition of the *Tyler Courier Times Telegraph*, the old Central Fire Station occupied one half of a building that also served as a City Hall and a high school gymnasium.

Although the building was constructed in 1886, there had been a volunteer fire department that operated in Tyler prior to that date. It had no equipment, however. One of the movers and shakers behind getting a "real" fire department for the city was a man named Joe Daglish. He had first arrived in Tyler as a railroad employee. He was instrumental in starting a volunteer bucket brigade before there had been any kind of organized fire department, water works, or any available equipment for fire fighting. Largely through his efforts, the dream of having a well-equipped fire department for Tyler became a reality.

When "Uncle Joe," as Daglish was called, became fire chief he was able to finally get together a staff of paid firefighters, an automobile gasoline fire engine, a chemical wagon, and other assorted equipment, as well as two fire stations.

The popular old bachelor, who actually lived in the upstairs dormitory of the fire station, was elected mayor of Tyler in 1915. He put the fire department high on his list of priorities as he continued to work to improve the department. Tragically, he could not continue to serve his city for as long as he would have chosen to do. He was a diabetic, and the crippling disease moved in on him so that he was forced to have both of his legs amputated. Although he had a brother who lived in Houston and two sisters who resided in Michigan, he preferred to spend his last years in residence in the fire station. Legless, he was confined to a wheelchair. The firemen took good care of him, and to Joe they were more than his friends. They were his family.

Daglish was happy keeping an eye on things at the fire station, playing dominoes with the firefighters when they weren't on duty, and visiting with friends who dropped by to visit. He always read all the daily reports of departmental activities.

The firemen were happy to carry the wheelchair and its occupant up and down the stairs of the fire station. He was a cheerful old man, with a white beard, snow-white hair, and intensely blue eyes that glistened behind little wire-rimmed round glasses. He tried not to dwell on his infirmities.

David Crimm, who researched the history of the Tyler Fire Department, said that when "Uncle Joe" died on November 27, 1935, he wasn't quite ready to let go of the fire department. During the twenty years between the date of his death and the demolition of the fire station, many firemen reported hearing his footsteps walking back and forth on the upstairs wooden floors, and they also heard him coming up the stairs. Some of the firemen said they had heard his shouts of "Get the hose!" and "Back off, boys!" Because so many of the men believed that Joe's spirit was still at the station, they got in the habit of leaving a window open a crack every night. They said it was to let Joe Daglish's spirit in and out of the building!

The old station was torn down in 1955. There's no way to tell where the spirit of the dedicated old fireman might have gone. Let's hope it's to a place of peace and rest, and big red fire trucks!

MYSTERIOUS NIGHTS
Docia Williams

There are happenings so mysterious
That they fill our hearts with fright;
There are rivers flowing, and lights a'glowing
And spirits that walk the night.

There are "things" that we as mortals
Just cannot understand
About the restless spirits
That haunt this ancient land.

Oh, would that we might help them
Find their way to peaceful dreams,
Beneath the spreading live oaks,
That shade the crystal streams.

Then we might freely travel
And never fear the sight,
Of these souls, so lost and lonely,
That wander in the night.

Section II

San Antonio and South Texas

While San Antonio may be the number one tourist destination in Texas, it may also be one of the most haunted cities in the entire state. Steeped in history and tradition, San Antonio has numerous buildings and locations that, many claim, are also home for some interesting and intriguing spirits. These include such places as the Alamo, the Institute of Texan Cultures, numerous hotels and restaurants, the city library, and the choir loft of a Methodist church.

Remember the Alamo

The most famous landmark in San Antonio is, of course, the Alamo. We have found much evidence regarding the spirits of the past which seem to cling to the historic old building. Checks into library and newspaper files and interviews with museum curators and librarians have brought forth many known, and some more recent, stories worth the telling.

First built as a Spanish mission known as Mission San Antonio de Valero, the old chapel and adjacent long barracks building have been the scene of many turbulent happenings over the years. There were Indian uprisings as well as the monumental Battle of the Alamo which was fought on March 6, 1836, at which time all of the valiant Texas defenders were killed by the overwhelming Mexican forces under General Antonio Lopez de Santa Anna.

General Santa Anna had decreed that there would be no mercy given to any of the defenders, and none was asked nor received. In just a few hours of fierce fighting, all the Texas forces were annihilated, their lifeless corpses left lying where they fell. Because there were none of their own number left to bury them, and the remnants of the Mexican army were busy taking their own dead off for burial, Santa Anna gave the orders to burn the Texan dead.

Old records indicate there were two, possibly three, funeral pyres prepared, and the bodies were stacked "like cordwood" to smolder for days. Denied the dignity of a Christian burial, killed in sudden and violent action, it is no wonder that even today there are many accounts of "strange things ... noises ... cold spots" associated with the Alamo and the long barracks museum where the fiercest of the fighting is reported to have taken place.

Although the exact locations of the funeral pyres are unknown, sketchy accounts handed down over the years, largely by word of mouth, indicate that at least one was located on the old "Alameda," a cottonwood-tree-lined avenue located where East Commerce Street is today. Just east of the location of St. Joseph's Catholic Church, there was a boardinghouse named Ludlow's at what is now 821 East Commerce. There was a peach orchard in back of the boardinghouse.

Witnesses to the events, both small children at the time, were interviewed by the late Charles Merritt Barnes in an article in the *Express-News* which ran on March 26, 1911. He had interviewed Don Pablo Diaz and Enrique Esparza, who had been around eight years old at the time of the battle. Both vividly recalled the burning funeral pyres and the stench of the smoke which filled the air for days. From these interviews, Barnes concluded the bodies were burned in two pyres, one in the Ludlow yard and the other on the south side of the street some 250 yards east.

We came across another story which concerned the location of the fire station now located east of the Alamo on Houston Street. When it was built in 1937, charred bones were unearthed at that location, which might bear out the possible theory there were three, instead of two, funeral pyres.

The Alamo

By coincidence, when we were browsing in the Brentanos book-store on the lower level of River Center Mall, the subject of books dealing with ghosts came up. The young man waiting on me was quick to volunteer the information that "strange things" had been happening in that establishment, and they might possibly have their own resident ghost. He said that lights would go on and off, books would be moved about, and the cash register would open and close of its own volition. He reported there was a "cold spot" in one corner of the shop. In checking around, it seems the shop is located just about where the Ludlow boardinghouse would have been, and the peach orchard in back where one of the pyres was reported to have been. He further went on to say that on March 6 of 1991 lights had gone off and on all day, and other unexplainable things had happened. That date is of course the anniversary date of the battle and the subse-quent burning of the Texan dead which followed.

Numerous historical accounts have mentioned that after Santa Anna and his forces surrendered to the Texans under General Sam Houston on April 21, 1836, at the Battle of San Jacinto, orders were sent to the small Mexican force remaining in San Antonio to evacu-ate and retreat south. They were ordered to destroy the Alamo before their departure.

General Andrade, who was in command, gave his subordinate, Colonel Sanchez, the order to send a party of men to blow up the chapel. Several men left for the task but soon returned, saying they could not destroy the building. Their faces showed stark terror, and no amount of persuasion could force them to go back to the building. They reported having seen strange figures which they described as "diablos" (devils) . . . six ghostly forms standing in a semicircle hold-ing swords, not of steel, but of fire, blocking their entry to the building. They were terrified and fearful of the consequences if they should destroy the building, they reported back to their commander. It is said General Andrade went himself to the place and was also confronted by the same figures. And so it was that the building was left intact, as the Mexican army marched out of San Antonio.

Although, periodically, someone reports hearing strange noises, such as voices, marching footsteps, and moans, the last known sight-ing of anything supernatural took place over a hundred years ago. In

1871 the city of San Antonio decided to dismantle the last remaining part of the original mission (other than the chapel and long barracks, which remain today). This section was the two rooms on either side of the main gate of the south wall. Late one evening, before these were destroyed, guests at the Menger Hotel watched in shocked amazement as spectral forms marched, perhaps in protest of the desecration, along the walls of the rooms.

The *San Antonio Express News* of February 5, 1894, had a most interesting article concerning the Alamo: "The Alamo is again the center of interest to quite a number of curious people who have been attracted by the rumors of the manifestations of alleged ghosts who are said to be holding bivouac around that place so sacred to the memory of Texas' historic dead. There is nothing new about the stories told. There is the same measured tread of the ghostly sentry as he crosses the south side of the roof from east to west; the same tale of buried treasure and the same manifestations of fear by the American citizen of African descent, as he passes and repasses the historic ground. The only variation appears to be in the fact that the sound of the feet on the roof has been heard as late as five o'clock in the morning by the officer in charge, who says that as a matter of fact, however, the sounds are never heard except on rainy, drizzly nights. He attributes the whole matter to some cause growing out of the condition of the roof during rainy weather, but forgot to give any reason why the same causes that produced the sounds at night did not produce like sounds in daylight hours." (Note: in 1894 the city was using the Alamo property as a police headquarters.)

The article continues: "A new feature of the case was presented Saturday night when the spirit occupants of the old building were for the first time brought to bay and made to disgorge the mission of their restless presence in the place. Leon Mareschal, an old and respected citizen living at 1001 San Fernando Street, accompanied by his fourteen year old daughter, Mary, called at police headquarters and introduced themselves to Captain Jacob Coy, who was on duty at the time, stating that they could establish communication with the ghosts. Captain Coy gave the parties two chairs and permitted them to use the little jailroom adjoining the station office. Mr. Mareschal placed his daughter in a trance and told Captain Coy to speak to the spirits through the medium. 'Do you see the spirits?' asked Coy. 'Yes, they are men,' came in a faint voice from Miss Mareschal. 'Then get them to form in line and ask them who they are,' continued Capt. Coy.

"The young girl nervously twitched her head from side to side and announced that the ghosts had fallen in line. Immediately thereafter the medium spoke again, saying: 'The forms say that they are the spirits of the defenders of the Alamo.'

"This answered the question in a very general way. It was not satisfactory, but Captain Coy decided not to press the matter until a little later on. 'Now, then,' continued Coy, 'what is the object of their visit and noise in the building at night?'

"After a few seconds the young girl in the trance spoke in a low but firm voice: 'They say that there is buried in the walls of the building $540,000 in $20 gold pieces. They also say that they are anxious to have the money discovered and have been waiting for a chance to communicate with the people on earth about it and have it discovered. They will relinquish all claim to the treasure in favor of the person who finds it.'

"'Now, just where is this treasure buried?' asked Capt. Coy.

"Miss Mareschal fidgeted a little nervously and her words were scarcely audible. 'It's in the wall near that room,' said the medium, pointing towards the dingy little apartment in the southwest corner of the Alamo without looking. 'It's in the wall at that ... ' here Miss Mareschal broke short feebly and rubbed her eyes and the trance was broken.

"It was after midnight, nearly one o'clock in fact, when Leon Mareschal and his mediumistic daughter left the old Alamo. Those who believe in spiritualism lay considerable confidence in the result of Miss Mareschal's interview with the spirits, and it is currently reported that the local Psychical Society will investigate the alleged phenomenon.

"Yesterday all sorts of rumors had gained currency, among them one that the officers in charge of the building were afraid to stay there. This brought a squad of four soldiers from the post who volunteered to hold the fort against the ghostly visitors. Their offer was declined with thanks."

That article was printed nearly a hundred years ago. Strange, but true, those who guard the Alamo now during hours of darkness have told of unexplainable sounds and the feeling of "presences." Is it because the gold is still there, being zealously guarded by spirits until the right finders come along?

Three years later, there appeared still another article about the Alamo in the *Express*, with a new explanation for the hauntings. This article described a visit to the landmark by a number of tourists from out of the state, and ran on August 23, 1897. The article stated: "As a climax to their visit the tourists are told the story of the ghosts of the Alamo and are shown the dark, gloomy recesses in the rear of the building where moans and hissing whispers and the clanking of chains are sometimes heard on wild stormy nights. The disturbing specters are supposed to be those of the errant monks who cried in chains for violating their monastic holiness in the old days when the Alamo was a Franciscan mission. That ghosts haunt the Alamo is claimed to be a well-substantiated fact. The discovery was made only a few years ago by the policemen who were stationed there when the building was used as a sub-police station, and created a great sensation at the time. Some time ago a number of prominent spiritualists held an all night seance there and are said to have had a very interesting and profitable conversation with the specters."

A more recent feature article in the Sunday magazine section of the *Express News* dated January 27, 1991, blared the headlines: "John Wayne's Ghost Remembers the Alamo." Seems the story first ran in the *National Inquirer*! Questions about ghosts at the Alamo museum are usually referred to Charles Long, who was curator of the Alamo museum for fifteen years and currently is the curator emeritus. Long did take Wayne on a tour of the historic mission when the actor was filming the movie *The Alamo* some years back. Wayne's widow, Pilar, wrote in his biography that the story of the Alamo is the epitome of everything he (Wayne) identified with and believed in: toughness, courage, and patriotism ... so if his spirit comes back to visit the Alamo, it is no doubt to just "visit" with the brave men who defended those ideals and were willing to die for them. (We haven't been able to locate anybody who has heard or seen "The Duke" around, but we thought it a story interesting enough to mention, anyway!)

The *News* article concerning Wayne also mentioned that Joe Holbrook, a widely known San Antonio psychic who counts his ability to communicate with spirits among his special talents, was called upon to visit the Alamo. "He agreed to visit the Alamo to see what sort of ghostly energy he could pick up," the article states. "Holbrook's psychic powers started kicking in even before he reached the shrine," according to the *Express* writer, Craig Phelon. "During his drive downtown he began to pick up images of the Battle of the Alamo.

"In particular, he tuned in on a figure unknown to Alamo history, who he says was one of the real unsung heroes of the Alamo. He was a humble bootmaker named 'Buttons' Morgan. 'Buttons' was obviously a nickname. The psychic said he couldn't pick up Morgan's real first name, but the man apparently was one of the bravest Alamo defenders. He also was devoted to taking care of the wounded soldiers."

Holbrook discussed the nature of spirits with author Phelon. "They don't just linger around the same place all the time," he said. "Anytime you have any place where people have died, you're going to have a spirit sighting from time to time."

Phelon goes on to say, "We enter the shrine and he says . . . 'with all these people in here it will be hard to pick up any energy.' But then he is drawn to the room to the left of the main entrance. 'There are six of them right in here,' he says.

"Even though the room appears empty, Holbrook says he can see the spirits. 'The funny part of it is, they're from the other side. They're Santa Anna's men, and they are still in their Mexican army uniforms.' Holbrook stands at the entrance to the room, as if listening . . . then offers to supply their names.

"He picks up the name of three of the spirits . . . two are brothers, Raul and Pablo Fuentes. They were seventeen and eighteen when they were killed. 'The other one is what we would call a lieutenant. His name is Pedro Escalante,' he says. 'They went over the line and helped these guys. They didn't want this battle. They came over to persuade the defenders to give up and stop fighting. For that they were killed.'

" 'The lieutenant spirit gives this information,' says Holbrook. Then he adds, 'You want me to ask about John Wayne?' After a brief silent conference with the spirit, Holbrook brings back the verdict. 'I confirm this is true,' Holbrook quotes the spirit. It seems Wayne's spirit doesn't hang around all the time, but he comes to visit about once a month or so, says the psychic. 'The reason John Wayne comes here, the lieutenant says, is that this place rejuvenates him in some way. To him, the Alamo stands for the freedom of all mankind.' "

The Alamo pulls at our heartstrings when we enter. We are filled with reverence and respect when we enter into this shrine to freedom. Under the gentle custodianship of the Daughters of the Republic of Texas, the Alamo has fallen into tender, loving hands. The dignity of those who died defending it is well preserved, and the turbulence of its past now rests in the pages of history. Our fervent hope is that the spirits of those brave defenders have at last found their eternal peace.

THE MEN OF THE ALAMO
Docia Schultz Williams

These hallowed walls hold secrets that we shall never know
About the brave and gallant men who died here long ago.
They did not shirk their duty when they were called to stand.
They knew their lives were soon to end with foe so close at hand.
When the army of the enemy blew their mournful bugle calls
They bravely faced a certain death within these cold grey walls.
They knew they were outnumbered. They knew they could not win,
But they chose to die for freedom's cause, these brave and valiant men.
In memory's golden storehouse we must ever hold them near
And take great pride in those who died for what they held most dear.
Oh, step inside with reverence, then bow your head and pause,
And say a prayer for those who died, defending freedom's cause.

Jose Navarro's Haunted Homestead

In downtown San Antonio, beside the Central Texas Parole Violator Facility, there is a quaint old world "compound" of houses, clearly dating from another era. The buildings, which are located on South Laredo and West Nuevo Streets, are a low one-story house, a two-story corner building, and a small adobe and limestone three-room building that is barely visible, out back. All are surrounded by a white fence on the Laredo Street side, and a stone wall down the West Nuevo Street side.

These buildings comprise the former homestead of a famous Texas patriot, Jose Antonio Navarro. One of the two native born Texans (the other being his uncle, Francisco Ruiz) to sign the Texas Declaration of Independence, Navarro and his wife, Margarita, purchased the land in 1832. The plot of 1.2 acres lay between the San Pedro Creek and the old road leading to Laredo. The neighborhood in which the property was located was called "Laredito," or "little Laredo," because it was situated on the old highway to the border city.

At the corner of the property there is a two-story limestone building that once served as Mr. Navarro's law office. The building is very much as it was when originally built, with quoined corners, and consists of two square rooms, one upstairs, and one directly downstairs.

The exact date the Navarros built their house and office is not known. It was certainly built sometime after 1832, as a two-room house with a one-room detached kitchen of adobe brick. The bricks were made of clay-rich soil, lime, and limestone chips and water. Each sundried brick weighed approximately thirty-five pounds. At some point the Navarros enlarged both the house and the kitchen. Workers joined three limestone rooms to the original adobe structure to make an L-shaped five-room structure. Two limestone rooms were also added to the original adobe kitchen.

Mr. Navarro was a member of the ill-fated Santa Fe Expedition in 1841. General Santa Anna sentenced the Texas patriot to life imprisonment in Mexico, but he was able to finally escape. He made his way back to San Antonio in 1845. The Navarros owned a ranch called the "San Geronimo," which was located some forty miles to the east of San Antonio, and they spent most of their time there. They used the town house on their visits to San Antonio. In 1853 they sold the ranch and made their permanent residence in town, where they lived until Jose passed away in 1871.

The Texas Parks and Wildlife Department beautifully maintains the restored complex of house, office, and kitchen. They've even planted a typical "kitchen garden" of the 1800s out back of the adobe kitchen. A pleasant porch shades the back portion of that building. Hollyhocks and roses and other old-fashioned plantings border the house and adorn the patio where the old covered well is located between house and kitchen.

Along with all this early South Texas charm, there's the opinion among people who have been closely associated with the house at one time or another that there are a few "spirits" lurking around as well!

Jose Navarro House

David Bowser, author of *Mysterious San Antonio* and resident of San Antonio, says that the house seems to be the main area of psychic disturbances. Footsteps have been heard, "cold spots" felt, furniture has been moved and rearranged, and there's a rocking chair that sometimes gets to rocking when there's no sign of wind or draft! David tells the story about the state employee who was working at the house on a restoration project and decided to sleep there at the house. He slept in the same room where Navarro died on January 13, 1871. Sometime in the middle of the night he suddenly awoke feeling very uneasy. Finally, feeling almost panicky, he arose and walked outside the room onto the porch. He chanced to glance upwards, and there, in one of the upstairs attic dormer windows, was a face staring at him! A careful search turned up nothing . . . at least nothing in human form!

Our friend, Sam Nesmith, who is both a historian and a psychic, visited the place and had a very strange experience. First, when he entered the house, a large cabinet started to teeter and would have fallen over had not a staff member come to assist him in righting the massive piece of furniture. Then, Sam said he went out of the house and crossed over to the kitchen building. There, in a room which he said he believed had been a laundry, he clearly saw the figure of a young man, cowering in a corner. His face was contorted with pain and he seemed to be out of breath. He had been shot in the leg, Sam believed, and was hiding in the room where he finally bled to death. Sam has never forgotten the look of intense anguish and fear that were reflected in the eyes of the youth he saw that day.

In 1834 Jose Antonio's brother Eugenio was the victim of a murder. Shot by what was referred to as a "vindictive assailant," Eugenio was only thirty-four years old at the time of his death. A lady who visited the Navarro house recently told members of the house staff that she had visited the San Fernando Cathedral Cemetery Number One, where she had seen the Navarro name. That is what prompted her to visit the house. They said that as soon as the women entered the house, she screamed, "Oh, my God! He's here!" "She claimed she could see Eugenio Navarro sitting in one of the chairs in the living room," according to the Park Ranger on duty. The Ranger said the woman told him that Navarro was just sitting there, waiting for someone to come and see him. It was very real to the woman, as she had "chill bumps" on both arms!

Other people have sighted various apparitions on the property at different times. There have been reports of a Confederate soldier, a bartender, and a prostitute. The "lady of the night" was apparently murdered in the room up over the main floor in the old corner office building, no doubt during the time it had served as a bar. Another story tells of a child who supposedly died in a fire on the second floor and whose little ghostly presence has been reported.

A former resident of the house, Mary Garcia, said she once saw an apparition of a woman going up the outside stairs. She and her mother lived in the house for about eight years and they saw the ghost "four or five times" during that period.

David McDonald, the Parks Ranger now in charge of the Navarro property, is quite an authority on the life and times of Jose Antonio Navarro. He speaks of the statesman with such familiarity one almost feels as if they were personal friends. There is one story McDonald told about Mr. Navarro's reported frugal nature. He hated to spend a lot of money, but at least once he did pull out all stops, because the big piano in the front parlor is really magnificent. Hopefully, his wife was a good musician to have convinced Jose to buy such a lovely instrument!

It is interesting to note that, although numerous ghost stories have surfaced over the years, none of them seem to implicate Jose himself as one of the ghostly visitors. He was apparently well satisfied with the house and grounds, which were comfortable and spacious; he was well respected in the community and had a thriving law practice, so his spirit apparently rests in peace over in the old San Fernando Cemetery Number One. The restive spirits who have made infrequent appearances over the years may have just been "passers-by" for the most part, just stopping off in that inviting little compound of houses as they made their way through town and on down the road to Laredo!

The Palace on the Plaza

It's called the Spanish Governor's Palace, but actually, the sturdy old stuccoed-stone structure that faces onto Plaza Del Armas (Military Plaza) was constructed to be the "Commandancia," or home of the Spanish Military Commander of the old Presidio of San Antonio de Bejar. It enjoys the enviable reputation of being one of America's finest examples of Spanish Colonial residential architecture, and what's more, unlike other Governor's Palaces scattered over the Southwest, which now serve a variety of purposes such as museums, restaurants, and shops, San Antonio's "Palace" is furnished with authentic antiques of the Colonial Spanish period and looks like a home would have looked in those days. Still easily visible over the entry doors is an "escudo," or coat of arms, bearing the old Hapsburg crest of the Double Eagle, a simplified version of the coat of arms of King Ferdinand VI of Spain. It bears the inscription, weathered, but still legible, "ano 1749, se acabo" (finished in the year 1749). The doors are of hand-carved walnut, copied from etchings of the original doors at the time of the restoration of the building which began in 1928.

There's an aristocratic air about the old building, and one can imagine how the "palace" nickname became attached to the building, since it was probably the most palatial building in San Antonio at the time of its construction! What grand fetes and parties and banquets it must have hosted, and what interesting and important guests must have enjoyed the hospitality of its candle-lit chambers!

The brochure given to visitors to the Governor's Palace offers the following historical information: The Commandancia, originally intended to serve as the residence of the presidio commander, came to represent the seat of Texas government when in 1772 Villa de San Fernando (San Antonio) was made the capital of the Spanish Province of Texas. Then, in later years, after 1822 (Mexico having won her independence from Spain in that year) the Spanish Governor's Palace served as a secondhand clothing store, a tailor's shop, a barroom, a restaurant, and a schoolhouse. In 1928 the building was purchased from the descendants of Jose Ignacio Perez of Spain for $55,000. (Perez had paid 800 pesos for the building in 1804.)

Only after thoroughly researching the original design and materials used in the building was restoration undertaken and completed at the cost of $29,514.61. Authorities state that the Governor's Palace is authentic to the last degree in room arrangement, fireplaces, the thick walls, and brick ovens. Furnishings of the palace include antique pieces from the early 1700s.

One real treasure, and of special interest to Texans, is the beautiful hand-carved secretary desk in the front bedchamber. It was the property of the famous frontiersman and Texas patriot James Bowie!

The Governor's Palace was dedicated in 1931 and since then has been under the capable supervision of the Department of Parks and Recreation of the City of San Antonio.

Spanish Governor's Palace

Today the "Palace" is one of San Antonio's most visited land-marks. Behind the main building there is a lovely shady patio, with a lily pond, a grapevine covered loggia, and a well. At one time this area was probably more utilitarian, as they must have stabled their horses nearby, and perhaps had a kitchen garden in the area, also. Now the restored patio is an integral part of the palace compound. The well, once used for drinking water, is no longer used for that purpose. Tourists toss coins into its depths, believing it to be a wishing well.

Patio at the Spanish
Governor's Palace

And therein lies a story, as told to us by present custodian, Jessie Rico. Rico says he was told in early days there was a robbery and murder that took place at the palace. Since it's a "word of mouth" sort of story, no one knows exactly when it all took place. But be it fact or fiction, this is what Jessie told us. It seems there were no banks in those days to safeguard family valuables. Once, when the family who lived there was away, they left the place in the care of a young servant girl. She was supposed to take care of the house and look after the gold, silver, and other valuables in the palace.

Robbers broke in, robbed her of the household treasures, and then bound her and threw her into the thirty-seven-foot well behind the house. She drowned, of course, and was not found until one of the robbers, unable to live with his terrible secret, told what had happened to her.

Rico says it is weird, but at night when he closes up the house and patio, he has often heard strange "gurgling" noises down in the well. Sometimes when he has to go down into the well to retrieve the coins tossed by the tourists he experiences "very strange feelings." Now, Jessie is a big man, and certainly doesn't look as if he'd scare easily...but he definitely doesn't like to be around that well!

We were also told that in the front room to the right of the entryway in the private chapel of the house, there was discovered, during the 1930 restoration, bones buried in the wall behind the small altar niche. They are believed to be the bones of a very small infant. Who it was, or why it was placed in the chapel walls, no one knows. It might be speculated that the infant was a stillborn who died in the house. Did weather prevent the little remains from being taken to a cemetery, or did they fear the Indians who often attacked the settlers as they made their way to the cemetery over where the Santa Rosa Hospital is today? Or was there some dark secret buried with those little remains? The spot in the wall, behind a lovely old statue of a Seventeenth Century Virgin is plainly evident, and the mystery still goes unsolved.

Jessie says he has had several strange experiences in the house, just little unexplained noises and feelings of cold spots in certain areas. Sometimes he feels he is being watched. As he closes up at night and turns off the lights in the ancient building, he says he just wants to close up fast and get out...and he never looks behind him!

A Museum That Has Both History and Mystery

The Institute of Texan Cultures, located at the corner of Bowie and Durango Streets, has often been likened to a flying saucer. The flat-roofed two-story building is accented with a wide, shady veranda floored in the same type of Texas-quarried pink granite that was used to build our state capitol in Austin. Terraced fountains centered in well-manicured grounds accent the front of the building. The sound of water rippling over the wide stone shelves tends to add an aura of refreshing coolness even on the hottest of South Texas' summer days.

The Institute was established by the University of Texas in 1968. It opened during the World's Fair known as the "Hemisfair." Unlike some structures constructed just for the exposition, the Institute was not built as a temporary pavilion. It was meant to be (and has served the purpose well) a teaching museum, emphasizing the importance of the contributions all the diverse ethnic groups who settled Texas in its early days have made. It is often filled with school children, who are well served by a fine professional staff and a large group of dedicated docents.

I had the privilege of knowing the first director, a fine gentleman and a brilliant historian, Mr. Henderson Shuffler. He passed away a number of years ago. Mr. Shuffler's office was located on the second floor level. He smoked a pipe. Numerous employees of the museum have reported smelling a strong pipe tobacco odor as they make their early morning or late evening rounds. A former researcher at the museum, my friend Sam Nesmith, said he used to come to work on Sunday mornings when he could work alone in the building and get more done before opening time. During those mornings he often smelled pipe smoke as it wafted from Shuffler's former office. No one else on the staff smoked a pipe at that time!

I believe Mr. Shuffler loved the museum so much his spirit still likes to come around and check up on things once in a while.

I received a cordial letter from Shuffler's son, the Reverend Ralph H. Shuffler, an Episcopal priest. He made some interesting comments after he had read *Spirits of San Antonio and South Texas*, the book I co-authored with Reneta Byrne. Shuffler observed: "Before he died, Dad 'haunted' the exhibit floor late in the evening and also, most often, early in the mornings. He habitually rose to get the papers, have a cup of coffee, morning pipe, muse and meander around looking for some good conversation with anyone available. There were usually plenty of early rising, flex-time workers, security guards, or maintenance folks to enjoy. He smoked an especially aromatic brand, called 'Amphora,' which reeks to high heaven and is smelled in the air for both a long time and a long way."

Shuffler continued: "Disregarding popular, contemporary management advice, he seemed to feel that he had to be pretty good at everything that went on there, was not too good to do anything that needed to be done, and besides that he liked it. One saw what a kick he got from every facet of the Institute's life—the research, writing, designing, giving production folks an often unneeded but apparently appreciated hand with some exhibit construction, welcoming visiting people of Texas (whom he recognized as the 'real proprietors'), academics, artists, business management, fund-raising, making friends with staff folks in every area, the social life, and even the necessary politics."

The clergyman concluded: "Even though I think of myself as one of those squeaky clean, contemporary, professedly Orthodox, and scientifically minded Episcopal priests (maybe that is a *non sequitur* in most circles), who has had to listen with amused patience to countless, confabulating jitters, I can imagine that Dad's spirit would really love a good, spooky story and just hanging around."

And, of course, there are so many displays all over the museum that have been touched, handled, loved by so many people one might be led to believe a great deal of energy must be attached to them. One employee named Roberto said he found working in certain areas of the museum so unnerving he asked to be relieved of that duty. He always sensed a strange presence and felt he was being watched. It made him extremely nervous.

In the section of the museum devoted to early French settlers, most notably the Alsatians who settled in Castroville, some thirty miles west of San Antonio, there is an old glass-sided horse-drawn hearse that was in use in that community from about 1889 to 1930. Often night security guards have reported the doors of the hearse will be open as they make their rounds. They close the double doors and securely fasten the catch. Then, when it's time for another round in that section, they often find the doors have opened again in the time it took them to make their rounds and return to that section. Maybe the spirit of someone who was carried on his final journey to the old Gentilz Cemetery in Castroville is still in that old hearse and is trying to get out!

Other employees at the Institute have recalled seeing a man clad in an orange work shirt. Seen from time to time, this man is said to have been a workman who committed suicide during the time the building was under construction. Many suicides do seem to try to come back. Probably regretting they ended their lives, these restless souls return for a look around the place where they might have been happy during their lifetime. This may have been the case with the orange-clad worker.

One of the most amazing and puzzling occurrences connected with the building took place in April of 1992. The Friday during Fiesta Week, a grounds maintenance man named Gerald had a heart attack and died. He had been ill for some time, but his sudden death came as a shock to the staff at the Institute. Gerald was a mildly retarded man, but he took great pride in his work. He loved the Institute and seemed to enjoy passing the time of day with his fellow employees.

On Saturday morning, the day after Gerald's death, one of the professional staff members, Vivis Lemmons, came to work as usual. As she came up to the back entrance of the building where the staff enters, she saw Gerald come out of the door on to the porch. She spoke to him and he returned her greeting with a smile and just a "hullo" as was his custom. She said she did not know him well, so she did not stop to chat. She did take note that he was very dressed up. He was wearing a tan suit, a white shirt, and a pretty bright blue necktie. She had always seen him dressed in the dark olive drab uniform worn by the groundskeepers, and she thought to herself, "Gerald must have the day off today."

Lemmons went on into her office. As she was putting her handbag away and getting her desk in order, she overheard the name "Gerald" mentioned by some of the staff who were already in the room. She said she turned around and said, "Did you mention Gerald? I just saw him outside, and he surely was all dressed up." There was a stunned silence for a moment, and then the others told her that she couldn't have seen Gerald. He had died the day before and his funeral was to be that day. She insisted that she had seen him, and later she went back to the door where she had greeted him and asked the guard on duty if he had seen her talking to anyone outside the door. He told her no, but he thought it rather strange she seemed to be talking to herself as she came in!

Lemmons said she learned later that day that a man who worked in the upper level of the museum in what is known as the "Dome area" had also seen Gerald. He had seen the custodian as he came out of the lower level snack bar, counting his change as he came out. He had not spoken to Gerald but plainly recalled having seen him.

He too noted that Gerald had worn a tan suit with a bright blue neck-tie and thought it certainly was different from his usual work attire.

Staff members who attended the funeral later that Saturday afternoon reported back to Lemmons that the clothing she had described was the attire in which Gerald was clothed for his burial. Mrs. Lemmons said she believed the museum was very special to Gerald. The staff almost seemed like family to him. He had just wanted to make one more trip there to make some final good-byes, and maybe just show everybody how nice he looked when he was "all dressed up." While everyone could not see him, Lemmons felt privileged that at least she and one other saw him that last time. She went on to say she felt some people are just more tuned in to psychic phenomena than others, and that is why she was able to see Gerald. He never came back again. He had said his final farewells.

On a recent visit to the Institute, I asked numerous staff members and docents if anything of a supernatural nature had transpired lately. It seems there have been no discernible manifestations in some time. I am not surprised. The Institute is so efficiently managed and has provided such a good service to the community, I should think all the spirits that manifested in the past may be so satisfied with the way things are going, they see no reason to hang around any longer.

A Watchful Spirit at the Witte

The Witte Memorial Museum at 3801 Broadway is located on the northeast side of Brackenridge Park. First headed by Ellen Schulz Quillin, who was director and curator for many years, the museum opened in 1926. It was named for stockbroker Alfred G. Witte, who bequeathed a large sum of money to the city with the stipulation a museum for the people be built within the confines of Brackenridge Park.

The museum includes natural history exhibits, a fine American Indian display, the Koehler Gallery of Early American Art, and a fine Texas collection. On the grounds numerous old pioneer homes have been relocated to the banks of the San Antonio River, which runs at the rear of the property. An enjoyable and educational day can be spent at the Witte, and the museum shop is a fine place to buy unusual gift items as well.

I was told by several current employees and docents that a ghost story is attached to the place. I contacted Linda Johnson, the museum director, and she said she had never seen or felt the presence of a ghost there but was aware of the stories that had been circulated. She referred me to an article which ran in the *San Antonio Express News* on July 3, 1988. The article by Ann Cain Tibbets was called "Witte's Ghost." The writer stated nobody she talked to had denied the possibility of there being a ghost in residence at the Witte. Of course, we all should know that a building so filled with artifacts of the past, belongings that once were treasured by persons now long departed, might take on a spooky appearance at night when all the tourists are gone. And, doubtless, a lot of energy from the past may still be going snap! crackle! pop! in the old building as well.

Dr. Bill Green, a former curator at the Witte who went on to become Capitol Historian for the State Preservation Board in Austin, seems to believe there's a ghost at the Witte. He said when he first came to the museum in 1981 he kept locking his door when he left his office, but when he returned it was always unlocked. The burglar alarm went off and he was blamed for it, even when he wasn't there, and no one else, including any intruders, was there either. This kept happening on a regular basis.

One staff member came to work early one morning and entered a vault through a heavy single door. She reached up on a shelf to get an artifact down, and at that moment a cold blast of air hit her and filled the vault. At the same time, off to one side, she saw a figure move out of sight. The employee was quite shaken by the sudden chill and commented to Karen Branson, the secretary seated near the vault, asking her if she'd suddenly moved from her desk. "No," was her reply, and then Branson added, "so you felt it too?"

Ms. Branson also told the *News* writer she had heard sounds in a room across from her desk. It sounded like screening trays were being shaken, she said.

At least four people told the reporter that papers move around on their desks.

The attic, which was formerly used as a library, seems to be the most active portion of the building. A gardener who went up there once on an errand said a bony hand touched his shoulder when he was alone up there, and he refused to go back.

One museum guard, when asked if he had ever encountered a spirit, replied off-handedly, "Sure. Who hasn't?" Then he went on to say it was a lady and she looked "like she always did. It's just Mrs. Quillin."

Another staff member spoke of unexplainable activity in the old library of the building. She said the coffee room was on the floor just below the library at one time, and she recalled when she was there drinking coffee she heard a sound like a wooden chair being scraped on the floor above her and then there were footsteps. The sounds were distinct. She also said she had heard footsteps on the metal stairs that led up to the library on numerous occasions, but when she got up to look to see who it was, no one was ever there.

Ellen Schulz Quillin, who almost single-handedly brought the Witte Museum into being, hung around there almost until she died. Many feel she was so involved and dedicated that even death will not separate her from her beloved museum. Towards the end of her long life she came to work when she was even then very ill and under her doctor's orders to go to the hospital for treatment of her high blood pressure. And ask the employees and docents. They think she's still there, at least much of the time. They take her presence for granted, and she is welcome.

Quillin especially loved the library because research was her big love. She wrote her book *The Story of the Witte Museum*, with Bess Carroll Woolford, there in the library. It is not surprising that it is her favorite spot to come back to for visits.

This remarkable woman was born around 1890. She grew up on a farm in Michigan and craved knowledge from the time she was just a little girl, literally "drinking up books." She went to the University of Michigan when she was only sixteen and majored in science and natural history, which were considered unusual studies for young ladies in those days.

In 1916 Ellen moved to San Antonio. She taught botany at the old Main High School. She loved to take her students on field trips to the woods around San Pedro Park to hunt for "specimens."

She and her students raised money to buy a collection of odds and ends, rocks, minerals, stuffed birds, Indian artifacts, and such from a Houston man named H.P. Attwater. Quillin and her young students begged for contributions on the street corners near the Gunter Hotel. They had bake sales, they sold bunches of bluebonnets for a dollar a bunch. (Now it's illegal to even pick bluebonnets, much less sell them.) At last they were able to raise the $5,000 that Attwater wanted for his collection. These items became the first collection handed over to the Witte Museum when it was built.

Then the feisty schoolmarm begged Mayor John W. Tobin for help until he finally gave her $7,500. A later gift of $75,000 from Alfred G. Witte made the museum a reality, and Quillin, the driving force behind it all, became the first director.

In October of 1960 Mrs. Quillin was forced to retire. She had served the museum for thirty-four years. She was given the title of director emeritus, but she still kept a watchful eye on "her" museum.

Ellen Quillin died at home on May 5, 1970. No one knew her exact age, but she was at least eighty years old at the time of her death. She lived a full and productive life. She was happy with what she had accomplished, which was to establish a fine museum for San Antonio. It was the most important part of her life. And there are those who would say she never left it.

Is the Hertzberg Haunted?

The San Antonio public library's Hertzberg Circus collection is housed in the old white stone former public library building at 210 West Market Street, just one block west of Alamo Street.

Back in 1993 I was invited by Barbara Celitans, curator at the museum, to come and tell ghost stories to a gathering of youngsters. It was around Halloween, when my storytelling seems to become most popular. After my program, several of the museum staff made it a point to chastise me for not including the Hertzberg in my book about San Antonio's ghosts. I promised them if I were to ever do another book I would certainly include their story.

The Hertzberg Museum

When Dr. Robert O'Connor, the museum administrator, sent me a copy of an article by Bruce Milligan that ran in the October 30, 1983 edition of the *San Antonio Express News*, I realized the museum did indeed have a fascinating story that deserved to be researched further. The article was titled "Murder Victim Haunts Hertzberg." It's a most intriguing story that takes us way back to the early days of Texas settlement.

John McMullen and James McGloin were two early Texas impresarios. In 1829 they founded the largely Irish McMullen-McGloin colony. It soon became known as the San Patricio Colony, and there is still a small town near Corpus Christi known by that name. McGloin stayed in San Patricio, but his friend McMullen, seeking a more affluent lifestyle, moved to San Antonio in 1837, just after the tragic Battle of the Alamo. He became a successful merchant and influential citizen. The wealthy, highly respected McMullen built a fine house which was located at the spot where the Hertzberg Museum is today. There he presided at many fine entertainments and lived the life of a prosperous businessman until 1853. It all came to an abrupt end on a cold January night when a thief slipped into the house, bound and gagged McMullen, rifled his possessions, and slit his throat, leaving him to bleed to death. The murderer was never brought to justice, and it still remains an unsolved crime.

The strangest twist to this story of heinous crime concerns James McGloin, McMullen's former partner and close friend. He had just arrived home from a trip to Matamoros, down in Mexico. He had experienced a severe case of depression, and a sense of foreboding had haunted him as he rode the last few hours towards his home. When McGloin got home, he unsaddled the beautiful Arabian horse he had been riding and went into his home on Constitution Square.

After supper McGloin settled into his favorite chair in front of the fire while his wife, Mary, went out behind the house to bring in her washing. Just then, McGloin heard the sound of wings beating frantically on the front door, and he was filled with a sense of terrible dread. Turning towards the door, which was barred against intruders, he saw a white mist float in and suddenly take on the shape of a human being. From out of the mist stepped the image of John McMullen. He was wearing a white nightshirt and blood was spurting, geyser-like, from a wound in his neck. Although his lips were moving, McGloin could not make out what his friend was saying, and the apparition soon vanished into the mist from which it had come, leaving McGloin extremely shaken.

Terrified, yet feeling compelled to find out why McMullen had appeared to him, he hastened to tell his wife he had to ride to San Antonio to take care of some pressing business. He went to the larder and packed up a few morsels of food, took his hat and coat, and resaddled his horse.

It is a long ride to San Antonio from San Patricio. The horse, already exhausted from its trip from Matamoros, still did the best it could to keep up the pace that McGloin demanded of him. Just outside San Antonio, near San Jose Mission, McGloin encountered a Texas Ranger, who asked him if he had seen a green-eyed Mexican boy on the road. He told the ranger he had not, and he and the horse, which was beginning to stagger, continued on their journey.

McGloin got to San Antonio just in time to hear the Angelus tolling from the bells at San Fernando Cathedral. He saw candles glowing from the lower windows of McMullen's house, and there were a number of men gathered on the front porch. As he dismounted, McGloin's faithful horse shivered, gave a loud snort, and dropped dead on the ground. He had served his master well.

One of the men assumed this was McGloin and asked him how he had heard. He answered that he had heard nothing, but he just felt somehow that he needed to hasten to San Antonio. The men led him into the front parlor where McMullen had just been laid out in a coffin. His throat had been cut!

Later, McGloin was told that McMullen had adopted a Mexican boy, and they all believed it was he who had murdered his wealthy benefactor. It was never proved, however.

The story of McMullen's death was told in Rachel Bluntzer Hebert's book *The Forgotten Colony*, according to the *San Antonio Express News* article. Hebert had the story from her mother, who had been told about the murder by Patrick McGloin, a nephew of James McGloin.

According to Dr. John Flannery's book *The Irish Texans*, a current story states that John McMullen's ghost walks the hallways of the library building that was built on the site of his old home, the home in which he was murdered, and his specter will continue to appear until such time as someone is able to bring to light who the perpetrator of the crime was. Since it was all so long ago and the players in the tragedy are all dead, it might seem the spirit will always remain there, within the confines of the library building.

As with most of my stories, I wasn't just content to read about the murder and subsequent haunting in the works that had already been written. I decided to question some of the current staff at the library building. I came to the conclusion that there is little doubt that some spirits of the past do indeed cling to the museum. Whether it's the spirit of John McMullen coming back to the site of his old home, or whether it's the spirit, or spirits, of some long-dead circus great whose personal effects are displayed in the museum, it's hard to say. Maybe even Mr. Harry Hertzberg, who so lovingly compiled the collection, comes back to see all is going well. Whoever or whatever it is, strange things continue to take place from time to time in the library building that today houses the circus collection.

A visit with Mario Lara, who has served as custodian there for a little over four years, brought forth some interesting information. Often Lara has felt cold spots in the building, especially in the basement near the bookstore where he often feels a sudden unexplainable chill as he comes to the stairs leading up to the ground level. He says the hair on the back of his arms stands up, he has goose bumps, and his skin crawls. He doesn't dare look behind him as he goes up the stairs! Often Lara has seen a dark, shadowy form moving about, out of the corner of his eye, as he goes about his work. He said recently an electrician doing some rewiring in the building asked him, point-blank, "Is this place haunted?" The workman went on to say he had seen a strange, dark, shadowy form pass by his peripheral vision and was quite sure it was a ghost.

Often, Mario told me, up in the rare books collection on the upper floors, the noise of keys jangling has been heard. He said Jill Blake and Thomas Smith, both former staff members, had heard this sound on numerous occasions but could never locate the source. I decided to talk to Smith, who was on the museum staff from October 1993 to April of 1996. He said he often heard keys rattling, and he also heard footsteps in the third floor hallway. He would look out and see no one. He finally heard the sounds so often he just ignored them. He said he was never frightened, as much as he was just curious as to what caused the sounds. He said he did most of his work on the third floor, in the Hemisfair Room, which faces the Hemisfair grounds and Convention Center, although the Hilton Hotel now blocks the view. Smith also said he often had the distinct feeling he was not alone, even when he knew he was.

One strange incident involved both men, Smith and Lara. One evening both of them were working rather late up on the fifth floor, unloading some papier-mache animals from the elevator, taking them into a storage area. The elevator only ran to the fifth floor, but Smith distinctly heard loud banging noises on the elevator door coming from the sixth floor. He looked up the elevator shaft (there was no ceiling on the open lift) and saw the door on the level above him shaking under the onslaught of someone banging hard on the door. He called to Mario to see if he'd gone up the stairs to the sixth floor, and if so, was he banging on the door? But no, Mario was there on the fifth floor, and he also had heard the commotion. Neither man could satisfactorily explain the noises, since they knew no one else was in the building that evening.

Lara told me that about the second year he was there, he was up on the third floor where a kitchen is located. Two female employees were there with him. He clearly heard someone softly say, "Mario." He turned to see who had spoken to him and was surprised to see the ladies had left the kitchen and he was just there alone.

One time when he was up on the fifth floor at work, Lara heard a lot of books drop. He ran down the stairs to the fourth floor and found a number of books on the floor but could find no reason for them to have fallen and could find no one who had heard or seen them fall off the shelves. Smith said on the fifth floor there were some bookshelves right in front of the elevator. He got to noticing that new books kept appearing on the shelves, and the books were rearranged nearly every day. Since the general public didn't go up there, he couldn't explain it. In fact, he said, there were just a lot of things that happened there he couldn't explain!

Lara also told me that he once saw a bright shimmering light that sort of moved around and floated between the book stacks, down the long aisle between them, going towards the wall. This was on the second floor. It happened during daylight hours, but because the room was rather dark between the tall book stacks, the light really stood out.

To this day, Lara says he often feels a presence as he works and knows he is not alone. Curator John Slate, who has not been on the staff long and to whom I spoke briefly, said he sometimes feels he is not alone when he knows he really is, up in his third floor office.

And so it goes. Is so much energy around, due to the collection of circus memorabilia stored within those white stone walls, that it must manifest itself to those who labor there? Or is the restless spirit of old John McMullen still seeking his killer after over a hundred and fifty years? Your guess is as good as mine.

The Haunted Railroad Tracks

Is it a legend? A made-up story? Or is it really true?

To be perfectly honest, there doesn't seem to be any documentation to substantiate this story. I've tried to find records in the libraries and newspaper files that would give a date and some details about a tragedy that is supposed to have happened a long time ago. The story, which has been a part of San Antonio's lore and legends for many years, concerns a train-school bus accident that is variously described as having happened in the 1930s or 1940s. I talked with a couple of elderly Southern Pacific Railroad men, and they said they vaguely recalled hearing about such an accident but could recall no details. It was a long time ago, and it doesn't look like anyone who might know about it is even alive now. The newspaper librarian has to have the date of such an incident in order to look up any news account in the microfilm files, and I just don't have it. It does seem like an accident of such magnitude would have been widely reported at the time.

So take it for what it is. A good story. A legend. But because it is so well known, it must be included in any ghost story book about San Antonio!

Years ago, the story goes, a school bus taking a group of ten youngsters home from the consolidated county school on the far south side, stalled as it started up over the Southern Pacific Railroad tracks. The driver couldn't get the bus to start. And suddenly, from out of nowhere, or so it seemed, the five o'clock freight train loomed into sight. The train couldn't stop and the school bus wouldn't start, and the result was a tragic accident at the crossing where Shane and Villamain Roads meet.

It is said that all the children and the bus driver were killed. Strangely enough, no mention has ever been made, to my knowledge, as to the fate of the train's engineer and his crew.

All we know, and this is what makes the story so fascinating, is that when a car is parked on Shane Road about thirty or so yards from the tracks, with the gears placed in neutral, and the driver's feet off both the brakes and the accelerator, it will suddenly start to roll towards the railroad tracks, gaining momentum as it progresses. The vehicle will cross the tracks, which are raised, and then come down on the other side, rounding the curve on Villamain Road.

Frequently people dust the trunks and rear bumpers of their vehicles with talcum powder or cornstarch, then when the rear of the vehicle is checked after its crossing over tracks, there always seems to be some small handprints visible in the powder. The oft-repeated story goes that the spirits of the little dead children don't want another bus or car to come to the tragic end that they did, and so they keep watch to insure a safe journey by pushing a vehicle up and over the tracks out of harm's way.

The area, which is pretty spooky anyway, with weed-overgrown stretches along the way, and trash and litter strewn along the roadside, is not a place where one would enjoy a pleasure stroll. Several murder victims have been dumped in the general vicinity of the crossing. One was as recent as August 1995, when the decomposed, blanket-wrapped remains of either a small woman or a young girl was found in a grassy ditch about thirty yards south of the intersection of Villamain and Shane Roads. The skeletal remains were judged to have been there at least two or three weeks when a man out walking his dog in the area discovered them. It's just not a nice place to be in the first place. My psychic friend Sam Nesmith told me there are lots of bad vibes in that general area.

Another friend, Jackie Weaverling, told me one time she was with a group on a trail ride on Shane Road. They were coming into town for the annual stock show and rodeo, and they paused by the side of the road to rest a short while. Jackie had her horse in a trailer. She said he nearly tore up the trailer trying to get out, and he was usually a calm, laid-back animal. She said some of the other trail riders had a lot of trouble getting their horses to go over the tracks. None of the animals were very calm out in that area, and it was only after they finally left that vicinity that they would settle down. I have always heard that horses are very perceptive to scenes of death and tragedy.

Numerous television crews have filmed cars going over the tracks. My husband and I have been interviewed at the crossing by the *Eyes of Texas* series, Fox National TV News, Discovery Channel's *Beyond Bizarre*, and Sci-Fi Channel's *Mysteries, Magic, and Miracles*, as well as numerous local stations. And so many people come out to the famous crossing around Halloween each year, the San Antonio Police Department has to send officers out there to direct traffic! Of course, I always include the strange crossing and tell the oft-repeated legend as the finale to my Spirits of San Antonio Tours. My tour participants would probably ask for their money back if I didn't!

The Aggie Spirit

Aggie Park, located at the corner of Loop 410 and West Avenue, has been the scene of many barbecues, meetings, parties, dances, Aggie Musters, and various other events over the years. In the past three or four years, numerous staff members at the big complex have reported there might just be something in the building besides the Spirit of Aggieland.

I doubt there are any Texans not aware of the indominable spirit of former students of Texas A&M University. Their fervor for their alma mater, football team, and one another is legendary! In San Antonio the "spirit" reached such a fever peak that a group of Aggies banded together and bought 3.3 acres of land back in the early 1940s on which to build a facility where they could have private Aggie barbecues and gatherings.

A man named Henry Wier owned a large dairy farm at that location when it was still considered to be way out in the country from San Antonio. Every year the local Aggies got together and rented a couple of acres from Wier, having the dairy man mow the tall grass as part of the deal. Then, according to all the stories I've heard, they'd have barbecues, reminisce, down a few beers, discuss the football situation, and generally enjoy some good fellowship together. These were strictly stag parties. Then, when Wier decided to get out of the dairy business and sell his property, ten members of the Aggie group got together, pooling their money, and for $999 were able to buy the three acres. They called this venture Aggie Memorial Park, in honor of several of their number who had passed away. The first thing they did was build a huge brick and concrete barbecue pit. Then, in 1953 they constructed a building so they could hold meetings year round. This building, which has been greatly enlarged since that time, was dedicated in 1954.

The San Antonio facility is the only one of its kind in the state. There are A&M Clubs all over the country, but none can boast a park and large meeting facility such as Aggie Park.

I recently learned the multipurpose building is believed to be haunted. I conducted one of my *Spirits of San Antonio* evening ghost tours for members of the Aggie Wives' Club, their husbands, and guests. Several of the group mentioned to me it was certainly a shame I had not included the story about Aggie Park's ghost in any of my books. Although I am a member of the Aggie Wives' Club, I seldom attend meetings because of work conflicts, and so I had not heard of the ghostly presence that is said to lurk around Aggie Park. Linda Turman, who got the group organized for the tour, told me she had recently been told by Kathleen Sheridan, the executive secretary of the San Antonio A&M Club, that the park was haunted.

Aggie Park

Telephone conversations with Ms. Sheridan and her assistant, Mildred May, revealed some enlightening information. Both ladies said they had started noticing things happening about two or three years ago. At first it was just lights mysteriously going on and off, then things would get misplaced and later reappear. They have both keenly felt the presence of someone or something in the building with them. This is most noticeable when one or the other of them is alone, working in the building after club members and the custodial staff have departed for the day.

Kathleen told me her ten-year-old daughter was in the building with her one afternoon when the child saw a whitish, misty form, which took on the appearance of a man's figure, in the vicinity of the bar. She actually saw the figure appear, then disappear, twice during the course of the afternoon.

Sheridan told me when work was being done on the building, a decorator was there quite late one evening. Suddenly he felt something holding him tightly to the spot on which he stood. For about sixty seconds he stood rooted to the spot, unable to move in any direction. Then, whatever the force was, it let go of him and he could move about. He says it was an absolutely unforgettable experience! Another man, a painter, came to work in the evenings when he got off his regular day job. He reported seeing strange shadows with human forms moving about in a deserted hallway where he was working. He was very unnerved by this occurrence.

Another worker, a military veteran who is now attending a local university, was so upset by seeing moving shadows and feeling he was not alone in the building, he said he would not come back and work in the building at night anymore.

Ms. Sheridan said one afternoon she was in the building with two ladies who had come to look at the building before they decided to rent it for an upcoming function. Because there are a lot of windows and it was a bright sunny day, Kathleen did not turn on the lights in the building. Then, suddenly, all the lights went on. There was no explanation for this at all.

Both Kathleen Sheridan and Mildred May told me they had never believed in ghosts before, but both women definitely believe the building at Aggie Park is haunted. Sheridan's theory, based on the fact the park is located on the banks of a creek where Indians used to camp and is only a short block away from where a large Indian burial ground was recently discovered, is that the ghost might be the spirit of an Indian hanging around the site of his former camping grounds. She thinks the spirit is an "old soul" that has been around for a long while.

Ms. May told me she has had numerous experiences with things moving around after she has placed them somewhere. Even chairs in the building have been mysteriously moved. These occurrences most often happen near the back of the building, the area closest to the creek.

Two Aggie Wives' Club members, Barbara Roberson and Marilyn Muldowney, the club president, told me they also believe there is a spirit in the building. Barbara recently went there to open the building for an evening meeting. The combination for the lock had been given to her by Kathleen Sheridan, who first warned her not to be by herself when she went into the building. When Barbara questioned her as to why she shouldn't be alone, Ms. Sheridan told her she might feel the presence there and be frightened by it as others had been.

Barbara proposed that the spirit might be a former Aggie club member who loved the place so much he just comes back now to keep an eye on things. I have another theory. After the creek flooded and inflicted a lot of damage on the building, the members decided to enlarge as well as repair and renovate the buildings. This was about five years ago. The ghost activity has only taken place in the past four or five years since so much remodeling has been done, and most students of ghost-lore know this often brings the spirits out. Maybe one of the former builders of the original building is the other-worldly visitor!

Many members, now deceased, were intensely loyal both to their alma mater and the local A&M Club. Several former members even requested that their memorial services be held at Aggie Park. At least two wakes have been held there. One was especially memorable. A former member, a prominent veterinarian, made arrangements prior to his death that a wake be held at the park for all of his old Aggie buddies and their wives, as well as his business clientele. Barbara and Ken Roberson attended, and they told me hundreds of people turned out for the party, which included heaping plates of barbecue with all the fixings, kegs of beer, assorted and unlimited libations, a dance band, decorations, and a gala atmosphere. The host also attended, in his closed coffin! Dr. Charles Wiseman, another veterinarian and a friend of the deceased, said a bottle of Jack Daniels was placed right beside the casket!

Every year on April 21 a muster honoring the dead is held at Aggie Park. It is a very moving ceremony, with the lighting of candles and the calling of the roll of deceased Aggies who have died during the previous year. There's seldom a dry eye in the crowd when the last strains of taps echo through the big building. These ceremonies are held all over the world wherever Aggies are able to gather together. Personally, I have attended them in four states and in England and Spain. So fervent is the Spirit of Aggieland that A&M men serving as officers at Corregidor in 1942 held a muster just prior to being captured by the Japanese!

For whatever reason Aggie park is inhabited by a spirit, Kathleen Sheridan and Mildred May are not afraid of it. They have learned to take it for granted. They believe whatever is there is a benevolent spirit, and only there to keep an eye on things. Personally, I think a friendly ghost would never find a more "spirited" place in which to dwell than the meeting place of Texas Aggies!

If you would like information about the available facilities at Aggie Park call (210) 341-1393.

Spirits at the Southwest School of Art and Craft

Many years before the fascinating cluster of old buildings at 300 Augusta Street became home to the Southwest Craft Center, renamed the Southwest School of Art and Craft, it was a Catholic girls' school known as the Ursuline Academy. Its story is very interesting.

The Ursuline order was founded in Italy by Saint Angela in 1535 as a teaching order. The Ursulines were the first to educate young women in Europe, Canada, and the United States. Their first school in America was founded in New Orleans in 1727. They brought education for young ladies to Texas when a group of them arrived in Galveston in 1847.

When it was realized that San Antonio had no school for girls, Bishop Odin purchased ten acres of land located on the San Antonio River that had formerly belonged to Erasmo Seguin. The bishop contracted with Francois Giraud, a fine French-trained architect, to design and build a school on the acreage.

There was a shortage of money in those days, so the building project moved along slowly, not really getting started until 1851. By then the main building had been constructed but not completely finished. The north wall was not complete, and some of the windows and frames were not as yet installed.

It was to this unfinished building, windowless, filled with rubble from the construction process, surrounded by high grass and weeds, and infested with all manner of bugs, scorpions, spiders, and snakes that seven sisters, four from New Orleans, and three from Galveston, came. The women were accompanied by a French priest, Father Claude Dubuis, of Castroville. The group subsisted for the first few months on offerings from the local residents. It was some time before their supplies, cooking utensils, and other essentials would be brought in by stagecoach.

The date the group arrived was September 17, 1851. Father Dubuis and the seven sisters worked almost ceaselessly until November 2, when they were able to open their little school.

The first students were children of German, French, Mexican, and Anglo backgrounds. They spoke different languages, so they had to be seated at dining tables with those who could converse with them as they spoke their mother tongues. Gradually they were taught to speak the languages they did not know. The sisters also taught geography, history, and astronomy. In 1852 two Ursuline sisters from Ireland arrived, and they added art, elocution, and music to the curriculum.

The Ursulines were a cloistered order. They wore unwieldy black habits with large white wimples and winged headdresses. No outsiders were allowed into the school. No men were allowed near the place except their priestly protector, Father Dubuis.

A beautiful Gothic chapel was built in the late 1860s, and a dormitory was built in 1866 to allow the boarding program to be expanded. The original school building was added onto in 1853 and again in 1870. The priest's house was added on in the 1880s.

A papal conference was held in 1900 that decreed the Ursuline order would no longer be cloistered. This influenced many facets of the school. To the original curriculum were added literature, spelling, composition, arithmetic, physiology, and gymnastics. The young ladies were also taught to sew and embroider. And of course, they were taught to be little ladies, minding their manners and respecting their teachers and elders.

Finally, because it had become increasingly difficult to maintain the old buildings, the sisters decided to sell their property and move to new, modern quarters. This was accomplished when they opened their new school on the northwest side of San Antonio, on Vance-Jackson, in 1962. They finally sold the old academy property to the San Antonio Conservation Society in 1965.

The Society did a great deal of restoration and repair work at tremendous expense. A few of the Ursuline sisters lived on there even after the new northside school opened. The last of the sisters moved out in 1965.

Although the order of nuns moved to the northwest side of town, it seems the spirits of some of the founding sisters remained in the old dormitory and classroom buildings where they spent such a great part of their lives.

Al Longoria is now retired, but the former security guard at the school told me there were many nights when he heard footsteps on the upper floors and stairs of the old dormitory building. As he sat on the first floor, keeping his nightly vigil, he heard little running footsteps, like those of little girls. Then, there would be heavier treads of adults, as the nuns apparently rounded up their small charges and sent them off to bed. Mrs. Longoria, who sometimes came down to sit with her husband and keep him company, told me she also heard the footsteps on numerous occasions.

The former chapel is now used for parties and receptions, and of course it is no longer consecrated. Longoria told me he could recall several times when champagne punch bowls had been turned over just prior to a reception, quite mysteriously. It seems quite apparent that the spirits of the sisters did not approve of alcoholic beverages being served in their former house of worship!

The Southwest School of Art and Craft, on Augusta Street

Another story I heard concerned a photography instructor who taught in one of the former classrooms. One evening when he was in his darkroom developing film, he suddenly was pushed quite hard from behind. Then he saw a large, dark, shadowy form fly through the adjoining classroom and out the door. Some months later he experienced another such encounter, except the misty form he saw float across his classroom was white this time! Explanation? Well, the nuns wore black habits during the winter months, changing to cooler appearing white apparel after Easter! Now, since it had been a cloistered order, with no men being allowed inside the buildings except for the priest, it is quite evident that the spirit of a sister who had once taught there did not approve of the presence of a male instructor in her old classroom!

From all that I have heard and the general atmosphere I sense when I visit the Southwest School of Art and Craft, the manifestations that have taken place indicate the sisters were protective of the place they had lived in for so long, and they only return with the most benevolent feelings towards the buildings. There is such a good and happy feeling around the place that I would almost like to think of them in terms of being guardian angels!

In 1970 the Conservation Society invited the school, which had been located in La Villita since its founding in 1965, to come and occupy the buildings. The invitation was accepted and the move began in 1971. The former academy again became a beehive of activity. Classes in drawing, sculpture, ceramics, weaving, fibers, paper making, jewelry and metal work, photography, and just about anything else creative and artistic were offered to the community. The buildings and surrounding grounds and gardens are beautifully maintained. Parts of the complex, including the gazebo and the former chapel, are available for parties and receptions. During weekdays, delicious lunches are prepared and served in the delightful Copper Kitchen Restaurant which utilizes the former dining hall.

Does all this sound interesting to you? A call to the school will bring forth information about classes and other available services at the Southwest School of Art and Craft.

The Spirits of Staff Post Road

Staff Post Road, adjacent to the historic quadrangle at Fort Sam Houston, consists of a row of limestone houses, constructed in 1881, the designs of British architect Alfred Giles. Although similar in style, the massive houses feature various floor plans. All are shaded by age-old trees centered in beautifully kept lawns. All of the houses front onto a green "parade ground" area. In front of each set of quarters, which are reserved for the "top brass" at the Army installation, there is a curbstone noting the name, rank, and key position on the post that the occupant holds. In keeping with military tradition, an American flag proudly flies along the curbsides at every set of quarters.

The Pershing House, so named because General of the Armies John J. "Black Jack" Pershing occupied the quarters in 1917, has long been the home of the ranking general on the post. The Fifth Army commander now occupies the house. Larger than all the others, it boasts a long, shady front porch and an attractive little bay windowed room on the side of the building. There are glassed-in sun porches, and spacious drawing rooms within. I have twice visited inside the beautiful Pershing house and can attest to the architectural genius of Alfred Giles.

I once spoke with Mrs. Dorothy Stotser, the wife of Lt. General George R. Stotser, who was Commander of the Fifth Army at that time. The Stotsers have since retired and now make their home in another state. Mrs. Stotser gave credence to the stories I had heard rumored but had not been able to substantiate, that the historic landmark is haunted. She said she believes the ghost is friendly and therefore no threat, but it does provide an interesting "topic of conversation," as she put it. She thinks the ghost might be that of General Pershing. At the time he resided in the house (February to May 1917) he had been newly and tragically bereft of his wife and three of his four young children. They had perished in a fire in the Pershing's quarters at the Presidio in San Francisco while the general was struggling to keep things in line on the Texas border. This was in 1916, during the Pancho Villa uprisings. Stunned by his great loss, a lonely and depressed widower, he was soon posted to Fort Sam Houston where he took up residence in the large commander's house. He did not remain for very long at Fort Sam Houston, however. In May of 1917 he was called to command the Expeditionary Forces in Europe during World War I.

Mrs. Stotser said that the main evidences of something unusual during their residency there were the frequent flushing of the commodes in the middle of the night and or the doorbell ringing when no one was there. There were also footsteps heard on stairways or in the halls. Mrs. Stotser said she believes the general's spirit gets bored, especially at night, and he wakes up the occupants for company.

Maybe General Pershing's spirit has returned to the house where he was so grief stricken and lonely after the loss of his wife and children. Or maybe, just feeling honored that the commander's house has been named for him, he just wants to check up on the general welfare of the house and its occupants. Military men are like that, you know.

Quarters Number One, which is at the very beginning of the road, adjacent to Grayson Avenue, was once haunted, too. John Manguso, curator at the Fort Sam Houston Museum, told me that museum visitors have said the quarters were once occupied by an officer who had access to government funds, as he was one of the finance officers. He evidently dipped into the funds and with his ill-gotten gains was able to build up a nice little nest egg to be used for his retirement. Unfortunately for him, he was caught red-handed. Rather than "face the music" (which might have resulted in a court-martial) the man committed suicide in that house.

After this incident, numerous residents of Quarters Number One reported that the toilets would flush when no one was around, and footsteps were heard and a definite presence felt. One woman felt something sit down on the bed next to her, but of course, no one was there! Many times these things happened when the military dependents were alone in the house, their husbands away on duty.

A close personal friend of mine, Colonel George Rodgers (USA, Retired), volunteered that he had lived in Number One during 1976-77 and that the house was indeed haunted at that time. He said his wife first heard the heavy footsteps walking on the upstairs hallways, and later, he also heard them on numerous evenings. His wife heard someone walking up the stairs as well. He was never particularly disturbed, but his wife found the presence of a night-walking spirit very unnerving.

It is my understanding that the spirit has not been active in several years. It is hoped that he has finally settled into a peaceful existence in his eternal resting place, forgiven for his indiscretions on earth.

Quarters Number One, Fort Sam Houston

A couple of years ago, when I was the guest speaker at a luncheon-meeting of the Fort Sam Houston Officers Wives Club, one of the women at my table volunteered that she was then living in

Quarters Number Twelve. She and her husband had experienced several occurrences that indicated the place might be haunted. When she told me what had happened, I had no doubt that spirits were about in her set of quarters. Besides the usual footsteps, lights going on and off, etc., the couple, upon retiring, would soon be awakened by a terrible clamor downstairs. It always came from the dining room, and it sounded as if the china cupboard had fallen, breaking all the dishes and crystal. Quick trips downstairs to find the cause of the noise would always find everything in order; nothing was broken or out of place! I have heard of this type of manifestation taking place in many houses in the course of my investigations.

The couple has since vacated Number Twelve, and I have not been able to contact the new occupants to see if the noises are continuing. I would be willing to bet that they are!

A Host of Ghosts at Victoria's Black Swan Inn

One of the most spirit-filled addresses in San Antonio is Victoria's Black Swan Inn, a large two-story special-events house that is situated on a grassy knoll overlooking Salado Creek. The address is 1006 Holbrook Road. The place has an interesting historical background, which I will share with you before I mention the spirits who inhabit the place.

The house is situated on ancient land that has known both turbulence and terror, peace and plenty. According to local archeologists, the Salado Creek site was utilized over a long period of time during the Archaic era of 5500 BC to AD 1000 by Native American tribes. Even now, people living in the vicinity find arrowheads, spearheads, projectile points, and various tools used by ancient man along the creek banks and in surrounding acreage. It is one of the few sections in the drainage area of the Salado at which prehistoric cultural activities can still be studied in a scientific manner.

During the uneasy times that followed the Texas War for Independence in 1836, another less bloody war with Mexico took place. There was a second invasion by the Mexican army in 1842. On September 11 of that year, General Adrian Woll, a French general serving Mexico as a hired commander, marched with about 1400 Mexican soldiers and captured San Antonio. Soon after the news reached the small city of Gonzales, over 200 volunteers under Matthew Caldwell gathered and marched to Salado Creek, which is about six miles east of downtown San Antonio. On September 18 Caldwell sent John C. Hays of Texas Ranger fame with a company of men to lure the enemy out of the Alamo where they were entrenched. The Mexicans took chase after Hays' men, who retreated to a protected site on the Salado where Caldwell and the rest of the Texans were waiting.

The clash of forces took place September 19, with the enemy sustaining losses of sixty dead and about as many wounded, while the Texans lost only one man killed and nine men injured. This battle took place on and around the grounds of a house that today stands atop a grassy natural knoll on Holbrook Road. A historic marker is located there stating that most of the battle took place between the hours of 1:45 and 2:30 on that September day. Just beyond the marker are the entry gates to the house that is now known as Victoria's Black Swan Inn.

It wasn't always known as the Black Swan. The beautiful white stately mansion has had several names and numerous owners and occupants. It also has been the habitat of some pretty interesting "residents" who don't seem in any hurry to go away. This brings us to the real reason for telling the story of this great white house on the hilltop.

Heinrich Mahler and his wife, Marie Biermann Mahler, immigrated to America from Germany in 1870 soon after their marriage. They wound up in Texas and, according to deed records in the Bexar County Courthouse, they purchased 200 acres of land on the east bank of Salado Creek, at what is now the corner of Rittiman and Holbrook Roads, on January 14, 1887, for the sum of $2,200. Here the Mahlers built their first house overlooking the creek.

In 1897 Mahler extended his holdings by purchasing 240 acres which adjoined his property to the north for $4,556.20. After buying this second acreage, the Mahlers built a new house and moved there in 1901. This was a gracious one-story farmhouse atop a high natural knoll, overlooking the creek. Heinrich, or "Henry" as he was known locally, had farming and ranching interests and also grew cotton. His main business was dairy farming, and he sold his famous Jersey Creamery Butter for many years. The dairy barn, water tank, windmill, and stables are still located on the grounds. The Mahlers had four children: Sam, Daniel, Louise, and Sarah.

Marie Mahler died in 1923 at age 73, and Heinrich was 83 when he passed away in 1925. Both are buried in the St. John's Lutheran Cemetery.

According to a family history compiled by a great-granddaughter, Pauline Gueldner Pratt, Heinrich left the house and farm to his two sons, Sam and Daniel, while the two daughters received two houses the Mahlers owned in San Antonio. Dan's portion of the inherited property consisted of the house, silo, and milk barn. Sam was given the "corner property." During the mid-1930s the Mahler farms were sold. Sam's property was purchased by Paul F. Gueldner, father-in-law of Sophie Mahler Gueldner, and was later resold. Dan's property was purchased by two families from Wichita Falls, the Woods and the Holbrooks.

Mrs. John (nee Katherine Joline) Holbrook and Mrs. Claude (nee Blanche Joline) Woods were sisters. They and their husbands were visiting San Antonio from Wichita Falls when they found and fell in love with the Mahler property and decided to purchase it. Much remodeling and enlargement took place, since the two families both planned to reside in the house and they wanted a house which would afford privacy to each family. The main body of the Mahler house was made into one extremely large drawing room, which looked out onto the long front porch. Several walls that had divided the house into small rooms were knocked out. Two long wings were then added to either side of the large center section, each wing having one large and one slightly smaller bedroom, and a large bathroom and numerous storage closets.

The kitchen and dining room, which the families shared, were to the rear of the main section of the house. There were lovely white gables on the front of the house, and the new owners chose to call their home "White Gables." Except for the wings, the house still generally carried all the characteristics of the original Mahler house of 1901.

Mr. and Mrs. Holbrook had no children. Blanche and Claude Woods had one daughter, Joline. She had been given her mother's maiden surname, since there were no boys to carry on the family name. Joline Woods lived there in the house with her parents and her aunt and uncle for a number of years until she married a young San Antonio man, Hall Park Street Jr. Street was born in San Antonio in 1909. He attended Washington and Lee University and graduated with a law degree from the University of Oklahoma in 1932. He later became the city's leading condemnation attorney for property owners for many years. The colorful and successful lawyer and his attractive wife were prominent in local society. Park Street served as president of the San Antonio Bar Association, president of the Order of the Alamo in 1940, and was a member of the San Antonio Country Club and the Texas Cavaliers. In 1948 he was selected as King Antonio XXVI for the Fiesta activities that year. In other words, the Streets definitely "belonged."

After Mr. and Mrs. Holbrook and Mr. Woods passed away, Mrs. Woods remained in White Gables. In order that she not be alone in the big old house, Joline and Park Street and their children, Hall Park Street III and Joline, moved into the house. They added a second story that included several big bedrooms and bathrooms. The home had expanded to sixteen rooms and had approximately 6,000 square feet of living space.

The socially prominent Streets entertained quite a lot in their spacious home. Among other notable guests were Mr. Street's good friends Earle Stanley Gardner and Raymond Burr. Gardner even dedicated his *Perry Mason* series to his good friend Park Street. Gardner was also an attorney, but his accomplishments as a writer were generally better known. Street was a member and one of the founders of the "Court of Last Resort." He investigated a number of cases for that court, of which Gardner was the prime founder.

In 1959 Street held formal dedication ceremonies for his Perry Mason room at his offices. He flew in the whole cast of the popular television show: Raymond Burr, Barbara Hale, William Hopper, William Tallman, Ray Collins, and of course, his old friend Earl Stanley Gardner came to help him celebrate. It is said that Gardner conceived several manuscripts for the mystery series while he was a houseguest of the Streets in their stately mansion.

While she was still young, only in her late thirties, the charming Joline Street succumbed to cancer. Her grandson, James Patrick Robinson III, was kind enough to give me a little family information. He said his grandmother died when his mother was only nineteen years old. He said that Joline had been a beautiful woman, slender and fair, with long, dark hair. James said Mrs. Woods, Joline Street's mother, also had been quite a beauty in her day. She was known as one of the "prettiest ladies in North Texas." Feminine pulchritude seemed to run in the family.

The elderly Mrs. Woods continued to live in the house after the untimely death of her lovely daughter, with her son-in-law and grandchildren. Park Street finally remarried, and he and his new wife lived most of the time thereafter in her home on Northridge Drive. In fact, it was there that Park Street was found dead on August 4, 1965, an apparent suicide according to the *San Antonio Express News* of August 6. The story goes that he was found by his wife, strangled, a belt looped around his neck and a bedpost. He had recently undergone some psychiatric treatment in Galveston. At the age of 55, Park Street was dead, bringing to an end a successful and brilliant career.

After Street's death, his daughter, Joline Wood Street Robinson, and her family moved into the Holbrook Road house with her grandmother. They remained there until she passed away, and then finally, in 1973, the house was sold to Mrs. Ingeborg Mehren.

Mrs. Mehren spent a lot of time totally refurbishing and restoring the house, clearing out the attics and storerooms, and making the house ready to become the "Mehren House." The old landmark soon became known as the "in" place to hold receptions, luncheons, dinners, conferences, and various social events. The floor plan with its tremendous central drawing room, elegant fireplace, huge kitchen facilities (which were added onto the rear of the house by Mrs. Mehren), and spacious side rooms lent itself well to such activities.

Ingeborg Mehren, a most attractive woman, is a native of Germany. Her late husband, Dr. George Mehren, was a former diplomat who once served as Ambassador to Thailand, and as an Under-Secretary of Agriculture during the Kennedy administration. The Mehrens lent a great deal of European sophistication and flair to the parties that were catered at the mansion. Finally, in 1984, Mrs. Mehren decided to sell the property and move on to other endeavors.

After Ingeborg Mehren decided to go out of the catering business, for a time, before she was able to sell the house, she leased it to Faye Leavitt, once the talk show host on *Our Turn*, a popular radio talk show for senior citizens aired on station KLUP.

Faye told me that during her tenure at Mehren House, where she also had a successful catering operation, it was not long before she and her staff realized that the house had numerous spirits in residence. She often heard music playing when no radio, stereo, or television set was turned on. Lights went on and off at will. Doors locked and unlocked by themselves. And there were numerous cold spots in the house that she could not explain. Faye vividly recalls one day when she was in one of the upstairs rooms, a former bedroom, where she had just launched a paint-up fix-up project. She had opened two cans of paint, one color for the walls and another shade for trim, and had begun to paint. She was suddenly called away from her task by a terrific racket that was coming from downstairs. Knowing she was alone in the house, she hurried down to see what had caused the commotion. After checking all the rooms and finding nothing out of place, she again went upstairs to continue her painting task. Lo and behold, while she was downstairs, someone or something had mixed the two cans of paint and created one entirely different color from the ones she had been working with! She is still talking about this strange occurrence, many years later!

One time Faye opened the door to the upstairs room which was used as an office-study. She was baffled when she discovered all sorts of papers and photographs scattered about the room as if someone had been rifling through the papers looking for something. As she gathered the scattered sheets together she was astounded to find they were photographs and old radio and television scripts of the *Perry Mason Show*! Of course, she knew that Park Street, the former owner, had been a close friend of Earle Stanley Gardner, who was often a guest in the Street home. How the scripts and photos came to be in the room (she knew all the contents of the room, and had never seen these items before) still remains an object of mystery to Faye.

When Faye, who had been a widow at the time she ran the Mehren House, remarried in 1984, although she no longer was associated with the business, she chose the lovely old gazebo at the foot of the hill as the setting for her garden wedding. Jack Leavitt, her son, escorted his mother down the hill. A photographer took a candid photo of the couple as they approached the gazebo. When the film was developed, a woman in a white dress appeared in the picture!

She was strolling along beside Faye, a ghostly, uninvited wedding guest!

Faye, who has a delightful sense of humor, volunteered that in spite of the romantic setting for the ceremony, the marriage didn't last very long. She thinks maybe it was "hexed" by the ghostly wedding guest!

The big house and its grounds have changed hands a couple of times since. Today it is known as Victoria's Black Swan Inn and caters largely to lavish wedding receptions, anniversary celebrations, and Sunday brunches. The owners are Jo Ann and Robert Rivera.

Victoria's Black Swan Inn

I have visited the house a number of times since the Riveras have owned it and have had many conversations with them. According to Jo Ann, some very unusual activities have taken place at the house since her arrival on the scene. She told me that in April of 1991 she was awakened at exactly 3 A.M. for about ten nights straight. Her bedroom door would unlock, and the light in the hallway would switch on. Then she would see a man, dressed in a white shirt and dark trousers, hands on his hips, standing at the foot of her bed. She never was able to get a good look at his face, and the apparition would disappear almost immediately. Since this was before she and Robert were married, the then single woman was quite disturbed to say the least. She finally repositioned her bed in the room, moving it to the other side, and since then the figure has not appeared, much to her relief.

It was 1992 when I first spoke to Jo Ann about the house. At the time, her daughter Meredith was about fifteen years old. Several nights when it was raining outside, the teenager awakened to find a man, old and wrinkled, definitely "evil-looking," peering into her upstairs bedroom window. There is no way a human being could climb up that steeply pitched roof to such a vantage point!

Jo Ann told me there are numerous cold spots in the house, too. Many doors will not remain locked. Others, especially the bathroom doors, will lock themselves from the outside, of their own accord. Lights often come on, especially in the south wing where Mrs. Rivera says she always feels a little uneasy. There is a large closet in the room on the end of the wing, and she does not like to enter that space. She says the hair stands up on her arms when she opens the closet door, and she feels like "something" is watching her.

In 1992 a George Strait special was partially filmed at the house, and during the filming all the lights in the south wing mysteriously came on without anyone's flipping the switches.

Rivera also said that the house makes strange noises at night, and men, more than women, seem to feel uncomfortable there. She added that teenagers seem to be especially uneasy in the house at night.

There is a grand piano in the drawing room. Mrs. Rivera heard it being played one night so she turned on the lights and ran downstairs to see what on earth was going on. As she came into the room, the music stopped, and of course, no one was there. She also has heard the sounds of a tinkling music box, just "coming out of the walls." Her brother, who used to live in a cottage on the grounds, was upstairs in the main house alone one afternoon, and he heard the distinct sounds of hammering downstairs. He hurried down to check, and there was no one there and the hammering ceased.

For a time, the room Mrs. Rivera used as her office was also a gift shop that she ran in conjunction with the party house. There were many dolls there. She said several times when she came down in the morning, the dolls would be all rearranged and the doll buggy out of its usual place, as if some little girl had been playing dolls in the room. For this reason, Mrs. Rivera thinks maybe one of the resident spirits might be a child-spirit. There is a beautiful old playhouse back of the house on the grounds, which was built by the Streets for their daughter, Joline, when she was small.

Jo Ann told me that soon after she purchased the place in 1991 she had a very unusual visitor. A woman from Dallas, accompanied by another woman and two small children, appeared at the house one day. The Dallas woman told Jo Ann she just wanted to look around and then went on to explain that she had visited the place when she was a child. This must have been sometime in the mid-seventies, after Mrs. Mehren purchased the place, but before all the refurbishing had been done, which took several years, as the woman said the house was then vacant. She went on to say at that time there were several "hippie" types that hung around the house, but they didn't bother her. She said she liked to go up into the attic area where there were trunks of old clothes and dolls to play with. She also remembered an old music box among all the belongings that previous owners had left behind. Then, she told Mrs. Rivera she really enjoyed "all the people" who would come and visit her up in the attic! She said she had lived in an adjacent neighborhood but did not say if she came with other playmates, or if she came to the house alone, which would have been strange behavior for a youngster. She went on to tell Mrs. Rivera she had been having disturbing dreams about the house lately and just felt compelled to come back and see it again. Mrs. Rivera has not seen the woman since that day, but she said something about her strange visit still gives her the "creeps."

I began to wonder if Mrs. Rivera's occupancy had brought out the restive spirits, or if they had been about during previous ownerships. James Patrick Robinson III, the Street's grandson, volunteered he had felt cold spots and heard noises in the house while he lived there with his parents and grandmother.

I decided to call Ingeborg Mehren to see if she had any unusual experiences in the house during the days it was known as the Mehren House. Well, she certainly had, and she was kind enough to share her experiences with me.

As an avid student of history, Ingeborg Mehren was fascinated by the house, which she said had a certain "aura of romance and mystery." She dreamed of turning the charming old mansion into a sort of exhibition house, a combination museum and tearoom, which would reflect its gracious years of occupancy. Along with the house and grounds, she came into the possession of countless boxes, cartons, trunks, and crates of old papers, newspaper clippings, photographs, and various memorabilia that, for some reason, the former owners did not wish to take with them. She went through every item very painstakingly and had finally sorted out some fascinating mementos of the house's history, when vandals broke into the place one night, carted off many of the most treasured items, and scattered other bits and pieces all over the property. She was absolutely devastated by this wanton act of destruction.

After the act of vandalism took place, Mrs. Mehren realized there was need for a resident caretaker to stay in the house and deter any further acts of vandalism, while she was sorting and cataloging all the belongings. The first "house sitters" were a young couple who worked part-time and attended a local college as well.

Ingeborg Mehren had been told by several local residents that she had purchased what was purported to be a haunted house, but not believing in such things, she took little notice. However, she did wonder when the young woman who had taken up residence there along with her young husband told her that there was "a lady, a beautiful lady, like a special presence," upstairs in the largest bedroom. She described her as young and lovely, and she said she was wearing a sort of headband, "like in the flapper days. It had a jeweled motif in the center over her forehead and a little feather in back." She told Ingeborg that she felt the woman, who had appeared several times, was friendly, and did not mind them being there. Ingeborg thought her young house sitter was beginning to see things!

Then, several days later, as she was going through a box of assorted newspaper clippings, she stumbled across one that announced Joline Woods, a local debutante, had been selected to travel to Washington, D.C. to represent San Antonio at a gala ball. The accompanying photograph showed her to be a beautiful young woman, and she was wearing a headband, complete with jeweled medallion in the center, and a jaunty feather in the back! Ingeborg said it was at that point that she started to believe.

When the summer ended, the young college student couple moved out, and Mrs. Mehren next hired an elderly Mexican man, who was quite hard of hearing, to move in and take care of things. Several days after he took up residence, she called on him to see how he was getting along. She noticed right away that he had moved his mattress and bedding out to the back porch of the house. She asked him why he wasn't staying in the comfortable bedroom she had arranged for him. He told her, "Oh, no, senora, hay muchos santos en la casa!" ("No ma'am, there are many spirits in the house!") He then told her that there was a lot of noise and music that disturbed him. The spirits must have been equipped with stereophonic sound, because Ingeborg said the man was almost stone deaf!

For a short time, Ingeborg had a distinguished guest who consented to stay at the house during an extended visit he made to San Antonio. He was Franz Wilhelm, Prince of Prussia. One time when he was entertaining a visitor from Austria, also of noble birth, the two men both saw a man appear at the upstairs window five or six times during the course of the evening. He was elderly, with a "menacing expression," they said. The Austrian, who said he was somewhat psychic, told the prince that he felt the man was evil and was somehow connected to a murder. When Ingeborg heard this she said for the first time she felt uncomfortable in the house.

Ingeborg often felt the presence of a woman in the house, especially in the largest upstairs bedroom to the left of the stairs. She said she got to where she would talk to the spirit, saying, "I hope you are happy that we are having such nice parties here." She felt a friendly benevolence in that room as if her messages had indeed reached the spirit.

Christa Rabaste, Ingeborg's secretary, had an office adjacent to Ingeborg's. They always locked up when they left in the evening, but at times, when arriving in the morning, they found the house unlocked and all the lights turned on! Mrs. Rabaste found desk drawers open, the closet door ajar, and things in general disarray on a fairly regular basis. However, neither she nor Ingeborg Mehren ever found anything missing.

Several waiters who worked at the house after it had finally been converted to a party house told Mrs. Mehren they didn't like to be in the house alone at night when they were cleaning up after a party. They said they heard a music box playing and the sounds would follow them all around the house. Mrs. Mehren said she also had heard both the music box and hammering noises, although she could never locate the sources. An elderly Mexican lady who came to clean there told Mehren she liked to work in the house because there was "such nice music playing in the house."

Ingeborg said just "lots of thing happened. It would take too long to tell everything." But she made it clear that she had certainly changed from the nonbeliever in ghosts she was when she first purchased the house. In fact, things got bad enough that she finally asked a friend, who was a Catholic priest, if he would come and give Mehren House a "blessing." This was not an exorcism, but she said she felt more comfortable after the priest had made his visit. She recalled one thing that happened while he was making his rounds of the house. When he got to the top of the stairs and headed for the bedroom on the left where the young woman in the headband had appeared to the house sitter and where Ingeborg often felt a definite presence, he told her, "For some reason I think I'd better give this room a double blessing!"

After hearing about so many manifestations from both Jo Ann Rivera and Ingeborg Mehren, I decided to ask my friend Sam Nesmith, a gifted psychic, if he would consent to visit the Black Swan Inn with me. At his request, I told him nothing that I had heard from either the current or the former owner. We drove to the house one sunny afternoon. Just before we passed through the gates that open up on the long driveway up to the house, Sam picked up on something. He said it was rather "unsettling." As we drove up the drive, he said he felt some "tumult" there. Of course, this is where the Battle of Salado Creek had taken place!

After we were greeted by Jo Ann Rivera, Sam started to walk all over the house and later, the grounds, to see what he might pick up. Jo Ann and I just followed along. He told us in the house itself he felt no violence, but he did feel it on the grounds. As we walked over the large house, Sam sometimes paused as he "felt something" somewhere. The south wing brought forth a comment that there was definitely "something" about the closet that Mrs. Rivera had mentioned that she did not like to open. The hair stood up on his arms as he thrust them inside the opening. He felt that someone might have had a safe or cabinet for valuables there at one time, and was still zealously guarding them. In the middle of the wing there is a small bedroom where he said he felt someone, most likely a woman, had been ill and confined to bed for a long period of time. There was a certain sadness in the room but no indication that a death had occurred there. (My visit with Ingeborg Mehren had included her telling me that the elderly Mrs. Woods was quite frail and confined to her room for some time before her granddaughter had to place her in a nursing home. This was apparently the room she had occupied. Ingeborg told me that a maid who had worked there told her that Mrs. Woods was very sad when she realized she was going to have to leave her beloved home.)

Sam was not at all comfortable on the steep stairs leading to the second floor. He felt something rather ominous in that area and in the area just below the trap door leading up to the attic, which Mrs. Rivera has had nailed down, so that it is pretty much inaccessible now. As he walked up the stairs, Sam said he "saw" a large gilt mirror on the wall at the head of the stairs. There is no mirror hanging there now, but Mrs. Mehren later told me there had been one there all the time that she had owned the house.

To the left of the top of the stairs, the largest bedroom, which also includes a dressing room, faces the rear yard of the house. This is where the house sitter had seen the young woman in the headband and where Ingeborg always felt the presence of a feminine spirit. The dressing area is completely covered with mirrors and has a lot of built-in cabinetry. Here, Sam strongly felt "a definite presence of a woman. She is a beautiful woman, an Yvonne DeCarlo type, with long, dark hair, lovely fair skin, and she is sophisticated and vibrant. She died fairly young, but she is very possessive of this area," Sam concluded. He went on to say she liked to be in charge of things and feels it is still her house, but she is not a threatening presence. He did say it would not surprise him if she made a "real physical appearance" in that room one of these days, as the energy was so strong there.

We went back downstairs. Sam strolled into the kitchen area. This was the old kitchen area that belonged to the original Mahler house, not the long addition that was added during the Mehren House era. Here he instantly picked up on another spirit. This one was also a woman, but a "very different type. She is rather short and stout, in her late sixties or early seventies, with her gray hair pulled back into a knot or bun at the back of her head. She is very busy here, either kneading bread or making biscuits or something... she is quite contented here," he concluded. In fact, he added, she is a sort of "guardian spirit." Later, when Jo Ann Rivera showed Sam a picture of the elderly Mrs. Mahler, he said she looked just like the woman he had seen at work in the kitchen!

And of course, after hearing Sam's description of the beautiful young woman spirit upstairs, we found it perfectly fit the description of Joline Woods Street that her grandson, James Patrick Robinson III, had given us. Sam was right on target!

The glassed-in porch to the rear of the house was one place where Sam felt some sort of "dominant spirit." This was a very dynamic male spirit. Sam said he felt the man was probably a "large, dark-haired middle-aged man"... also very possessive of the house, but not a violent presence. Of course, Park Street was a large, middle-aged and dark-haired man, and from all accounts a strong personality as well.

Some time after the visit with Jo Ann, I had a telephone chat with her, and she told me the latest news about the Inn. For some time the staff has been seeing a white-gowned, dark-haired young woman spirit come out of the front door, stroll across the porch, and walk down the front steps onto the grassy knoll upon which the Black Swan Inn sits. The wraith always walks to the gazebo at the foot of the little hill, and then she disappears from view. This has become such a frequent occurrence of late that the Riveras and their employees pay little attention to her comings and goings!

In December 1996, a reporter and camera crew from Sci-Fi Channel's show *Sightings* visited the Inn. They brought Peter James, their psychic consultant, and he agreed the place is literally overrun with spirits. He found a woman on the stairs, another in the main reception room, two spirits in the south wing, and another in a hallway. He also saw a man looking into a window. The renowned psychic also told Jo Ann that Park Street, the former owner, is trying to contact her, and he wants her to find something he left behind in the house.

The findings of the nationally known psychic, coupled with those of San Antonio psychic Sam Nesmith, only serve to solidify my own opinion that Victoria's Black Swan Inn has to be one of the most fascinating and spirit-filled places I have ever visited or written about! It is obvious that the hospitable Innkeepers, Jo Ann and Robert Rivera, have made their spirit-residents feel just as welcome as they do their local clientele!

A Gathering Place For Ghosts

A favorite place to take my guests on my nighttime Spirits of San Antonio tours is the Alamo Street Restaurant, located at 1150 South Alamo Street. Here we begin our tour with a delicious buffet dinner. The restaurant is located in the former Alamo Street Methodist Church. Marcia Larsen, the affable owner, admits the place is haunted! She is always glad to tell how she came to own the old church in the first place, and how she and her late husband, Bill, who passed away in 1996, made it into San Antonio's first nonprofit little theatre. She readily talks about the latest antics of her live-in spirits, who certainly keep things lively around the old building.

Back in 1976, Marcia, who prefers to be called "Marcie," and Bill were out on a Sunday drive. They had recently inherited some money which they'd thought about investing in a little apartment house or duplex, that would bring in some rental income. They happened to pass by the corner of Wickes Street and South Alamo and spied an old closed-up church, which Marcie says was looking quite neglected and forlorn. "Look," Bill said, "there's a church but no cars are around. Isn't that something?" Bill went on to comment that an old church like that sure would be a dandy place to have a dinner theatre. Marcie told him he'd lost his mind! By that night, the Larsens owned the former house of worship!

Then began the long, arduous task of cleaning up, fixing up, repairing, and repainting. The building had been vacant since 1968, and vagrants had just about torn the place apart. The building itself was sound. It was built in 1913 and served the King William District as a neighborhood church until the congregation dwindled to the point the Methodist District decided to close it, merging the small remaining congregation with a larger one nearby.

Marcie says work on the old brick building, built with two towers, in the popular mission style of its day, is still going on to this day.

Through Marcie's efforts, the building is now listed on the National Register of Historic Places.

The Larsens knocked down some of the walls in the basement level, making a large dining room out of the small Sunday school rooms used by the former church. The old punched tin ceiling is still in place. Good food of a wide variety with a definite home-cooked flavor has been served there since the beginning.

The Alamo Street Restaurant

Bill, who hailed from Michigan, held a degree in music and drama from the University of Michigan and had much experience as an actor and director of various playhouses both in this country and overseas. He had been connected with the USO during World War II and was the director of entertainment for a time at Fort Sam Houston. He was the founder of the Little Theatre at Fort Sam, now known as the Harlequin Dinner Theatre. Bill was a natural showman, and the theatre the Larsens established was an instant hit. Marcie, a graduate of the Rhode Island School of Design, was at one time the Executive Director of the Southwest Craft Center here in

San Antonio. And both of the clever Larsens brought the talents of gourmet cookery to their new enterprise. The dinner theatre was the first nonprofit venture of its kind in the country and they called it their Bicentennial project since it was launched in 1976. Dinner has always been served downstairs and many times the groups move upstairs for a theatrical production in the former church sanctuary, which has been secularized and converted into a playhouse. I recall attending some great plays there as far back as 1976.

The theatrical productions were produced by various people for a time. One of the earlier directors was popular Jerry Pollock, who was there from 1984-87. The Larsens took over the theatre operation when Pollock moved on. Today there are plays presented upstairs on weekends, directed by various people well known in San Antonio's theatrical circles. There are also small, intimate productions, often original works by Marcie Larsen and her theatrical director, a very talented lady named Deborah Latham. These are mostly mysteries or comedies that include a great deal of audience participation. They are popular and great fun!

Just about the time the Larsens really got going with their project, they began to hear from some of the actors that there was a mysterious lady hanging out in the raised former choir loft in the back of the theatre. The figure of an attractive young woman in a white Victorian dress had been sighted by quite a few of the theatre people. She would appear and then disappear almost immediately. Although the choir loft was her favorite place, she also was seen seated in one of the seats (former church pews) where the audience sits during performances.

Over the past twenty years, many people have seen the figure. Most of her appearances occur during the rehearsal or actual performance of a play. The Larsens hadn't a clue whom the lady might be until a few years ago, when after learning about the ghost, I asked them if I might bring some psychics over to see what they could find. All three, Sam Nesmith, Robert Thiege, and Liz Null, were able to see the entity in the prop room just behind the raised choir loft. I was with them and while unable to see or converse with the spirit, I did see a faint white misty glow of something in the darkness. The psychics saw her clearly, and she communicated with them that her name is Margaret.

Since that time, Marcie Larsen has come to believe that the woman seen in the theatre might be a woman who was a prominent resident of the King William neighborhood whose name was Margaret Gething. Gething, who passed away in 1975, was very attractive as a young woman. She was brought up on a ranch in Bandera, had wealthy parents, and led a most interesting life. At one time she lived in El Paso, where she took part in theatrical events. Quite a good amateur actress, she was asked to travel with a touring company when one of their lead actresses suddenly took ill in El Paso and was unable to complete the tour. Margaret agreed to step in and save the day. Later the young actress went on to perform in the legitimate theatre in New York, once even starring with Clark Gable in a production! The former debutante, who served as an Order of the Alamo Duchess in the 1917 Fiesta court (only high society young ladies are in the royal court each year!), adopted the stage name of Nancy Allen in order not to embarrass her strait-laced parents, who didn't approve of her theatrical career. Marcie and her staff think it is quite possible the former actress, who spent her last years in her lovely Guenther Street home just a short block from the old church, must surely have attended some services there, weddings, funerals, etc. and would have been well acquainted with the building. She was no doubt acquainted with a lot of the parishioners. And of course, she had always loved the theatre! She had only been dead about a year when the Larsens bought the church and turned it into a theatre. Her spirit must have been attracted to this gathering place for like-minded people.

People to whom I have spoken who actually knew Margaret Gething said she was "different." She was never quite of this era, preferring to wear white Victorian style high-necked, lace trimmed blouses and long skirts of lawn and lace. She had most of her clothes especially made for her. Tall and slender, she had a dignified look and has often been described as a gracious, soft-spoken "Southern lady." She never married, although it is said she had many admirers and could have married had she chosen to do so.

All of Margaret's beautiful furnishings were Victorian. She had money and excellent taste in spending it. In fact, the talented Gething had studied interior design at the Parson School of Design in New York, with an emphasis on historic preservation. As a consultant, she once worked on the Mark Twain house in Hartford, Connecticut; the Jay Gould Mansion in Tarrytown, New York; and the White House restoration headed by the late Jacqueline Kennedy Onassis.

There is a photograph of Miss Gething as a young woman in her twenty-room home, which was built around 1860. Each year during Fiesta week the home of the former duchess is opened to the public for viewing for just that one week. People who have seen the lady in the choir loft in the Alamo Street Dinner Theatre say that's exactly how she looked, leaving little doubt as to the identity of the spirit.

The trio of psychics I took to the theatre said Margaret is not alone in the building. They also identified three other spirits as well and said the old building has become a popular gathering place for former residents of the neighborhood.

One of the spirits, who is rather quiet and passive and doesn't do much of anything, is supposedly a seamstress named Henrietta. Since Margaret Gething had most of her clothes custom made, Henrietta might just have been the seamstress employed by Gething, and she may have followed her employer into the realm of the spirit world! There's also an old man who doesn't do much at all, but he has been sighted by several people. He and Henrietta often hang around one of the old church belfry towers, observing people driving past the church on Alamo Street.

The liveliest ghost, and the one that is the most fun, is known as "little Eddie." This mischievous youngster seems to have arrived at the theatre when they brought an old Victorian wicker wheelchair in as a prop for one of the plays. Eddie, a youngster of ten or so years, was confined to a wheelchair in life. Not so now! He enjoys playing pranks and is making up for lost time as he enjoys being an active little boy spirit—far more active than he ever was in life. The old wheelchair is still upstairs in a prop room, and that is where the psychics first met and visited with Eddie. He told them his name was Edward, but he preferred to be called Eddie. The boy-spirit is very active and playful as one might expect a youngster of that age to be. He is especially fond of teasing Victoria Sotello, the cook.

When Victoria arrives in the mornings, the first thing she does is light the oven to get it ready to bake the bread and muffins for the noon meal. But Eddie often turns it off just as soon as Victoria's back is turned. Finally, in exasperation, she'll say, "All right, Eddie. Let's cut that out!" Usually he gets the message and the oven stays on. Sometimes when Victoria leans into the big commercial-size refrigerator to retrieve something, she feels a push from behind as Eddie tries to shove her into the 'fridge. A few times he has gotten so carried away with his pranks, he has pulled shelves out of the refrigerator!

Several times, Marcie says a big serving spoon has risen up off the steam table, levitated across the room, and landed on the floor among the dining tables. Numerous customers as well as staff members have witnessed this phenomena.

Once when Marcie offered to help an elderly patron carry her plate from the buffet, something suddenly snatched the plate out of Marcie's hands and hurled it to the floor, spilling the food and breaking the crockery. Marcie swears she did not drop the plate. It was literally snatched from her grasp!

A couple of years ago I spoke with a former director at the theatre, Brian Cobb. He had some interesting experiences there also. His were connected with Margaret, and he said they were unforgettable. Once, when he was seated in the audience area watching a couple of actors as they ran through their lines, he heard someone nearby softly saying, "Brian ... oh ... Brian .... " He said he definitely did not imagine it.

Often, when several people were seated and chatting quietly while a rehearsal was in progress, they'd hear a definite "shhhhh!" in their ears! Margaret, having been an actress, knew how distracting it can be when one is trying to recall lines and the audience is not paying attention. Another time the spirit was heard to call out, "Help me! Help me!" Paul Gaedke, Cobb's partner, also heard the voice.

Once during a performance, which was NOT a musical, a female voice was heard to start singing. The singing wasn't all that good, either. It was coming from the area where the audience was seated, during an especially quiet and dramatic moment in the production. Cobb said he had never seen Margaret, as had many of the actors, but he certainly will testify to having heard her any number of times.

A frequent happening is ongoing. Frankly, I think this is more like something little Eddie would do than what Miss Margaret would do. She had far too much dignity. It seems the former choir loft is used to store sound and light equipment now. Often when the technicians get everything all ready for a performance and go off on a break, they return to find all the electric cords unplugged and tied in knots and various equipment disturbed enough that they know someone has tampered with it.

Back in 1990, Marcie said a couple, who were tourists from another state, came to eat at the restaurant. Their names were Barbara and Edward Kulis, and they lived in Florida. Barbara told Marcie she was a psychic, and she had a "funny feeling" about the place. She asked if Marcie would take her to see the upstairs theatre. It was the middle of the summer and the air conditioning was cut off upstairs. Marcie told the couple it would be exceedingly hot. They didn't mind; they wanted to go upstairs anyway. Marcie said it was stiflingly hot when they got upstairs, but within a few minutes of their arrival the temperature plummeted down to the freezing point. They were literally shivering! And Barbara said she felt a presence there. The couple took a Polaroid photo of the entryway to the sanctuary-turned-theatre, and when it was developed there was a figure of a woman in white standing in the doorway! The photo is prominently displayed in the restaurant for one and all to view.

Although Marcie readily admits she has never seen Margaret, Eddie, or any of the other spirits, she has heard one of them. This may be Margaret or Henrietta the dressmaker. Marcie had stepped inside the ladies' room when she heard someone plainly calling "Marcie . . . oh Marcie!" She didn't linger there long!

A few years ago there was an Elvis Presley collection of memorabilia on loan at the restaurant. One of the items was a life-size full-figure photo of Elvis, which hung on the wall. One day when a group of the actors were in the dining room discussing an upcoming play, the figure suddenly came off the wall and "traveled" across the room, landing on a table. It did not fall. Deborah said, "Little Eddie

...put that back!" And would you believe, the cutout figure of the rock-star arose from the table and backed across the space to the wall where it reattached itself to the picture hanger! A number of people saw this and swear it is true. Oh, my!

Marcie told me that New Years' Eve 1995 was a gala time of celebration and festivities at the restaurant. The party was just about over; 1996 had been duly ushered in. The band was packing up to leave, just one couple remained at a table, and Marcie and some of her staff were just about ready to close up and go home, leaving the shambles of paper hats, confetti, noisemakers, and dirty dishes for the morning clean-up crew to tackle. All of a sudden Marcie saw a champagne flute rise from an empty table and hover in the air for a moment. Then the stem snapped in two and the flute fell back on the table. Marcie is still talking about this episode.

The manifestations are ongoing. Lights still go on and off and doors lock and unlock by themselves. The temperature, especially in the upstairs theatre area, can go from extremely hot to freezing cold in a matter of minutes. Newly washed dishes in the kitchen area can be suddenly removed from the drain board and plunged back into the soapy dishwater by unseen hands. Once a blender started up on its own and could not be turned off until the cord was jerked from the wall socket! These ghostly happenings are so frequent and so varied that almost every time I drop by the place, Marcie or Deborah or one of the other staff members has a new episode to tell about. In fact, the ghosts are so well known that there is a printed give-away sheet on the cashier's stand for the diners to take and read. All the staff members just accept the ghostly residents. In fact, when someone suggested an exorcism be held to get rid of them, they were all horrified! Marcie thinks the ghosts bring good luck to the place, and it might be really boring if they were to suddenly depart.

And so it goes on. Good food. Good drama. A gaggle of ghosts! All are available at the Alamo Street Restaurant and Theatre!

The Ghost Wears White
at the Cadillac Bar

My friend Franklin Roe was at the Cadillac Bar at 212 South Flores one morning in April 1996. He had loaned the restaurant some saddles, harnesses, chains, and other tack to add atmosphere to a Western party that was held the night before in the upstairs party room. Now, he'd come for his paraphernalia and was in the midst of half dragging, half carrying the heavy items down the sweeping staircase that leads to the upstairs party room. Jesse Medina, the owner of the Cadillac, remarked, "Good grief, Frank, that sounds just like some of our night noises around here." When Frank asked Medina just what he meant, Jesse told him that they often heard strange noises late at night after the customers had all left, noises like chains rattling and heavy saddles and bridles and such being dragged down the stairs. He also said that childish screams and laughter of children at play were heard around the place at various times. They've also frequently heard the sounds of glass shattering as if a car might have driven right through one of the plate glass windows there on South Flores Street, but thorough checks always reveal nothing is broken or out of order. Frank asked Jesse, "Are you trying to tell me the place might be haunted?" When Jesse told him yes, that was indeed what he and his employees thought, Frank told him he knew just the person he should talk to about the situation . . . me!

Frank called me the next morning to tell me of his ghost discovery. He asked if I might be free for lunch that day and asked if I would meet him and his business associate, June Bratcher, who was also interested in the whole thing. I had no pressing plans, and I always enjoy learning of another "new" ghost, so I accepted his invitation. I hurried on downtown to meet Frank and June and one of their employees, Chris McKinney, who also wanted to learn about the ghosts at the Cadillac. We had a delicious Mexican lunch and a good visit with Medina, who told us he'd been there for about twelve years and had heard all sorts of weird night noises over that time. He also said the alarm often turns on and off by itself, usually very late, just before closing time. Sometimes large utensils, such as serving bowls and chafing dishes, fly off the shelves in the kitchen. He recalled one day when the water faucet turned on and off all day long. It did this at least six or seven times. They actually saw the faucet slowly turn as if unseen hands had hold of it, and then the water began to flow! Finally, not understanding what on earth was going on, they called a plumber. He checked the faucet and said there was absolutely nothing wrong with the spigot, and there was no possible way it could turn on by itself. The only thing . . . it did!

When Jesse first came to work at the Cadillac and he'd hear a strange noise late at night when he was there alone in the building, he would just lock up fast and go home! It happens so frequently now, he is used to all the strange noises and takes them all pretty much for granted. He says he expects something to happen nearly every night after midnight.

I felt I needed to know some of the background of the building,

which is actually two old buildings which have been joined. One is a large stone-walled room, where the main restaurant operation is located, and this is then joined to an older two-story structure, which has two large party rooms, one on each floor. Jesse gave me a menu, which has some of the history of the place on it. I would like to share some of this information with you:

The nation of Texas was young. Just two years earlier in 1845, the Alamo had fallen and rebel Texicans had won independence from Mexico. Herman Dietrich Stumberg, a young German immigrant, left Missouri for San Antonio. Time passed. Texas became the 28th state and Herman and his son George became successful in the general mercantile business. In 1870, they built a fine new limestone building on land Herman had purchased in 1863. Their business flourished. Farmers and ranchers from across South Texas drove wagons to the campyard behind the store, checked their guns with the storekeeper, bought supplies and headed for the saloons to the north or maybe the red light district to the west.

The nineteen twenties brought wild times along with Prohibition. Mayo Besan, the owner of the Cadillac Bar in New Orleans' Roosevelt Hotel, was not satisfied to sit out this country's moral evolution, so he packed up and headed for Nuevo Laredo, Mexico. Although he found the liquor laws more permissive, he also found that Nuevo Laredo already had a Cadillac Bar. Besan opened as the White Horse Bar and a year later, when the competition closed, changed the name back to his beloved Cadillac Bar.

The Depression changed the face of the country and part of that change was the demise of the Stumberg General Store in 1932. After its closing the building was used for many purposes. John Wayne had a saddle made for Queen Elizabeth by one of the tenants. The Cadillac flourished.

Time passed. Mayo Besan was succeeded by his son-in-law, Porter Garner, who retired in 1980 and left the Cadillac to its employees. Shortly thereafter, they sold to "Chito" Longoria and Ramon Salido.

The 1980s also brought change to the old Stumberg General Store. The buildings were restored and renovated in a redevelopment known as Stumberg Square. The project won the 1985 San Antonio Conservation Society Award for Excellence. The Cadillac Bar became the project's flagship tenant in 1984 when the operation returned to the United States for the first time since Prohibition.

In December 1991, the latest chapter in these two histories was written when the partnership in Nuevo Laredo split. This event saw George Stumberg, the great-great-grandson of the German immigrant, become the operating stockholder of the Cadillac Bar in San Antonio.

After I had read over this information, I was even more fascinated by this unusual old building. When I questioned the former owner, George Stumberg III, about the saddle shop, he said a family named Carvajal had run this shop and it had been popular and successful. Sounds of chains and the sort of equipment associated with a saddle shop come from the area of the building where the saddle shop was located.

In addition to strange noises, numerous employees have actually seen the ghostly figures of some former occupants of the building. No one seems to have a clue as to who they might be. One of the kitchen helpers told my husband that he had seen an older man on the back steps leading from the kitchen to an upper storage room. The man had a white handlebar mustache and was tall and thin. George Stumberg said he has a photo of his ancestor Herman, and he was clean shaven. George, Herman's son, once had a full beard. Neither man wore a handlebar mustache as far as George could determine.

However, Stumberg volunteered that there had been an "Uncle Herman." He wasn't sure what he had looked like, but he might have had a handlebar mustache. He was sort of a family "black sheep." While he did hang around the mercantile business quite a bit, he was a habitue of the old Silver Dollar Saloon, which was located at the corner of Main and Commerce, where now stands the old Frost Bank Building, now used for city council meetings. In fact, he was such a frequent visitor to the saloon, the management gave him one of the old gaming tables when they closed up! Uncle Herman just may be the man that the cook saw on the back stairs that night.

After my initial visit to the Cadillac with Frank, June, and Chris, I discussed the place at length with my psychic friend Sam Nesmith. Sam concentrated hard on the building, and he called me to say he believed that there were two spirits hanging around the building. One, a man, was tall, thin, and had a handlebar mustache, and he believed his name was either Herman or Henry! He told me this before my husband had visited with the cook or before I talked to Mr. Stumberg!

Nesmith also said there was a young woman, a rather sad spirit, hanging around. He couldn't determine just why she was there. The place stood on the outer fringes of the notorious red light district, and she might have been one of those nighttime ladies. I mentioned this to Mr. Stumberg, and he said he was positive the building had never been a brothel or anything like that. The upstairs portion was used for a long time as a storage place for goods and supplies needed for restocking the mercantile business. It once was served by a hand-operated elevator. However, the amazing thing here, Sam told me the girl might have been named Beatrice. This was the name he kept picking up on, and he said she was not particularly attractive. She knew she was homely, and this made her sad. She was very thin, had stringy dishwater blonde hair and protruding teeth. For some reason she has more or less taken up residence in the upper floor party room of the building.

Several of the employees of the Cadillac Bar have actually seen a woman matching the exact description Sam gave me. She has always been seen upstairs as the viewers glance up towards the glass windows of the room. Two waitresses at the establishment, twin sisters Deborah Fresco and Linda Frazier, truly believe there is someone there. Linda, a vivacious blonde, says she saw a girl spirit late one night as she was cleaning up a bar she had been working at on the lower level next to the stairs. She chanced to glance upstairs and saw a slender young woman in a white dress standing behind the glassed-in portion of the party room, just looking down at her. She said the woman bore an angry expression on her face. It wasn't a "nice ghost," she said. She went on to say the wraith had stringy, brownish-blonde hair, a thin face, and could not be considered at all pretty. This was much as Sam had described the live-in ghost. We later spoke to Brenda Cordoway, a comely brunette bartender. She has also felt a presence and says whenever she walks up the stairs at night she feels somebody is there, staring at her.

Lorenzo Banda Junior, a security guard who works on Friday nights, said he often feels a presence up on the second floor, and it gives him chills because he feels like he isn't alone, although he knows he is.

June and Frank and my husband and I went to the bar one Friday night, right at closing time. However, we didn't sense anything out of the ordinary on that one evening. I think there was too much noise from the serving staff as they cleaned up the place, and when they heard that "ghost hunters" were there, they all wanted to come up to the party room where we were to tell us of their own particular experiences. It just wasn't the right time for one of the spirits to appear.

However, just a few days after our fruitless midnight visit to the Cadillac, we got a call from Linda Frazier. She and several others had again seen the female wraith. They were all out on the patio in the rear of the building which is lighted by some wonderful old lamps. In fact, they were the first electric street lights in Texas. As they went about their work of cleaning up after a patio party, they chanced to glance up to the second floor windows. There she was! The ghostly young woman was just standing there, looking down at them. She walked away, then turned and walked back to the window. Then she sort of knelt down and peeped out of the window from a lower position. The group of Cadillac employees were all just fascinated by what they saw!

When I reported this latest sighting to Sam Nesmith he said he thinks this type of haunting is a replay of something that took place in the past and is a registered emotion, rather like a photograph. It can continually reoccur. He thinks the young woman either lived or worked in the vicinity and for some reason has become so attached to the old building she doesn't want to leave it.

All of the people we spoke to at the Cadillac Bar are convinced the place is haunted. No one knows who the spirits might have been in life or why they've decided they want to hang out at the Cadillac. But they are there, and they don't appear to be in any hurry to move on.

There's one thing I can tell you. The Mexican food is great, and the icy margaritas are memorable! I can't guarantee you'll see or hear a ghost, but come on down to the Cadillac anyway. I'll guarantee you'll have a good time!

The Mission Walls
Still Shelter Spirits

Mission San Jose de San Miguel de Aguayo was founded in 1720. Situated on Roosevelt Street at Mission Road, it is the best restoration of all the missions. A visit within its walls is like taking a trip back in a time capsule to the early Spanish colonial days.

The National Park Service has recently added a fine new visitor's center to the San Jose Mission complex. A beautiful twenty-five-minute film outlining the history of San Antonio's five missions is shown every half hour. The photography is exquisite. While mystical sounding music plays in the background, the narrator takes the viewer through a series of vignettes of mission life peopled by the spirits of long-dead mission Indians whose names and faces have been lost in time. The film leaves a definite impression on those who see it. I believe, as the screenwriters obviously did, that the missions are still peopled by the spirits of those who lived, toiled, and finally died within the confines of those thick, gray stone walls.

Marjorie Mungia, a Park Service volunteer, enjoys meeting people who come to the new visitor's center at San Jose Mission. She was born just a few blocks from the old mission and has been a life-long member of the parish of San Jose, which was known as the "Queen of the Missions."

The little houses where Marjorie's parents, Claude and Alvina Guerrero, and her aunt, Della Flores, lived, were torn down to make way for the construction of the visitor's center.

Marjorie recalls hearing lots of ghost stories about the mission when she was a little girl growing up just outside its walls. There were numerous stories about a Franciscan monk clad in a dark robe. (The earlier priests wore dark indigo blue habits instead of the brown ones worn by Franciscans today.) This figure was seen walking in the convent courtyard on moonlit nights. Sometimes he appeared to be headless! The courtyard must look eerie at night anyway, with the moonlight shining through the Gothic arches that once were the windows and doorways in the ruined portion of the mission. Add a headless friar, and it could really get your attention!

Once, in the mid-1940s, when Marjorie was a small child, she recalls the family talking about seeing a tall figure of a priest clad in a dark robe as he came out of the gate where tourists enter today. The gate was tightly closed off then, and the monk actually came right through the wooden gates. Marjorie remembers that her parents said he was "very, very tall," and they were extremely frightened!

Mission San Jose de San Miguel de Aguayo—The Church

Mission San Jose de San Miguel de Aguayo—The Convento

Once, Marjorie believes it was around 1969, her mother and father saw a group of young boys come running down a path that used to run along the side of the mission and on across to Mission County Park. It was obvious the kids were terrified. They'd seen a figure of a dark-robed, headless priest walking near the stone rectory which is just outside the mission gate.

After Marjorie's mother died, her father remarried. Marjorie said her stepmother was active in the parish. Once she recalled entering the church through the sacristy when she saw a priest standing with his back to her, near the little altar. She turned around for just a moment and looked out the back door. When she turned back around the priest was gone. He couldn't possibly have gotten out of the chapel that quickly. She walked on through the church and was astonished to see the parish priest, whom she thought she had seen in the sacristy, out in front of the church, chatting with some of his parishioners. When he was questioned, it turned out he'd been there for some time. She is convinced the priestly figure she saw in the sacristy was a ghost!

Not just the clergy haunt San Jose. One of the ushers at San Jose church told Claude Guerrero, Marjorie's father, that recently an old lady had come up to him and asked him the hours of the masses. He told her to wait there just a moment and he would go and get a church bulletin for her that listed the times of the various services. When he returned, the old lady, who had told him her name was Mrs. Iluizar, had disappeared. He mentioned this to Mr. Guerrero, and he told the usher that he had known that lady, and she couldn't have been there asking for information. He said she had been dead for over fifty years!

Just a few miles down Mission Road from San Jose is the quiet little compound of Mission San Francisco de la Espada, built around 1731. I have been told that something strange exists, or at least used to exist, around the old church. A friend of mine told me that a priest, now deceased, who used to live on the property, told her he had once seen a large, dark, hairy animal, that looked like a wolf or a big, black dog, with a broken chain dangling from around its neck. He had seen it from the window of his quarters at the mission late one evening. It was clearly visible in the moonlight as it darted across the courtyard and disappeared in the vicinity of the well outside the chapel. A search outside for the animal revealed nothing. Then, when two young priests were visiting the elderly padre in his study on another evening, he reported that all three of the men had seen the same thing. Another search outside revealed no trace of any animal in the vicinity.

A recent conversation with a woman who lived in the neighborhood of the old mission during her childhood verified that she also had heard of such a creature, and her mother had always warned her to stay away from the mission grounds at night.

A young woman acquaintance of ours told us that her mother, while visiting the chapel as a young girl, had clearly seen the figure of an Indian man standing near the altar. The apparition, clad in ceremonial regalia, suddenly appeared, and then just as suddenly it disappeared.

Mission San Francisco de la Espada

Mission San Juan de Capistrano, which was founded in March of 1731, located in far south San Antonio near the river, has a lovely little jewel-box of a chapel, which was actually built as a temporary place of worship. A larger church was begun in 1760, but for some reason it was never completed. The little chapel is small, probably seating no more than a hundred people. The retablo is of polychromed wood, beautifully carved. Featuring several carved images, it is centered with a fine likeness of San Juan de Capistrano, the namesake of the mission. It is still a parish church, and many of its parishioners are descendants of the original mission Indians.

It was to this lovely little house of worship a young tourist couple wandered in the late afternoon hours of a summer day in 1994. Most of the other tourists had already departed, and the park ranger was about ready to close his little visitor's center and call it a day. Suddenly, the young couple burst into the center and excitedly told what they had just witnessed. As they sat in one of the little pews, absorbing the beauty of the chapel and the quiet tranquillity of the afternoon, there appeared to them the figure of an Indian man, standing beside the altar. Then, just as suddenly as the apparition had appeared, it vanished, absolutely disappearing before their very eyes. It was readily apparent to the park ranger that this couple was not making up ghost stories. They were fully convinced that the spirit of a long-departed mission Indian had come back from out of the distant past, perhaps to welcome them, to the place where he had found the Christian faith so long ago.

Mission San Juan de Capistrano

A Magical, Mystical Place: The Grey Moss Inn

As many times as I've passed through Helotes en route to the "Cowboy Capital of the World," Bandera, for some reason I've always just zoomed right past the cut-off marked "Scenic Loop Road." My goodness, what I've been missing!

Recently, my husband, Roy, and I had occasion to drive out to visit in the small community of Grey Forest, where we understood we'd find a good ghost story or two. We were not disappointed.

The two-lane Scenic Loop Road traverses a valley through which flow Helotes Creek and various other small spring-fed streams. The whole area is lush and green with plants and trees in contrast to the Hill Country's arid rocky slopes just to the north.

Wildflowers, mostly little yellow ones, were blooming in profusion on the day of our visit, and most of the yards in the small community of Grey Forest were overgrown with tall grass, the result of a recent downpour. There was a magical, mystical aura about the whole place. I would not have been at all surprised if a band of little leprechauns had materialized to escort us as we turned into the driveway leading to our destination, the historic Grey Moss Inn.

Because I had heard from various sources, including an interesting article by the *Express News* writer Paula Allen, a few ghost stories connected to the inn, I called the present owner, Nell Baeten, and made an appointment to drive out and see her. While my husband and I waited for Nell to appear, her bookkeeper-secretary Linda Young proved an able guide as she showed us around the lovely dining rooms and spacious patio with tables shaded by colorful umbrellas. The four dining rooms were all appointed with various antiques, lots of green plants, hand-painted china plates, and lovely portraits and still-life paintings. The place has the look of what it is; an old-fashioned country inn. I could well see why it is a favored spot for anniversary celebrations and romantic rendezvous. There are huge candles formed from many small tapers of various colors which have dripped and built up the colored waxes over the years. These illuminate the tables at night. The mantle in the main dining room boasts a pair of candles over three feet tall! They have doubtless been around a good many years.

It was not long before Nell Baeten, the attractive proprietor, appeared, and a fascinating visit ensued. First, she filled us in on the background of the inn which she and her husband, orthodontist Dr. Lou Baeten, have owned since 1987.

Grey Moss Inn owner, Nell Baeten

A woman named Mary Howell, a part-Cherokee Indian, who was brought up in Oklahoma, arrived in the valley with her husband, Arthur, back in 1929. They had come here from Waco, where previously they had made their home. Arthur was a fireman with the Katy Railroad. When they drove through Grey Forest, Mary fell in love with the area. She noticed a big rock building, which had once served as the headquarters for the old Requa Realty Company, was up for sale. It looked like just the place where she could make her longtime dream of owning her own "tearoom" come true! She had already had experience with the restaurant business, since she had managed a tearoom in Waco for the Business and Professional Women's Club.

After Mary and Arthur purchased the building a big kitchen was added and the open front porch was eventually closed in. Mary named the place the Grey Moss Inn because it is circled with giant live oak trees from which long fronds of silvery Spanish moss slowly wave back and forth in the breeze. The Grey Forest Playground, which was close to the inn, was a popular weekend attraction for wealthy San Antonio families. Many of them built cottages and cabins of limestone and wood close by the playground area which featured a beautiful natural limestone swimming pool fed by springs. The pool is still there. The walls of the little changing houses are there as well, on the high banks overlooking the pool. The old metal stand for the diving board is still firmly anchored in the limestone escarpment. What a beautiful place it must have been in its "heyday." Nell took us to see it and said the pool, which was empty, still fills up after a rain. Lush green ferns and watercress grow along the banks of the creek and the dam which was built to hold the water in the swimming area. In the 1930s and '40s artists and various celebrities flocked to the playground to enjoy the scenic landscape and the pleasant climate. Mary Howell often cooked for such well-known "neighbors" as John Floore, artist Robert Wood, and movie star Sonny Tufts. She sold homemade candy, too, made in the kitchen at the inn.

It didn't take long for Mary's tearoom to catch on. Nell told us that many families who were regular customers came every Sunday and always insisted on sitting at the same table. Mary was a fabulous cook, and the recipes used today are still from her files of tried and true favorites. The recipes and techniques have not changed in over sixty years. Four meats are served: steak, chicken, lamb, and seafood. Only choice, heavy-aged beef is used, lightly basted with what Nell calls "witch's brew," an original inn recipe. The water used at the inn is drawn from fresh spring wells, and all the desserts they serve are made "from scratch."

Across the driveway leading to the inn there is a little cottage which was where Mary and Arthur Howell lived. It is built of old limestone, and its quaintness calls to mind the dwarfs' house in *Snow White and the Seven Dwarfs*. Consisting of just one big room that was a combination bed-sitting-dining room, with a kitchen and a little bathroom, which was obviously a later add-on, it today makes a charming small party house. At one time, Nell told us, it was a part of Requa Realty's properties. The building converted to the inn was the company headquarters and the small building housed the Realtors who lived there and ran the business. The Howell's twin boys, Arthur Junior and Tynus, lived in another small stone cottage situated just behind their parents' small house.

When Mary opened her tearoom she decorated it with some favorite plates and antique bric-a-brac. Arthur was busy with his railroad job and left the operation of the restaurant to Mary. From what the current owner told us, the place hasn't really changed all that much in its over sixty-five years of operation, except for a few additions which have added to the capacity of the restaurant.

The Baetens purchased the inn from Mary and Jerry Martin who owned it for several years. The Martins had purchased it from Mary Howell's son, Arthur Junior, who managed the property for a number of years after the death of his mother.

Nell Baeten was a most gracious hostess to my husband and me during our visit. She not only took us on quite a tour of the inn and to the little house that had belonged to Mary and Arthur, but we visited her small office which is housed in the tiny building where the Howell boys lived. Nell is not only a restaurateur, she is also a licensed family counselor and a reflexologist as well, and she uses the office for her work in those professions.

Just visiting the inn wasn't enough. Nell insisted on taking us on a long drive over the green hills and valleys of Grey Forest. We saw many of the old original playground houses, many doubtless purchased from Requa Realty! We learned much of the colorful local history from Nell, who is a former city councilwoman of the small community of some 400 inhabitants. She knows every rock and rill in the area! While we came away thinking the inn is certainly a special place, I would have to say that Nell Baeten is the real treasure of Grey Forest!

We finally, of course, got around to talking about the spirits who are said to inhabit the area. Nell told us numerous incidents have occurred during their ownership to convince the Baetens that the inn is frequented by several spirits. Mary Howell's spirit seems to be the most dominant. It is evident she likes to know what is going on at the restaurant. Why not? The inn was the culmination of her dream to own her own place. She was very happy there, made many friends, and was undoubtedly proud of her accomplishments. Why wouldn't she want to return to see that things were kept up to her standards?

Nell says if Mary is at all displeased, she usually manages to make it known. Sometimes Nell gets a strong whiff of the rose cologne she has been told was Mary's favorite fragrance. It is most often evident in the main dining room, where Mary's presence is often sensed near "her" table, which is located close to the kitchen door.

Linda, Nell's bookkeeper, told us she had an experience where she heard a big coffee maker fly apart in the kitchen when no one was around. She has often witnessed the alarm system going off for no reason at all, too.

Nell said when Mary is not pleased with the operations at the inn she causes the tray jacks to fall over, ice buckets full of water and ice to fall, and dishes to break. Once, when a couple was there to celebrate a wedding anniversary, they were given what Nell says was a warning from Mary. The wine bucket next to the table fell over, although there was no plausible reason how it could have done this. In six months the happy celebrants had parted, headed for the divorce court!

One employee of Nell's has reported the adding machine sometimes starts to add figures all by itself. The same woman also reported that once, when she had her arms full of things, the gates suddenly opened up right in front of her. She thanked Mary for helping her! Linda seems to have a lot of trouble with the computer. When the new system was installed a few years ago it looked as if Mary was reluctant to accept the new technology. The technician, who was a computer science instructor, was baffled when the programs failed, hardware stalled, and discs died. The day we were there, Linda had a lot of trouble getting the computer to work for her, and she's apparently a skilled computer operator! Mary just doesn't seem to like any kind of change!

Nell has placed Pennsylvania Dutch hex signs in all the dining rooms, and in Mary's little house that is now the party house. Mary Howell's upside-down horseshoe (holding the good luck in, you know!) still hangs over the front entrance, which is now the entrance to the main dining room as one comes off the former porch.

Nell said whenever she plans to leave on a trip she always goes into the main dining room, which seems to be Mary's favorite baili-wick, and she talks to her, "like she was still a live, human being." She tells her that she is going away for a few days, but capable peo-ple will be running the inn in her absence and everything is going to be just fine. She started doing this after a number of manifestations occurred during her absences. This past New Year, however, Nell forgot to tell Mary she was leaving. Right after Nell left, the alarm system went completely haywire, going off every fifteen or twenty minutes for no reason at all. This went on all night long. Dr. Baeten, who did not go out of town with his wife, had the alarm people out the next day to check out the system. They cleaned and checked the system and said that absolutely nothing was wrong, and there was no earthly (what about unearthly?) reason the alarm should have acted up like that.

One room at the inn, the Garden Room, seems to have another spirit attached to it. Unlike the benevolent spirit of the former owner, this spirit seems to be rather hostile. One strange event took place there about five years ago. That night Nell had personally checked to see all the candles had been extinguished before she locked up the inn. A last glance revealed not a glimmer of light from any of the candles. Satisfied, Nell went home. The next morning they were startled to find that there had been a fire in the Garden Room! It was just at one table, underneath a giant hex sign on the wall that stands for "Justice." The placemats, which had been placed over the tablecloth, had totally burned up. But the stitching, a series of round concentric circles, was still there on top of the charred tablecloth, which had been reduced to just a black tissue-thin bit of ash, except for the area just beneath the hex sign, where the cloth was intact and had not burned at all. There was also a basket of sugar packets there on the table. Neither the little basket nor its contents had burned at all. The napkins on the table for two had burned up completely except for the portions under the forks. The candle on the table had completely burned down and the wax had formed a big puddle on the floor beneath the table. The plate that had been beneath the candle had cracked in two. The fire alarm had never gone off and there was absolutely no smoke smell in the building!

Furthermore, the table top, which was formica, was unharmed, but the woven straw back of one of the chairs pulled up to the table had completely burned away.

A visiting psychic recently told the management that there was an unfriendly or malevolent spirit that hangs out in the Garden Room. They believe it must be a male entity, but no one has a clue as to whom he might be.

Once, after work, a few of the cooks were just "hanging out" and visiting while drinking a cold beer after work. They were out by the little stone building Nell uses as an office. Nell had left a light on in the building. The men suddenly saw a large shadow go by the window. At first they thought Dr. Baeten might be inside. Then, whatever it was (they just call it the "spirit") materialized into a big black form that literally walked through the wall and went out to the bird bath. It didn't take long for those cooks to all take leave!

Nell claims an Indian woman spirit has been seen walking from the herb garden to the area where a big fallen tree now lies in the meadow. She said there is a vortex of waters under the tree, and the woman, according to Nell, may be headed towards that water source. There are underground springs all over the area, according to Baeten. Sometimes water literally oozes up in the patio area of the restaurant.

It wouldn't be at all strange to surmise there are Indian spirits around. There were Indian trails all over the area, and the heavily forested area was a favored hunting ground for Indian tribes for hundreds of years. The first white family to arrive was a man named Juan Menchaca, who obtained a land grant and brought his Aztec Indian wife to settle down there. Later on, the little road that ran through the valley became a stage route and often the stagecoaches were raided by either Indians or bandits. There are a lot of caves in the area which provided both cover for the stage robbers and a handy hiding place for their loot. Pioneer Texas Ranger Captain Jack Hays pursued many a bandit through the area, and for a time the famous lawman was the main source of law and order in the little valley.

Nell also cited an experience some of the help had fairly recently. They were in the employees' parking lot across from the inn, chatting and have a cold drink after work. Suddenly they heard the tremendous clashing of cymbals coming from the inn! They hurried over to see what was wrong. The sounds had set off the alarm system, and soon the police arrived. Nothing could be found out of order, however. Later on, that same night, the Baetens, who live in a house adjacent to the inn, had just retired for the night, when the same cymbal clash routed them from their bed. Again, nothing was out of place and there was no explanation for the racket. This same thing happened one more time that night. Nell still doesn't know what set off the sound of cymbals.

Nell firmly believes there are several "old souls," as she prefers to call them, living both in the inn and in her home. She takes them for granted. Mary Howell's is the presence that Nell most often senses. Because she is such a loving spirit, Nell feels comfortable having her there. Strong as her presence is, Nell says as far as she knows, no one has ever actually seen her apparition.

If you would like to experience an evening spent dining on delicious food served in an atmosphere of country charm and romantic seclusion, you might look no further than the Grey Moss Inn, which is the oldest continually operating restaurant in South Texas. It's long been popular with generations of South Texas diners, so we suggest you call (210) 695-8301 for reservations. You're sure to enjoy a memorable, magical evening in this special place.

Haunted Historical Landmark: The Bullis House Inn

The beautiful white mansion which stands at the corner of Grayson and Pierce Street, just across from Fort Sam Houston, boasts a fascinating history. Construction began in 1906, and the house was completed down to the last detail almost three years later, in 1909, when its owner, Brigadier General John Lapham Bullis, moved in. Unfortunately, Bullis was only able to enjoy a couple of years in his fine home before he died in 1911. Perhaps the old general was in ill health when he built his house, or maybe he was just the type of person who liked to plan ahead. At any rate, I was told that the reason the huge front door is so much wider than ordinary doors was because the general planned it that way. He wanted to be sure it would be wide enough to admit his coffin, flanked by pallbearers on either side, when he was brought home to lie in state in one of the big front parlors. And, I was told, that's where he did lie in state, for a whole week, in fact!

Today the mansion is a spacious bed and breakfast inn, owned by Steve and Alma Cross and ably managed by Michael J. Tease. And, it's said, the old house just may have a resident spirit or two who comes around from time to time.

General Bullis enjoyed a colorful military career. A Union officer during the Civil War, he ended up in Texas during the Reconstruction period, where he served with considerable distinction under the famous Colonel Ranald McKenzie at Fort Clark, near present-day Brackettville. While at the fort, Bullis was promoted and given his own detachment as a reward for his valiant service during a raid on a hostile band of Indians camped across the Mexican border.

While the old Indian fighter was known to be a tough officer, he is said to have treated his men fairly, and he was respected and well liked. He later served as an Indian agent in New Mexico and

Arkansas before he was transferred, with the rank of major, to Fort Sam Houston.

After his retirement, Bullis moved into the big white mansion he had built just across the street from the fort. His family lived there after his death, until they finally sold it in 1949 to another famous general, Jonathan Wainwright. General Wainwright commanded Fort Sam Houston after his return from a Japanese prison camp in World War II. Known as the hero of Corregidor, Wainwright survived the infamous Bataan death march and became the highest ranking military officer to be incarcerated in a prison camp during the war. Although Wainwright purchased the Bullis house, for some reason he decided not to live there. He preferred a smaller house, which he named "Fiddler's Green" on Elizabeth Road, in Terrill Hills.

After 1949 the house was leased to various insurance companies for office space. Then for a time it was a child care center. In 1983 its present owners bought it, renovated and restored it. A popular bed and breakfast inn today, its spacious parlors and dining room are frequent choices of San Antonio brides for wedding receptions as well. It is a Texas Historic Landmark.

Bullis House Inn

Manager Michael Tease says he's only had one brush with the resident spirit at the inn. A few months back, a very excited guest arrived at the front desk with an unlikely story. He told Tease he had been coming down the back stairs when suddenly he'd been blocked, for several minutes, by some sort of invisible barrier. It was like he was pushing against a rope or barricade. He literally was unable to continue his progress down the steps. He was absolutely astounded by this. Tease, not quite believing what the gentleman had told him, went right away to the back staircase and started going up. Suddenly, his upward movement was stopped. He could not proceed up the stairs. Something was holding him back, some invisible resistance that kept him from moving forward. It was like some sort of barrier had been erected across the stairs. The stubborn resistance which impeded his progress lasted only a few minutes, but both Tease and the guest were totally baffled by the strange experience.

Tease told me that was his only experience with anything super-natural, but he knew Alma Cross had some strange experiences, and he felt sure she would be willing to share them with me. I finally was able to reach the busy owner, and we enjoyed a nice visit. Mrs. Cross told me for the first three years that they had the house, she and Steve lived downstairs while they worked to restore the place. When their work was completed, they began to rent out the upstairs por-tion as a bed and breakfast. They don't reside there now, but Alma is frequently on the premises.

One evening soon after they purchased the Bullis House Inn, the couple was upstairs working, when they suddenly heard loud men's voices involved in what sounded like a heated argument. The sounds came from downstairs in the vicinity of the entrance foyer. Knowing they were supposed to be alone in the place, they hurried to the staircase and yelled down, "Hey, what's going on down there?" Then they rushed down to see for themselves. But there was no one there. The front door was locked. They looked all over the big house, even going down into the basement. They found absolutely nothing.

Alma said Steve, an engineer, is pretty much of a skeptic where ghosts are concerned. But that night he heard the voices. He searched the house. He started to believe!

Once, when Alma's mother was visiting the couple, she was sleeping in a downstairs bedroom. Alma occupied the next room, now used as the inn manager's office. At 3 A.M. Alma suddenly awoke with a start, and in the moonlight she could plainly see the figure of an Indian man standing by her bed. She saw his face, his long black hair tied back with a bandanna around the forehead, and his body down to about the waistline. About the same time she saw the figure, her mother let out a blood-curdling scream! Still in a daze over having seen the Indian form, Alma leaped from her bed and dashed into her mother's room. She asked her mother why she had screamed, and her mother told her she had the most awful nightmare, about an Indian man standing right by her bed. The women each described to the other what they'd just seen, and the figure had looked just the same to them both. Alma said they decided to go to the kitchen and make some hot chocolate to try and settle their nerves.

Alma said she had never thought much about the types of dress of the different Indian tribes that once lived in the area, but the more she got to thinking about it, the man she saw that night looked like an Apache. And General Bullis was instrumental in capturing the most famous Apache of them all, the Chiracahua head man, Geronimo! Maybe that's why the spirit of an Apache brave came to the Bullis house. Come to think of it, it might have been Geronimo himself!

Alma told me one time her mother tried to get into an upstairs bedroom, which they call "Room G." It wasn't locked, but try as hard as she could, she couldn't open the door. Finally she went downstairs to get Alma. When the two women got to the room, the door was standing wide open!

There are just lots of little occurrences that take place in the inn, giving weight to the possibility that there are several rather interesting spirit personalities clinging to the historic old mansion.

For a night spent reliving history, call (210) 223-9426 where the owners guarantee you'll find "affordable elegance in the classic Southern style."

A Spirit Filled Chateau: Terrell Castle

One of San Antonio's truly grand mansions is a magnificent limestone pile known as Terrell Castle, located at 950 East Grayson Street, facing Fort Sam Houston's beautiful Staff Post Road. Until recently the owners were a charming mother and daughter team, Katherine Poulis and Nancy Haley. The two purchased the thirty-two-room house, complete with turrets and towers, in 1986. They spent several years and a great deal of money and effort in restoring a building which was in a slowly deteriorating condition at the time of purchase. Almost every room, ceiling, and floor had to be completely restored and refinished in order to return the house to its former grandeur and elegance.

Edwin Holland Terrell, a lawyer and statesman who served as ambassador and plenipotentiary to Belgium under President Benjamin Harrison in the early 1890s, was greatly impressed with the castles and chateaux he had seen in Belgium and France. A wealthy man, Terrell commissioned the noted English architect Alfred Giles to supervise the building project for him. He sent Giles to Belgium to more or less duplicate the plans of a castle he admired, a home that would exemplify the elegant style of living enjoyed by wealthy Europeans of that era. Terrell had recently remarried. His second wife, a member of the influential Maverick family, was a widow with several children, and Terrell wanted to provide a lovely big house for his new bride and ready-made family!

The Terrell name, by the way, is well known in San Antonio and around the state of Texas. Both Terrell County and the city of Terrell, Texas, bear his name.

When Terrell commissioned the building of his fine home, he also selected a name for it. During his lifetime it was called Lambermont after a favorite business associate. When Terrell died in 1908, the house fell into the hands of a succession of owners. The name its current owners have bestowed upon it, Terrell Castle, seems most appropriate.

This grand home, which boasts over 12,000 square feet, nine fine fireplaces, many curved windows, galleried porches, and beautiful woodwork, is now a comfortable bed and breakfast inn. It is also haunted.

Terrell Castle

Nancy says that often when she knew she was all alone in the house and was sitting in the downstairs den off the main entry hall she heard footsteps moving back and forth across the floor above her. It sounded like a woman's high-heeled shoes clicking across the hardwood floors, rather rapidly. This happened only when Nancy was alone, or when her mother was there but already asleep. I asked Nancy if she ever went upstairs to investigate. She said, "Who, me?" The sounds of the footsteps continue to the present time, and Nancy grew quite used to hearing them, but she still had no inclination to go upstairs to find out who was doing the walking.

A couple of years ago a nice couple from San Angelo spent several days at the popular inn. The first two nights were spent in the Alfred Giles suite, named for the architect. The last night they were in San Antonio they had to move to another room because the Giles suite was already reserved. They moved up to the fourth floor room, which is decorated in red, white, and blue and is called the "Americana Room."

This was a friendly, outgoing couple, Nancy recalls. When they returned to West Texas, they wrote the innkeepers a letter. Besides saying they had enjoyed staying in the beautiful house, they also said they wanted to say some things they thought Nancy and her mother should know.

It seems while they were staying in the Giles suite they heard a crash in the middle of the night, which sounded exactly like the toilet seat had dropped down. They got up and checked the bathroom, but that wasn't the cause of the noise. Several more times that night, at about thirty-minute intervals, they were awakened by the same noise. They got very little sleep during their stay in the Giles suite.

Then, when they moved up to the fourth floor, they settled in for a comfortable night of watching television. They decided to move the small TV set from its perch atop a cabinet to a small coffee table which they moved to the foot of the bed, so they could lie in bed and view a movie.

First, the ceiling fan began to spin. All by itself! The switch was on the off position. It did this off and on during the whole evening. It would spin really rapidly. Then it would stop. Then it would start up again. They checked all the switches and just couldn't figure out what was causing it to do this. Then, in the middle of the movie, the TV set just up and jumped off the table, landing upside down on the floor, just as if it had been hurled off the table! They were really dumfounded!

Recently, when I visited the Castle with a group on one of my nighttime Spirits of San Antonio tours, I took a psychic along. He was interested in the house and said it had one, possibly two, spirits, but they were friendly and harmless. Since Nancy has never been frightened by the sudden noises she has heard, this must be true.

When Nancy recently mentioned to her two housekeepers she was having the ghost tour people in that night, they confided that they, too, have had their experiences. They had never mentioned this to Nancy before. Mostly they hear footsteps or glimpse someone passing by in the hallways outside the upstairs rooms as they go about their cleaning. At first, each woman thought it was the other housekeeper, but when they checked and found out that their counterpart was working downstairs and was definitely not the figure they'd seen walking in the hallways, they realized there was something "different" going on at Terrell Castle!

I asked Nancy if she knew any stories of deaths or violence associated with the mansion. She told me there was one story, an unsubstantiated rumor, really, that she had heard about the original building contractor that Giles had hired. She didn't know his name. It seems he was using a number of government workers on the project, on government time, and he had been found out. He is said to have plunged off one of the upper balconies during the construction of the house, rather than face the exposure of his wrongdoing.

Then Nancy told me that just a short time ago a lady came to the house one afternoon and asked Katherine if she could just see the old house where she had once lived. It seemed the place had been divided up into numerous little efficiency apartments for military families at Fort Sam Houston during World War II. This lady had lived in one of them.

The woman asked Katherine if the bloodstains were still on the floor at the foot of the stairs. Katherine didn't known what on earth the woman was talking about. The lady went on to say that while she was living there, a man and his fiancee were occupying a third-floor apartment. The soldier came home early from the Fort and found his sweetheart with another man. He was enraged! He supposedly killed the man and got into a terrible argument with the woman, which extended out into the hallway. He apparently struck the girl and then either pushed her, or she fell over the stair railing, plunging three stories below to her death. The lady said that there was a big ugly bloodstain on the floor for a long time. Nancy told me that all the parquet floors had been redone prior to their purchase of the place. Neither she nor her mother had ever heard of this incident.

At this writing, Nancy and Katherine have just negotiated a sale of the Inn. The new owners are Victor and Diane Smilgin who plan to continue operating the bed and breakfast.

If you're interested in spending the night in what has been described as one of Texas's most elegant bed and breakfast inns just call the Smilgins at (210) 271-9145.

The Marvelous, Mysterious Menger

The venerable old Menger Hotel, a beautiful inn situated on Alamo Plaza, has long been the locale of history in the making and mystery for the taking! Built in 1859 by German immigrant William Menger and his wife, Mary Guenther Menger, the hotel has been the scene of many a gala ball, extravagant reception, and candlelit dinner party. Generations of debutantes have been presented to local society in its grand ballroom. The hotel has seen a lot of life whirl by, with vignettes of tragedy and pathos sometimes mixed in with all the glamour, glitter, and excitement it has known. Little wonder it has become the favored habitat of numerous ghostly residents!

William Menger was an enterprising young brewer who was reputed to have made the "best beer west of the Mississippi." A natural extension of his first business, a tavern, was an inn to provide lodgings for his customers. Some of the early history of the hotel is rather sketchy, but it's logical to assume the intact basement walls, two to three feet thick, of hand-cut rock, provided the right place to store hops and malt, imported from New York for this, one of the finest breweries in Texas.

Historical documents also indicate the Alamo Madre ditch, which forms one of the several existing tunnels beneath the original building, was once used for chilling the beer made on the spot. It was in the lower cellar of the building that it is said the renegade Apache, Geronimo, was held prisoner for a time before being transported to a reservation. Today, in this most mysterious part of the hotel, there is a steel door with a metal bar and two padlocks. Behind the door is a ten by twelve-foot rock-walled room with an arched ceiling. This room, in spite of its strong security, contains nothing. Perhaps it's where Geronimo was held captive. And perhaps the woeful sounds that maintenance men have reported hearing are echoes of the mournful chants that the Indian made as he endured captivity. And maybe they are just wind drafts whistling through the old basement. Who knows?

When Mr. Menger decided to expand his small inn, he really did it up right! People from far and wide came to the grand opening on February 2, 1859, and they've been beating a path to its doors ever since.

The hotel's old ledgers and registration books reveal the autographs of many famous people. For instance, Presidents William Howard Taft, William McKinley, U.S. Grant, Benjamin Harrison, Dwight D. Eisenhower, and Richard Nixon have all signed the guest register. There's a photograph of Harry S. Truman in the hallway just outside the Menger Bar taken during a visit to the hotel. Great stage and opera stars such as Sarah Bernhardt, Lillie Langtry, Anna Held, Sir Harry Lauder, Maude Adams, Richard Mansfield, and Beverly Sills enjoyed the Menger hospitality. There were the famous writers and poets Sidney Lanier and William Sidney Porter (better known as "O. Henry"). Gutzon Borglum, the creator of the great Mount Rushmore monument, once maintained a studio at the Menger.

The Menger Hotel

Roy Rogers and Dale Evans spent so much time at the Menger that the management named a suite for them.

Military heroes often visited the Menger. Robert E. Lee, while a colonel in the Union army prior to the Civil War, was stationed in San Antonio. He often visited the hotel and enjoyed their famous turtle soup, venison steaks, and other delicacies. General John Pershing, General Phillip Sheridan, and Texas Ranger Captain Leander McNelly were often Menger guests. Buffalo Bill Cody, the famous Indian scout and showman, loved the Menger. General William Simpson actually lived in the hotel until his death.

With all these famous people visiting the hotel and so much activity going on all the time, there is little wonder that some ghostly visitations might take place. Theodore ("Teddy") Roosevelt is caught up in the big middle of the tales of ghosts and hauntings that are just taken for granted by today's Menger employees. You see, Roosevelt is said to have done much of his recruiting for his famous Cavalry unit, the Rough Riders, from the convivial atmosphere of the Menger bar. This was back in 1898, during the Spanish American War. Teddy was given the formidable task of recruiting and training a cavalry unit to be shipped out to Cuba as soon as possible. He sort of held court at the Menger bar, plying the local cowboys with Mr. Menger's famous brew and promising them an interlude of excitement and adventure. Evidently a lot of those cowpunchers got just mellow enough that they did sign up, because it wasn't long till Teddy had his conscripts signed up and shipped out. During that training interval, the locals called these recruits "Teddy's Terrors," although Roosevelt preferred to label them the Rough Riders.

During the spring of 1996 there was quite a spate of manifestations, many of which centered around the Menger bar. Why this was such an active period, I couldn't say. Then I spoke with my psychic friend Robert Thiege, and he seemed not at all surprised, explaining that he believed there would be more and more activity as time approached 1998, the hundredth anniversary of the recruitment of the Rough Riders. Robert thinks there are a lot of old vibes from the days Teddy and his buddies hung out at the old bar. Why, even the ultra wealthy financial titans Cornelius Vanderbilt and Hamilton Fish came clear to Texas to sign up with "Teddy's boys!"

The dark cherry wood paneled bar, with its charming little balcony and big mirror, has been a busy place of late. I first received word that there might be something new going on at the Menger when I received a phone call from Cindy Shioleno, a friend who lives up in North Texas, in Kennedale. She told me she'd recently been to

San Antonio and had stayed at the Menger. She was told about a custodian who had a strange experience at the bar. She also told me that while she occupied her fifth floor room, she had felt a strong presence of someone or something there. Several times she suddenly smelled the unmistakable aroma of cigar smoke in the nonsmoking room. The smell of the smoke would come and go and was noticeable in the early morning hours.

I decided to see what I could find out about the recent manifestations and called several hotel staff members, who were very cooperative in telling me what they could.

Ernesto Malacara, assistant hotel manager, has been at the Menger for many years. He knows every employee and every nook and cranny in the hotel. He and night desk manager Yvonne Saucedo told me what they could about the custodian's strange experience that Cindy Shioleno had referred to. It seems on an April night in 1995 one of the custodians had gone to clean the bar. It was in the wee hours of the morning when both patrons and bartenders had called it a night. The young janitor, a husky man over six feet tall, was the kind of fellow you'd want on your side in a fight. He looked like he wouldn't be afraid of the bogeyman himself!

That night he'd opened the inside double doors to the bar and put the kick-stools in place to hold the doors open so he could wheel his cart of cleaning supplies down the center aisle of the narrow barroom. He started getting his cleaning equipment organized, and just happened to glance towards the bar over to his right. He noticed one of the barstools was on the floor. All the others had been placed, as was customary, upside down on the bar to facilitate cleaning of the floor. Another glance revealed a man, dressed in what the custodian later described as "an old-fashioned dark-colored military uniform" suddenly had materialized! He sat on the end barstool and beckoned a "come here" signal with his index finger to the startled janitor. The young man hastily headed for the open doors. But something was terribly wrong! The double doors had slammed shut. And, they were locked! It took a few minutes for the shaken janitor to gather his wits, yell, and make enough noise to attract the attention of passing security guards, who got him out of the locked barroom. All the while the unusual guest still sat upon the barstool.

Yvonne Saucedo was on duty at the front desk that night. She had been chatting with one of the night security guards. The pair were startled to see the young janitor, breathing hard and visibly shaken as he came stumbling into the lobby. He headed for one of the lobby chairs, and as he slumped into the chair, Yvonne feared he might be having a heart attack. He was gasping for breath, sweating profusely, and shaking violently. He managed to blurt out, "I think . . . I think, I saw a ghost . . . . " Because he seemed to be in shock and was white as a sheet, Mrs. Saucedo dialed 911. In only a few minutes the EMS crew arrived and transported the shaken young man to a nearby clinic for observation.

The custodian has never come back to his job at the Menger.

Later, Yvonne and the security guard went into the empty bar and looked around. She said they must have stayed there for at least half an hour, but the strange visitor did not make another appearance. However, just a couple of weeks later another custodian glimpsed what may have been the same spirit, and again, it was in the Menger bar. The employee was in the bar at 2 A.M. when he chanced to glance up to the balcony area. He noticed a man dressed in a dark gray suit, wearing a little hat. He just sat there for a few minutes, at the railing of the balcony on the side closest to Crockett Street. The surprised janitor ran out to summon another staff member. When the men returned to the bar a few minutes later, the apparition had vanished and did not return.

Rodney Miller, who works in the valet parking area, told me he understood that one night recently all the glasses in the bar had begun to tremble and shake, and this phenomenon was witnessed by a number of guests, as well as the bartender.

Mr. Malacara told me one night all the glasses on the bar, which had been artistically stacked in a pyramid by the bartender, fell over, many falling to the floor, and yet not one was broken!

Just a short time back, a couple who remained until closing time in the famous bar was preparing to leave. The woman stood in the center of the bar area and her husband was standing slightly off to one side. Suddenly a man entered the bar and started walking towards the woman. Her husband stepped in front of the man who seemed to be purposely striding right up to the woman. Just as the guest stepped in front of the figure, it vanished right in front of their eyes!

The bar is not the only part of the Menger that's haunted. Not by a long shot!

An article in an old *Express News* stated that guests had reported seeing a "woman in blue" walking silently through the hallways on several occasions. Historian and writer David Bowser wrote about this particular lady in his *Guidebook to Some Out of the Way Historical Sights in the City of the Alamo*: "There are a host of interesting stories about this grand old hotel. One of the most fascinating and little known of these is that of the Lady in Blue."

Then Bowser goes on to tell about numerous rumors of odd occurrences in a second floor room in the older section of the hotel. This room looks out over the beautifully landscaped patio.

After I read David's story, I checked around with numerous people who work at the hotel. It seems a figure of a young woman, dressed in an old-fashioned blue dress, with blonde shoulder length hair, has been seen sitting in a chair by the window, pensively looking down upon the patio. Most often she has been seen by one of the chambermaids, who as they clean the room, suddenly feel as if someone is watching them. When the girls turn around, the young woman, who is always seated, briefly appears, and then just as suddenly disappears. No one has been able to explain who this figure might have been in life, or why she always comes to just this one room.

Probably the best known of the Menger's ghosts is the spirit of Salie White. Many employees and hotel guests have seen her. Her restless spirit roams mainly around the second and third floors of the original portion of the hotel. This ghost always wears a full, floor-length skirt and has a bandanna or scarf tied around her head. A long necklace of beads dangles around her neck, and she wears an apron. Often she carries a broom or a feather duster, much as she did as she went about her chores during the time she worked as a chambermaid at the hotel back in 1876. She worked hard and was well liked and appreciated by the hotel staff. Unfortunately, her young life was cut short on March 28, 1876, when, as she was leaving the hotel one evening, she was shot by Henry Wheeler, her insanely jealous common-law husband. She hung on for two agonizing days at the hotel, where the staff did all they could to nurse her. She had lost too much blood to survive and passed away on March 30. I have seen an entry in an old hotel ledger, which is displayed out in the lobby in a glass case. The entry, written by one Frederick Hahn, was in the "cash paid" column, and it stated "to cash paid for coffin for Salie White, chambermaid, deceased, murdered by her husband, shot March 28, died March 30, $25 for coffin, and $7 for grave, total, $32."

From what I have been told, some of the maids prefer to work in pairs in the section of the hotel that Salie frequents. Also, a rather unnerved executive from the sales staff once confessed to me that she too had seen Salie, and it was an "unsettling" experience.

Another famous Menger guest is said to have made an appearance or two at the hostelry. Captain Richard King, founder of the world-famous King Ranch, south of San Antonio at Kingsville, always stayed at the Menger when he came to San Antonio on business. The King Ranch Suite is still furnished with period furniture used during his stays there, including the lovely four poster bed complete with canopy in which King expired in August of 1885 after a lingering illness. He loved the hotel so much that his funeral service was conducted in the big front parlor under the stained glass skylight.

A young man with a local security company, who once worked as a night security guard at the hotel, told me one night when he was patrolling the hallways of the older section of the hotel, he saw a man going down the hall quite late. The man was wearing a dark suit and a broad-brimmed Western style hat. The guard said he followed the gentleman, and then as the figure came up to the entrance to the old King Ranch Suite, which has a recessed doorway, he didn't bother to unlock the door. He just seemed to drift right through the door and then disappeared! The guard said he went down to the lobby and asked the other guard on duty if he had ever seen the mysterious visitor. He had not. The young man also told me that several times when he was on duty at night and got into the elevator it would always stop at the third floor no matter what floor button was pushed.

Ernesto Malacara has a lot of stories to tell about the hotel. One evening as he stood at the front desk chatting with three employees, all four men noticed the big double front doors of the hotel as they slowly swung open. Only, nobody came in! These doors are very heavy, made of brass and beveled glass, and they just wouldn't blow open. According to Malacara, there was absolutely no wind that night. These doors are not right on the outside of the building, either. They are located in a covered and protected entryway that also has doors. There is no way of explaining why these big, heavy doors opened that evening. Since then, I have spoken with Mr. Malacara, and the doors have opened several other times, always to admit no one.

The affable manager told me one woman who operates a shop off the main lobby reported that she actually witnessed a display of little shot glasses she had just arranged on a counter get up and move, one by one, from the left to the right side of the counter. They were lifted, moved, and then set down by careful invisible hands as the astounded shopkeeper watched!

And, there was the time, several years ago, when a hotel maid saw a male figure appear just before she stepped into an elevator on the fourth floor one evening. She had just pushed the elevator button and happened to look over to the left. She distinctly saw the figure of a man dressed in strange-looking clothing, a jacket or tunic with big puffy sleeves, and a funny peaked hat, definitely not ordinary 1990s attire. Mr. Malacara said the maid was visibly shaken. It sounds a little like someone from the Spanish period of our city's history to me. This isn't so strange. The land on which the Menger is located was part of the earliest Spanish mission in San Antonio, the Mission San Antonio de Valero. I am sure many soldiers, grandees, and notables of that era walked all over that property at one time or another.

Several years back, a gentleman who was checking out of the hotel questioned some items on his bill. There were a number of telephone calls billed to his room, and he said he had made no calls at all. Then, glancing again, he noticed that the phone number he had supposedly called, and which appeared on the room charge, was his mother's old telephone number. But, she had been dead for years! When I mentioned this to one of my psychic friends he interpreted it to be a signal that the spirit of his mother was somehow trying to reach her son.

On a recent evening when we were down at the hotel to visit friends who were guests there, we ran into another hotel executive, Gil Navarro. He told me recently when he was in the older section of the hotel, standing outside room 205, he distinctly felt someone brush by him very closely, actually touching his shoulder. He whirled around to see who had collided with him, saying "pardon me" at the same time. But no one was there. There had not been enough time for whoever it was to have totally disappeared. When ghosts at the Menger are mentioned, just like Ernesto Malacara, Gil Navarro never laughs. Like many of the hotel staff members, he just takes them for granted as being hotel "fixtures."

I recall one incident I personally witnessed. Before the remodeling job done on the front registration desk, there used to be a little bell that guests could ring to summon a room clerk. It was plugged into an electric socket at one time. Well, it was disconnected for some time, but they just left it out on the desk. Periodically, even though it was disconnected, it would ring loudly as if someone was summoning a clerk. The desk staff decided it might be Teddy Roosevelt's ghost, demanding the usual prompt service he experienced at the Menger. It even went off during an interview I conducted with some front desk personnel, so I can attest to its performance. The bell has now been removed, so it's no longer available for Teddy or any of the other spirits to ring. I miss it.

Recently, according to Mr. Malacara, a maid cleaning a room suddenly saw an Indian man standing in the doorway of the room, just staring at her. He was there a moment and then disappeared. He was probably one of the early mission Indians just "visiting" from next door at the Alamo grounds!

One morning when I was at the hotel ready to do a radio interview about the Menger spirits for KTFM, I ran into Mr. Malacara. He told me that he had just had "an incident." It seems he and Tom Brady, the chief of security, were strolling down the hallway that leads to the parking garage. They both happened to glance through the glass doors to the executive offices and they saw a man sitting in the office, which they knew had not yet opened. They'd passed the door when they stopped, looked at one another, and said, "Who was that?" They backed up a few paces to glance into the office again. The man they had both seen had vanished into thin air!

Another time Mr. Malacara was walking along a corridor when he saw a door standing ajar. He glanced in as he strolled by and saw that a maid was cleaning the room. But he noticed there was no cleaning cart in the hallway. He took a few steps backward and looked into the room. The maid wasn't there at all!

Several of the restaurant employees have seen a ghostly maitre de dressed in old-fashioned frock coat and gray pin-striped trousers, not the standard attire worn today, as he goes about greeting invisible guests at the tables, obviously still intent on doing the best job possible!

A guest reported he needed some towels. He went into the hall looking for a maid. He saw one working in a nearby room. He asked her if he could get some towels. She paid no attention to him. He repeated, in a louder voice, "I need some towels." No reply, again. Finally, he went to his room and called the desk and reported the maid was totally unresponsive, which he found strange. The desk said there was no maid working that floor at the time. The desk clerk asked what she looked like, and the man described the maid and the uniform she was wearing. The staff member told the guest that the uniform he described had not been worn by any maids in the hotel for many, many years! This was a typical case of a replay ghost; this type of spirit will occasionally surface, do a scene over and over, paying no attention at all to anyone around them. Of course, the guest was quite astounded by his experience.

I am sure that spirits from San Antonio's by-gone days will continue to find this beautiful hotel with its charming Victorian furnishings a lovely place to visit. There's absolutely nothing to fear about these spirits who frequent the hotel, and many guests are hopeful they might run into one of the wraiths, who all seem to be friendly and benevolent. In fact, it's my opinion that an occasional manifestation just adds a little touch of mystery to the elegant hotel, another fascinating facet to the elegant gem that so beautifully adorns Alamo Plaza!

Glories and Ghosts at the Gunter

Since the beginning of the Republic of Texas, there has been an inn at the corner of Houston and St. Mary's Streets. In 1837, just one year after the Battle of the Alamo, the Frontier Inn opened its doors to the waves of new arrivals surging into Texas from the East. In that same year, Bexar County was created by an act of Congress of the Republic of Texas, and John W. Smith was elected mayor. Mayor Smith, known as "El Colorado" because of his red hair, was a hero of the Texas Revolution and the last messenger sent out from the Alamo by Travis. His wife was the former Maria de Jesus Curabelo, whose family arrived with the Canary Island settlers in 1731.

For over twelve years the Frontier Inn saw many changes in the Republic of Texas from its vantage point on El Paso at El Rincon (now Houston and St. Mary's Streets).

In 1845 Texas became a state of the Union. U.S. troops were dispatched to serve in San Antonio. When the army arrived, there were no government headquarters, storehouses, or living quarters. The Alamo was repaired sufficiently to serve as a quartermaster depot.

In 1846 a man named William Vance, an Irishman from New York, was appointed commissary agent for the United States and came to San Antonio. Soon after his arrival, his brothers, who had operated successful mercantile businesses in both Arkansas and Louisiana, followed him and opened a general store on Alamo Plaza. At the request of General Percival Smith, the brothers Vance agreed to erect a building the army could lease. They negotiated to purchase the old Frontier Inn for $500, choosing it because of its good location. It was soon replaced with a two-story structure facing on Houston Street. In the rear of the building, on St. Mary's at Travis, a barracks was built around a quadrangle, the first army quadrangle in

San Antonio. Among officers stationed there were Col. Albert Sidney Johnston and Lt. Col. Robert E. Lee.

The Vance brothers took back their buildings, and they established their business as the Vance House. In 1882 Stanley Gould wrote in his *Alamo City Guide*, "We have another strictly first-class hotel, and very favorably located, handy for those who come here for business or for pleasure; quiet and cool, yet central, near all the churches, it combines all the elements needed in a hotel home. The proprietor, Mr. E.C. Everett, has made this hotel his hobby, and guests can rely on receiving first class accommodations at reduced prices. The table has the reputation of being one of the best provided and served in Western Texas." *The Guide* continued: "Terms are $2.00 a day. Reduced rates by the week or by the month. Guests arriving by trains at either depot can take the horse cars and be carried to this hotel for five cents."

That same year a gentleman from Germany arrived on the scene. His name was Ludwig Mahncke. He was a friend of Kaiser Wilhelm I, and with him he brought customs of his "fatherland." He soon opened a family saloon-restaurant which was characteristic of many European coffeehouses, a place where people could gather and exchange news, make business deals, enjoy refreshments and the camaraderie of others.

Shortly after Mahncke opened the saloon and restaurant, he decided to venture into the hotel business. He took a partner, Lesher A. Trexler, already a successful hotelier, and together they took over the Vance House, adding innovative new conveniences, and renamed it the Mahncke Hotel. It soon became one of the city's leading hotels and a favorite meeting place for cattlemen and businessmen to gather. In the late 1880s the Mahncke, which was an anchor for Houston Street, advertised that it had "no superior in the State." It stated that its rooms were "airy, comfortable, and cleanly." It had all the modern conveniences. Its table was said to be beautifully supplied with everything in season and everything first class. Its rates were reasonable, and last, but by no means least, the managers, Dr. Trexler and Mr. Mahncke, were said to be "especially attentive to its guests."

By the turn of the century San Antonio had become a metropolitan city. Tourism was a big business, and the Mahncke site was central to the city's business section. At this time a group of civic leaders banded together to organize the San Antonio Hotel Company. They decided to buy the corner occupied by the old Mahncke and build the most modern hotel in the country, "a palatial structure that would meet the demands of the state's most progressive city." Real estate developer L.J. Hart, along with twelve other local investors, including Jot Gunter, purchased the site from Mrs. Mary E. Vance Winslow in 1907 at of a cost of $190,000. Mr. Gunter died before the hotel was completed, but the hotel was named to honor him, as he had been a major financial backer of the project.

The new hotel officially opened on November 20, 1909. It was an eight-story, 301-room structure of buff brick, steel, and concrete, the largest building at the time in San Antonio. It ushered in an era of grand social life in the city. The November 21, 1909 edition of the *San Antonio Light* gave a glowing write-up of the formal banquet that heralded the opening. It was a grand affair, with covers laid for 382 guests.

The designer of this grandest of hotels was J. Russell of the St. Louis firm of Moran, Russell, and Gorden, the same firm that had also designed the Hotel Adolphus in Dallas, the Galvez in Galveston, and later, in 1912, the Empire Theatre in San Antonio, which is just across Houston Street from the Gunter.

The new hotel became the center for cattlemen to gather (there was a separate reception room for women, with a private entryway!) It had its own laundry, heating plant, barber shop, and water system with an artesian well in the basement.

In 1917 a ninth story was added, and then, in 1926, three more stories were added, with the "Gunter Roof," which boasted a Japanese garden, as the final icing on the cake. It became a popular place for dining and dancing under the stars. During two world wars the Gunter became "home" to both the Army and Air Force personnel stationed here, continuing its importance as the "center of everything."

The Gunter was a home away from home to many famous personages over the years. General John "Black Jack" Pershing, feted for his service on the Mexican border with a banquet at the Gunter, was presented a fine thoroughbred horse in the hotel lobby! Western film star Tom Mix also was photographed registering at the lobby reception desk astride his favorite horse, Tony. Will Rogers dispensed his homespun humor there; Max Baer and his brother Buddy spent their free time there while stationed at Lackland Air Force Base; John Wayne called it home during the filming of *The Alamo*. While Harry S. Truman was President, he stayed in the twelfth floor Presidential Suite, right across the hall from Speaker of the House Sam Rayburn. Mae West, B.C. Forbes of *Forbes Magazine*, and Gene Tunney were other famous guests of the hotel.

Photo courtesy of the Camberley-Gunter Hotel.

In 1979 Josef Seiterle, representing a Swiss investment group, bought the Gunter and spent over $20,000,000 completely refurbishing the hotel, restoring it to its past glory. In the spring of 1985 a new porte cochere entrance from St. Mary's Street, topped with a swimming pool, landscaped deck, and exercise room, and flanked by a parking garage, completed the costly restoration.

In July 1989 the Gunter joined the huge global network of Sheraton Hotels, becoming the fourth of the Sheraton Corporation's
historic hotels. Then, in 1996, it was again sold, becoming a part of
the Camberley Corporation, and is now known as the Camberley-
Gunter.

Along with all the pomp and ceremony, and all the big business
deals that have transpired over the many years the hotel has served
San Antonio, a little intrigue and mystery have crept into the
archives of the old hotel as well. Probably the most unusual, fascinating, bizarre unsolved crime in San Antonio police files occurred at
the Gunter.

On February 6, 1965, a blonde man in his late thirties checked
into room 636 at the hotel. He registered as "Albert Knox" of Youngstown, Ohio. Later, police found the address he gave was a vacant
lot, and the only Albert Knox in Youngstown was a black man who
had never visited San Antonio.

During the next three days the man, who was about five feet
nine inches tall and weighed around 160 pounds, occupied the room.
He was seen going in and out of the hotel several times, always
accompanied by a tall slender blonde woman who appeared to be in
her thirties.

On the morning of Monday, February 8, the maid on duty, Maria
Luisa Leja, said she changed the linen in the room and straightened
it up. On the same day, the afternoon maid, Maria Luisa Guerra, prepared to check the room. Thinking the occupants had forgotten to
remove a "Do Not Disturb" sign on the door, when there was no
answer to her knock, she opened the door with her passkey. As she
stepped inside, she saw an Anglo man standing beside a blood-
soaked bed. According to an account in the *San Antonio Express
News* that ran on February 10, the maid, upon discovering the man,
screamed. The man laid a finger against his lips as if cautioning her
to be quiet. Then, he scooped up a large bundle wrapped in a blood
soaked blanket and disappeared out the door.

Searching the room for clues, the police found what they said
were the small footprints of the apparent victim. They also found
several cigar butts, one of which bore the imprint of lipstick!

A police tracking dog was brought in to follow the suspect's apparent trail. It led to a window leading to the sixth floor fire escape. There police found some drops of blood, but the trail turned cold, apparently washed away by a light rain.

In the room they found a suitcase containing a man's shirts, some cheese, sardines, and several empty wine bottles. Officer also found blonde hairs in the room, as well as nylon hose and women's underwear.

On the bed, officers found the shell of a fired .22 caliber bullet. A .22 caliber slug was found embedded in a wall near a bloodied chair. This led detectives to believe the woman had been shot, possibly with an automatic pistol, from the bed, as she sat in the nearby chair. Bloody trails indicated the slayer had to make several trips to the bathroom, presumably to wash the parts of a dissected body. A recent interview I had with former Detective Frank Castillon, who was a Homicide detective assigned to the case, revealed that during the investigation, a bloody "water line" was found in the bathtub. Detective Castillon's theory is this is where the body was butchered and washed.

Mrs. Guerra, the maid who discovered the man in the room, said the bloody bundle she saw was about a foot high and some 20 inches or so long and wide. Officers said the body of a small boned woman, dissected and blood drained, could have fit the dimensions Mrs. Guerra described.

The whole room was a bloody mess. The mattress and floor were covered with blood. The commode was sticky with a "red substance." The bathroom was literally covered with gore. While no body was found, it was theorized by some that the body had been butchered in the bathroom and perhaps then run through a meat grinder. At that time, Dr. Ruben Santos was the assistant medical examiner. He agreed that there was enough blood to indicate a butchering. Dr. Robert Hausman, the medical examiner, was out of the country at the time of the occurrence. He disagreed that there had been a butchering, saying that he believed from police photographs there was not enough blood. He also discarded the theory that a body was slowly run through a meat grinder and then flushed down the hotel bathroom commode. He projected the theory that the woman had given birth and the blood came from that, a theory Frank Castillon has never agreed with. And then what would explain a bullet hole in the chair and the wall if this was what had taken place? And people in the hotel who had seen the blonde with "Knox" said she was tall and slim, certainly not the description of a pregnant woman! No, Castillon still stands firmly by his belief that there was definitely enough blood to indicate a murder, then a butchering, took place in room 636.

Checking out any clues they could find, Detectives Castillon and his partner, Bob Holt, discovered the suitcase they found in the room had been purchased on February 3, just prior to the time the man going under the name of Albert Knox had registered at the hotel. It was bought at the San Antonio Trunk and Gift Company at 211 Alamo Plaza by a man who had used a personalized check of a Mr. John J. McCarthy. Mr. McCarthy turned out to be the stepfather of a Walter Emerick, the real name of the man going under the Knox alias. The detectives then checked local restaurants to find the source of the cheese, wine, and sardines. When they visited Shilo's Delicatessen, at 424 East Commerce Street, they learned a man, later ascertained to be Emerick, had dined with a "blonde woman" and had later purchased $12.80 of take-out food, including the cheese and sardines. He had used a similar check to the one used to purchase the suitcase at Alamo Trunk. When questioned about the John J. McCarthy who signed the check, a restaurant employee surprised the officers by answering, "Oh, Mr. McCarthy didn't sign the check. It was his stepson, Walter something or other...I believe it is Urick. The McCarthys are regular customers." Evidently, the restaurant management recognized McCarthy's stepson and didn't want to make a big deal over his signing his stepfather's check.

Now suspecting a forgery case, district attorney 's investigator M.R. Nugent, who had joined Castillon in his investigations, went to the hot check section where he learned that Walter "Urick" was really Walter Emerick, and a forgery charge had indeed been filed against him only the previous week. Emerick was Mrs. John J. McCarthy's son by a previous marriage. He had a forgery record and had served time. Fed up with her son's habits, his mother had accused her son of taking fifty personalized checks on January 17.

Learning that Emerick had a previous police record, fingerprints expert Captain A.M. Davenport matched up the fingerprints found in room 636 of the Gunter with those on Emerick's police record. The police finally had a suspect!

A statewide alert went out for Walter Emerick, a thirty-seven-year-old unemployed accountant. But just hours later, the police were to come to the end of a dead-end street.

Sandor Ambrus Jr., a security guard at the St. Anthony Hotel, located just a block away from the Gunter, became suspicious of one tenant who had checked into the hotel under the name of "Robert Ashley" on Tuesday. Arousing his suspicions was the fact that Ashley had not allowed the maids to enter the room to clean it.

Ambrus called in city and county officers and they went to room 536 at the St. Anthony. The hotel revealed that the man who signed in as Ashley had tried to rent room number 636 at the hotel, but when he found it was already occupied he settled for room 536.

Detective Castillon was with the security guard and asked him to use his key to unlock the door, fearing a sudden knock on the door might upset the man, who was thought to be armed. The guard was quite nervous, according to Castillon, and jangled the keys against the door, thus alerting the occupant. A shot rang out from within the room. Detective Castillon said he pushed the door open and was the first to reach the man, who had shot himself in the temple. He was still clutching his .22 caliber pistol. The detective asked him if he had killed anyone at the Gunter Hotel, but the man could only make a few "gurgling noises" before he expired.

In the St. Anthony room, a shirt was found which had been washed or rinsed out in an effort to remove bloodstains. Also, cigars of the same brand as those found in the Gunter room were among the effects. And, of course, as police had no doubt, "Ashley's" fingerprints matched those found in Gunter room 636.

No body of a victim was ever found. Police were never able to match fingerprints that were lifted from the room, which may have belonged to the woman. No woman was ever reported to be missing. One police theory is that she may have been a prostitute from another city. Emerick was known to hang out with attractive ladies of the night.

One interesting twist did come to light during the investigation when two sales clerks in a downtown department store later identified Emerick as the man who had come into the hardware department and purchased a very large meat grinder!

At the time all this occurred, there was a lot of downtown construction going on, and green dye, used to color cement, was found hardened on Emerick's shoes. One theory remains alive that he may have entombed the remains of his victim in still-wet cement at one of the downtown construction projects.

The case is still open. The body was never discovered. The murder suspect was dead by his own hand. A homicide detective was heard to say, "The best case we have is malicious mischief over $50. It took a couple hundred dollars just to get the room cleaned up."

When the hotel staff took me up to see the room, I found it to be a small inside room, very close to the elevator. I was told the original room had been divided into two rooms, so what I saw was only a portion of the original crime scene. And of course, all drapes, bedspreads, upholstered pieces, etc. have been replaced. Only the tiny octagonal bathroom tiles, so popular in years past, are original to the room. Although I looked very closely, I could see no trace of bloodstains on them!

Strangely enough, Liz Wiggins, a former KENS TV newswoman, told me she did a special telecast from the Gunter for Halloween in 1995. She took Kathleen Bittner, a well-known local psychic, Kathleen's husband, and some news photographers, and the group all spent the night in room 636. Bittner felt a lot of strange vibes and supposedly "saw" a re-enactment of the heinous murder that took place there. Although no one had told her, Bittner announced that the room was much smaller now, and she believed it had been divided. She was right on target!

Other chats with members of the hotel staff have revealed that there have been some unusual happenings in the hotel from time to time. Whether or not they are connected to the murder, there is no way to tell.

An executive who has been there for some time says that a woman in "ghostly garb" has been seen a number of times in the vicinity of room 636 where the activity took place. Two security guards reported sightings at different times, usually very late at night. On at least two occasions, hotel guests have been awakened by loud hammering noises in the rooms adjacent to theirs. When guards were summoned to investigate, the rooms next door to the complainants were found to be unoccupied. The guards would check around, then leave, going back downstairs, and the noises would resume with renewed vigor!

Former staff member Jackie Contreras, who worked in the sales office, said in 1990 she had a frightening experience. She had gone to check on a room that had been made ready for some very important hotel clients. She went to the door and knocked. When no one answered, she opened the door with her passkey. The room was pitch black inside. She thought this was rather strange, since the maids customarily would draw the drapes to allow sunlight to come into a room that had been made ready to receive guests. As she groped in the darkness for the light switch, she said the light coming in from the hallway revealed a "woman standing in the room. She was looking straight at me, her hands reaching towards me. She looked very old and very stooped, and was white as a sheet. She was wearing a long white gown." Jackie said she backed out fast, closing the door behind her. She went down to the lobby and told the people at the desk they must have given her the wrong information, as the room they had sent her to check out was occupied. They assured her this was not the case, the room was not occupied, as the maid had just finished making it ready for the new occupants. Jackie told me as she thinks of it now, she is fully convinced the woman she saw was a ghost, and she still gets cold chills whenever she recalls that afternoon and the woman she saw in that dark room. (I noticed as Jackie spoke, the hair on her arms was standing up straight—she had been truly, unforgettably frightened!)

Christina Richards, an accountant at the hotel, had hotel guests tell her they had seen ghosts when she was working at the front desk. She just thought they might be trying to get out of paying their bills until she saw one herself! Once when on an upper floor in a hallway, Richards said, "I saw something that crossed from one side to the other side. I turned to look and saw somebody dressed in a long white dress go right through a wall."

In 1996 former sales manager Lydia Fischer and I had a nice chat over lunch. I first met Fischer when she was interviewed for a TV special filmed in the hotel, in which I was a participant. She is convinced that she saw a ghost as she made her rounds on one of the upper floors. She saw this lady clad in a long white dress, going down the hall, sort of floating from room to room, sometimes going through the walls and coming out again. The figure had long black hair, upswept on both sides and hanging down long in the back. It was rather like the Belle Epoch style worn at the turn of the century by the famous "Gibson Girls." Lydia said she thought to herself, "Am I seeing what I think I am seeing, or what?"

At Christmas time in 1990, a group of the hotel employees gathered together to celebrate at an informal Christmas party up in the grand ballroom. One of those in attendance took some photographs of the gathering. One developed photo revealed an extra person in the picture. Someone showed up with the group who was not in the group, and nobody knows who it was, except another human form was plainly visible in the picture!

The police still don't have all the answers to the 1965 murder in room 636. But call it a strange twist of fate, just about a year ago Gil Lopez, who was then the hotel's general manager, received a strange envelope in the mail. It was a post office envelope bearing no return address. The envelope was addressed to the Gunter (not the Camberley-Gunter) Hotel and the zip code was the old, now outdated one used in 1965. Inside the envelope was a room key, the key to room 636. This was a regular old-fashioned room key, like the hotel used back then, not the credit-card-like plastic door openers used today. No one has the slightest clue as to who mailed the key, or why!

So there you are...an old and venerable hotel, situated in the very heart of downtown San Antonio! The remarkable hostelry has been the scene of many gala balls, elegant gatherings, memorable speeches, and visits by the rich and famous. It also has the distinction of having a certain aura of haunting mystery contained within its sturdy walls. It is a wonderful hotel, a great place to dine in style, to spend a night or a long vacation. And what is more, they won't charge you a penny more for room 636!

Spirits at the St. Anthony

One of the stately hotels known as the "grand old ladies" of San Antonio is the elegant Crowne Plaza St. Anthony, located on Travis Street between Navarro and Jefferson Streets, facing onto the shady square known as Travis Park. Built in 1909, the hotel was designed to offer comfortable lodgings to cattlemen and their families, the discriminating traveler, and visiting tourists.

F.M. Swearingen, a former manager of the Hot Wells Resort Hotel, first thought of the idea of building the hotel. He was financed by two prominent cattlemen, B.L. Naylor and A.H. Jones. Jones later served as mayor of San Antonio. He died in 1913 while still in office.

Today's hotel has been greatly enlarged but has lost none of its early charm. It is beautifully furnished with fine antiques and cut crystal chandeliers. The walls are decorated with fine tapestries, original oil paintings, and nineteenth-century French mirrors. The hotel was the first to have electric eye entrance doors, to provide drive-in garage registration facilities, as well as the first auto lobby. The garage permitted guests to drive their cars in and take an elevator directly to their floor to change clothes before entering the main lobby, often referred to as "Peacock Alley." All the china and glassware in the hotel bore the crest of the establishment. The modern kitchen was located at the basement level and boasted such state-of-the-art accoutrements as mechanical dishwashers and potato peelers!

Built during the days before integration, there were two dining rooms provided for the guests' servants, one for white and one for black servants. Now I wouldn't know of anybody even traveling with servants! Times have indeed changed!

In 1959 the St. Anthony Club was founded. It was one of America's finest dinner clubs and drew its members from around the world. Known as "the" nightclub of the Southwest, it was rated third in the nation. Every week it boasted one of the top bands in the country. The big band sound was broadcast live nightly from the club to radio fans all around the country. Sadly, today it no longer exists. The rooms once used for gala dinners and balls are now offered as dining facilities for conventions and such. Its beautiful mural walls, reminding one of enchanting Mediterranean balconies, have been replaced with more conservative wall coverings.

Unlike the Menger, where the identities of the spirits in residence are pretty well known, it seems that no one really knows who the St. Anthony's spirits might be. There are no clear-cut stories of sightings of identifiable apparitions, but there are enough stories that have come filtering down from various hotel employees to leave little doubt in anyone's mind that the hotel hosts its share of ghostly guests.

Mark Eakin, one of the bellmen, who admits to being sensitive to the presence of other-worldly spirits, says he has often felt a presence in the basement-level male employee's locker room. He told me as he is putting away his belongings he hears sounds of someone washing up in the lavatory area, but when he takes a look to see who it is, there's never anyone there. He has seen strange shadowy outlines and generally has a feeling he is not alone. He also said that when he is called to deliver the newspapers on the tenth floor level he always feels as if he is being followed. He added that he knows the doors that open out onto the old former roof garden, where San Antonians used to dance on summer nights, have been known to open up all by themselves!

A front desk employee, said once a couple checked into their room, and soon afterwards they came right back down to the registration desk and asked to be checked out! They said the room assigned to them was already occupied. When they unlocked the door they saw a man and a woman sitting in the room, drinking cocktails. They were quite upset to find their room was already taken. An immediate and thorough check by the hotel staff revealed that the room was empty, and there were no empty glasses scattered about. One staff member confided that several times people have just checked out because something in their rooms spooked them! We were told by a hotel executive that recently a woman thought someone got in the bed in her room. She hurriedly checked out. The executive thinks the spirits may be upset because the hotel is undergoing a lot of renovations just now, and we all know that situation often causes unrest among the ghostly population.

Warren Andrews, another hotel bellman, says that he has heard the sound of footsteps following him as he walks on some of the upper floors. They sound as if the walker is wearing old-fashioned galoshes, as they squeak and squish as they stride along. He has turned around to find nobody there, but he usually gets a really cold feeling just as he stops. Also, he has heard the lavatory faucet turned on or the shower running in the men's locker room, just as his friend and fellow bellman, Mark Eakin, reported.

Mark also told me he had heard of a ghostly lady in a red dress, but he has never personally seen her. A couple of ladies who worked in the sales department in the executive office section up on the mezzanine have seen ghostly feet! Cindy Waters, who used to work in sales, and Jet Garcia both told me they had seen them. Housekeeper Manuela Espinosa also reported she had seen the dark-stockinged legs with slim ankles clad in black old-fashioned pumps in the first stall of the mezzanine level ladies' powder room. The lady never comes out. Her feet and legs eventually just disappear. No one seemed to have a clue what might cause the phantom feet to appear. I promised Cindy I would try and bring a psychic to check out that facility. More about that later.

I also spoke at length with two security guards. I questioned them if they'd seen or heard anything unusual that might be construed as a ghost or spirit. They did not laugh at me. One man mentioned that when he made his usual rounds on an unoccupied floor, he heard television sounds coming from rooms he knew were unoccupied. He opened the rooms to check, and the TV would suddenly turn off. As soon as he closed the door and started to walk away, the noise would start up again.

Warren Andrews told me that one of the room clerks told him that he had seen a tall man, clad in dark clothing, with a decidedly Lincolnesque look to both his dress and stature, get off the elevator. The minute the man stepped out, he disappeared!

Al Langston, one of the security staff and a former ranger at the Alamo, is a levelheaded and trustworthy individual who says he thinks the Anacacho Ballroom is haunted. Once when he was there alone, checking the room for security, he both saw and heard a deadbolt lock fall into place. And the same night, he heard a kick against a closed door, and of course, no one was there. He said a cold chill went up his spine, and he is convinced he was in the presence of some unknown entity that night.

After hearing so many things from a number of staff members, I contacted Sam Nesmith and Robert Thiege. They agreed to go "ghost hunting" on a night when the moon was full, always a favorable time to seek out the spirits. Sue Baker, former sales director, and Shari Thorn, the executive secretary to the general manager, Mr. Peter Ells, were our hostesses. Our party consisted of Sam and his wife, Nancy; Robert and his wife, Joie; my husband, Roy, and myself. As we trooped around the hotel, we also picked up housekeeper Manuela Espinosa, who had been alerted to our coming and had agreed to accompany us.

Sam and Robert said that their late evening visit to the mezzanine's powder room was definitely a "first" for them. Both psychics picked up the image of the woman to whom the mysterious black-clad phantom feet belonged. They both "saw" the same image, an elderly gray-haired woman wearing a tailored black suit. They said she was wearing a little round black hat with a veil. After she entered the stall she was stricken with terrible chest pain and was terrified she was going to die. She finally was able to make her way out and into the hallway where her son was waiting for her. He called an ambulance. Sam and Robert say they think the woman's name was either Claire or Clara. She was taken to a hospital, and recovered, but later died from a stroke. Sam told us that this was such a frightening and traumatic experience for her that the energy remained and the scene periodically repeats itself.

One strange thing happened while seven of us were in the powder room: Sam, Robert, Joie, Sue, Shari, Manuela, and me. We were suddenly assailed by the fragrance of a very sweet perfume. We all smelled it. Then it went away just as suddenly as it had come.

Although we had been told that there had been a number of manifestations, including the rather frequent appearance of a gentleman wearing a tuxedo coming into the laundry room and housekeeping department, the night we paid our visit to the basement level of the hotel, nothing was discovered in that area by the psychics. Manuela told us she had once seen a male figure in the housekeeping section, and he disappeared even as she watched him. And one early morning she had seen a woman in a white uniform in the inner corridor which connects the two main hallways that run the length of the basement. Of medium build, the figure had dark hair. She had not seen the face as the woman was walking away from her. Sam and Robert located this entity in the corridor, and she communicated to them that her name was Anita. She was an Hispanic employee who loved the hotel where she had worked in the 1950s, and because she was so happy there she frequently returns. She communicated to Sam that she wanted to know what all of us were doing there. Sam told her we were just visiting and she need not let our presence disturb her. He also told her she was not bound to the place and was free to move on to the light if she so desired.

We also visited the once-lovely roof garden. Quiet, dark, and deserted though it now is, it still retains some vestiges of its former beauty. The moon was full and the stars were out. A soft breeze caressed our faces as we strolled in the moonlight. We could imagine how glamorous and romantic it must have been as couples swayed to the sounds of music that drifted out over the dark, quiet streets of San Antonio. The heyday of the garden nightclub was during the World War II years. The big band sound was in. Music was romantic then, and so was the setting. Doubtless, in this atmosphere, many proposals were made, and probably many tender and sad good-byes were said as the military men prepared to go overseas to fight for their country, leaving their sweethearts and wives behind. Much of this poignancy seems to linger there. Sam felt the strong presence of a young woman wearing a white ballgown. He said the spirit was in a storage or service room behind the bandstand, probably where service people brought up food and drink from the kitchens below. Sam said she seemed very sad. Her sweetheart had brought her to the roof garden to dance on his last leave before shipping out. He never returned. Now her sad little spirit comes back to linger where she had once been young and happy and in love.

A short time after our late night visit to the hotel, a guest had an unusual experience which she shared with me. Karen Martin, of Odessa, New York, called me from the hotel to see if I had any openings on my Halloween week Spirits of San Antonio tour. I was able to accommodate her, and I picked her up at the hotel and drove her to the restaurant where we joined the other tour participants. In the course of the evening I told Karen that I had collected several interesting stories about the hotel where she was staying, and they would appear in my latest book. I mentioned that the tenth floor seemed to be the most "populated" area as far as ghosts were concerned. Karen said, "Oh dear, that's the floor where I am staying."

Shortly after Karen returned to New York she wrote a note to me saying that night, and the next one as well (this would have been October 28 and 29), she had a very strange experience. At precisely 5:45 A.M. on Monday, the 28th, she heard a loud "whacking or snapping" sound against the door to her room. It was loud enough to wake her from a sound sleep. She rushed to the door to see what had caused the sound at that early hour of the morning. She stuck her head out of the door and saw that no one was in sight. But she heard a succession of "whacks" as whatever it was hit each door all the way down the hallway. People rushed to their doors just as Karen had done, to see what had made the sounds.

Karen went on to say the same thing happened the next day, at 6:15 A.M. Again, all the doors were hit by a snapping or whacking noise, which Karen likened to a bullwhip or heavy leather belt being snapped against the doors.

I called Shari Thorn to tell her about Karen's experience, since she had so recently escorted me and my psychic friends around on our ghost-hunting venture. She told me that recently Mr. Peter Ells, the general manager of the Crowne Plaza St. Anthony, his head housekeeper, and one of the resident engineers were making a routine inspection up on the sixth floor of the hotel. As they stood talking in the stairwell, the engineer was whistling a little tune. Then he stopped whistling. Just then something whistled right back at him! All three looked at each other and said, "What was that?"

They all clearly heard the unseen whistler. Shari said Mr. Ells had been skeptical of the ghost stories about the hotel until he had this experience. Now he has begun to believe there really might be some spirits in his fine old hotel!

The St. Anthony, which has been a home away from home to many famous people, celebrities from all walks of life, politicians, military leaders, stage and screen stars, and outstanding athletes, has seen it all in its long lifespan. Since 1909 it has been the scene of many grand balls, receptions, banquets, and wedding parties. It is still one of the most elegant and splendid hotels in South Texas. No wonder some former guests and employees just couldn't bear to leave it permanently! Frankly, I find just knowing that this fine old hotel is among the haunted places in San Antonio adds another fascinating dimension to an already wonderful place. But its elegance, beauty, tradition, and Continental ambiance, combined with a gracious staff always eager to please, is what makes it truly unique!

Photo courtesy of Crowne Plaza St. Anthony Hotel

Spirits on the South Side

On a quiet street on the south side of San Antonio, near Brooks Air Force Base, there is a house that has been the site of frequent unexplainable visits over the years, from not one, but several, other worldly presences. It isn't an unusual house ... nothing in its outward appearance would separate it from its neighbors. But the family that has resided there has many tales to tell of unexplainable happenings at that address.

We learned of this "house of spirits" through a chance conversation with John Silva. Later, we also spoke with his sisters Maria and Sandra, all children of the widowed owner, who still resides in the house alone since the death of his beloved wife in June of 1990. The family of ten children grew up in an active household presided over by a loving mother who enjoyed her children and the various nieces and nephews and their friends who filled the house with laughter and childish pranks. Much of the time, their father, Juan, a serviceman, was away on active duty overseas, and later, after his retirement, he worked night shifts at Kelly Air Force Base, so naturally the children became very close to their mother.

John told us about many unusual and strange events that took place in the house. He said he recalled that as a child, when some of his young cousins were visiting, his mother had heard the children laughing, with obvious glee, in one of the bedrooms. She left her work in the kitchen and went to the bedroom to see what on earth was so funny. They were all in there, convulsed in laughter. She asked them what was so funny, and they told her they were laughing at "the funny stories that man sitting on the bed is telling." She saw no one. The children described him as a man wearing blue jeans and a red flannel shirt and thought it strange that Mrs. Silva did not see him, too. Many years later, John said his young son Jeddy was talking, apparently to himself ... and when his grandmother asked him who he was talking to, he said, "to the ghost, grandmother... but don't worry, he's a nice ghost."

Maria Good, John's sister, spoke with us and told us one time one of her sisters, who now resides in California, was resting in one of the bedrooms. She heard children laughing and then felt someone tickling her feet. She opened her eyes to see a small blonde boy, dressed in short pants with suspenders and a striped shirt and wearing round wire rimmed glasses, standing at the foot of the bed. She thought he was a friend of her younger brother, Timmy, and told him to stop it so she could go back to sleep. He ran and opened the closet door and went inside. She closed her eyes and drifted back to sleep, and then, once again, was awakened by her feet being tickled. She told the little boy to stop once more and then called to her little brother to come tell his friend to stop. Her mother heard this and came to the room. The youngster again went into the closet. Maria and her mother opened the closet door. No one was there! The boy was never seen again!

When the Silva children were small, their dad worked a night shift. Often the children would go into the master bedroom and watch television with their mother. Sometimes they would crawl into bed with her to sleep. Once, Maria was lying in bed with her mother, when they heard a tremendous crash coming from the roof. They couldn't imagine what it was. Almost simultaneously, there was a blinding red light in the room, so bright they could not see one another, and they were literally paralyzed with fear. Maria said they couldn't even move. Then, suddenly the bright light disappeared as quickly as it had come, and they could move around again. This never happened again, although there were often loud noises heard on the roof, which sounded very much like heavy footsteps.

We also talked with Sandra, another of the Silva girls. She said she felt, as a young girl growing up there, that there was an evil presence in her bedroom. She said several times, when she was about seventeen, she had heard heavy breathing at the window and thrashing about outside. Her father had gone out to investigate and found nothing. She said she had at times felt a "black... evil presence" in the room... and often, while trying to sleep, she would hear footsteps in the hall that would always stop at her door. When she ventured a peek, there would be no one there.

When they were teenagers, Sandra said the children had played with a Ouija board. Once, when they were playing with it in her room, all the curtains fell, and the Ouija marker flew off the board, while the family cat screeched and, its hair standing on end, bounded from the room!

Sandra also added that one of her brothers had distinctly heard a baby crying in one of the bedrooms one day while he was alone in the house. An investigation turned up nothing.

Several remarkable occurrences have taken place in the house, since Mrs. Silva died in June of 1990. For instance, there was a ring, not an expensive piece of jewelry, but just a costume piece his mother had liked and had misplaced. After her death, John said he had found a picture he liked of his mother and had it framed. He showed it to his son Jeddy who was nineteen at the time. He was very close to his grandmother. He said, "Dad, looking at her picture I get the feeling she's trying to tell me something." That night, he dreamed about his grandmother, and she told him to go over to her house and look in a "high place" and he would find the lost ring. He did go to the house the next day, and he looked on an upper shelf of her closet. Way at the back . . . was the ring!

Mrs. Silva was buried at the Fort Sam Houston National Cemetery. The services were conducted, as is customary, in a special staging area where parking is accessible. Then after the family left, the casket was removed to the designated gravesite for burial. A few days after the funeral, John's son went to the cemetery. He had never been to his grandmother's burial plot, but in all the maze of look-alike graves, he went straight to his grandmother's resting place, as if drawn there by radar. He said the night before she had appeared to him in a dream, wearing a long white gown. She told him she was fine and asked him to come and see her.

Maria told us of a strange occurrence when she first returned to visit the cemetery. She knew the section where the burial plot was located and thought she could just search until she found the exact location, never dreaming what a large area the section covered. She said the cemetery was totally deserted that day, and there was no one around to ask about the grave location. She said she looked and looked and when she could not find the grave, she said out loud ... "Oh Mom, I just can't find you," and started to walk back to her car. She distinctly heard a voice say, "No!" She stopped suddenly, and there at her feet was her mother's marker!

When Bobby, one of the Silva boys, was home on Christmas leave from the Navy in 1990, he decided to take a nap on the living room couch. He dozed off to sleep, but was soon awakened by a whispered voice saying "Bobby... Bobby...." He thought it was his girlfriend, who was at the house for a visit. He said, "Oh, Janell, leave me alone ... I'm trying to sleep." He dozed off again, and once more was awakened by the same voice. This time he got up to see who had called him. He looked, and found his girlfriend was outside in the yard talking to some members of the family. Then, he recalled the way his mother had always waked him up ... with a gently whispered, "Bobby, Bobby...."

Mr. Silva still lives in the house he shared so many years with his wife. John told us that recently his dad had seen a "dark shadow" pass through the bedroom, just as he was retiring for the night. The next morning he was awakened, as his wife had often done ... by someone shaking his feet.

Maria said that prior to her death, her mother had been ill for a long while. Since she lived just across the street from her parents, Maria would go over to bathe her mother and to keep her company. Her mother knew that she was dying and often told Maria that she didn't want to die and leave her family. She asked Maria, who is the oldest daughter, to try and take care of the family. Maria feels that her mother, who was just 58 at the time of her death, still has the ability, through a loving spirit, to return to keep an eye on those she loved.

There is still no explanation for all the other "spirits" who were either seen or heard in the house for many years. Only Mrs. Silva continues to return.

DID YOU EVER SEE A GHOST?

Is there anyone who'll boast
That they've ever seen a ghost?
Or heard a footstep on the stair?
Did you ever freeze with fright,
In the middle of the night,
Knowing, surely, "something" was out there?
Have you ever really seen
On the night of Halloween,
"Something" out among the costumed hosts,
That seemed out of place
Because it didn't have a face,
Well, my friend, I think you saw a ghost!

Docia Williams

Section III

South Texas Coast

This section contains stories of ghosts that have appeared around the coastal plains and low-lying marshes and woodlands that constitute the Texas Gulf Coast. The windswept beaches, offshore islands, and mysterious swamps bring forth tales of buried pirate treasure and adventurers such as the legendary buccaneer, Jean Lafitte. There are "big city" stories about Galveston, Corpus Christi, Brownsville, and the great metropolis of Houston. And there are tales centered around the Golden Triangle, which is comprised of Beaumont, Orange, and Port Arthur, and the area surrounding those cities. Some spirits guard hidden treasures or valuables, so the sighting of an apparition might possibly indicate that something of value may be hidden close by. And then, some of them just "hang around" for no particular reason at all!

THERE ARE GHOSTS...
Docia Williams

From the sunburnt town of Brownsville,
'Way down near Mexico...
There are ghosts and roaming spirits
Where'ere you chance to go.
They come back to roam the beaches
And the farmers' sun-parched land.
They're in the far flung reaches
Where rolling waves meet sand.
They're known to roam the islands
And the marshlands by the sea.
Their graves cannot contain them,
For their souls roam wild and free.
They're in Galveston and Houston,
Port Arthur has a few;
They're in dark and hidden places,
And in hotel rooms with a view!
Wherever men have worked and lived,
Wherever men have died;
Wherever women laughed or danced,
Wherever they have cried;
They're anywhere and everywhere,
And forever they must roam.
The Texas Coast... their cordial host,
And the ageless land, their home.

Ghostly Guardians of Buried Treasure

Now, Jean Lafitte was a pirate bold,
A pirate bold was he!
He boarded ships and plundered gold
From sea to shining sea.

Now buried on the Texas coast
Just where, we've not a clue;
His gold is guarded by his ghost,
If what we've heard is true!

Tales of buried pirate treasure and the ghostly guardians still standing watch over the ill-gotten booty of the buccaneers who raided shipping off the Texas coast have been around for many long years. By now, what is fact and what is fiction is a bit hard to sort out, as there are so many conflicting tales. However, most all the stories make mention of that most famous of pirates known to sail the waters off the Texas shores, the dashing swashbuckler Jean Lafitte.

Although the *Encyclopedia Americana* lists Lafitte as "American, Pirate and smuggler," he was actually born in a small village on the Garonne River in France in the year 1780. Little seems to be known of his youth. At one time he was known to have been a privateer in the employ of Cartagena for the purpose of the destruction of British and Spanish commerce. He soon turned to piracy (where he could be his own boss!) and around 1809 he turned up in New Orleans, along with his brother, Pierre, and a stalwart band of followers of the same persuasion. Jean opened up a blacksmith shop in New Orleans that may have been a "front" for his real vocation, which was smuggling slaves into New Orleans. The hapless blacks were offered at $1 a pound, and the Lafittes did a big business. At the same time, they supplied New Orleans' citizenry with contraband goods, which they often sold at Grand Terre Island in the Barataria Bay. From this locale, it was easy for the pirate band to plunder shipping in the Gulf of Mexico.

Jean was a handsome, dashing figure of a man, and he became a well-known personality in the gambling salons, quadroon ballrooms, at the opera, and at theatrical productions in New Orleans.

The United States government eventually launched a number of expeditions against the Lafittes, but they all failed. A revenue inspector who had been sent to examine their goods was murdered in 1814. Legal proceedings against them in United States courts had to be abandoned because John R. Grymes, the U.S. District Attorney, resigned his office in order to help the pirates! It seems Jean Lafitte's whole career was built more or less on duplicity and double dealing. So successful was he in his various endeavors that he succeeded in transforming himself into a legend while he was still alive!

Now, Pierre was finally captured. During his captivity, Captain Nicholas Lockyer, of the British navy, offered Jean a captain's commission, the sum of $30,000, and pardon for all "past mistakes" if he and his followers would join the British expedition against New Orleans. While pretending to deal with Lockyer, Lafitte informed the American authorities of the British plans. The Louisiana authorities, with the exception of General Jacquez Villere and Governor William C. Claiborne, suspected a plot from the pirate, and they sent an expedition against Lafitte at Barataria. Many of the pirate company were captured, but the Lafitte brothers escaped. Later on, they, and a number of their followers, honorably served under General Andrew Jackson. In fact, Jean Lafitte assisted in the construction of the defenses of Barataria Bay. In command of a detachment of his pirate band, he participated most creditably in the Battle of New Orleans on January 8, 1815. For his services, Lafitte and his men were granted full amnesty by President James Madison in 1815.

Even though the Lafittes were pardoned, they probably felt like their welcome had worn thin in Louisiana, because in 1817 they founded a "pirate commune" called "Campeche" (sometimes spelled "Campeachy") on Galveston Island, which was first called "Galvez-town" after Bernardo de Galvez, viceroy of Mexico. Jean Lafitte ruled over Campeche as "president," and in 1819 for a short time he was governor of "Galveston Republic." In the administration of his far-flung piratical empire, Jean made use of the islands off the coast of Texas. One of his bases was Culebra Island, composed of Matagorda and St. Joseph's, separated only by Cedar Bayou.

For the purpose of protecting commerce against depredations of freebooters and to safeguard the port of Caparo, the Spanish, and after them, the Mexicans, maintained the small fort of "Armzazu" on Live Oak Point. In retaliation, Lafitte maintained a fort of his own on the southwest part of St. Joseph's Island. The village of Aransas (now Aransas Pass) was later laid out near the site of the pirate's fort.

In 1821 the U.S. government, in reprisal of an attack on an American ship by a Lafitte follower, sent Lt. Lawrence Kearny to disrupt the community, although it was Spanish territory at that time. Lafitte is said to have burned Campeche and "disappeared." Actually, after being ousted from Galveston Island, many of the pirates just settled down in the coastal area. The final meeting of the great buccaneer and his men is reputed to have taken place at False Live Oak Point after they had been cornered by British and American navies. Here the booty was divided up and Lafitte supposedly cached most of it at False Live Oak Point in heavy chests, among the oak trees. This done, the pirate and his remaining followers attempted to slip through the American and British blockade. For three days and nights a cannonade was heard by the residents of Cedar Bayou, and Lafitte finally eluded his pursuers.

Historic marker at Galveston

Later on, it is said that Lafitte conducted most of his activities on the "Spanish Main," which could have been just about anywhere in the Gulf of Mexico or the Caribbean. The famous pirate died of a fever at Losbocas, on the north coast of Yucatan, about fifteen miles from Merida, in 1826. He was forty-six years old. He was buried in the "Campo de Santos" in the little Indian village of Silan.

Now, there are lots of legends concerning Lafitte and his crew. Their latter-day haunts greatly resembled the Barataria waterways they had known in Louisiana. They centered in the marshy Texas coastland below Beaumont and Port Arthur, and around the vast, brackish Sabine Lake, which emptied into the Gulf of Mexico at dark-running Sabine Pass. These secretive waterways and marshes harbor stories of buried treasure and pirate ghosts to this day.

According to a story that appeared in the *Houston Post* many years ago, one of Jean Lafitte's ships was chased across Sabine Lake and made anchor in Port Neches at the mouth of the Neches River. To keep the treasure aboard the ship from falling into the hands of the Spanish pursuers, it was carried ashore and buried in a marsh. Maps purported to show where this treasure was secreted have appeared from time to time, and there has been much digging for it. It is supposed to have never been found. Maybe this is because it was never placed there. Lafitte's treasure simply can't be buried at every place it is said to be!

Now, it's hard to tell whether Jean and Pierre Lafitte and their pirate crew spent more time plying the ocean deep in search of ships to plunder, or whether they spent more time ashore, digging holes in which to bury their ill-gotten goods, if we are to believe all the buried treasure stories that are often told. These stories run the gamut of the Texas coastline, from Cameron County, down near Brownsville, clear up to Jefferson County near the Louisiana border. Why the pirates didn't come back for their treasure is anybody's guess. Maybe they had poor memories, or maybe they partook of too much rum while out burying their loot. I'd buy the theory that the shifting sands on the windswept seashore caused the terrain to change in appearance sufficiently to make the burial spots unrecognizable. And, we must remember, the pirates more than likely buried their chests under cover of darkness as well. It would have been a real chore to find a certain spot among all the almost identical sand dunes and tufts of sea oats and marsh grasses that dot the coastline.

Conversations with psychics, and time spent reading and researching the subject of "ghosts" in general and "pirate ghosts" in particular, have brought out several interesting conclusions. Ghosts, which are the spirits of dead people who can't quite accept they are dead, do come back. In the case of Jean Lafitte and his pirate-followers, they return to guard the treasure they buried so long ago, and never got around to dividing up. But are they there just to protect their treasure? Might be they are there to lead a selected someone to the site of their buried treasure.

For some unknown reason, there has always been a certain amount of romance and mystery attached to pirates. It must have something to do with all that buried gold, because they really were dastardly individuals. Boarding and looting and sinking ships was NOT a wholesome occupation!

Before we can begin to think about the ghostly guardians that protect the pirate treasure, we have to have an idea of where the booty is buried.

Using Thomas Penfield's book *A Guide to Treasure in Texas*, we will come along on a make-believe trip along the Texas coast, from the southernmost portion, near Brownsville, in Cameron County, where Penfield reported, "unconfirmed is the report that the pirate Jean Lafitte sank an unidentified Spanish galleon off South Padre Island in 1811 with a cargo of $500,000 in gold and silver. One treasure writer speculates this may have been the *Santa Maria*, and the treasure was valued at around a million dollars." This event took place during the time the Lafittes were still operating from their Barataria headquarters near New Orleans.

Moving on up along the coast, we come to Kenedy County, where it is noted that off the shore of Padre Island there is the wreck of the Spanish galleon *Capitana*. This ship was assigned to defend some smaller Spanish vessels against a band of pirates. In a furious fight, the *Capitana* went down with all hands, and so did the treasure in her hull, said to be over $1,000,000.

Moving eastward up the coast, we hit Kleberg County, where the famous King Ranch is located. There is a peninsula that juts out into

Baffin Bay that is known as "Point of Rocks." A Lafitte treasure chest is said to have been buried there and the site marked by a copper spike driven into a crack in a rock.

Penfield reported there are three hills, called "Money Hills," on Mustang and Padre islands. The original Money Hill on Mustang was the highest sand dune, about three miles south of Aransas Pass. Because of the wind, the sand dunes shift a lot, and the highest dune one day might not be that way the next! Therefore, nobody knows where the original "Money Hill" was located. Sometimes it was called "Big Hill" or "Three Mile Hill" because of its location three miles south of Aransas Pass. According to local legend, a pirate ship blew ashore on northern Mustang Island, and the treasure from it was buried under "Money Hill" because it was a good landmark for the pirates to locate. Many coins have been picked up in this area over the years, so the main cache may already have been found.

When Lafitte was forced to quit Galveston Island, the remnants of his organization drifted on down the coast to the many islands and coastal towns where they were safe from patrols. It was at this time that the legend was born that Lafitte had personally buried a vast fortune under a millstone on the northern tip of Padre Island. A printer from New Orleans named Newell spent a great part of his life, and finally lost it, searching for this elusive treasure. No one ever learned just what information he had that made him so persistent in his search, but it was believed by some that he had befriended one of Lafitte's men while living in New Orleans and was told the secret of Lafitte's treasure in repayment. The markers sought by Newell were a single Spanish dagger (a type of yucca plant) and three silver spikes. He found hundreds of Spanish dagger plants but not a single silver spike. In 1871 Newell's small boat was found drifting in the Gulf, and a few days later his body was washed ashore.

In Calhoun County, where the ghost town and former seaport of Indianola was located, Penfield's treasure guide states: "A number of Texas treasure stories start with Jean Lafitte's inland flight as he was pursued by a U.S. man-of-war. This was soon after he was ordered to leave Galveston Island. One story has it that he sailed into LaVaca Bay and, with the help of two men, buried treasure valued at a million dollars at the mouth of the LaVaca River, across the bay from the town of Port LaVaca. It is said that a long brass rod was driven into the ground directly above the treasure and left emerging to indicate the treasure site.

"One of the pirates who helped to bury this treasure is said to have told of the incident on his deathbed in New Orleans, giving rough directions to the treasure. This story was heard by a man named Hill, who eventually bought the ranch on which the brass rod was believed to be located. One day a man out herding cattle for Hill noticed the rod and pulled it from the ground, not realizing its significance, and he took the rod with him that night. When Hill saw the rod he recognized its meaning at once, but the old cowhand could not retrace his steps to the place where he had found it. Hill is said to have searched for years for the Lafitte hoard, but he never found it.

As might be expected, since Lafitte and his pirate followers lived on Galveston Island for a time, there are many stories of buried treasure connected with that area. Penfield's book cites a number of pirate treasure locations around Galveston. It's said that there may be as much as $27,000,000 in pirate's treasure on Pelican Island, whose 4,000 acres are used largely by industry, including ship repair facilities. The small island is connected with Galveston by a causeway.

Then, Penfield mentions that Dr. James Long of Natchez, Mississippi, who was among the last of the Texas filibusterers, led two expeditions into Texas in 1819 and 1821. For a time, he and 200 followers lived on Bolivar Point at the southern tip of Bolivar Peninsula, opposite Lafitte's fort on Galveston Island. While Lafitte was robbing Spanish ships in the Gulf, Long and his forces seized one of the pirate's small boats which had been left in the harbor at Galveston. Long described this action in a letter he mailed to General E.W. Ripley in Louisiana in 1820. He also mentioned that "some men of Mescatee" (referring to Lafitte's men) knew of $130,000 buried nearby. It is believed that Long had planned to recover this money, but he was killed before he could get around to finding it. It is believed this little known treasure has never been located.

Harris County is home to La Porte, in Trinity Bay. Lafitte is said to have sailed a ship into La Porte and taken a treasure chest ashore, where it was buried. Lafitte was accompanied by two trusted lieutenants, who helped carry the chest inland a short distance. Lafitte is said to have returned to his ship alone. Supposedly, the lieutenants were blindfolded as the treasure was buried, but Lafitte saw one lift his blindfold to note the location of the buried chest. In a rage of anger, the pirate chief killed both of the men. They say the treasure chest lies under an old house, which was built over it without the owner's knowledge of the treasure's being there.

Sabine Pass, over in Jefferson County near the Louisiana border, was a thriving village in the days when Lafitte and his pirates roamed the Gulf Coast. Tales of buried treasure abound in this area. According to a story that appeared in the *Houston Post* many years ago, one of Lafitte's ships was chased across Sabine Lake and anchored in Port Neches at the mouth of the Neches River. To prevent the treasure aboard the vessel from falling into the hands of Spanish pursuers, it was carried ashore and buried in a marsh. Maps purported to show where this treasure was secreted have appeared from time to time and there has been much digging for it, according to Penfield in his Texas treasure guide. It is supposed to have never been found, but maybe, just maybe, an article that ran in the *Port Arthur News* on October 28, 1984, will shed some light on this tale. The writer, Denny Angelle, related the story of a man named Marion Meredith. It seems many years ago Meredith told a Houston newspaper reporter about a neighbor of his who had bought a map from an old Mexican woman. It was supposedly a pirate's treasure map. Now Meredith lived over near Port Neches, and the buried loot was supposed to be somewhere near the mouth of the Neches River, not far from his home. Here, pirates led by Jean Lafitte were said to have escaped their pursuers into the shallow waters of Lake Sabine. This one particular ship, bearing a fortune in treasure, was supposedly floated into the headwaters of the Neches where the crew cut the anchor chain, leaving the anchor as a marker. The treasure is supposed to have been buried in the marshy land nearby.

Well, Meredith's neighbor found the rusty old anchor and located the spot where the treasure should be. Naturally, he began to dig! But before he got too deep, something unseen and icy gripped him! The man was seized with such a nameless horror that he fled the place. So terrified was he that he lost his voice entirely, and he is said to have died a few days later, without ever speaking a word to anyone!

Meredith later obtained the map, but he decided he wouldn't undertake the treasure search alone. He enlisted the help of a man known only as "Clawson," a crusty old woodsman with a bit of pioneer salt throbbing in his blood.

The two men set out down the Neches River and, following the map, they soon discovered the ancient, rusty chain. Pointed in a certain direction by the chart, they searched for a tree with a heart cut into its bark, as was noted on the map. Sure enough, they found it with no difficulty.

From the marked tree, Meredith and Clawson paced off a certain distance and soon found themselves high and dry on a small island in the marsh. They found the tools that Meredith's unfortunate neighbor had left behind him, and the hole that he had begun to dig. Meredith grabbed a pickax and eagerly started to dig. It wasn't long before he found a human skeleton, still wearing rotting clothing and boots. Meredith and Clawson put the skeletal remains aside, and Clawson jumped into the hole in order to dig deeper. Suddenly, he leapt from the hole, his eyes wild in a face as white as a sheet. "For God's sake, man, let's get out of here," he told Meredith. Meredith didn't understand, but Clawson begged him to go, saying, "I've just seen hell and all its horrors! We have to leave this place."

The two men fled, leaving their digging tools on the little island.

Several years later, Meredith ran into Clawson in Beaumont. He recalled the day that they had gone digging to Clawson. The man never would reveal to Meredith what he had seen, but he did tell him that "that day" had haunted him every day of his life since then! It truly had to have been a horrifying experience!

Meredith later returned to the spot to retrieve his tools, but taking Clawson at his word, he did not attempt to dig again. Instead, he carefully reburied the skeleton, then hid the map away and never again went near the little island at the mouth of the Neches.

Once, when some young men approached Meredith and asked him to lead them to his "treasure island," he told them, "I'll take you out there, and I'll even watch you boys, but there ain't enough money in Texas to get me to dig that damned hole."

Nobody knows what became of Marion Meredith. It was a long time ago. Maybe he finally learned the secret of just what is guarding that pirate treasure, or maybe he really didn't want to know what that dreadful unknown thing was that his friend Clawson saw and described as the "dark side of hell." He was probably content to just let well enough alone. No doubt the treasure is probably still out there.

There is, without a doubt, a lot of buried or sunken treasure scattered all along the Gulf Coast area of Texas. Maybe someday some of it will be found, since now there are metal detectors and other devices that can aid in such searches. I learned in speaking with Dr. Joe Graham, of the Department of Sociology at Texas A&M in Kingsville, that "ghost lights" are said to shine around an area where treasure is buried, also.

From time to time somebody finds a doubloon from a wrecked ship. An occasional gold coin will turn up in a sand dune somewhere, proof that there is still some gold out there. Whether or not there are pirate guardian ghosts at all those purported treasure sites, we have no way of knowing. Since we haven't seen any publicity about pirate treasure being discovered, we're reasonably sure that there are a few "sentries" on duty. After all, it was tough work, dragging those treasure chests ashore and digging those deep holes in which to bury them. We can't blame the pirate-specters for not wanting to give up their loot! They must still be out there, patrolling the beaches, guarding their treasure, so that neither you, nor I, nor even the IRS will discover their secret hiding places!

> *The pirates' gold is still around*
> *The legends will not die.*
> *In holes dug deep within the ground,*
> *Their treasure chests still lie.*

House Plays Host To Live-in Ghost

When Clouis and Marilyn Fisher moved into their "new" Victorian home in 1979, little did they know the charming old house was already occupied! The Fishers first saw the house while they were driving around Rockport, a quiet little town on the Texas Gulf Coast. A yard sale was being conducted in the front yard of the place and the Fishers stopped to browse. Of even more interest to them, however, was the "For Sale" sign on the house. The place was pretty run-down, but Clouis, a dedicated "fixer-upper," and Marilyn welcomed the challenge of restoring the place back to its circa 1881 splendor.

The Bracht-Fisher House

The previous owners neglected to tell the Fishers that the house came complete with a ghost, but it wasn't long before Clouis figured that out for himself!

At the time the Fishers and their three children moved in, the house was badly in need of rewiring. The wiring would not even support an air-conditioner, which was badly needed during the hot summer of '79. One July night stands out even now in Clouis' memory. It was about 1:30 A.M. when he awoke with a start and realized that a light was faintly glowing in the room. He described what he saw to be a "glowing fog" that floated into the room, sort of circled around, and then went out and into a large room next to the bedroom. The night had been unusually hot. But suddenly, Clouis felt an arctic blast of cold air enter the room. He said he was literally petrified.

Clouis did not mention the strange incident to Marilyn, who had slept soundly through the night. Nor did he mention his strange experience with any friends or other family members. He just tried, with little success, to put the occurrence out of his mind. Soon after this initial encounter, Clouis also began to hear strange, unexplainable noises as well.

Several weeks after the purchase, Clouis, who is a Realtor, attended a company sales meeting in nearby Corpus Christi. A new employee, a woman he had never seen before, walked into the room. After she was introduced to Clouis, she very matter-of-factly inquired, "Have you seen the ghost in your house yet?" It was then that Clouis realized, with some relief, that he hadn't been imagining things.

The lady went on to explain that in 1946 she had come to Rockport as a young single school teacher. She had rented a small upstairs apartment in the spacious old house that Clouis had bought for his family. Soon after she moved in, she came home from school one afternoon and went straight upstairs to her apartment. She heard footsteps of someone walking outside her room, and then the footsteps went down the stairs and out the front door. Frightened, because she thought she was alone in the house, she cautiously went to the front window and peered out to see who had exited the house. No one had come out the front door! A careful search revealed no one was around. She mentioned what she had heard to the daughter of the owners from whom she had rented the apartment. She told her it was just "our ghost." The family thought it might be the spirit of a woman.

After Clouis and Marilyn learned they had a ghost, they began to understand why they had heard the sound of footsteps, and why other unusual things had been happening at the house. Clouis says the antics of the spirit are actually more annoying than frightening. While the Fishers have never seen their resident ghost, except for an occasional glow of light, Clouis and Marilyn both believe it is the spirit of the first man who owned the house, Leopold Bracht.

It seems the Bracht brothers came to Rockport back in the mid-1800s. Leopold ran a successful mercantile business and thus was able to provide a large and spacious home for his growing family. The house was actually built at another location by a builder who hoped to sell it. Today we would refer to it as a "spec house." But the house did not sell right away, standing unoccupied for several years. When Leopold Bracht bought the structure, he had it cut in half and moved to its present site by mule train! This was in 1889, when the structure was about eight years old. Here it was reassembled and made ready for occupancy. In the early 1900s, Bracht remodeled the house considerably, modifying the mansard roofline into a two-storied, gabled-roof house with wrap-around porches on two floors. Space was added to the living areas until it reached its current size of over 4,000 square feet ... the better to accommodate the Bracht family of six daughters and one son!

Marilyn Fisher told me that a few years after they had moved into the house, one of the Bracht daughters, then a very elderly lady past ninety, called and asked if she could have someone bring her over to see the house in which she had spent much of her childhood. Marilyn said they had a wonderful visit, and the lady told her many interesting stories about the family and the old house. She said her father, Leopold Bracht, was very strict with his daughters. He kept careful watch over them. In fact, two of the girls never married. It seems the girls had to observe strict curfews or Leopold would be angry.

Soon after the Fishers moved in, their daughter, Laura, who was in high school, started dating. She had several dates with a nice young man from Rockport and always tried to be in by the deadline that Clouis had set of 10 P.M. Several times as she arrived at the house, just in time, the front porch lights would start to flicker on and off, off and on! Laura found this both annoying and embarrassing, and when she went in the house, she went upstairs to tell her father she didn't appreciate that, only to find that Clouis was in bed, fast asleep! The same thing happened numerous times, and they had no explanation, except that Leopold Bracht was keeping tabs on Laura just as he had on his own daughters!

Almost from the time they moved into the house, Marilyn said, the side door, which enters the kitchen off the front porch, would open every afternoon at 5:15 sharp. Even if the door was locked, it would somehow manage to swing open! Now, Mr. Bracht had owned a mercantile store a few blocks from his home, in the business section of Rockport. He apparently closed at five o'clock, and it would be just about 5:15 when he would arrive at home, using the side entrance. Even after they installed new locks, the screen door would often still shake as if someone were trying to gain entrance. A good "talking to" with Leopold finally put an end to that particular problem.

The Fisher family cat, Samantha, a big black feline, was just a kitten in '79 when they bought the house. But ever since she has been a resident of the place, she has been especially sensitive to Leopold's presence. At times, she just bristles, the hair standing up in a ridge behind her neck, for no apparent reason. And sometimes she will hiss and make a sharp swat with her paw at some unknown entity. Then Clouis will say, "Well, I see it's gotten to old Samantha again" (referring to the ghost).

The Fishers have just learned to accept the presence of Leopold, who has been with them the entire fifteen years they have lived there. Sometimes he doesn't make a sound for weeks at a time. Then, for no particular reason, he will make his presence known. He seems to get especially active whenever the Fishers are into a project, changing or remodeling some part of the old house. Leopold must have liked it just as it was when he lived there, and he doesn't want any changes made. Although he did not die in the house, Bracht spent most of his time there and was probably happy there as head of the household. It is just the most natural place for him to turn up. Fisher says many times he and Marilyn have both felt someone was staring at them. This most often happens when they are in the kitchen standing in front of the kitchen sink. When they turn around, they feel as if they almost see something out of their peripheral line of vision, but then, there is never anything there. The strange feeling that something, or someone, has been watching them still remains, however.

Clouis told me about one night when he had just finished rewiring the house. The family was sitting around the dining room table having supper when suddenly the dining room lights went out. His daughter, Laura, looked up at the light fixture and said, "All right, Leopold, that's enough out of you tonight." Evidently the ghost got the message because the lights came right back on again!

When the Fishers' son, James, was in high school, he had three of his friends over to visit one evening. The boys were around 16 or 17 at the time. One of James' friends had brought a Ouija board along to provide some entertainment. Clouis said all was quiet and peaceful when suddenly he and his wife heard a terrible racket as the boys ran down the stairs and out the front door, slamming it hard behind them! When the youngsters calmed down, they explained that they had started talking to Ouija and asking it some questions, when suddenly the bedroom door, which they had locked from the inside, flew open! There must have been something else that happened, but they would never discuss it. Two of the boys would not even come back into the house. Clouis said one of the young men, the son of the local Baptist preacher and now a young man in his mid-twenties, still tells the Fishers he will never, never, forget that night!

Currently, the Fishers are doing a lot of work around the house in anticipation of turning the spacious dwelling into a bed and breakfast inn. Leopold is not always happy with the new project! Recently, Clouis was adding extra bathroom space to the upstairs area where the guests will be accommodated. He leaned the door for the new upstairs bathroom against the stairs and went downstairs for a minute. He heard a tremendous crash and felt sure the door had fallen over. A careful search revealed nothing was out of place; nothing had fallen. Yet the noise had been very real, and very, very loud!

Leopold has been destructive only once. When the Fishers hung a watercolor picture of purple iris in the newest bathroom, they came home to find it on the floor, the glass shattered. The heavy multi-strand wire on the back had stretched taut and broken at one end, but the picture hanger was still in the wall. Now, the picture had hung for some time in another room. It was just after it was moved to the new location that it was forcefully removed from the wall.

The Fishers have both resorted to talking to Leopold, telling him that the place is going to be nicer and more attractive than ever when the work is all done. They stress that they are trying to bring it back to its original state of elegance, when Leopold and the rest of the Bracht family lived there. They hope by acknowledging his presence and making him feel a part of the project, that his spirit will be happier. They hope maybe he will calm down so that the bed and breakfast guests can spend peaceful, restful nights in the pretty old home that's painted a cheerful yellow with white trim. Its spacious rooms and cool, inviting porches will offer a wonderful haven for Gulf Coast visitors.

If you would like to stay with the Fishers, and Leopold, of course, you might call them at (512) 729-3189 for rates and reservations.

Someone's in the Kitchen
at Beulah's

The Tarpon Inn, located in the waterfront area of Port Aransas, has long been a favorite resting place for visitors to Padre Island. In fact, the historic inn has already celebrated its 100th birthday!

The town of Port Aransas sits on the northernmost tip of Padre Island, a barrier island which protects the bay and harbor of Corpus Christi. The harbor was discovered by the Spanish on Corpus Christi Day in 1519, hence its name. It was not fully explored until a Frenchman mapped the area in 1720. Padre Nicholas Balli acquired the title to the land, which is a 100-mile-long strip of sand dunes and grass, for the sum of 400 pesetas paid to King Charles IV of Spain in 1880. The padre set up a cattle ranching operation on the island, and in

Beulah's Restaurant, at the Tarpon Inn in Port Aransas

time, the land took on the nickname "Padre Island" rather than its official name of Isla de Corpus Christi.

According to Rand McNally's *Weekend Escapes, Southeast Texas Edition*, in about 1855 an English settler built a ranch house up at the northern tip of the island. He established a small town, eventually to be called Port Aransas, which sprang up around his homestead.

During the Civil War, the site of the Tarpon Inn was occupied by a barracks for Confederate troops, and in 1886 the Tarpon Inn was built from materials which had been salvaged from the old barracks. The inn was named for the tarpon, huge game fish with extraordinarily large scales that were found in the waters around Port Aransas.

The first Tarpon Inn was destroyed by fire in 1900. It was rebuilt in 1904 and was destroyed by a hurricane in 1919. In 1923 it was rebuilt in its present form, a two-storied, long frame building, with long galleried porches both upstairs and down. The original building was painted white. Today, it is sky-blue. Mr. J.M. Ellis, the builder in 1923, wanted to assure the hotel would not fall victim to another hurricane, so he sank pier pilings in sixteen feet of cement for the foundation and then put a full pier at the corner of each bedroom for added strength in case of a storm. Hence, the hotel has withstood many storms and quite a few rambunctious young people on spring breaks as well!

A lot of well-known personalities have stayed at the inn, but the one they still talk about most frequently is President Franklin Delano Roosevelt, who came down for a few days of tarpon fishing and left his signature on a tarpon scale which is proudly displayed in the hotel's lobby.

Right behind the inn is a lovely little garden area. Here there are two frame buildings, each a part of what is called Beulah's Restaurant. The long building at the rear of the property, which mostly serves as a bar and overflow dining room for the larger Beulah's, was at one time the original Tarpon Inn's location, the site that burned.

Beulah's Restaurant has had several names over the years. At one time it was the bar to the original Tarpon Inn, and after this, it was known for a time as the Silver King. Since mid-1992 it has been called Beulah's. The head housekeeper at the Inn for many years was Beulah Mae Williams, and it is in her honor that the restaurant was named. She resided in a very old, long frame building that still stands behind the restaurant on a little side alley. Beulah is currently living in a retirement home in Lamar, Texas.

Ms. Julie Caraker, who manages Beulah's, describes the place as one in which the atmosphere is "upscale, down-home," and combines good home cooking with the added flair of gourmet cuisine. After a recent visit and a delicious lunch, we can attest to this being a pretty accurate description. The food is excellent, attractively presented, and not inexpensive.

When I first approached Ms. Caraker, via telephone, and asked her, point blank, if there might be a ghost at the establishment, she did not seem at all taken aback. She quite freely described her feelings and experiences.

Paula Bonillas, of Corpus Christi, and her husband, Steve, own a restaurant by the name of Blackbeard's in Corpus Christi. Their place is haunted, too. Knowing of my research project, Paula had sent me a copy of an intriguing article that had run in the *Silver King Newsletter* some years back. That is why I decided to contact the present management of the restaurant and learn more about the place.

The *Silver King* article stated that Beulah's (then the Silver King) was haunted. It mentioned that while Beulah Mae Williams had never seen the ghost, she had definitely heard it. Beulah cited one particular day when she was walking outside past the kitchen and had heard quite a clatter within, such as would be going on during a very busy day. She knew the restaurant was closed, however. Curiosity beckoned, and she went inside and found everything in its place. There was no explanation for the din she had heard. It had to be the ghost that she had heard other employees mention. This ghost must have been hard at work in the kitchen that day!

The article went on to say that Mr. Kent Marsh, an evening chef at the Silver King, had witnessed what he called "an eerie haze" in the form of a "woman of middle age and medium height." Mr. Mike Buvosa, a former employee, also saw the apparition and thinks she is from a past era since her hair was pulled back in a severe bun, a style not often worn today

Ms. Caraker informed me that the fire in the original Tarpon Inn building had caused massive damage. It is rumored that the cook lost her good pearl necklace in the fire, and she still comes back in search of her lost gems. This might explain the hazy figure seen in the kitchen by both Marsh and Buvosa. However, Ms. Caraker believes the "main ghost" is a man who once worked as a cook at the restaurant. Caraker said a lady who said she was a psychic from Colorado stopped at Beulah's recently and asked Julie if she knew the place was haunted. When Julie answered that she did indeed believe that there was a resident spirit, the psychic asked her if the ghost's name started with an "S." Julie said she believed the ghost was a former cook who was named Samuel, but everyone always called him Sammy.

According to Julie, Sammy still comes around, often at breakfast time, to help her cook. Recently, after the kitchen floor was freshly mopped, Julie was astonished to see large footprints following her much smaller ones on the kitchen floor! Sammy was following her all around the kitchen as she worked!

The mischievous side of Sammy often comes out. He turns lights on and off in the original portion of the old inn, the part of the building that was no doubt his bailiwick.

Mark Wilks, another employee at Beulah's, spoke with us on a visit we made to the inn in August of 1993. He also believes there is a ghost there. He told us about an incident that took place a number of years ago when he and his wife, Janet, were just teenage friends. Janet had left her bicycle leaning against the wall of the restaurant one afternoon. Later that day, she asked Mark to accompany her to get it. Since it was beginning to get dark, she was afraid to go alone. Just as the two retrieved her bike, they heard the "wildest clatter imaginable" coming from inside the kitchen. Mark said it was so loud he was sure that they could hear it across the bay in Aransas Pass! It sounded as if all the pots and pans were being thrown across the kitchen and knocked down from their racks. They knew the place was closed for the day, and that no one was inside. Mark says that even now Janet will not go into the kitchen, and she's always uneasy even in the cheerful restaurant and bar section of the building.

And Julie Caraker said that whenever she goes into the little room behind the bar in the old building she gets "prickly sensations" and knows that the ghosts are still there!

Paula and Steve Bonillas told me about a recent visit they made to Beulah's. As they were enjoying their meal, a door near their table suddenly flew open from the inside. Although there was no breeze, no person to open the door, and no reason for the door to open, it just did. When they questioned their waitress, she matter of factly stated it was "just the ghost." Paula told me I would just have to see for myself why that particular door cannot open by itself. Well, I did. And it can't.

THEY ARE HERE
Docia Williams

Graceful fronds fan tall palm trees
That gently sway in the evening breeze,
As twilight falls on far-flung reaches
Of coastal swamp land and sandy beaches
The sunlight fades, and darkness falls
And ghosts come out, to make their calls
Back to where, in the days of yore
They lived, and breathed, and walked the shore;
And dreamed their dreams, as now we do,
And loved the homes that they once knew...

Their stories now I bring to you.

Fort Brown, Where
Old Soldiers Never Die

Way down at the very bottom of the Rio Grande Valley at what one might call the "jumping off place," lies a beautiful city of some 95,000 souls, called Brownsville. The city sits just across the Rio Grande from its sister city, Matamoros, in the Mexican state of Tamaulipas. The two cities are in one of the most interesting and intriguing regions in Texas, dating back to Spanish Colonial days, and covering periods of exploration, wars, revolutions, banditry, and "you name it ... it was there."

General Zachary Taylor established Fort Brown in 1846 to maintain the United States' claim to the Rio Grande as the international boundary, the line won some ten years earlier by Texans in their battle for independence from Mexican domination. The old fort housed troops during the Mexican war, defended the border, and later exchanged hands during the Civil War. By a strange quirk of fate, the last engagement of the Civil War, the Battle of Palmito Ranch, was fought near Brownsville in May of 1865. Confederate soldiers under the command of Colonel John S. Ford, not having heard of Lee's surrender a month earlier, completely routed and captured a Federal force in a fierce running two-day encounter. Only after the battle did the victorious Rebels learn of Lee's surrender. The victors then became the formal captives of their former prisoners! That battle was the final one of the Civil War.

Fort Brown's hospital was where the famous Dr. William Crawford Gorgas did much of his yellow fever research. During the Spanish American War, he was appointed chief sanitary officer in Havana and did much to clear that city of yellow fever. Then he was sent to Panama, where in five years he succeeded in greatly reducing the death rate from yellow fever during the time the canal was being built. Later, Gorgas became Surgeon General of the U.S. Army and was promoted to the rank of Major General.

Today the hospital has been converted to an administration building for the University of Texas at Brownsville (formerly called Texas Southmost College) and is called Gorgas Hall.

The former fort has its ghosts, too.

Yolanda Gonzalez, librarian at the Arnulfo L. Oliveira Memorial Library on the University of Texas campus, was kind enough to share some interesting happenings with me. "There are supposed to be ghosts everywhere," she says, as she related personal sightings and experiences she has had. She believes the college's ghosts are friendly, and she doesn't fear them. On several occasions, she has seen books in glass-fronted cabinets move slowly, as if someone were searching the shelves for a certain book.

One night while working late putting up a display to go on view the next day, she saw a door to the Hunter Room open, then close. She thought the janitors might have opened the door, and ignored it until she saw both janitors come in together from having dinner. The three then investigated and found the door was still locked. Gonzalez said they told her it was "just the ghosts of the college."

According to an article which appeared in the October 31, 1993 *Brownsville Herald*, one of the most widely told stories concerning the old fort was related by a janitor, who early one morning walked out of the building and heard the "thundering of horse hooves and the stomping of marching soldiers." When he looked out, he saw an entire regiment of soldiers on parade, saluting the American flag!

Ms. Gonzalez talked at length to the janitor who had viewed the strange dawn ceremony. She said he described in great detail how the soldiers and horses looked, and said a bugler was standing near the flag. He said the sound of the horses' hooves was so loud he got scared and tried to run away.

Later that same morning, the janitor found a button from a uniform, and a buckle. He kept the button but gave Gonzalez the buckle, which she took to the Historic Brownsville Museum. The museum director, Bruce Aiken, authenticated it as being a buckle used in some type of harness like a backpack or horse harness. It could have been used anytime from the 1860s to the 1910s, he said.

The ghostly soldiers also bothered another college employee. When John Barham, former Dean of Continuing Education, first arrived in Brownsville, he was given a room in the old commandant's house until he could find a place to live. Barham, now Provost of Suffolk Community College in Long Island, N.Y., said that for three mornings he was awakened by the sounds of marching feet and of prancing horses' hooves. He said he could distinctly hear the hoof beats and the jingling of spurs.

Barham told the college officials he had been awakened by the ROTC cadets marching early every morning. Imagine his great surprise to learn that the college didn't even have an ROTC program! He later learned the old parade ground ran right in front of the former commandant's house where he was staying.

Gorgas Hall, the former fort hospital, has its share of ghostly visitors, also. Numerous people have reported sighting a lady dressed from head to toe in white in the style of nursing uniforms a hundred years ago. She walks into locked offices and sits behind desks. No one has been able to engage her in conversation thus far.

Several janitors have sighted a woman dressed in black mourning attire. She asks for directions to the hospital and inquires about the condition of her son. Several janitors have seen the same woman, and sometimes the incidents have taken place several years apart! Some of the janitors who saw the lady and didn't realize that Gorgas Hall had been a hospital during the old fort days, directed her to the hospital across town. Only later did they realize they had encountered a ghost!

Then there's the puppy story. A little stray puppy has been sighted by many people over the years. He will follow a group of friendly people as they walk from class to class. When they stop and sit down, the puppy literally disappears! Administrators point out that the walkway which spans the length of the campus, connecting all the buildings, is at almost the same location as a similar dirt road that ran the length of old Fort Brown. The similarity was discovered after comparing old pictures of the fort and modern photographs of the college. No doubt, the friendly pup is just trying to find his way home!

La Abuela

This is another story told by Felipe Lozano in his barbershop in Brownsville in 1963 and written down by Peter Gawenda for inclusion in the book *Studies in Brownsville History*, edited by Milo Kearney:

Before the turn of the century several incidents occurred on ranchitos around Brownsville in which children and young mothers were helped by an old woman. Two of these stories are as follows:

The Garzas lived in one of the ranchitos right outside of Brownsville. Every morning they would head out into their fields and work all day long. Their only child, the four-year-old Consuelo, would be with them and she would usually play at the edge of the field or under the mesquite trees. She would chase butterflies. Very often one could see her interrupt her activities to look for her parents, and only after she saw them would she continue her play.

One day, though, when chasing a butterfly, she started wandering off, and neither the parents nor she herself realized that she was getting lost in the mesquite brush. When dusk set in, the parents called their daughter, but they did not receive any response. As they always walked the same way to the fields and then home again, they finally hoped that Consuelo had already found her way to the house. But this was not the case; the parents looked and called in vain. They walked to all of the neighbors, but no one had seen or heard Consuelo. The father went to the sheriff's department for help, and that same night a search party was assembled to look for the girl. Three days later the search was discontinued, and Consuelo was given up as having died either from hunger or from attacks of coyotes or snakes. The parents and relatives were broken-hearted, and especially the mother, who blamed herself for not having watched the four-year-old. On the fifth day, right after the parents had returned from church and were preparing to again search for their daughter, an old, frail-looking woman in a strange outfit approached the house, led by little Consuelo. The girl showed no signs of hunger or thirst and was in excellent spirits. In fact, she was "flowing over," telling her parents about the nice treatment by the "abuela" (this means "grandmother" in Spanish). As the parents were so busy caressing and kissing their daughter, they had completely forgotten to take notice of the old woman. When they finally turned around to thank her, she had disappeared. All three ran first inside the house, then to the back, but in vain. The girl's "abuela" was gone.

The grateful parents made a novena at the church and the father set up a marker where the girl had been returned from the mesquite brush. But the old woman never returned, although the girl would always remember her "abuela," even when she herself was already in her seventies. She would always remember a beautiful smile.

Another incident happened right across the river on the road from Matamoros to Reynosa where a woman was about to deliver a baby in one of the desolate little farms. The young woman's husband had gone to town on his horse to get the midwife, but was held up for some unknown reason. As the young woman was in pain, she screamed several times, and suddenly an old woman wearing an old outfit walked into the hut. Without saying a word she quickly boiled water, put cold compresses on the young woman's head, massaged her abdomen to ease the pain, and then helped a healthy little boy into this world. The old woman then washed the baby, cleaned the young woman, and left the son with his mother.

By the time the young father returned with the "partera" (midwife), he found only his wife and son, both sound asleep. The mother always remembered the beautiful and very soothing smile of the old woman, who was lovingly referred to as their "abuela."

In all such incidents, the outfit of the "abuela" was described to be similar to an old Indian costume as can be seen carved on some of Mexico's ruins. Some of the people therefore believed that she must have been, and maybe still is, the good spirit of an Indian medicine woman.

The Light on Bailey's Prairie

Down near Angleton there's a place known as Bailey's Prairie. "Brit" Bailey, for whom it is named, was one of the most colorful of Texas' frontier characters. What was the truth, and what was fiction, has all gotten sort of tangled up over the years as different tale spinners talk or write about the colorful figure.

Brit, a hard-living, hard-drinking, sometimes controversial but always highly interesting Texas frontiersman, still seems to appear from time to time! At least that's what folks around Bailey's Prairie say. Bailey's appearances, which take the form of a big ball of light, known as Bailey's light, seem to take place about every seven years. Old Brit has carved himself a unique and permanent niche in the "Hall of Fame" of Texas "ghostdom."

Having read numerous accounts of Bailey's life, death, and subsequent hauntings, all of which did not always agree, I was delighted when I was contacted by his great-great-granddaughter, Mary Lou Polley Featherston, of Port Arthur. Her letter stated, "I was a Polley, great-granddaughter of Mary Bailey Polley, daughter of Brit Bailey. She married Joseph H. Polley who was also one of the Old Three Hundred. (This refers to Stephen F. Austin receiving permission from the Mexican government to bring 300 Anglo families into Texas in April of 1823.)

James Briton "Brit" Bailey was born on August 1, 1779, in North Carolina. He took pride in being descended from Robert Bruce of Scotland. As a young man, he moved about a good bit and lived in both Tennessee and Kentucky. During the War of 1812 he served as a U.S. Navy captain.

In 1812 he packed up his wife, Edith Smith Bailey, and their family of six offspring, and came to Texas where they settled on a piece of property along the Brazos River in what is now known as Brazoria County. This land grant was under Stephen F. Austin's jurisdiction.

At first, it's said that Austin tried to oust Bailey and his family when he (Austin) learned that Bailey had served time in the Kentucky state penitentiary for forgery. Bailey often stated it wasn't serving in the pen that caused him embarrassment; it was the term he'd served in the Kentucky legislature that set heavy on his conscience. After paying his debts to society, Bailey packed up his family and came to Texas, just wanting a new start where they could be left alone. The settler finally got squared away with Austin, and while they were never really friendly, Austin accepted Bailey in July of 1824 as one of the "Old Three Hundred." He was able to live and die on his original land claim, a "league of land."

In 1824 Austin used Bailey's cabin to meet with settlers who lived along the lower Brazos, where they took an oath of loyalty to Mexico's federal constitution in 1824. At the same meeting a company of militia was organized, and Brit was appointed as a lieutenant. That same year he took part in the Battle of Jones Creek. This was a no-win fight between Captain Randel Jones and his group of some twenty-three settlers, and a party of thirty or so Karankawa braves who were camped on a tributary of the San Bernard River. The Indians had massacred some settlers, so Austin authorized Jones to go after them. Both sides suffered losses in the skirmish, and no one came out the victor.

Because he was a good talker, Bailey was often called upon by Austin to negotiate with the Indians.

Tired of the cramped conditions of his little cabin, in 1827 Bailey contracted with Stephen Nicholson and Peter Reynolds to build him a frame house eighteen feet square, with nine-foot galleries on all sides. The finished house was painted bright red! Bailey paid the builders the sum of $220 in cash and the balance in cattle and hogs. A visitor to Bailey's place in 1831 wrote to a friend that Bailey's red house "sure had a novel appearance."

Bailey became very successful as a cattle rancher and cotton grower and gradually expanded his land holdings until he owned a great deal of real estate from Houston south to the Gulf Coast.

The Mexican government evidently thought highly of Bailey, because in 1829 General Viesca commissioned him a captain in the militia.

Brit could be the epitome of the solid citizen; responsible and trustworthy, a good businessman and a good leader. But he had two faults. He loved his liquor, and he had a very short fuse. He thoroughly enjoyed a good fight, and when he was bored or just a little too liquored up, he'd pick a fight just for the sheer fun of it!

His short temper showed itself on many occasions. One time, when a horse he was riding wasn't behaving to his liking, he reached down and bit the critter's ear until the blood flowed. The mustang, not taking kindly to such ill treatment, bucked and threw Bailey to the ground. Not to be bested, Brit promptly took out his hunting knife and slit the poor horse's throat!

One afternoon when his family was away, old Brit got pretty well inebriated. He hadn't counted on the circuit-riding preacher knocking on his door to seek lodging for the night. Brit greeted the churchman with his customary greeting, "Walk in, stranger." He told the preacher he could stay the night if he would agree to abide by the house rules. Not quite knowing what the "rules" were, the man of the cloth hesitated a minute, but needing a place to stay, he agreed, feeling quite sure the "house rules" couldn't amount to much. After supper, Brit picked up his rifle and told the preacher to disrobe and then get up on the table and dance a jig that was called the "Juba," an African dance popular with the local black population. The preacher told Brit he didn't know how to dance, but a shot aimed at the preacher's foot convinced him he could dance pretty well after all! He stumbled around on the table top, "jigging" as best he could while one of Brit's black servants played "Juba" on the fiddle!

It was said that Brit was just about the hardest drinker in all of Austin's colony, a dubious honor. The Bailey family history records tales of some of his most noteworthy sprees. One Saturday night, Brit, accompanied by a black boy named Jim, rode into town for a little partying. There was a revival going on, and most of Brit's usual drinking companions had been dragged to the camp meeting by their wives. Brit was pretty let down. He and Jim rode on back out to Brit's place, and after sitting under the old oak tree pulling on his jug for a good long while, Brit decided to liven things up a bit. He really lit up the night when he set fire to the corn crib, and sat drinking and admiring the flames till all his corn had gone up in smoke. It's said he probably would have set fire to the house as well if his favorite daughter hadn't arrived and talked him out of it!

There are all sorts of tales about Brit's drinking escapades, and unfortunately, most of them are true!

Finally, the hard-drinking character took sick and died of what they called cholera fever on December 6, 1832, at the age of sixty-three. At the time of his death his marital status was a subject of controversy, also. When he arrived in Texas in 1821, he brought his wife, Edith Smith Bailey, and their six children. However, an 1826 census of the Austin Colony lists his wife's name as Nancy. In his last will and testament he left his property to his "beloved Nancy and our two girls, Sarah and Margaret." The three surviving children that Brit and Edith brought with them to Texas were disinherited, without any "just cause." In 1838 Elizabeth Milburn and Mary Polley petitioned to have the will declared null and void, claiming they were Brit's legitimate children and that Nancy was only "represented" to be Brit's wife. (She might have been a common-law wife.) The plea was first denied, and then the will was set aside in January of 1839, some seven years after Brit's death.

Now, Bailey made some mighty strange requests concerning his burial, too. For one thing, he insisted he be buried standing up because he had "never stooped to any man while alive, and didn't intend to change after death." He wanted his gun placed over his shoulder and his powder horn nearby. He wanted to be buried facing west, because he'd been moving in that direction all his life and wanted to be facing in that direction when he crossed over into the next world. And one last request, he wanted a big, full jug of whiskey planted right at his feet!

Nancy Bailey saw that his instructions were carried out. A huge hole, over eight feet deep, and "big around as a wash tub," was dug in a pecan grove near the red house. The remains were placed in a pine coffin and provided with a gun and ammunition as requested. But when Bubba, a favorite slave of Bailey's, a giant of a man, came up with a huge jug of whiskey to plant at Bailey's feet, Mrs. Bailey would have none of that. Bubba insisted that it was what his master had requested, but on that one request Mrs. Bailey flatly refused. It is said she jerked the jug away from Bubba and threw it out the window. She said Brit had had more than enough of that stuff on earth, and she didn't think he needed any wherever he was headed to in the great beyond. And that's evidently what caused all the trouble to start out on Bailey's Prairie!

Bubba used to talk a lot about old Brit. And he would always conclude his stories saying that "Marse Bailey don't stand easy in his grave. He's still out huntin' dat jug of whiskey."

A few years after Brit died, the place was sold to John Thomas, who brought his wife, Ann, there to live. He had heard tales that the old red house was haunted, but he hadn't told his young wife. Soon after they moved in, business called John away. On a dark night, Ann and a servant girl were sleeping in the bedroom when something suddenly awakened Ann. The night was very dark, but darkness had never frightened her. No, there was something different, a "presence" that she felt. She gazed towards the door and could barely make out the form of a big man. She instinctively knew that this was no mortal man. She knew she was seeing a ghost! As the figure seemed to drift towards her, she was far too frightened to scream. As it came to the foot of her bed, it seemed to stoop and grope around under the bed. Then the figure retreated to the doorway and disappeared.

The servant girl, named Malinda, had also been awakened by the figure. She was too petrified to cry out. She told Mrs. Thomas that she (Mrs. Thomas) was sleeping in the very bed in which Brit Bailey had died four years before! This thought brought no comfort to the frightened Mrs. Thomas, and she promptly changed bedrooms!

As soon as John Thomas returned from his trip, Ann told him of her experience, which he explained away as a nightmare, or just a figment of her overactive imagination. But she said she wouldn't sleep in their bedroom again. He said he would go sleep in the room and show her that there was nothing to fear. In fact, he said, Old Brit had been a friend of his, and if he made another nocturnal visit, John joked he'd just get up and shake the old man's hand!

Well, in the bedroom opposite to where she now slept, a few nights later Ann heard a terrible, unearthly scream. She could, and did, move this time. She burst into the room and found her husband sitting on the side of his bed, rigid with fear. His face was streaked with sweat, and he was just able to gasp... "I saw him! It was old man Bailey. I saw him plain as day!" It wasn't too long after that that the Thomases moved away from the big red house.

As the years rolled by, the old house that had belonged to Bailey stood vacant and forlorn. But something was still around. As new dwellings rose up on the other side of Bailey's Prairie, people began to report seeing strange lights. In 1850 Colonel Mordello Munson was awakened by the mournful wails of his hounds. When he went outside to investigate, he found his dogs crawling on their stomachs, cowering in fear. Then he saw a great column of light, the size of a big man! It was some distance away. Although he and a friend pursued it for most of the night, on horseback, they were never able to catch up to the elusive and mysterious light.

People living around the Prairie still talk about the lights. It is my understanding that Catherine Munson Foster, the well-known Brazoria-area folklorist and writer, now owns Bailey's Prairie. She wrote about it in her book *Ghosts Along the Brazos*. She says the light would most often appear on late fall nights. It would circle around as if searching for something. Everybody who knew about Brit Bailey and his strange burial rites were convinced that his ghost was still abroad, searching for his jug.

Gradually the lights have lessened in size and intensity, until they seem to appear only once in a great while. Around West Columbia these days they say that Brit can only work up enough strength to shine his strange light every seven years. Some folks say he has caused cars to stop dead on the road, and some even say he caused a gas blowout when oil well workers worked too close to the site of his grave, an unmarked site somewhere up on Bennett's Ridge that no one can seem to locate now.

After so much looking for years and years, Brit may have found his lost jug by now and be well settled down into an eternal stupor.

Reeves Thicket's Ranch House

Between Victoria and Goliad, off Highway 59, there's a small community called Reeves Thicket. It used to be one huge ranch, but over the years the land has been subdivided and sold off in large lots where over 300 families reside today. The original ranch belonged to one man, John Reeves Sr., who came here from Pikes County, Georgia, in the early 1840s. It is believed his wife probably died in childbirth, because Reeves came to Texas alone, leaving his father and oldest son, John Jr., behind for quite some time. Finally, after he acquired considerable land holdings and established a law practice, he sent for his son John and his father to join him. John Jr. brought his wife, Cady, and their nine children with him. Later, another child, their tenth, William Worth, was born after they had settled into their new Texas home.

After a few years, John Jr. and his family moved to the banks of Coleto Creek, in the area now known as Reeves Thicket. John Sr. was pretty old by then (he was born in 1779) and needed looking after, so John and Cady cared for him until he passed away in 1863. His grave is one of those in the rather sizeable Reeves family cemetery that sits on what is known as Reeves Hill today.

John Reeves Jr. died in 1868, and at that time, one of his sons, Jonathan, whom they called Tobe, moved the family home from the banks of the Coleto Creek to its present location. It was a big house and had to be moved uphill about half a mile. Evidently it was slowly (how else?) moved uphill by being placed on huge logs, which were rolled along by teams of sturdy mules. The place that we visited recently is smaller than its original size. According to the present owner, it suffered considerable storm damage a number of years ago.

Today's owner of the Reeves ranch house, the old cemetery, and quite a few acres of the original holdings, is a direct descendant of the founding Reeves family, and he is "obsessed," as he puts it, with taking care of, and preserving, the old family homestead. A young man in his mid-forties, Charlie Faupel is a storehouse of knowledge of regional history, both factual and legendary. During a visit to the ranch, he was kind enough to tell us a lot of interesting things about the house and the land surrounding it, and about the spirits he feels still guard the place. According to Charlie, Tobe was probably the most colorful of the Reeves family members. He took over the ranch shortly after the Civil War ended, endured drought, hard times, outlaws, and a yellow fever epidemic. Tobe was called the "law west of the Coleto," and he was said to have administered justice in his own way. For instance, one hot summer day in the 1870s he'd been out with his men rounding up some cattle. When they got home, they found someone had stolen some of their horses. Along with some of his ranch hands, Tobe rode out to catch the culprit. They crossed over Reeves Creek and rode over to Fleming Prairie, where they found the horse thief. A shootout was the result. Tobe remained on his horse; the thief took cover and managed to shoot Tobe's left ear off. This really made Tobe angry, according to Charlie (well, who wouldn't be mad about losing an ear?). Now, Tobe had planned to be "fair" with the culprit and give him a hearing before hanging him, but he was so enraged that he just up and shot him right there and buried him somewhere out there on the land. Charlie says there's some evidence of that gravesite today, and there are probably numerous other graves scattered over the vast estate.

There was quite a big outlaw gang around in the 1860s and '70s known as the "Brookins gang." They lived on the Coleto and made raids on ranches in the area, but it is said they gave Tobe Reeves' place a wide berth!

When the Reeves family first settled the area, they decided to call their ranch Reeves Thicket because of the thick brush that dots the countryside. It was in an area once crossed by the Old Spanish Trail, and signs of the trail are evident even today. There was also an old wagon road that followed Coleto Creek. Charlie Faupel said his great-great-grandfather Tobe was a "really, truly" cattle baron of his time, and he showed us the old live oak hanging tree that was used to put more than one desperado out of business. It has a huge limb that sort of stands out, and this was probably the hanging limb.

Charlie says it's hard to get a horse to ride by the tree. In fact, he says, there are lots of places on the ranch that just naturally spook a horse, sensitive as those creatures are to otherworldly beings!

The "hanging tree" at Reeves Thicket

Charlie loves to talk about his rambling old wooden ranchhouse and the surrounding land, which he inherited and in which he takes great pride. He says it is strange, but his feeling for the old house is like the house owns him, and he is sort of possessed by it and the ties it has with his ancestors. Well, it is very old. And very charming. And not many people can boast of living in a house that so many generations of their family have lived in, and died in, as well. Charlie said if his old bed could talk, it could tell lots of stories, as it came by wagon over 135 years ago from Georgia, and was where the colorful Tobe died of pneumonia in 1890, and where his grandmother, Isabel, was born in 1901. There are pictures and mementos everywhere depicting important events in the Reeves' family history: old photographs, portraits, and memorabilia of all kinds.

The house wasn't always a homestead, however. Charlie says for a time it was sort of abandoned and used to store feed and hay. Six generations just sort of wore it out, but Charlie, of the seventh generation, is doing all he can to keep up the place. That's why the spirits which Charlie thinks are peaceful and just kind and gentle presences are there, because they are happy he is looking after the place. He also revealed that the house was placed atop the hill overlooking the creek where once the family slaves had been buried in unmarked graves. He thinks his office and bedroom are probably located right over the old slave cemetery!

Charlie told me that Union soldiers once rode right through the house on their horses, and once the roof caught fire during an Indian attack. There's still a lead bullet embedded in the front porch banister, and there are also three bullet holes in the dining room wall. A large section of the house was destroyed by a storm in 1942.

Today, Charlie believes that UFOs make regular visits to Reeves Thicket. His cousin Susan Purcell, with whom I later spoke, believes this as well. Not in the realm of ghosts, but very fascinating nonetheless, Charlie says the big attraction at the ranch, besides his pet llamas, is frequent sightings of what must be described as unidentified flying objects. The bachelor owner of Reeves Thicket Ranch and his frequent visitors enjoy sitting on the long front porch of the ranch house to watch the hovering lighted objects. They will hover for quite a long time, sometimes, and then dart off with great speed, into space.

Yes, Reeves Thicket is a fascinating place. The old ranch house is interesting, and the owner, Charlie Faupel, is a unique and interesting man. So why wouldn't any watchful spirits out there be pretty fascinating, too?

The Ghosts at Goliad

"Remember the Alamo!" "Remember Goliad!" These were the rallying cries shouted by General Sam Houston's forces on April 21, 1836, as they attacked the slumbering forces of General Antonio Lopez de Santa Anna at the Battle of San Jacinto. This battle won independence for Texas from Mexico's domination. Now, today, the whole world recognizes the shout, "Remember the Alamo!," but not nearly so well known, especially among non-Texans, is the poignant story of the massacre of Colonel James Fannin and his Texan forces that were stationed at the old Presidio of La Bahia at Goliad.

The establishment of the Royal Presidio of La Bahia ("the bay") in the year 1721 was in direct response to the encroachment by the French into the Spanish Province of Texas. The first La Bahia presidio was located on the banks of Garcitas Creek near present-day Lavaca Bay, on the remains of the ill-fated French Fort St. Louis which Robert Cavelier LaSalle had built. In 1726 the Spaniards decided to abandon this location and relocate in an inland position near Mission Valley, just above present-day Victoria. Finally, in 1749, the presidio was relocated to its present location just outside of the town of Goliad.

This presidio became the only fort responsible for the defense of the coastal area and eastern province of Texas. Soldiers from the presidio assisted the Spanish army, which fought the British during the American Revolution. This action gives Goliad the distinction of being one of the only communities west of the Mississippi River that participated in the American Revolution!

Another little-known fact is that the cattle industry of Texas had its real beginnings at La Bahia, with the soldiers overseeing the herds from the missions of Rosario and Espiritu Santo, which were located nearby. Troop escorts for the cattle drive which supplied other Spanish settlements of the Southwest were commanded by the garrison at the presidio.

When Mexico won her independence from Spain in 1821, the La Bahia became a station for Mexican forces. On October 9, 1835, a group of Texas citizens, led by Captain George Collinsworth, entered Goliad, attacked the presidio, and succeeded in taking possession of the fort. Later, at the presidio, the first Declaration of Texas Independence was signed by ninety-two citizens of Texas on December 20, 1835. In the Declaration, which was distributed throughout other municipalities in Texas, the settlers boldly stated their desire for full independence from the dictatorial government of the self-styled "Napoleon of the West," General Antonio Lopez de Santa Anna.

Texas forces were soon stationed at the old presidio, under the command of Colonel James Walker Fannin. One of the darkest days in Texas history was Palm Sunday, March 27, 1836, when Fannin and 352 of his men were executed a week after they were captured at the Battle of Coleto. First, Santa Anna had put every man at the Alamo to the sword. Joining that valiant force of 189 men in death were all the men stationed at Goliad. As the grim news of the needless execution of so many men reached the United States, volunteers streamed forth to assist the Texans who were at war with a dictator who was determined to fight a war of extermination!

Today, over one hundred and fifty years later, the old walls of the historic fortress and its adjacent Chapel of our Lady of Loreto sometimes echo with the mournful sounds of spirits returning from that troubled and turbulent time in the history of the great state of Texas.

Kevin Young, San Antonio historian and writer, was the museum director at La Bahia some years back. He recalls that his living quarters at the presidio were just a few paces away from where James Fannin and his men were summarily executed. Many a day, and night, Kevin said he felt "cold spots" and uneasy feelings like someone was watching him. He never actually saw a ghost, but he says he knows they are there!

Kevin suggested I contact the current museum director, Newton Warzecha. Warzecha said he has had no ghostly encounters "yet," but he didn't doubt the stories he had heard from many people who had reported either seeing, or hearing, the unearthly visitors to the old presidio.

The *Victoria Advocate* on Sunday, November 8, 1992, ran a very interesting feature article by a staff writer, David Tewes. Tewes had interviewed Jim Leos Jr., a guard with Triple D Security Company who had been assigned to guard some equipment at the presidio that was to be used for the Cattle Baron's Ball. Leos, long used to night-time duty, expected just a routine evening at the quiet old former fort. But just before midnight, strange things began to happen. The quietness of the night was broken by the "eerie, shrill cries of nearly a dozen terrified infants." It sent shivers down the spine of the veteran security guard and former deputy sheriff from Victoria. Leos said the cries indicated "pain and suffering." He couldn't locate where they were coming from at first. He finally realized the cries were coming from one of the dozen or so unmarked graves that are located near the Chapel of our Lady of Loreto.

As suddenly as the crying started, the sounds ended, only to be replaced by the singing of a woman's choir. Although he could see nothing unusual, the mysterious music sounded as if it were coming from the back wall of the old fort. Leos said the women were singing words, but he couldn't make out what they were saying, and the tune was also unfamiliar to him.

The strange singing ended in two or three minutes, but then a much more frightening event occurred. A small friar suddenly appeared! At first, there was a vaporous form arising from the ground in front of the double door that leads into the chapel. Leos said the little friar was only about four feet tall. The robe he wore was black, tied around the waist with a rope. He was barefoot and his face was concealed with a hood.

Leos recalled having heard other people talk about the same apparition. The words of warning came back to him: "Remain perfectly still because this is an aggressive ghost." The shocked Leos just froze where he stood and watched as the priest wandered around from one corner to the other of the old church. The figure then went to each corner of the quadrangle. Leos says he thinks the hooded figure was praying in Latin.

About an hour and a half after the friar disappeared, the apparition of a woman wearing a white dress, which looked somewhat like a wedding dress, materialized in front of one of the unmarked graves that are situated in front of the chapel. It was the same grave from which Leos had heard the cries of the babies, and Leos said the woman appeared to be looking for one of the infants.

The article in the *Advocate* stated, "Then she turned around and looked at me. She drifted maybe a foot or two off the ground and headed towards the back wall."

Leos said the ghostly figure just floated over the wall and out of sight as she headed towards an old cemetery established in the 1700s.

Although teased by his coworkers when he told of his nocturnal adventures, Leos is convinced that what he saw was real, and not a bad dream. After all, he doesn't ever sleep when he is on duty! And Leos knows he isn't the only person who has reported bizarre occurrences around the old presidio.

Presidio of La Bahia at Goliad, Chapel of our Lady of Loreto

Many residents who live near the fort have related similar stories. Although Newton Warzecha hasn't seen anything since he has
become museum director, he says, "I do not know whether there are
spirits there, but I could understand if there are such things, because
of all the violence that has taken place there." His assistant, Luiz
Cazarez-Rueda, who sometimes lives on the presidio grounds, is
rather guarded with his comments when questioned about ghosts.
However, the expression on his face indicated to David Tewes, who
wrote the article in the *Advocate*, that Rueda knew more than he
wanted to tell.

Dorothy Simmons, owner of the Souvenir Closet in Goliad, was
watching the museum within the fort one spring day for John Collins,
a former director, while he was out running some errands. As she
walked through the museum and got to the third room, she heard
what she called "celestial humming." A beautiful soprano voice was
singing. There was nothing scary about it. She could detect the
music only in that one room. When she walked out, it stopped. When
she returned, it began again. Although she tried to reason it was the
wind, it just wasn't enough to account for the very real sound of
music which she heard. Simmons says she believes that we can
experience time warps or see just a fleeting glimpse of the other
side.

Then, there was the time that Irma Valencia, owner of Irma's
Cafe in Goliad, agreed to do some volunteer work at the presidio. It
was a hot, humid summer day. As Irma began to clean the furnishings and to wax the floor after the last tourist had departed, only Luiz
Cazarez-Rueda, the assistant director, was still there. He had gone
outside to take down the flags. As soon as he left, Valencia said, she
heard organ music begin to play, accompanying the celestial humming of a woman. She said the music was just all around her, but it
stopped when Casarez-Rueda came back inside. At first she thought
he had been playing a portable radio, but he said, no, he didn't have a
radio. Then he asked her, "So you heard it too?" Although she had
been there as a volunteer many times before, Irma said she had
never heard the music previously. Once was apparently enough for
her, as she has stopped going out to the presidio entirely.

It seems that visitors, often complete strangers to the presidio, have reported strange happenings, also. Cazarez-Rueda said a mother and daughter visited the fort just before closing time. The mother soon came back to the entrance and asked Cazarez-Rueda if there were historical reenactors on the property, people dressed up in period costumes to add "atmosphere" to the place. He told her, yes, they were there sometimes on special occasions, but there was no one there on that particular day. The lady assured him she had just seen someone, a lady dressed all in black, with a black veil over her face. She was in the chapel, by the candles, and she was crying as if her heart would break. At the daughter's suggestion, the mother stepped forth to ask the lady what was wrong, to see if she could help. In that instant, the figure totally disappeared!

Cazarez-Rueda tried to get the visitor's name, but the lady didn't stay long enough to say who she was. She just said she wanted to get out of there, and didn't ever plan to come back there again!

There was an interesting article in the *Texan Express* back on October 31, 1984, written by Sandra Judith Rodriguez. She mentioned in her story that many people have reported hearing "mumbling noises," like a group of people praying, when they pass the Chapel of our Lady of Loreto in the evenings.

And several people from the La Bahia area have reported that every so often when they are in their cars, driving alone, they will suddenly see someone sitting on the passenger side of the car. This happens usually when they are just passing over the San Antonio River. In their confusion, some people have said they first thought somebody was in the back seat of the car and had moved to the front seat. They start to talk to the person, but the person does not reply. As they glance again, the person has disappeared. Some people even claim that the person they saw was headless! Talk about goose pimples!

And the La Bahia Restaurant crew, who work pretty late at night, have reported that some evenings when they pass by the old buildings they notice the chapel lights are burning. They know they had been turned off earlier in the evening. They also have reported hearing the cries of a baby, but no babies are ever found in the area.

During the restoration of La Bahia, one of the workmen stayed late doing some paperwork. He had his dog with him. Suddenly the animal started growling and moving towards its master. The dog seemed agitated and frightened. About this time, the man heard the cries of a baby outside the door. It seemed very close. He thought a mother with a sick child might be outside, seeking help. He waited for a knock but heard nothing, so he opened the door and peered out. He was surprised when he found no one there. He said the hair stood up on the back of his neck and he was all "goose pimply." He looked all around the presidio and could find absolutely nothing. He just left his paperwork and headed off to town as fast as he could drive.

And so the stories continue; a new one now and then, or a repeat of an oft-told tale. Who are these restless spirits? The crying babies, are they little lost souls of pioneer infants? Or, are they the offspring of Spanish militiamen and their wives? How did the little ones die? Did the Indians kill them in a raid, or was there an epidemic that snuffed out their little lives? The young woman in white ... is her own baby buried somewhere out there in an unmarked grave near the chapel? And who was the little friar in the black robe? Was he a chaplain brought to the presidio to serve the Spanish forces? Is his soul in turmoil because the Spanish forces had to depart when Mexico won her independence from Spain? Or is his spirit disturbed because so many brave men were executed right there next to his beloved chapel? The lady in black who cries in the chapel ... was she the widow or mother of a soldier who served there? Why does her sorrowing spirit return to weep at the altar? And the music, angelic voices singing long forgotten canticles and hymns; are they songs of praise, or of supplication?

They are all there, caught in a web of timelessness, a multitude of lonely, lost souls, searching ... sorrowing ... seeking ... singing ... none quite prepared to let go of that life which they lived so briefly, so long ago, in a lonely outpost called La Bahia.

The "Great Blue Ghost" Has Ghosts of Her Own!

After serving her country for nearly fifty years (1943-1991), the great aircraft carrier U.S.S. *Lexington* (CV16) has come to a permanent safe harbor, at the port city of Corpus Christi on the Texas Gulf Coast. As a naval museum, under the custodial care of the Corpus Christi Convention and Visitors Bureau and many devoted and dedicated volunteers, she will be visited and suitably honored for many years to come.

During World War II, the *Lexington* was often referred to as the Great Blue Ghost, a name bestowed upon her by Tokyo Rose, who gained notoriety during the war for her propaganda broadcasts to Allied troops. Painted in Measure II "Sea Blue," the ship blended well with the azure seas she sailed. Hit once by a torpedo in December of 1943 and severely damaged by a kamikaze attack in December 1944, the Japanese reported her sunk at least four times. But after repairs and restoration, she came back each time to contribute greatly to the U.S. war effort in the Pacific theater. The valiant ship received the Presidential Unit Citation: "For extraordinary heroism in action against enemy Japanese forces in the air, ashore, and afloat in the Pacific War Area from September 18, 1943, to August 15, 1945." The "Lady Lex" earned battle stars and awards for operations in the Gilbert Islands, Asia-Pacific raids, Lyte, Luzon, and Iwo Jima, as well as the Third Fleet operations against Japan. She was everywhere, and anywhere, she was needed, with her crew of 2,500 men and 250 officers and her hangar bays capable of handling at least forty aircraft ready to strike.

The huge ship with its 910-foot flight deck (so large that 1,000 automobiles could be comfortably parked upon it!) has been "home" to literally thousands of seamen and aircraft crews over its fifty-year history. There were many casualties during her years of service, including nine men killed and thirty-five wounded after being torpedoed, and forty-seven men killed and one hundred twenty-seven injured after the 1944 kamikaze attack. There were probably many other deaths as well, from illness, fever, and various accidents on board ship.

Today the ship is no longer sailing; she is no longer the launching pad for countless naval aircraft. She is no longer painted blue, either. When she was given a streamlined island structure and a new mast and her deck was angled to accommodate the coming of the jet age, she was also given a new paint job. Today she is "haze gray."

From 1962 until November of 1991 she served as a training carrier, based at Pensacola, Florida. From her first training operation in 1963 until her decommissioning in 1991, an average of 1,500 pilots were carrier-qualified on her each year.

The U.S.S. *Lexington* after modifications to superstructure and deck, 1960s.
(U.S. Navy photo courtesy of the National Archives)

Now, men are known to love their ships. That's probably why they have always referred to them as being of the feminine gender. As for the "Lady Lex," there are some men whose spirits have never left the ship they served and loved so well. They still remain in the staterooms, briefing rooms, decks, passageways, and sick bays of their ship. Therein lies a story, or several stories, in fact.

Soon after my husband and I visited the *Lexington* in February of 1993, I spoke with a friend about having seen the great ship. This gentleman, Sam Nesmith, is a well-known military historian, and he also possesses great psychic powers. After I mentioned my visit, he told me that he and his wife, Nancy, had recently visited the ship as well, and he said he felt the ship had a number of "resident spirits," earthbound to the ship and either unable, or unwilling, to leave. He said he especially felt a deep sense of pain and sadness in the dark corridor near a first-aid station, and in the "fo'c'sle" area, near the anchor, he also noted a very strong "presence." But it was in the Pilot's Ready Room Number One that he felt an overwhelming presence. It literally filled the room! Sam had brought a camera, with high-speed film. He took a direct shot into the room. When the film came back from being developed, there, quite visible, was a pilot, seen from the shoulders up. Also discernible was a collar and a head with a World War II era pilot's helmet and goggles. The face appeared to be "skull-like," according to Nesmith, who strongly believes it was the spirit of a pilot who did not make it back after a sortie, and is still struggling to return for his debriefing.

As we were planning another trip to Corpus Christi in August 1993, I decided to try and contact someone connected with the Lexington Museum to see if anyone there had experienced any unusual encounters of a supernatural nature. A telephone call to the curator's office brought me in contact with Derek Neitzel, assistant to the curator and the resident graphic artist at the ship museum. He didn't laugh when I asked him "Could there possibly be a ghost on the *Lexington*?" Instead, we made an appointment to meet on the ship on Friday, August 13.

I met Derek, a very personable young man, at 10 A.M., and we spent the next two and a half hours in conversation as he showed me some places on the ship not on the regular tourist route. He also told me about some of his personal experiences, as well as those of his coworkers. He showed me a short videotape made by a local television studio, that included an interview with Derek speaking about some of his experiences with "spirits" as he took the TV crew over various parts of the ship, where he later took me. He said one of the first experiences he had was at twelve noon on a Saturday, when he was working alone in his office. This was soon after he had come to work on the ship. He heard, in a passageway near his office, the loudest banging and rattling imaginable! He traced it to the metal door to the ship's former radio station, WLEX. The door was actually shaking and vibrating. Derek said, "Hello," to which there was no response, and no letting up. Then he went to find the "D.C." (damage control) personnel. This is the name used on the ship for the firemen, paramedics, and security staff people. When the man arrived, there was no one there, of course, and no way to explain the vibrating, banging door. Incidentally, the door, which Derek pointed out to me, is a heavy metal sliding door which is secured by a sliding metal bar.

We discussed various "happenings" that Derek recalled during the months he worked on the ship. One night stands out above all the others. It was the night of February 13-14, 1993, and the "spirits" were really active all night long! In fact, there was no holding them back! Derek gave me a Xerox copy of the ship's log with the hourly reports noted by the "D.C." personnel as they signed in at all hours of the night while making their rounds. Derek said he had been there in his office, working, most of the evening. Since so much activity was taking place, he just stayed on throughout the entire night.

As various members of the Damage Control staff made their entries in the log, it became apparent this was a most unusual night, and a wet one as well.

Some of the entries noted included the following:

0010: Water still coming down in Hangar #1, due to problem in C.O.'s room above.
0155: Smoke detector 02-126-1 malfunction. Checked out. All ok, reset system.
0300: Made routine round of all tour areas. Found two areas with water running into sinks in C.C. Admiral's quarters. One sink full of water. Unknown why water running. Still can hear water running in pipes in bridge area.

0345: Found sink in Admiral's quarters with water running, sink full, water on floor, this seems very strange why fresh water left running.

0400: Made rounds of pier area. Unable to go to fo'c'sle area due to fresh wax.

0410: Wayne notified about water running. He advised D.C. to secure all water running in heads.

0530: Made rounds of bridge and flight deck. Raised flag.

0630: Made rounds of pier, opened gate, water leak in hangar stopped.

And so it went. Derek attached his own personal notes to the D.C. log for the night of February 13-14 as follows:

In addition to those incidents reported in the D.C. Log by Richard Longoria who was scheduled at the time, Wayne, with D.C., was there with Wayne Fellers of Ship's operations at the Admiral's galley at about 9:20 on the night of the 13th. I overheard a radio report of water running in the Admiral's galley which was locked and sealed at the bottom with screws. It has a two-part door.

I ran up to help, in that I might be able to find a key since I have access to the locksmith's shop. I was told to bring either a key or a crowbar. I was gone approximately 7 to 10 minutes. When I returned, the group of Wayne F., and his son, Wayne with D.C., and Art Smith, the ship's electrician, had already pried the door open. I came down to the hangar deck and caught up with Wayne to ask what the cause of the water running was. I was told that a water faucet had been turned on. I know for a fact (for I was there) that I witnessed Pete Valentine (the ship's locksmith) lock the door a number of weeks previously and I had installed the screws on the back side. This was just a day before we opened this tour line. I also know Pete was the only one who had a key. One final note: I was in the next compartment aft (the admiral's stateroom) at 6:00 the same evening working on lashing ropes for the stanchions in the same room and I would have heard it had it been occurring at that time.

And then on February 17, Derek notes:

Addendum. Today I talked to D.C. "Shane" who was on
duty during that night (February 13) He reported that two of
the sinks were behind locked doors and one instance was the
shower being on in the captain's sea-cabin on the 06 level.
This was accounting for the water running sounds which he
and Richard Longoria traced to the sea cabin. All in all, it was
four sinks total, plus the shower and a faucet in the galley.
D.N. 2-17-93.

Derek, in discussing this strange night, said that some of the faucets that were running hadn't been turned on in a long while, and he
added they were so stuck tight that it would have taken a strong man
with a wrench to turn them on. Yet there they were, running freely,
and in compartments behind firmly locked doors! He said the whole
week centered around February 14 was "very active" and he
referred to it as "hell week."

Derek went on to tell how the swivel chair that the bookkeeper
uses often would swivel and squeak when she wasn't even there.
This chair is in the photocopy office.

A man named Wayne, on the Damage Control staff, has a son
whose name is John. This young man told his father that he had a
strange experience on the ship. He suddenly felt terrified for no particular reason. Then, he heard a distinct voice speaking to him,
saying, "You'd sure hate to be here when them planes were taking
off." The voice was very clear, and there was no mistaking what it
said. John has never forgotten this incident.

Numerous times Derek has experienced the sensation of being
followed down various passageways. He hears the sound of heavy
military type shoes following along behind him. When they come to
the coamings (raised door openings in the passageways) they do not
break cadence as they should. He has also been followed by the
same heavy treads as he comes out of the "head" (restroom) near
the officer's dining room. These footsteps have followed him for
some distance.

Another time, as he was disassembling a table in order to move it from the galley where it was located to the passageway outside, Derek could hear footsteps. There were no lights on in the passageway, but he had a flashlight. The steps were going from aft to forward. He asked, "Who is it?" but of course, there was no answer.

Derek took me on a tour over many areas that are off limits to visiting tourists. I felt the presence of "something" in several areas, sort of a feeling of loneliness and emptiness. The place that drew the most shivers in me was the former brig where there were a number of small, dark, barred cells. However, my host said that there had never been any reports of any ghostly happenings around that area.

Derek told me many of the ship's staff members have discussed their own experiences with an "unexplainable presence" on the huge vessel. One of the volunteers, John Dau, told Derek he had served on the carrier in the 1960s, and he knew then there were ghosts on the ship even while it was still on active duty.

One of the janitorial staff working there on contract, Jimmy Caldwell, told Derek he actually saw a medical corpsman in the sick bay about 5 A.M. one morning. He saw the figure just briefly, and then it totally disappeared.

Although Derek, who spends lots of hours on the ship at night in the print shop or doing artwork, is not fearful of the resident spirits, he says that they are at times "disturbing." Finally, after one particularly exasperating night, he asked them to "Just lay off...just quit bothering me and trying to frighten me. I can't do my job as well with you disturbing me." He said he believes they are really intelligent entities, and they understood him, because he has had a relatively peaceful time of it since he made that request!

I might add a postscript to this story:

A more recent visit with Derek aboard the *Lexington* revealed the spirits are still active. Two security guards have reported hearing voices when no one is around on several occasions. Derek, who is convinced that these otherworldly seamen will never leave the *Lexington,* is not worried about any more disturbances. He's moving to West Africa.

Miss Bettie's Still in Charge at Ashton Villa

In September of 1992, my husband, Roy, and I were the guests of the East Texas Tourism Association on a familiarization tour of Southeast Texas communities. Included in our jam-packed itinerary was Galveston Island. The representatives of the Galveston Convention and Visitors Bureau pulled out all the stops to show our group a wonderful overview of the historic landmarks of that great city on the Gulf of Mexico.

Our group was treated to an elegant progressive dinner. After the salad course, which we enjoyed at the beautiful Moody mansion, we moved on to Ashton Villa, where the main entree was served. This magnificent mansion, a project of the Galveston Historical Foundation, is located at 2328 Broadway. The splendid villa was built by James Moreau Brown in 1859. Brown, a hardware magnate, was one of Texas' leading businessmen, and his home became a meeting place of the great and near-great from across the land. While no mention was made of Mrs. Brown, we were told that his colorful daughter, Rebecca, generally known as "Miss Bettie," served as his hostess and presided over the household for many years. And therein lies a story....

After our group had dined in a large reception room, we were given a tour of the beautiful residence. As I wandered through one of the upstairs bedrooms, I felt something... a little shiver, perhaps just a feeling as I looked around. Then I walked down the broad staircase and strolled into the main parlor known as the Gold Room. I felt some presence was with me as I walked. Then, as I moved towards a beautiful antique piano, the hair stood up on my arms and a real shiver went right through me. I stopped, walked out of the room, and sought out one of the Galveston hostesses. I asked her if she knew whether or not Ashton Villa was haunted. She said, "Well... there are stories." I couldn't get much more from her as it was time for our group to move on to still another landmark, the Old Opera House, where we were served our dessert course.

Having felt something, some special energy in the Gold Room, I was most anxious to pursue the subject further. Finally, some time later, I obtained some printed material from Galveston's famous Rosenberg Library. Casey Edward Greene, the assistant archivist, sent me copies of articles from the files in the library that substantiate that I had, indeed, almost had a "close encounter" with "Miss Bettie" Brown.

In the days when the Browns entertained in their grand mansion, guests were often shown into the formal reception room, or salon. There, elegant Victorian galas and musical recitals were held. "Miss Bettie," who never married, would have been quite at home in today's liberal society. She was way ahead of her own day; a liberated woman before the term "women's lib" existed! An accomplished and multitalented artist, she traveled, alone and unchaperoned, all over Europe. She smoked a pipe, and was said to have urged at least one of her male admirers to drink champagne from her golden slipper!

Ashton Villa, at 2328 Broadway in Galveston
(photo courtesy of Galveston Historical Foundation)

"Miss Bettie" was definitely an individualist and possessed a very strong personality.

An article from Galveston County's *In Between* (the October 1978 issue, featuring Galveston County's ghosts) stated that the furnishings of the Gold Room at Ashton Villa were true reflections of the lifestyle of Rebecca Brown. Many of her most treasured possessions are shown displayed in a small alcove. There are costumes, fans, an Egyptian mummy's head, and a diamond-studded cat's head she purchased in Paris. Two of her original paintings also hang in the room. One depicts a demure Victorian lass on a swing; the other portrays two rotund cherubs, one of whom boasts the wings of a butterfly!

In the adjacent dining room there is a photo on display which shows a servant standing in a doorway. But what sets the picture apart from the ordinary is that to the left of the mantel pictured in the photograph, the image of another man's face is plainly visible. Could it possibly be a ghost?

Then, there's that magnificent piano ... the same instrument I stopped near when the feeling of a presence overtook me. The story from *In Between* stated that a caretaker who had lived in the carriage house adjacent to the villa vividly recalled a night when he was awakened from a sound sleep about 3:30 A.M. by the sounds of a piano playing. Because there had been some attempted break-ins, he decided to go check the villa. As he entered, he heard the music emanating from the elegant Gold Room. As he came into the room he was startled to see the faint image of a woman in nineteenth-century clothing seated at the piano bench. In just a moment, both she and the music which was playing faded completely away. The caretaker was quoted as saying that he turned on every light in the building and stayed awake for the remainder of the night!

Steven Long, a newswriter for the Houston *Chronicle*, wrote an interesting feature for the October 29, 1993, edition of that paper. The article, which was titled, "Haunted Houses," stated that Lucie Testa, weekend manager at the villa since 1988, had experienced several strange happenings there. On February 18, 1991, the alarm system went off, for no particular reason, three different times. Then, as Testa prepared to close the house for the day, she noticed the ceiling fan at the top of the staircase had come on. She climbed the stairs to turn it off, only to find it running again when she arrived the next morning! She noted that Miss Bettie Brown had been born on February 18, 1855! Extrovert that she was, maybe she just wanted to make sure somebody remembered her birthday!

Testa also told about feeling a ghostly presence in Miss Bettie's former day room. At the end of the single bed there is an ornate chest that she purchased on a trip to the Middle East. The key was lost many years ago. Sometimes the chest is locked. Other times it is unlocked. There is no explanation whatsoever for this.

Long's article in the *Chronicle* also related that a volunteer who came to work at the villa during the "Dickens Christmas on the Strand" weekend reported seeing a lady standing at the top of the grand staircase. She was wearing a beautiful turquoise blue dress. He reported seeing her to Testa, but there had been no one in the house wearing that color on that day. Turquoise was known to have been Miss Bettie Brown's favorite color!

When I made a recent telephone call to Ashton Villa, one of the docents to whom I spoke confided that there was one upstairs bedroom in which there is a bed that never stays properly made up. No matter how many times a day the staff members straighten the spread and smooth out the wrinkles, it always appears rumpled and wrinkled. She said this was in Miss Bettie's bed-sitting room. I wondered if it was the room in which I had first felt that strange otherworldly presence.

One might make a final conclusion about the Ashton Villa and all the strange, unexplainable things that have occurred there over the years. The former mistress of the household is still around, at least in spirit, and she's just keeping everybody aware of the fact that she is still very much in charge!

The Haunted Portrait

Mrs. Catherine Polk makes her home in La Marque, a small city on the Texas coast just north of the causeway leading to Galveston Island. This charming, friendly lady warmly welcomed my husband and me into her large, two-story Tudor English house, where we enjoyed a nice morning visit and a lively discussion concerning the other "occupant" of her spacious home.

The ghost is that of Elvie Bertha Weller, Catherine's great-aunt, who died at the age of fifteen in 1904. Elvie's spirit has long clung to a portrait made of her when she was about thirteen years old.

Elvie was born in the small town of Sublime, Texas, on August 24, 1889. She was one of five daughters in the loving, close-knit Weller family. When she was very young the family moved to Brownsville. All the girls except Elvie were sent off to various convents and private schools in Brownsville and San Antonio. Elvie, always sweet and rather shy, was apparently the family pet, according to Catherine Polk. Her parents elected to have her remain at home, receiving her education under the tutelage of the family governess. Musically talented, she played both the piano and organ, and by the time she was twelve years old she played the organ for services at her church. She was also the only Weller daughter whose portrait was made. Catherine is not sure if it is a good watercolor or an old photograph which was hand colored, as was the custom in those days prior to the invention of color film. I personally believe it is a photograph because of the sepia tones of Elvie's face.

Young Elvie was highly esteemed in the city of Brownsville. The summer of 1904, when she was fourteen, she became seriously ill with Bright's disease, a then-fatal kidney ailment. The Brownsville city officials became very concerned. It was an extremely hot and humid summer, and the windows of the young girl's bedroom had to be left open to allow ventilation to flow through the house. The city sent out wagonloads of sawdust to be spread in the street in front of the Weller home to muffle the sounds of horses and carriages passing by, which might disturb her rest.

As Elvie's condition worsened and the family realized she would not last much longer, the entire Weller family, except for one absent sister, gathered at her bedside. Just before she died, only two weeks after her fifteenth birthday, Elvie exclaimed to her assembled family, "Look! don't you see them? The angels! They're so beautiful, and they have come for me!"

Nancy Polk, Catherine's oldest daughter, who lives in Houston, shared the death notice announcing Elvie's passing, which ran in the Brownsville paper. It stated:

> Dead in this city, last night at twelve o'clock, Elvie Bertha Weller, born at Sublime, Texas, August 24, 1889, aged fifteen years and thirteen days. The friends and acquaintances of the deceased and of the family, are respectfully invited to attend the funeral from the family residence, corner of Levee and Eighth Streets, this afternoon at three o'clock. Brownsville, Texas, September 7, 1904.

In those days, news must have traveled very slowly. Nancy has in her possession a copy of the eulogy which ran in the Cuero, Texas, newspaper, on December 18, 1904, some three months after Elvie's death. Cuero is in DeWitt County, which borders Lavaca County, where the tiny town of Sublime, Elvie's birthplace, is located. Supposedly named by early German settlers to the area, Sublime bears the name of a town in Germany. According to Fred Tarpley's 1001 *Texas Place Names*, Sublime had a population of seventy-five people on June 14, 1875.

The Cuero paper may have been quoting from the Brownsville paper, or the article may have been composed by a Cuero staff writer. The words formed a beautiful tribute to the young girl:

> It is best. Too beautiful and too pure for this world's sin and sorrow, Elvie Bertha Weller closed her eyes in death in Brownsville, Texas, September 6, 1904. Of rare physical

beauty, with a mind exceptionally bright, combined with a gentle, loving disposition, she readily won the love of those she met. Though a sufferer for many months without the knowledge of those who loved her best, she patiently bore her sufferings, only saying, "she did not feel well." A fair flower of only fifteen summers, God, the Father, took it back to bloom only once more in the great celestial garden.

Calmly calling each loved one, she bade them "kiss her goodbye." And then, with faltering lips came the words, "Mama, I have seen God; I have prayed to Him and He said, 'Elvie, I have forgiven all your sins. Come home and rest.'" To her, death was only "the gentle nurse, whose goodnight kiss precludes one's entrance into bliss."

"Oh," she said, "the other world is so beautiful." And love borne on a faith in Christ, she prayed that she might be spared to see an absent sister.

Oh, my friends, what sublime faith and trust in one so young. She asked that "Nearer, My God to Thee" and "The Haven of Rest" be sung at her funeral. So they laid her down to rest, far from her childhood home, on stranger soil.

The dead and the beautiful rest but her soul has entered into immortal life.

Oh, dear ones, all be comforted; such a beautiful death is full of the Balm of Gilead. Although with bruised and breaking heart, with sable garb and silent tread, you bare her senseless dust to rest. You say she is dead, ah, no, she has but dropped her robe of clay to put her shining garments on. She has not wandered far away. She is not dead, or gone, and when the trumpets sound and the dead be raised, incorruptible, not changed, but glorified, Elvie, bright with the beauty and celestial glory of an immortal grace shall meet the poor broken-hearted mother, with the same face that you have loved and cherished, divinely fair.

Whom God loves, He chastens, and when His finger touching our loved ones into sleep that takes them from us, He whispers into our aching hearts, "let not your hearts be troubled; in my Father's house are many mansions." Cuero, Texas, December 18, 1904.

Elvie's grief-stricken mother kept the portrait of her deceased daughter in her bedroom. Catherine recalls, as a youngster, she would go and gaze up at the picture of the young girl, admiring the sweet faced image, which was gowned in a white dress with a white rose caught at the neckline. She told her great-grandmother that she would love to have Elvie's portrait someday. She was very disappointed when Mrs. Weller left the picture to her youngest daughter, Katherine Lenora, whom Catherine Polk called "Aunt Kate."

Portrait of Elvie Bertha Weller

When Catherine visited her great-aunt Kate in Brownsville, back about 1960, Kate asked her if there was anything among her effects that Catherine might like to have at her death. Without a moment's hesitation, Catherine said she would like to have Elvie's portrait. Kate gave it to Catherine right then and there, saying that her grandson, who was living with her at the time, had removed it from where it hung in his bedroom because it "gave him the creeps." Catherine took the portrait back to her home in Harlingen where she was then living with her Air Force husband and children.

As the years went by, Catherine and her family noticed little things that were a bit peculiar, but at first they did not attach any significance to them happening around the portrait. The events have become much more pronounced since Catherine bought the big old family home in La Marque from her parents, some years back. The Tudor house on an acre lot, shaded by giant oaks, is furnished with lovely family antiques, many of which once graced the childhood home of Elvie and her siblings. And then, of course, her portrait is there, hanging on the wall at the first landing of the staircase leading up to the second floor. Her spirit seems to be there, as well, its baili- wick centering around the staircase, the upstairs and downstairs halls, the entryway, the dining room, and the butler's pantry.

Many times, by day or night, definite sounds of footsteps are heard on the wooden stairs. Catherine said the first time her daugh- ter Nancy heard the footsteps she was alone in the house. She was so frightened that she telephoned her mother, who was at a meeting, to please come home at once, as she thought an intruder was some- where hiding in the house!

When all her children were still living at home, at night they sometimes saw what they thought was the shadowy form of a woman descending the stairs. There is a big window at the landing, and the walls of the house by the staircase are painted white, so a dark, shadowy form would be easy to see. At first the children thought it was their mother, but when they tiptoed to her bedroom, they found her fast asleep!

A few years ago, when Nancy was spending the night at her mother's home, she heard what she described as a "whispering" noise, and then she saw the dark form of a woman descending the stairs. She thought it was her mother, Catherine, taking one of her cats outside. Not really sleepy, she decided to get up and go have a visit with her mother. She was certainly surprised to find that it was not Catherine she had seen, or heard whispering, on the stairs. Her mother was sound asleep in her bedroom!

Nancy told me when she was just a small child, about seven or eight years old, she had a frightening experience which she has never forgotten. The family was living in Florida at the time. One night Nancy was restless and couldn't sleep. She got out of bed and went into the living room and lay down on the couch with the family pet, a big dog named Homer. She gazed up at the portrait of Elvie, which was hanging over the mantel. Imagine her shock as she saw the chest heaving up and down, as if the portrait were breathing, and then the lips started moving, as if she were speaking to Nancy. Nancy was so terrified she ran back to her bedroom, dragging the dog with her to sleep with her the rest of the night! She said it was a long time before she told her mother, as she was afraid no one would believe her, but she is convinced to this day that what she saw that night was real and neither a dream nor a figment of her imagination.

Catherine, who today lives alone in the big house, says she isn't afraid of Elvie, and indeed, rather enjoys having her spirit around. She does find it a bit annoying when the ghost plays childish pranks, probably to gain attention. We must remember, Elvie was barely fifteen when she died, and she had led an extremely sheltered life, in Victorian days, so she really was very much a child at the time she passed away.

To illustrate what Elvie's spirit will do to gain attention, Catherine said she often removes her red earrings when she talks on the telephone. When she takes them off, they usually disappear right away. They will always reappear a few days later, generally in the middle of the dining room table or in the butler's pantry. Also, her favorite sewing scissors frequently quit their usual spot in Catherine's sewing box, which is kept in the pantry. Sometimes they are gone for weeks at a time. Then they always reappear in the box after their sabbatical with Elvie.

Catherine showed us a dear little china tea set that belonged to Elvie. The saucers are in the shapes of faces of cats and dogs. It is displayed on an antique whatnot stand. Catherine often hears the clinking of the china dishes as Elvie rearranges the pieces of one of her beloved former possessions. After hearing this, Catherine often catches a brief glimpse of the bottom of a long white skirt flying up the stairs! She has never seen the full figure of Elvie. But Nancy has!

About two years ago, when she was visiting her mother, Nancy decided the carpet in the front entry hall needed vacuuming. She was busily at work when she chanced to glance upwards. There, in the upstairs hall, peering over the stair railing was a full-length figure of a young girl, smiling down at her. The face gazing at Nancy looked exactly like the face of the portrait, except she was smiling. The hair, which in the portrait is arranged in corkscrew curls, was brushed out loosely about the shoulders. The apparition wore a white gown which looked to be a peignoir or granny gown, instead of the lace-edged blouse of the portrait. Nancy stood staring at the figure for several seconds, utterly in shock at what she saw. She finally looked down at the floor. When she glanced up again, the figure had totally disappeared!

The figure Nancy saw was probably how Elvie looked at the time of her death. Her hair would not have been so carefully arranged in long curls during a long spell of sickness, and she would have probably been wearing a long nightgown, also. Nancy confessed that seeing Elvie so plainly was pretty frightening.

We had such a lovely visit with Catherine that we were sorry we could not have spent more time with her. Catherine is head of the English department at the high school in La Marque. She is quite contented there in her lovely big home with a trio of friendly cats, lots of friends, and frequent visits from her children, all grown up now. And of course, there is the sweet, playful spirit of Elvie to keep her company!

Spring's Haunted Saloon

Spring, Texas, is a small city a few miles north of Houston on Interstate Highway 45. The Harris County town was founded by German immigrants in 1840. But it wasn't until the early 1900s that the little town began to flourish. When the Great Northern Railroad came to town, a real building boom took place. Seven saloons and a number of small hotels sprang up, practically overnight, to accommodate the railroad workers and the travelers the rails would carry on this Galveston-Houston-Palestine line.

Jane and Carl Wunsche were children of some of the German immigrants who first settled Spring. Two of their sons, Charlie and Dell, who were former railroad men, acquired a piece of property near the railroad depot in what today is called Old Town Spring. Along with another brother, William, or "Willie," as he was called, they constructed a two-storied frame structure on the property. It was the very first two-storied building in Spring!

The new establishment, which opened for business in 1902, was named The Wunsche Bros. Saloon and Hotel. The main purpose of the new business was to accommodate railroad employees on overnight stopovers.

The town prospered, and so did the Wunsche brothers, until 1923, when Houston and Great Northern (now known as the Missouri Pacific) moved the Spring railyard to Houston. By 1926 most of the little town's wooden buildings had been torn down, the lumber salvaged for barn construction and firewood. Somehow the Wunsche establishment survived. The saloon was the last one to close in Harris County when Prohibition hit.

In 1949 a lady named Viola Burke leased the building, renaming it the Spring Cafe. She was known for her delicious homemade hamburgers which the railroad workers passing through town delighted in ordering. In fact, word of her wonderful burgers spread far and wide, and soon the cafe had the reputation of having the best hamburgers anywhere in the country! When Viola died in 1976, her daughter, Irma Ansley, inherited the business and continued making the famous hamburgers.

In fact, the entire shopping village of Old Town Spring traces its origins back to the famous hamburgers! Back in the 1970s, just getting one of the burgers required a long wait, because all were made to order. Sensing a good opportunity, an enterprising couple opened a gift shop for cafe customers to shop and browse in while they waited for a table. Slowly, more and more houses and buildings were converted into shops, until quite a variety of gifts, crafts, antiques, and works of art were made available to the cafe patrons.

As Old Town began to flourish, the little cafe that helped to bring about its birth was going downhill. Finally, the building, now quite dilapidated, was sold in 1982 to an enterprising couple, Brenda and Scott Mitchell. The old building was carefully restored by Scott, a Woodlands builder, and his wife. Today, the building, which bears a Texas Historic Landmark plaque, is a popular restaurant. Staying in tune with its pioneer heritage, the Mitchells call the place, The Wunsche Bros. Cafe and Saloon. (It's no longer a hotel, so don't plan an overnight stay!) From the looks of the menu and a delightful cookbook entitled *The Wunsche Bros. Cafe Cookbook*, written by owner Brenda Greene Mitchell and offered for sale at the cafe, there are plenty of good viands available at Wunsche Bros. including the famous made-to-order hamburgers.

In addition to great food, there's also a ghost! Well, maybe more than one; the owners aren't really sure. Telephone interviews with Brenda Mitchell, who now resides in Austin; her current manager, Sherry Sinini; and former employees Alma Lemm and Ilona Langlinais all indicate that Charlie (they're pretty sure that he's the "haunting brother") still comes around to check up on things at the place.

Lemm, a cook who retired a few years ago, is now in her seventies. She loved working for the Mitchells and it was only on doctor's orders that she finally hung up her apron. She said in about 1988 (she recalled it was in the fall of the year) she had a real shock when she went to the linen closet to get a hand towel and heard the unmistakable sound of a man's voice. "It was sort of mumbling. I couldn't understand the words he said but I definitely did hear a voice," she said. She was so startled that she shut the closet door and scurried to the kitchen to tell a fellow worker what she'd heard. She says now she wishes she had had the presence of mind to ask it what it wanted. This was the first time she heard a voice, but there were a lot of unexplained occurrences all during the time she worked at the cafe.

Wunsche Bros. Cafe and Saloon, Spring, Texas
(photo courtesy of Donna Brown of "Portrait Copyint")

Lemm said she and Gladys Barton, another employee, were in the habit of having a cup of coffee together early in the morning to kind of "get going." The tables in the cafe had candles on them that were lit each evening for the dinner hour. They were always extinguished when the last patron had departed. But on Saturday mornings, Lemm and Barton kept finding one candle lit when they opened up the restaurant. Each Saturday the lit candle would be on a

table closer and closer to where they customarily sat for their morning coffee visit. When the candle finally "arrived" one Saturday and
was glowing on their table, it never came again. There is no possible
explanation except that Charlie finally had a silent Saturday morning
visit with them!

Back in 1989 and 1990 the ghost was more active than he is now.
Lemm said every time a new manager came in there would be quite
a bit of unexplained activity. (This is not unusual. Ghosts dislike
change, and until Charlie was reasonably sure the managers were
doing things that met with his approval, he would naturally have
become more agitated.) Sometimes when she came in early, about 5
A.M., Lemm said, the chairs would "rattle and move about quite a
bit."

When she first went to work at the cafe, an upstairs room in the
section that had been part of the old hotel was rented out to a young
man who was an artist, according to Lemm. One morning when he
came downstairs, he asked the cooks if they knew something
strange was going on. They told him, yes, indeed they did.

Soon after this, a former waitress with whom I also spoke, Ilona
Langlinais, actually saw the ghost! The young artist who lived
upstairs was able to draw a sketch of him from her accurate description. Langlinais said one October day in 1984, around 9 a.m., she was
in the upstairs section, which in those days was used as a dining area
to accommodate the overflow from downstairs. She had just made a
fresh pot of coffee and was carrying it down the hallway. Langlinais
was startled when she glanced into a room off the hallway and saw
an elderly man seated at a table. Although he had his back to her, she
could see he had longish white hair, worn over the collar, and he had
on a tall-crowned black hat and a black suit. He was sitting sort of
hunched over at the table, and to her he looked dejected, just from
the way he was sitting. Langlinais said a feeling of great sadness suddenly came over her as she saw him there. She thought a cup of
coffee might be just what he needed, so she asked, "Would you like a
hot cup of coffee?" As she spoke, she said, a gust of wind hit her with
a tremendous "whoosh!" and at the same instant, the man she had
seen so plainly literally vanished in front of her eyes!

After she spoke to the figure, whom she feels might have been the spirit of one of the Wunsche brothers, she said she never again felt or heard anything strange at the restaurant. She believes the spirit left... at least during the rest of the time she worked there. She was glad, because she said seeing the figure, then having it disappear so suddenly, definitely gave her a good case of the "heebie jeebies."

Several waitresses reported that salt and pepper shakers and sugar packets used to be scattered all about the tables and on the floor when they would open up in the mornings. And pictures on the walls of members of the Wunsche family would often be crooked as if intentionally rearranged. No other pictures were ever touched, just the Wunsche likenesses.

Owner Brenda Mitchell says she has never seen or heard the ghost, but she believes in the veracity of her employees and therefore acknowledges the existence of a ghost at her restaurant. The place is very busy these days, with the restaurant operating on the ground floor and a successful gourmet food mail order business operating out of the former hotel rooms on the upper floor.

Why don't you drop by the Wunsche Bros. Cafe and Saloon next time you're in Spring? You might not run into Charlie, but the homemade hamburgers are worth the trip anyway!

Joe Lee Never Left Nederland

When I first began this book project, I sent out letters to numerous South Texas newspapers, hopeful they would run an article about my project and that people who had a "ghostly encounter" to share would contact me about their personal experiences.

I was not disappointed. Many people who had previously kept secret their encounters with the supernatural did contact me. I believe they were relieved to at last talk about what they had experienced, having found someone who would believe them and not question either their veracity or their sanity.

One such person is Anne Malinowsky Blackwell, of Nederland, a small town midway between Port Arthur and Beaumont. We have been in contact by mail and telephone for the past year. Her story is most interesting, and heretofore, unknown and unpublished.

Ms. Blackwell stated in her first letter to me, dated March 5, 1993, "Your letter caught my attention because six years ago I bought a house in Nederland that was built around 1922. I knew nothing about its history nor did I believe in ghosts prior to living here. After several years of strange occurrences that were totally inexplicable, I have accepted the fact that there is a ghost in my house. In fact, when I finally met a descendant of the man that built the house my first question to her was 'Who died in this house?' 'My grandfather,' she replied, 'on New Year's Eve on the stroke of midnight.' "

In another letter, in which Ms. Blackwell enclosed a photo of her home, she stated, "I've also included background information on me so you'll know I'm not a lunatic (at least not yet!). Actually, I'm the least suitable person I know of to be haunted. Certainly, if you find this of interest, you have my permission to use my Ghost Story, and my name if you wish. Maybe, with some exposure, we can find someone who appreciates him. I certainly don't!"

Nederland house built around 1922 by Joe Lee at 1616 Elgin Street

Anne Malinowsky Blackwell is indeed a fascinating and accomplished lady. The personal photograph she enclosed in one of her letters also shows her to be as beautiful as she is "brainy." In fact, her brunette good looks would certainly border on "extremely glamorous" in finding words to describe her appearance. The owner of Maco Construction Company, Blackwell was the first female contractor in Southeast Texas, the first female to be licensed as a civil contractor by the state of Louisiana, the first female contractor to perform underground construction for United States Environmental Protection Agency projects, and the first female contractor to be utilized on United States Department of Energy projects. Well qualified as an independent construction consultant, she has testified in numerous cases in state and federal courts and has been sought by a variety of federal agencies, senate committees, and the EPA, which have incorporated many of her suggestions in their regulations. She is a member of Sigma Lamda Chi, the National Construction Honors Society, the Southeast Texas' Women's Hall of Fame, received the Jefferson Award for Public Service, Avon's Women of Enterprise Award, Female Entrepreneur of the Year, and holds membership in the National Association of Female Executives. Her honors, accomplishments, and educational background fill two single-spaced typewritten pages!

This lady, to use her own words, is definitely "no lunatic." And therefore her story is to be believed, just as she wrote it to me, in her own words:

I heard about the house in Nederland months before I ever saw it. I had lived in Beaumont or Port Arthur for most of my life and for the past seven years had resided in Louisiana. I had made frequent trips back to Southeast Texas, where I also had a business.

In 1986, I realized it was time to move back to Texas. Since I owned a second home, a townhouse, in Port Arthur, I didn't really need another house, but became intrigued by the house in Nederland that two of my employees frequently discussed between them. This house, I heard, had formerly been a run-down shack that someone had bought and spent several years remodeling. Now it was for sale. The more I heard about the house, the more I realized it sounded "like me." Finally, I asked for directions, and found it. It was exactly right for me. Not large ... two bedrooms when I bought it (one's now my home office), a small formal living room, and a very large, open kitchen-den area with lots of windows giving an almost "beach house" effect.

It sat on two lots that were covered with huge live oak and pecan trees. The old, quiet neighborhood suited me very well. I live alone and like my privacy. There was even a dog pen for my beloved "Beaux," who I had acquired in Louisiana earlier that year. I bought the house at 1616 Elgin and moved in that October of 1986.

I knew little about the house's history beyond the prior owners, a young couple who only lived there three or four years before divorcing. It had been built around 1922 by a man named Joe Lee. It was empty for many years prior to being remodeled in the early 1980s. There's not much more I know about its history now, except that Joe Lee died here of a heart attack on a long-ago New Year's Eve, just at the stroke of midnight. He was survived by a wife, who was, according to his granddaughter, a "witch" (what kind, I don't know, and I don't even know what became of her). But somewhere between learning that Joe Lee built the house and that Joe Lee died in this house, I have come to believe that Joe Lee has not ever left this house.

For the first year and a half that we lived here, Beaux and I were quite content in our home. My only complaint was a shortage of closet space in my bedroom. It finally occurred to me by taking out the folding door closet that ran along the bedroom's east wall (the wall between the bedroom and the kitchen) and building a walk-in closet off the north wall (the back of the house) I could increase the size of my bedroom and my closet space. Since I am a contractor, it was a simple matter of bringing my carpentry crew in and lining them up.

First, we built the addition onto, but not yet accessible to, the bedroom. Then we took down the wall of folding closet doors and finished the former closet's interior. After a week or so of work, we were ready to cut a doorway through the north bedroom wall into the new closet. The carpenters pulled my bed out to the middle of the room in preparation, with Beaux's dog bed a few feet away from the right side, as usual. That night, actually about 2 A.M., I was jarred out of a deep sleep by a violent shaking of my bed. Beaux and I jumped up at the same time. For a minute we just stood there, stunned. I fully expected a "boom!" The last time I'd experienced such a tremor was during my childhood when the Texas City refineries blew up! There was no sound to follow. Beaux laid back down. I stayed up, looking out the windows for the glow of a fire from one of the Port Arthur refineries. There was nothing but darkness outside.

The next few days I asked everyone I encountered if they had felt any sort of tremor that night. No one had. Meanwhile, the carpenters finished the doorway and moved the bed to the east wall. We looked over the bed, the floor, and even under the house for any clue to what had caused the bed to shake. There was simply nothing to explain the event. After a week or two, I decided it was just some sort of a freak one-time occurrence.

And then it happened again . . . and again . . . and again! Just about every week, and sometimes twice a week, the bed would suddenly start shaking violently for five to fifteen or so seconds. I literally tore the house apart trying to find a reason, any reason. There was none. Eventually I realized that it wasn't the house shaking, for never did glass rattle or pictures shift during these occurrences. I started sleeping (when I slept at all) with one eye open and the lights on. But I never saw a thing. Beaux, after the first time or two, slept through the rest, just a few feet away, undisturbed. Not me! After four months, I was a wreck. The bed-shakings were now occurring two to three times a week, happening most often right after I fell asleep, no matter what time of night. I continued to explore every possibility with no results. Finally, I simply left the house for two weeks.

When I came back, things eased up somewhat. The bed-shakings now were only happening two or three times a month, then once, or twice. By fall of 1989 I had acquired a second dog, a female named Char, and it seemed as though the bed-shakings lessened in frequency when she started sleeping at the foot of my bed, under a bench I have there.

After a few months of relative peace, a new and terrifying event took place. I was in bed watching TV. The lights were on and both dogs were asleep. Suddenly, something hit the side of the bed, eight times in succession. It was like a giant fist hit the side of my mattress! I had time to sit straight up and clearly look in all directions while the bed jumped from the invisible blows. There was absolutely nothing to see. That was sometime in 1990. The bed wasn't "touched" by unseen hands again. But I was.

One night about a year after the eight "bed-thumps" I was lying crossways across the bed on my stomach, reading. Suddenly, someone tapped me on the shoulder . . . hard! I leapt up in absolute terror prepared to face an intruder. I was even more terrified to see no one there.

Last year, I was again in bed, reading, wide awake. I was sitting, my back against the pillows and my hair had fallen over my forehead, almost in my eyes. Gently, very gently, something lifted my hair off my forehead and brushed it back into place. I froze for a second and when I finally got the courage to lift my eyes I saw, for just about two or three seconds, a faint, white mist. That is the only time I have seen anything. Occasionally there is a loud thump or crash that I can't explain. Then, again, there are those I can explain.

The most awesome event took place in the living room. The previous owners had installed brass wall sconces with glass chimneys on each side of the fireplace. I had inspected these very closely to see if they could be moved, but found that they were each held by two sturdy screws through the sheetrock into the solid wood wall behind. One day, the dogs and I were outside when I heard an enormous crash in the house. I ran inside to find one of the sconces on the floor, with glass everywhere. I couldn't believe my eyes. There was no way it could have simply come out of the wall. I looked at the wall. If the sconce had fallen downward, the bottom hole through the sheetrock should have been elongated by the screw pulling loose. But it was the top hole that was elongated, upward! The sconce had been pulled upward, and out, by some tremendous force!

Then there was the night I came home to find no hot water at any faucet in the house. But when I checked my gas water heater it was running fine. I called several people, including a plumber, and no one could give me any possible reason. After making arrangements for the plumber to come out the next morning, I shut the hot water heater completely off, figuring something had to be wrong with it. Two hours later, I went to the kitchen to fill a pot to heat water to wash up in, and the instant I turned the faucet on, hot water came out! The plumber found nothing wrong. There was no possible explanation!

The most recent incident happened only a week or two ago. [Note: This would have been in March 1993.] The dogs and I (I'm up to three now) were in the den one evening when I heard a crash in the bedroom. I ran in to find a heavy, nearly solid crystal perfume bottle smashed on the carpeted floor. This bottle had been on a tray on my dresser surrounded by a dozen or so smaller, more fragile perfume bottles. But all the other bottles still sat undisturbed. I cannot possibly explain how one bottle in the middle had fallen, or how such a sturdy bottle could shatter on . . . thick carpet. Actually, I can't explain any of this.

Char, my female dog, now weighs fifty pounds, about the same as Beaux. She sometimes wakes me up in the morning by jumping up on my bed. And a fifty-pound dog jumping on my bed does not shake it with near the force of the unexplained bed shakings.

While the dogs don't appear to sense anything, there have been many times one of them, usually Beaux, has suddenly yelped, jumped, and slunk away to hide in a corner and look at me with hurt eyes, as if to say, "Why did you hit me?

The bed-shakings seemed to have stopped about the time that Joe Lee's granddaughter visited. When I told her about all my incidents she did not seem at all surprised. She simply nodded and said "Paw-paw's still here. You need to tell him to either behave himself or leave." I did. And at least I can get a decent night's sleep now.

The only pattern I have been able to think of is that the events have happened after men were in my house. The bed-shakings started while the carpenters were here; the wall sconce crashed the day after a party, the perfume bottle fell after a young man had dog-sat for me for a week.

As I said, I don't "believe in" spirits. I don't talk about this often because people often act like they expect me to try to convince them there are such things. I've found it's not a matter of believing or convincing. It's simply a matter of realizing and finally accepting the fact that Joe Lee (or someone else) lives with me at 1616 Elgin in some form or another. I don't like it, and I don't want it. But, whoever, or whatever, it is here.

The Mysterious House at Browndell

An article that ran in the Jasper, Texas, *News Boy* just before Halloween in late October 1993 interested me enough to do some investigating. It was written by Diane Cox, managing editor of the paper, and was sent to me by my sister-in-law, Juanita Williams, who used to live in Jasper.

On a recent trip to visit in that interesting and pretty old town, I managed to meet with Diane, and she took me to see her house, which she wrote about in her story.

The old Browndell Community, some thirteen miles north of Jasper, was once a well-established mill town, consisting of 143 buildings. There were houses for the mill workers, a post office, general store, depot, and various other buildings. The town was built by the Kirby Lumber Company. In 1903 they built a large house for the mill manager and his family. The sawmill eventually burned down and was rebuilt. The mill burned a second time, and this time the company did not rebuild. The community rapidly dissolved as workers had to move elsewhere to seek other employment. Today only the mill manager's house remains, although a sign on the highway still states it's the "Browndell Community."

The old house, which originally consisted of two large rooms located on either side of an open gallery, or "dog trot," has changed hands, and appearance, numerous times in its long and rather colorful history.

The Walker family purchased the place in 1928. It was used, over the years, for various purposes: as a residence, a rental property, a hotel, a rooming house, and even for a time, standing unoccupied, was used as a place to store hay! The house finally underwent extensive remodeling and restoration in 1965.

Today, the rambling structure sports a new tin roof, which has replaced the original. The "dog trot" has been sealed in, becoming a long and spacious central entry hall. A large kitchen, a laundry room, and a bathroom were also added during the restoration period, as was a large carport at the side of the house.

Mill manager's house built in old Browndell community by Kirby Lumber Company in 1903

Diane Cox, who is the present owner, is an interesting story-teller and a talented artist as well. The old house is filled with her paintings, mostly beautiful landscapes and still lifes. Cox says many people in the Jasper area lived in, or visited, the old house at one time or another, and it was the scene of many memorable, and some-times turbulent, events. She feels there is a lot of "energy" attached to the house and the land where it is situated.

By 1974 Claude and Sybil Walker were the owners of the place. They also owned and operated the Browndell Liquor Store on High-way 96. It probably did very well, because Jasper, the nearest town of any size, was "dry." According to Mrs. Cox, Claude Walker came home one Saturday night with the day's receipts in his pocket. As he climbed the steps from the carport and entered the house through the laundry room, an assailant (or perhaps more than one) awaited him in the dark laundry room, armed with one of Walkers' shotguns taken from the house. Walker was apparently first struck with the butt of his own shotgun, then brutally shot several times with the weapon. His wife, Sybil, arrived home a little later and was shocked to find her husband lying mortally wounded in a pool of blood on the floor. (Police reports later noted it took every sheet they could find in the house to mop up the blood.) Although Mr. Walker was still alive when the ambulance arrived, he died en route to the hospital. Even today, twenty years later, one of the square white acoustical tiles on the ceiling bears deep brown stains, bloodstains, dating from the night of the murder. Mrs. Cox did not offer any explanation why she had not replaced the gruesome reminder of the tragedy.

The police later discovered Walker's wallet lying on the Highway 96 right-of-way, where it had been tossed aside after being emptied by the perpetrators of the crime. Several firearms were also missing from the Walker house. The killer, or killers, have never been brought to justice, and the unsolved crime still remains on the Jasper County criminal records. The murderer must have known Claude Walker and his custom of carrying large sums of money late at night as he made his way home from the liquor store. Because the house was in a remote area and the people in the area all knew their neighbors, the Walkers probably left their house unlocked. This would have made it easy for the assailant to enter the place prior to Walker's arrival.

Soon after her husband's brutal murder, Sybil Walker decided to sell the property. Fearing another attack, she was terrified to remain alone in the rambling country place. The Coxes, who came to Jasper from Alabama, purchased the house and the sixteen adjoining acres from her.

Diane Cox vividly recalls the first Halloween night she spent alone in the old house. It was 1976. Her three teenage children were in town attending a football game, her husband was away on business, and she was all alone. She made herself a cup of hot cocoa and sat in her kitchen, trying not to think too much about the heinous murder that had taken place in the laundry room adjacent to the kitchen where she now sat.

Just to make sure all was well, she timidly peeked into the room. As she stated in the article which first touched off my interest in the house, "The hair stood up on my arms, just recalling what had happened in that room. Although I was terribly frightened, there was nothing there, and I breathed a sigh of relief."

Then Diane heard a ghostly wail . . . an "Oooooooh" sound that really got her imagination going. She first thought it might be her three youngsters just trying to give her a good Halloween scare! The sound was repeated several times. Finally, when the young people arrived home she accused them of standing outside and making weird noises to frighten her. They assured her they had just that minute arrived home, and to back up that claim, they all heard the same mournful moan as they stood together in the living room!

Several times during the next few weeks the sound was heard again, always at night. Cox became increasingly nervous whenever she was in the house alone.

Then, about three weeks after the strange noises began, Mrs. Walker, from whom the Coxes had purchased the house, called Diane to say she hoped that she wasn't afraid, but their old "yeller dog" kept running back to his old home. Anytime the hound would hear a train whistle or a siren off in the distance, he'd start to howl. Mrs. Walker said she'd gone to bring him back home several times in the daytime, when the Coxes were all away, but she still had trouble keeping him home at night. This explained the "Oooooooh" sound that had slowly been driving Diane up the walls for nearly a month!

At least that problem was solved. But Diane says there are other strange things that keep happening in the old house. The children are all grown and gone now. Mr. Cox has passed away, and Diane lives there all alone, except for two very large dogs that I'd hate to tangle with.

Diane says there are several "cold spots" in the living room, with a "magnetic place" in the air, that makes the hair stand up on her arms and the skin prickle. Lights go on and off at will, and then there are the "voices" which are heard, engaged in nocturnal conversations in various parts of the house.

Several years ago, Diane decided to have what she called a seance to try and learn more about the house in which she lives alone. A gentleman named Ray Nevels from the nearby community of Brookeland whom she variously described as an herbalist, an Indian shaman or healer, and a hypnotist, was invited to come and help her make contact with the spirit world. Besides Diane, her mother and stepfather and a lady friend were present. The hypnotist succeeded in placing Diane into a hypnotic trance. While "out," she said she distinctly saw a young woman who looked to be in her early thirties standing in the kitchen in front of an old wood stove, which is no longer there. She wore a long dress with an apron. Diane said the dress was in a geometric type print that was popular back in the 1920s. The woman also had a hair style that dated to that era. Diane said she recalled the apron had a bib front and was safety-pinned to the bodice of the dress she wore. A toddler, no more than about two years old and still in diapers, was hanging on to her skirts. The woman was stirring something up in a big mixing bowl, and Diane distinctly felt that she was making a birthday cake! Diane also had the name, "Rini," come to her while in the trance-like state.

Then, Diane said, she suddenly felt she was in the laundry room and had "become" the victim of the Walker crime. She said she "saw" and "felt" the awful murder that had taken place there. She said she could actually feel the bullets as they entered her body! And she experienced a terrible fear, just as Mr. Walker must have felt, on that last night in his life. She said she then snapped out of the trance, but the memories of that evening still remain fresh in her mind.

A couple of years after the seance, or psychic experience, Diane met a lady whose husband's grandmother had once lived in the house. She described her vision to her and also asked her if the name "Rini" meant anything to any of her family. The woman's husband said, "Why, Rini was a close friend of my grandmother's," but he had not heard her name mentioned in many years!

Diane said she also once had a distinct vision of a group of men, probably sawmill workers, engaged in an animated conversation on the back porch of the house. (The porch is no longer there. It was altered to make room for a bathroom.) It must have been a hot evening, as the men were shirtless, wearing just their customary work overalls.

To this day, Diane says, often when she is reading in her front living room she suddenly hears a lively conversation "like a party going on," in the kitchen, or when she's in the kitchen, the same sounds emanate from the living room! She does not find these "otherworldly" conversations particularly frightening. By now she seems to take them for granted.

Those two big dogs that live with Diane won't go into the central hallway (which used to be the open "dog trot") after dark. And her brother absolutely refuses to remain in the house at all after the sun goes down. Diane herself admits she always reaches around the corner and flips on the light switch before entering a darkened room. However, she is not particularly uncomfortable about living alone in the mysterious old house. She says she's trying to take good care of the place, and she calls herself a "caretaker." She has a theory that "they" don't threaten "caretakers."

It's an interesting house. And Diane Cox is an interesting lady ... and pretty brave, too, in my opinion.

West Texas Plains

West Texas, with its rich heritage of pioneer settlers, cowboys, bands of Indians, soldiers who served at the cavalry posts, and Spanish speaking explorers who roamed the high plains, has its ghost stories. They are fascinating reminders of the glorious days when the West was won at the sacrifice of many lives. Spirits not quite done with what they set out to do keep returning. Haunting the high mesas and rolling plains, these departed souls seem gripped with a purpose not realized in life. Whether they linger to protect, seek revenge, or complete a task, these "spirits" appear doomed to an elusive world between the living and the dead.

PHANTOMS OF THE PLAINS

Over broad and rolling prairies
'Cross the dry and dusty plains
Souls of men from days gone by
In phantom state remain.
On nights so still and lonely,
In the moon glow's yellow light,
Their earthbound spirits wander
In the stillness of the night.
On steep and rocky hillsides,
And on dusty plains they roam,
Those spirits that refuse to leave
The place they once called home.

Docia Williams

It's a Mystery

I often wonder why there are so many stories connected with hauntings at the West Texas forts that were built to protect the early settlers from Indian depredations!

Life was terribly hard in those far-flung outposts, designed to protect the settlers as they steadily moved westward. The soldiers stationed at them often had to live in crude tent shelters while they struggled to build more permanent facilities. All the while they were doing this, they also rode patrols, fought Indians, planted gardens, and traveled long distances for supplies.

They suffered miserable weather conditions, too. The West Texas summers were blistering hot. Dry winds brought dust storms and dried up the streams. The gardens they planted died from lack of water. And then, when the winters came, the days were freezing cold. Often there was no wood for fires. Blizzards blew down from the Rocky Mountains, covering the rustic little forts with blankets of snow. Poor diets resulted in cases of scurvy, and many soldiers suffered from malnutrition. Many of the soldiers died from fighting Indians, from disease, from snakebites, and from numerous accidents. For the most part, these men were young, and they should have enjoyed many more good years. The army wives who followed their husbands suffered right along with the men. And many of them also died in childbirth or of disease and hardship.

According to reliable sources quoted in the individual stories, there are numerous accounts of ghosts and hauntings connected with the old West Texas forts. With such miserable surroundings and living conditions, it's a mystery to me why anybody, even in spirit form, would want to continue hanging around those lonely, desolate ruins out on the West Texas plains.

The Army Left, But the Spirits Remain

Fort Clark, near the town of Brackettville on Highway 90, west of Uvalde, was founded as a cavalry post in 1852. It had a long and colorful history, and the sturdy limestone buildings that formed the main section of the installation are now a part of the Fort Clark Springs Resort, a private retirement and recreation community.

Back in its beginnings, like so many other West Texas forts, this one was established here because of the plentiful water supply. There were natural springs here, called "Las Moras" for the mulberry trees that grew around it, and it was a favorite campground of the Comanches and the Mescalero and Lipan Apache tribes. It was an ideal place to locate a fort, as a plentiful supply of building stone was available, and there were also plenty of pecan and oak trees in the area.

Major Joseph H. LaMotte was in charge of establishing the fort. Companies C and E first encamped near the springs, and later the complete garrison was moved up the hill a short distance from the springs. By 1853 the soldiers' quarters were completed, and in 1854 three grass-covered officers' quarters were added. Finally, a stone hospital and a two-story storehouse were erected in 1855.

At first, all the supplies had to be brought in by wagon train from Corpus Christi, a thirty-day trip! Later on, supplies were brought in to Indianola (a seaport that is no longer on the Gulf Coast) and from there, transported by wagon to the fort by way of San Antonio, still about a thirty-day journey.

According to a pamphlet prepared by the Fort Clark Historical Society (copyright, 1985) of Kinney County, the Federal soldiers departed from the fort on March 19, 1862. The Second Texas Mounted Rifles moved in and stayed there until August of 1862.

Then the fort served as a supply depot and a hospital for Confederate troops as well as civilians who lived in the surrounding area.

Although the post headquarters had been built in 1857, prior to the Civil War, most of the area referred to today as the Historic District was built between 1870 and 1875 after the Federal army returned. By 1874 the installation had quarters for 200 men and nine officer's dwellings. All of these were of stone. A second storehouse known as the "old commissary" and a granary capable of storing 3,000 bushels of grain was built in 1882. During the major construction period (1874) 104 civilian stone masons were employed! Most of the stone was quarried there on the fort property, but some was brought in by wagon from other locales. This was because the quarry at the fort did not provide the best quality of building stone.

Up until about 1881, when the last Indian depredations ceased, the fort was a busy place. Lt. John L. Bullis, who later became a famous general, served as commander for the famous Seminole-Negro Indian Scouts who were stationed there. Later on, Colonel Ranald S. Mackenzie's raiders were stationed at the fort. Their mission was to lead raids into Mexico punishing renegade Indians. During this era, Comanches came down from the north on their famous "Comanche moonlight" raids, raiding, killing, raping, taking horses and cattle, then escaping across the Rio Grande into Mexico where they continued to kill and plunder. The Lipan Apaches and Kickapoos from Mexico came over the border on raids, killing and stealing and causing general havoc. Outlaws fled from one side of the border to the other, and the pioneer settlers lived in a state of upheaval and general terror. Many abandoned their homes. On May 17, 1873, Mackenzie's men and Bullis' Seminole-Negro scouts led troops of the 4th U.S. Cavalry into Mexico on a punitive expedition against the Lipans. Finally, in 1878 a large peacetime army crossed the border and effectively stopped the Mexican-Indian hostilities forever.

During its heyday, the old fort was home to many famous military personalities, including General Wesley Merritt, Commander of the Philippine Expedition; General William R. Shafter, Commander of the Cuba Expedition; General George C. Marshall, U.S. Chief of Staff during World War II; General Jonathan M. Wainwright, hero of

Bataan and Corregidor; and General George S. Patton Jr., famous for his daring exploits in North Africa, Sicily, and from France into Germany during World War II.

The last mounted Cavalry Division, the Second Cavalry, trained at Fort Clark until its 12,000 troops were deployed in February of 1944. During the war, there was also a German prisoner of war sub-camp located on the 4,000-acre reservation.

Unlike many of the West Texas forts, whose careers were short-lived, Fort Clark lasted until June of 1944. In 1946 the property was sold to Brown and Root Company for salvage. Later it was used as a guest ranch. Finally, in 1971 it was purchased by a private corporation and developed into a recreational community. A large golf course, tree-shaded picnic areas, an amphitheater in the old rock quarry, and a beautiful swimming pool fed by the springs make the place a peaceful and idyllic spot for retirement. And, some of the old residents must have been reluctant to let go.

Many of the quarters along old Colony Row are large two-story two-family buildings, which were used by the officers stationed at the fort. My friend Barbara Niemann owned one of these, at Number 11. She has moved back to San Antonio, and the house was sold. Much work was done to restore the old set of quarters, and it is a lovely and spacious two-story duplex with a beautiful garden. During the time Barbara lived there, she experienced the presence of a benevolent, friendly spirit, whom she believes was a man, probably an old soldier who had once lived in the house. Perhaps he was an orderly, assigned to some officer's family, as was often the custom in early days. Barbara often awakened in the wee hours of the mornings to the strong aroma of fresh coffee brewing and bacon frying! The Niemanns did not drink coffee and made it only when they had houseguests. Especially around the kitchen area, Barbara felt someone was there many times. Once she heard a deep sigh, and of course, no one was there but her! For some reason, she refers to the spirit as "John," but really can't say why she chose that name for him. She also told me that often, Bucky, her big Doberman, would suddenly prick up his ears and look alertly around the room as if he had seen someone go by, but he never seemed disturbed or upset.

Quarters 10 and 11, Old Fort Clark

Barbara introduced me to Georgia and Pete Cook, who lived a couple of doors down Colony Row at number 8-9. This is a large one-story set of quarters. They quite freely admit to having had a resident spirit, or maybe more than one.

Pete Cook said the reason he decided to buy the house when it came up for sale was because it had once been in his family, when an aunt by marriage, Ollabelle Dahlstrom, had owned it. The house changed hands a couple of times, belonging first to Tully Pratt and then to A.J. Foyt, the race car driver. When Foyt decided to sell, Pete was delighted, although Georgia did not at first share his enthusiasm. She was quite happy in her lovely home in Hunt, Texas, up in the Hill Country near Kerrville.

Georgia believes their live-in spirit might have been Ollabelle Dahlstrom, rather than an early army wife who might have once lived there. Several times she had cause to believe it's Ollabelle, but whether it is she or another, Georgia definitely thinks the ghost is of the female gender.

Soon after the Cooks moved into the quarters, while Georgia was lying on the floor shoving boxes under a high four-poster tester bed in the guest room, someone grabbed her leg and tugged it hard. Thinking it was Pete or one of the relatives who was assisting them in getting settled, she said, "Oh stop that!" only to discover no one had been in the room with her when it happened.

Georgia told me that in the 1960s, Pete's cousin, Nina Dahlstrom, and several ladies in the family were there at the house spending the weekend. This must have been during the time Ollabelle owned the house. Well, Nina and her mother occupied the master bedroom. At the time, Nina's son Graham was just a baby, less than a year old. The infant was sleeping in a bassinet near the fireplace. During the night, Nina was awakened by a tug on her arm. Then she heard a baby crying. She got up to check on her little son and found that the baby was sound asleep. She went back to bed. Then, a little later on she was awakened by the sounds of a woman crying. She heard her say, "Help me! Help me! Help my baby!" and it was then she saw the apparition of a young woman with her arms outstretched to her, as if imploring her to come and help her. While the woman's appearance was rather misty, it was definitely a woman's figure. Of course, she woke up her mother when this upsetting event took place.

The only explanation they had for this strange encounter with the spirit world was that perhaps a former resident of the house, an army wife who once lived there, might have had a very sick infant who needed help. Maybe her baby had died there before she could get help, and the coming of a small infant in the person of Nina's little son, Graham, had triggered the appearance.

Georgia said the Dahlstroms also told them of a time in the late 1960s when they entertained several couples at a weekend house party. One young couple from Houston occupied the family room, sleeping on couches that made into twin beds. Because it was a very cold night, they moved their beds up close to the fireplace. In the middle of the night, the young man's bed began to shake violently. In fact, it actually raised up off the floor, going up and down, shaking all the while. At first he thought his wife might be playing a joke on him, but then he glanced over and found she was asleep in her own bed. She was expecting a baby, and the young husband was so terrified that whatever it was would affect their unborn child, he insisted they leave early the next morning. Georgia said the couple absolutely refused to ever come back for another visit!

When the Cooks moved in, they had a lot of things happen that defy explanation. Pictures moved about, and Georgia's jewelry often moved around, was missing a few days, and then appeared on the dresser or back in the jewelry box where it was kept.

One of the strangest things that happened, soon after they moved in, concerned a bottle of brandy! Since Ollabelle liked to party, they believe this was in keeping with her character. It seems they had a couple of bottles of brandy on the bar, but neither had been opened. Yet, one day they found a brandy snifter on the bar with about a jigger of brandy left in the glass. There were no unsealed bottles of brandy anywhere in the house. Who poured the brandy, and from what? And plainly seen on the rim of the glass were little dainty lip prints, doll-sized prints as Pete described them. The next night someone, or something, again set out a brandy snifter on the bar and set the two unopened bottles of brandy on the bar beside it, removing them from the sideboard behind the bar. They have yet to find any plausible explanation.

Cook's Quarters, Old Fort Clark

Often Georgia and Pete smelled bacon cooking, usually in the wee hours of the morning, when it was still dark. Once, Georgia woke up after Pete had already left for the day. When she came out to the kitchen to get some coffee, she saw some sausage patties that had been in the refrigerator had been cooked. Several of them were on a plate by the stove, and there was grease in the skillet where they had been prepared. Although she found it unusual, she figured Pete had been hungry, found the sausages in the refrigerator, and decided to cook them for breakfast. She went on and ate some of the cooked meat. When Pete came home later she told him she had eaten the sausage patties and they surely were delicious. He said, "But I didn't cook any sausage." In fact, Pete had seen the sausage there when he got up and thought how strange it was that Georgia had gotten up in the night and cooked sausage! To this day the Cooks can't figure out how that meat got cooked, unless, of course, it was their ghost!

The Cooks took me over to visit with Joy and Russell Williams, who live in the other side of Barbara Niemann's former quarters, at number 10 Colony Row. The former Houston residents told us that they have often been awakened in the wee hours of the morning by the strong smell of coffee brewing and bacon and eggs cooking. Usually this is around 4 A.M. (Just about the time the old army folks would have been getting up for the day!) Joy told me that there's a metal candleholder that hangs as a decorative fixture on the kitchen wall. Sometimes something pulls it off the wall and throws it on the floor. Most of the time the frame is bent and must be straightened out. Yet, the nail on which it hangs has always remained in place on the wall, indicating the piece was removed and did not just fall off the wall.

Joy told me that soon after they purchased their retirement home, she spent some time alone in the house while Russell was winding up their affairs in Houston. One night she was awakened by their little dog, who sleeps on their bed. It was very agitated, growling and barking like something was there in the room with them. She reached over to nudge Russell and then realized he was not there. She said the dog has been visibly disturbed by something in the room several times.

On a recent visit to see the Cooks before they moved, we also walked over to Barbara Niemann's former home, which was empty. The Cooks had the key in order to show it to prospective buyers for Barbara. As soon as we headed toward the kitchen at the rear of the quarters, we were assailed by the strong aroma of bacon cooking! It absolutely permeated the room! The smell lasted only a few moments and then was not at all evident by the time we left. A later check with the Williams next door revealed they hadn't cooked any bacon in quite some time, but they said it's just a "happening" that goes on all the time in both their quarters and in Barbara's old home.

The Cooks said a lot of other people along Colony Row have similar stories to tell. We just didn't have time to talk to all of them. I remarked to Georgia and Pete that the fort is such a tranquil retirement spot today that even the ghosts of the past hesitate to leave such a delightful place!

Ghosts at Fort Worth's Miss Molly's

It's said to be "where the West begins." At least, that's what any Fort Worth native will tell you!

The little town that began as a military encampment on the high bluffs along the Trinity River was established on June 6, 1849. It was just after the Mexican War when General Winfield Scott brought in forty-two men of Company F, Second Dragoons, to set up the camp which he named after General Williams Jenkins Worth, who saw distinguished service in the Mexican War.

The year after the small fort was organized, the Fort Worth-to-Yuma, Arizona, stage line was established. In 1860 the place, now a growing township, became the county seat of Tarrant County. After the Civil War, the economy really took off, as the settlement became a gathering place for the trail riders who drove their herds of cattle up the Chisholm Trail to the Kansas railheads. Between 1866 and 1890, more than four million cattle were driven north up the trail via Commerce Street, before fording the Trinity River into what is today called "North Side." (My paternal grandfather, William Schultz, was a drover on the very same Chisholm Trail!)

During the last half of the century the railroad came to Fort Worth, making the city a major shipping point for livestock. Then the meat packing industry came into the city's north side. Some prominent Fort Worth citizens built large holding pens, forming the stockyards that were to bring fame and fortune to their city. In 1902 two large packing companies located their plants in the stockyards area, and Fort Worth soon became the second largest livestock market in America. Within ten short years, sixteen million cattle passed through the stockyards. Now, that's a lot of beef, and probably how the city acquired its nickname, "Cowtown."

I've always had a special nostalgic feeling about Fort Worth. I grew up in the North Texas town of Garland, just northeast of Dallas. My father, John Schultz, was a district sales manager for Ralston Purina, and his home office and the big mill were located in Fort Worth. A graduate of Texas A&M University with a degree in Animal Husbandry, Dad was a fine livestock judge. Sometimes, back in the forties when I was a youngster, I'd be allowed to accompany him when he went to the Fort Worth Stock Show to judge some of the livestock events. I learned a lot about the fine points of judging cattle and horses from Dad, and unlike a lot of matrons my age, I do know a Hereford from a Brahman!

Fort Worth is a very Western city. A visit to the stockyard area, where some of the best steaks in the world are served up in the good restaurants that pepper that area, and a look around the antiques and Western-wear shops is a "must do" on any itinerary. It's a great city, rich in Western tradition, and it's home to numerous ghostly residents as well!

Our first encounter with a ghostly habitat in Fort Worth was at Miss Molly's, a great bed and breakfast inn that is situated right smack in the heart of the stockyard district.

Fort Worth in the late 1800s and early 1900s was the place where the cowboys came to have their last flings before taking off on the long dusty trail to Dodge City and Abilene, Kansas, via the route named for old Jessie Chisholm. These flings usually included a good soaking bath, a shave and a haircut, and a night of liquoring and gambling at one of the many saloons in the old settlement. And it was even better if it could be spent in the company of a pretty little girl-for-hire!

There were plenty of bawdy houses in Fort Worth in those days, and at least one of them has survived till now. This particular one isn't as old as some of those frequented by the trail riders. But it's similar in plan and right down in the stockyard area where the red light district used to be. Of course, it's taken on an entirely new purpose and is now a respectable and attractive eight-room bed and breakfast inn called "Miss Molly's." Located at 109 West Exchange Avenue, it's just a hop, skip, and a jump from the famous coliseum where the world's first indoor rodeo was held in 1918.

Back in 1910 when the place first opened, it was a proper boardinghouse for visitors, "drummers" (traveling salesmen), and cattle buyers who came to the stockyard area. Sometimes rodeo cowboys riding for either a fortune or a fall found their way up the steep staircase as well. The rooming house was arranged with nine rooms encircling a large central hall used as a parlor and reception area just as it is today. In the 1920s the place was managed by one Amelia Eimer, a sedate and proper lady, who called her establishment "The Palace Rooms." Hers was a very successful and altogether respectable rooming house.

Then for a time another management took over and it became known as "The Oasis." It remained a short-term boardinghouse for Fort Worth visitors until the 1940s when the big packing companies moved into the stockyard area. Armour and Swift brought in many workers. There were a lot of cowboys who came to compete in the rodeo events, too. Then, the war years brought a lot of servicemen looking for a good time before shipping overseas. The time was right for "Miss Josie" King to take over.

The former boardinghouse became a "sporting" or bawdy house, a bordello managed by Miss Josie that she called the "Gayette Hotel." Her "ladies" entertained their clients in any one of the nine available rooms. Many of the girls had regular clients, cowboys and businessmen who stopped by from time to time to pay their respects and play out their pent-up passions in the company of Miss Josie's pretty girls. And of course, the packing house workers always dropped a goodly portion of their weekly paychecks at the Gayette.

One such young man visited Miss Josie's weekly. He always requested the same young lady, who occupied room number 9. He became so enamored of her that he even proposed marriage. The young woman did not return his affections. In fact, his attentions and obvious sincerity had begun to disturb her so much, she finally decided to pick up stakes and move on. When the young man found she had left Miss Josie's with no message for him and no forwarding address, he was crushed. The madame, feeling pity for the lovestruck youth, told him she had just what he needed, a beautiful new girl who would soon make him forget the young woman to whom he had become so attached. He was told which room to go to. Deciding there was nothing to lose, he knocked on the door. The young woman who opened the door to his knock was the absolute spitting image of his own mother in her youth! He was so stunned that he turned and fled down the stairs, never to return to Miss Josie's again! This true story was told years later by the very man who gave up the sporting life that night and later became a prominent minister and religious leader.

After Miss Josie's closed down, the place became an art gallery and the rooms were used by individual artists as studios. Today the former boardinghouse-bordello-art studio has entered still another new phase in its long and colorful history. Mark and Susan Hancock have made Miss Molly's Bed and Breakfast Inn a unique place in which to spend a night or two in the old stockyard section of Fort Worth. It's up a long flight of stairs, over the famous Star Cafe. If you can't climb, you can't come, but if you can possibly manage the stairs, the view at the top is well worth it! The Hancocks have done a superb job of restoring and decorating the former bawdy house, and their good taste is only surpassed by their warm and gracious hospitality.

I asked Mark how they arrived at the name of "Miss Molly's." He said that the lead cow on the cattle drives was often referred to as a "Molly." They just kind of liked that name and said since their place was located near the stockyards where a lot of Mollys started off on their long treks north, they thought it an appropriate one.

Each of the eight rooms has a theme reminiscent of the heyday of Miss Josie's bordello. And at least two of those rooms are haunted. Hancock told us about a night when a local journalist spent the night in the Cowboy Room, which is furnished, in Hancock's words, "Texas sparse" fashion, to resemble a bunk house. The writer awoke suddenly in the middle of the night to find a very attractive blonde young lady had suddenly materialized at his bedside. Although he admitted it wasn't too bad a way to be awakened, he did realize that his visitor was an apparition, and this was a trifle unsettling. Hancock could shed no light on whom she might have been.

The Cattlemen's Room, which is done up with a big oak double bed beneath mounted longhorns on the wall, a splendid accommodation for the cattle barons of that era, was the scene of another visit from the beyond. This time the occupant was an English gentleman who was traveling alone. In the night he awoke and saw, in the light coming in from the transom over the door, the figure of an elderly woman standing at the foot of his bed. She just stood and stared at him. She was attired in old-fashioned clothing and was wearing a sunbonnet and was an altogether proper-looking lady. Hancock thinks perhaps this specter might have been the spirit of Miss Amelia Eimer.

Hancock said once three ladies came up the stairs to tour the former bordello. One of the women, who was psychic, said she felt the overwhelming presence of a female spirit in the kitchen adjacent to Miss Josie's former room. The kitchen is where the Hancocks make the coffee and serve up the delicious breakfast pastries that are daily offerings at the bed and breakfast. Mark is convinced that there are presences there, but he says they are friendly and nonthreatening.

Miss Josie's bedroom at Miss Molly's Bed and Breakfast

Mark told us he encourages visitors to the stockyards to come upstairs to tour the establishment, to get a look at an authentically furnished rooming house of the early stockyard era. Visitors are shown around at no charge and seem to enjoy their visits very much. They are shown the various rooms, each of which has a special theme. All of them are furnished with antiques and beautiful hand-made quilts. There are the Cowboy's Room, the Oilman's Room, the Railroader's Room, the Gunslinger's Room, and the Rodeo Room. As a tribute to the former proprietress of the "Palace," there's Miss Amelia's Room, primly decorated with a white iron double bedstead, lace curtains, immaculate linens, and a beautiful pastel quilt. My husband and I stayed in Miss Josie's, a flamboyantly elegant corner suite with an old-fashioned bathtub sitting up on claw feet, rich wall coverings, and a high-backed carved oak bed with a satin spread. It was a very appropriately furnished suite, named for the former madam.

For a comfortable, restful, and thoroughly enjoyable night, we heartily recommend a stop at Miss Molly's! A call to (817) 626-1522 will guarantee your reservation. But as to whether one of the resident ghosts will come to visit you, we can make no promises.

Spirits at the
Old Schoonover Mansion

They say it's haunted. The old Schoonover house at Eighth and Pennsylvania Streets in Fort Worth is no longer a residence. Built by a prominent jeweler as a family dwelling in 1907, the Victorian style buff-colored brick mansion is located close to the Harris Hospital in what was once referred to as the "silk stocking district." It has led many lives since it was a beautiful residence.

An interesting article that ran in the *Fort Worth Star Telegram* on October 31, 1993, a Halloween special, no doubt, stated that some of the odd occurrences in the old house might be brought on by the women who lived, and later died, in the house. Ann Maurine Schoonover Packard, who lives in Birmingham, Alabama, grew up there. She recalled her grandmother, Velma Simmons, had died in the house. Her father's office secretary, Lorene DeLipsy, also passed away there. DeLipsy had no family and had a crippled hip. They found out she was dying of Hodgkin's disease and brought her there to live out her days. DeLipsy died in a little upstairs back bedroom. That same room was also once occupied by Elsie Scaman, an English nanny employed by the family. Packard also recalled that at one time the room had served as a schoolroom where the children were tutored by their mother until Ann was ready to enter the sixth grade.

The large basement once housed a coal bin, laundry, and canning closet. It also had a storage place where houseplants were kept during the winter months. There was a large room under the dining room where the housekeepers lived. Two couples served as housekeepers at different times. First there was Mamie and John Henry Jones, and later, Frances and Grady White. But no one ever died in the basement.

Although Mrs. Packard did admit some puzzling things happened as she helped her parents move from the house, she never thought about any ghosts being there.

Fred Cauble, an architect, and his partners, Larry Hoskins, John Esch, and Toby Harrah, purchased the house from the estate in 1981 and set up their offices there. They were to find out soon enough that they weren't the only occupants of the old house.

Cauble said one night soon after they had purchased the house, he went down into the basement, which at the time smelled very musty like a house does when it's been closed up a long time. When he reached for a light switch he felt cold fingers clutching at his shoulder. When he turned around, there was no one there, but he knew he had not imagined this. Later real estate agent Trish Bowen had a similar encounter in the basement. She was out of there in short order!

Although Cauble did not have the same encounter again, he still experienced some strange happenings during the years he occupied the building. However, he said he wasn't afraid. He thought the ghost was either inquisitive or maybe trying to be helpful. Once the ghost opened a door for him when he was having trouble moving a big box into a room at the head of the stairs. The door was closed. As he bent to put the heavy box on the floor so he could open the door, it suddenly opened for him! He said sometimes when he would search for plans and couldn't find what he was looking for, he'd come to the office the next morning and they would be on his desk. It wasn't just a coincidence, he is sure of that!

Cauble even heard the sounds of piano music drifting up the stairs to his second-floor office. He'd pause to listen but never bothered checking it out. He just accepted the fact that his building was "different." One of his friends and fellow architects, the late Bill Pruett, recalled a day in 1981 when he had a strange experience in the attic. According to the news write-up in the *Star Telegram*, Pruett said while they were working on the renovation of the building on a cloudy, cool, wet day, he saw a ball of light about the size of a softball. It just seemed to zoom from one side of the attic to the other. While Pruett said he wasn't a believer in ghosts, it surely was strange and he couldn't explain it. The ball of light just danced around from one place to another and seemed to be all over the place, all at once.

Cauble said the occurrences grew less and less noticeable, until by the time the building changed hands again in 1990, there had been no encounters for over a year. That is probably because the ghost had accepted the architects and trusted them to take care of the house.

Then, with new owners came new manifestations. This, of course, is not unusual. Ghosts seem to get active whenever the status quo changes, be it ownership of the property, or renovation. They really don't like things changing around in their old bailiwicks.

Currently, Dr. Roger Harman's offices occupy the main, or first floor, of the old mansion, while the basement level is occupied by the advertising firm of Marketing Relations, Inc., partnered by Denis Russell and Jerry Gladys. A recent visit to Fort Worth to see the house and visit with the two advertising executives revealed they still are having encounters with the unknown occupants of the house. Gladys said the evening of the first day the firm occupied their new quarters he worked late at his desk. He recalled it was around 10:30 P.M. when he suddenly started hearing strange, loud clanking sounds, metallic sounds coming from an air duct high in the wall behind his desk. The noise continued for quite a long while. There was no one else in the building at that hour. Gladys knew he was all alone. Finally, having been alerted to the presence of a ghost in the house, he told the spirit, "Look, I've got to get all this work done and I just don't have time to fool with you." It must have worked, because the noises stopped.

Russell, an Emmy award winner for the work he did some twenty years ago in optical effects for the TV series *Star Trek*, had another unnerving experience. One afternoon he was alone in the offices painting the walls. A door that he knew was locked suddenly opened, slammed shut, and then came to rest, slightly ajar.

A continuing irritant exists in the offices. The temperature is impossible to regulate. The partners will turn the air conditioning thermostat to about 70 degrees, since they both like it cold. Soon the place will be hot, and the thermostat will be up to 80 degrees or above. They'll reset the thermostat and soon the temperature goes down, but it won't be long till it's up again! They've even put heavy tape over the setting and arrived the next day to find the tape has been removed and the temperature control has again been set at 80 degrees. This happens when they are positive that no one was there during the night. This is a constant irritation to both partners.

After our visit with Gladys and Russell in their attractive offices, we climbed the stairs to enter the offices of Dr. Harman on the first, or ground, floor. We chatted with Bobette Vroon, Harman's medical assistant, and Kimberly Bradley, the office manager. Both young ladies openly admitted there was something "different" about the office space they occupy.

Vroon made the same observations about the temperature of the offices and said they also had placed duct tape over the thermostat control, but it would always be peeled off in the morning, with the control set way up, leaving the temperature much warmer than they wanted it to be.

There is a kitchen down in the lower level of the building. Both young ladies said they had often heard water running when they worked late at night. They knew they didn't turn it on, and they could never find anyone else who would own up to doing it.

The Cchoonovor houoo, Fort Worth

The big chandelier in the main reception room often turns itself on and off, as do some of the other light fixtures in the place.

Bradley said she once heard the sounds of something, "like a ton of bricks," falling upstairs, but a thorough search revealed nothing out of place. Vroon said she'd heard stacks of books and magazines falling in the office area, but again, nothing could be found to explain the disturbing noises. (Note; this is evidently a common denominator with many ghostly encounters. People often report hearing sounds of things breaking and falling and then when they search, there is never any sign of anything being out of place.)

Both of the women said that on numerous occasions they would search and search for a patient's chart and would be unable to find it anywhere. But on arrival at the offices the next morning, the first thing they would see would be the missing chart, either on top of the manager's desk, or atop the file cabinet where it was ordinarily kept.

The front doorbell frequently rings. But many times no one is there. The door sometimes opens by itself. From a small office to the left of the main entrance in a room which was formerly the Schoonover breakfast, or morning, room, Bradley has frequently heard the doorbell ring and then has seen the front door slowly inch open. From her vantage point she can plainly see through the beveled glass front door, and if anyone were to ring the doorbell she would be able to see the person standing there.

The ladies told me that the receptionist, who was not there during my visit, has often mentioned that she felt someone was walking up behind her, but there's never anyone there. Both Vroon and Bradley also said often they encounter strange smells that suddenly permeate the reception and examination rooms. Sometimes they are pleasantly floral, and other times a very offensive "rotten egg gas" sort of smell is in evidence. They have absolutely no explanation for any of this.

Creaking footsteps on the winding stairs leading up to the second-floor level are frequently heard. There used to be a beauty salon on that level, but after constantly having her bottles of shampoo, skin treatments, and nail polish fall off the shelves, the beautician decided she'd had enough, so she isn't in the building any longer.

Both of the women I talked with said one of the strangest things they have experienced is how the plants get watered. They said they hardly ever water any of the beautiful house plants that decorate the reception area, in what was once the big Schoonover parlor. The plants aren't just damp, either. Sometimes they are almost overflowing with water. None of them have watered the plants, and they can't explain who has. Maybe one of the former residents was an avid gardener.

There's an old-fashioned radio in the reception room. They always turn it off when they go home. For a while, when they arrived in the morning, they would be greeted by loud Mexican music coming from the radio! For some reason this finally ceased.

Both ladies said they and several others had seen a dark shadow drift past one of the side windows. This has happened a number of times. All anyone can make out is the shape of a man in a dark suit going past the window. He always looks the same to everyone who sees him. However, thorough searches, inside and out of the building, have revealed no such person is anywhere around.

There is no creepy feeling about the building. It is light, airy, and pleasant, with the ambiance of an old, venerable building that's there to stay. Evidently its ghost is also there for the long haul!

The Ghost of the Gage Hotel

Far West Texas is just about as large and lonely as the Western films depict it to be. And if you're driving down Highway 90 between Del Rio and Alpine, you'll notice that stopping-off spots are few and far between. So if you're looking for a good comfortable hotel room or just a delicious meal that'll stick to your ribs, as you're headed down that long stretch of highway, you'll do no better than to slow down and take a breather at the old Gage Hotel in Marathon.

You'll probably be astounded to find such an attractive, beautifully appointed hostelry in a small community that's not much more than a wide place in the road. In 1882 Albion E. Shepherd, a former sea captain turned engineer for the Southern Pacific Railroad, named the fledgling community Marathon because it reminded him of the mountain wilderness terrain he had once seen in Marathon, Greece.

Alfred Gage was the first owner of the hotel, which he had designed by a renowned architect of that era, Henry Trost. It is now the only building in Texas that Trost designed as a hotel that still serves that purpose. A native of Vermont, Gage arrived in West Texas at the age of eighteen, ready to seek his fortune. He worked hard, first as a cowhand in the Panhandle, and later on he and his brothers organized the Alpine Cattle Company. Finally, Gage became a successful banker and businessman in San Antonio. He owned a 500,000-acre spread outside of Marathon, and it was for his convenience when visiting his property that he planned and built the Gage Hotel to serve as a combination home and ranch headquarters. He opened it to the public in 1927. Unfortunately, his time to enjoy the fine structure built in the middle of a wilderness was short-lived. He died the following year, in 1928.

According to a feature article in the March 1985 edition of *Texas Highways Magazine*, at the time of its construction the Gage Hotel was considered the most elegant building in Texas west of the Pecos.

Before driving out to Marathon, I had a good telephone visit with General Manager Bill Stephens. He manages the property for absentee owners J.P. and Mary Jan Bryan of Houston. It has been during Stephen's tenure at the Gage that extensive additions have been made on the property. A large section adjacent to the old brick building called "Los Portales" has brought the number of rooms up to thirty-seven. About 100 guests can be accommodated nightly, making it a fine stop for tour groups as well as individuals. The addition, which is covered with a shady porch featuring inviting benches for sitting and enjoying the West Texas breeze, is in a traditional Chihuahuan desert style. Stephens said that 110,000 handmade adobe bricks went into the addition, as well as 40,000 dried sotol stalks, which have been used as cross beams. The vigas, or larger beams, are of ponderosa pine shipped in from New Mexico. Several beautiful patios and a fine Mexican tiled cross-shaped swimming pool form an oasis for guests to enjoy.

Front of Gage Hotel, Marathon

Of course, since I had heard it rumored the Gage was haunted, the conversation just naturally took a turn in that direction. When questioned, Stephens said a manager who worked there before him mentioned he had heard footsteps in a hallway, and there probably were guests who also heard, but just never mentioned, such sounds. Stephens cited one occurrence about three years ago that might lead one to believe there is a resident spirit at the old hotel. A young man employed as a dishwasher at the hotel was an excellent worker, willing to work late into the night doing extra chores, such as cleaning floors, polishing ashtrays and brass, and cleaning the fireplaces. He worked at whatever needed to be done, as he was very ambitious and liked to earn extra money for his family. Then, suddenly, he changed. He stopped working overtime. He wasn't so cheerful anymore. Instead of being willing to stay late and work extra hours, he'd up and leave before he'd even completed his regular chores. Such a sudden change in his personality and work habits was exceedingly strange, totally out of character for the young man.

Stephens said he was determined to get to the bottom of it. The young man finally broke down and told the manager that one evening when he had been in the basement level working into the wee hours, he suddenly felt a presence, a distinct feeling that someone was there in the room with him. He felt a hand upon his shoulder, and as he turned, he confronted the figure of Alfred Gage, which he recognized from the portrait hanging in the hotel. Gage's apparition looked straight at the startled worker and said, "I do not want you in my hotel any longer."

That's when the man quit staying late and working alone. Then came one night when he had to go down into the basement again. This was about two weeks after his first confrontation with Mr. Gage's spirit. Again, he felt a strong presence in the room with him, although he knew he was alone. This time he left the basement, climbed the stairs, and went out the door. He has not returned to the hotel since that night.

The rooms in the main building are furnished with antiques and are kept as authentic to the era in which they were built as possible. There are no television sets in the rooms. Many of the accommodations have been given names, such as Panther Junction, Persimmon Gap, Dagger Mesa, and Stillwell's Crossing. Furnishings are in simple ranch style, but there are some good antique beds and tables and some interesting Western and Native American artwork. Some rooms are Western in theme while others are Indian or south-of-the-border in their decor. All are comfortable and attractive!

Now, there's one room that has an added bit of ambience. That's room number 10. There are a couple of old violins hanging on the wall as part of the decor. Guests and staff members alike have reported hearing music playing in that room. It's hard to recognize the tune, but it's definitely music, and it's only heard in that one room. The evening we checked in, the desk clerk, Allen Russell, told us that several guests who have occupied number 10 have reported being awakened by a gentle tap on the arm, and they hear the soft voice of a woman reciting poetry.

Lobby, Gage Hotel, Marathon

Haunted guest room, Gage Hotel

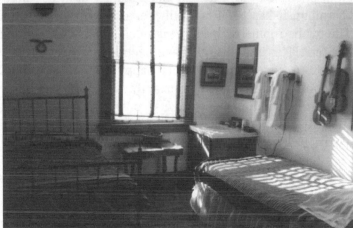

As we checked out of the hotel after a restful night in beautiful surroundings, the morning desk clerks, Richard Lott and Gilda Martinez, mentioned that fairly recently a gentleman who stayed in room number 25 in the new Los Portales unit was awakened by someone tugging on his arm. He then plainly saw the figure of a young woman standing by his bed! She appeared to be in her early thirties and was rather misty in appearance. As the startled man stared at her, she slowly faded away.

Miss Martinez suggested I look up the grounds maintenance man, Jesus Tercero, whose nickname is Chuy. I did, and he told me a young woman also appeared to him one evening as he stood by the Coke machine in the Los Portales area. It was about 10 P.M. but he plainly saw her, as the unit is well illuminated at night. She was a youngish woman, somewhere in her thirties, had short brownish hair, and was wearing a white blouse and a dark skirt. He believed the skirt was a dark blue color. I asked him if it was long, and he said, no it was the modern street length women wear now. She just walked by him, but she looked sort of misty. He stared after her, and as she walked towards the courtyard where the swimming pool is located, she just slowly melted away, finally disappearing completely. He is positive she was a ghost!

Today, the Gage is just about the most attractive, inviting stopping-off place in that part of the state. The cuisine is as good as one might find in a fine restaurant in a major metropolitan area. The atmosphere of the place is outstanding; warm, comfortable, and charming. It has been faithfully restored to its original appearance. The public rooms with their high ceilings, transomed windows, and fine fireplaces and mantels have been lovingly restored.

Alfred Gage should be very happy with the way the hotel looks and operates these days. It certainly is a credit to him and his architect, and it's the perfect place to spend a peaceful night out in far West Texas!

For reservations or information call the Gage at (915) 386-4205.

The Scent of Magnolias

About fifty miles to the northeast of Lubbock is the small city of Floydada. Some 4,000 people make their homes in the community which boasts it's the pumpkin capital of the U.S.

Floyd County was named for a hero of early Texas, Dolphin Floyd, a man who gave his life at the Battle of the Alamo in 1836. Originally the county seat was called Floyd City, but when a post office was applied for, it was discovered there was already a Floyd City elsewhere in Texas. A prominent local citizen, a rancher named T.W. Price, suggested the name "Floydada," in which he combined the county's name with his own mother's Christian name, which was Ada. And it's remained Floydada to this day!

There's some mighty good ranch country around the community, and a popular stopping-off place for locals and visitors alike has long been the Lamplighter Inn, which was built in 1912 and opened for business in 1913. Three generations of the Daily family operated the hotel until about four years ago. In 1991 Evelyn Branch and her daughter, Roxanna Cummings, purchased it. They are restoring and redecorating the old hotel, bringing it back to its original ambience. Today they offer many services other than just bed and breakfast. They specialize in wedding receptions, luncheons, and special parties, and every day lunch is served to the public in the gracious old dining room.

Mother and daughter have enjoyed their years as innkeepers at the Lamplighter, where they reside on the top floor. And by now they've also accepted the fact they must share their address with at least two ghosts. Who they are or why they hang around at the Inn is only a matter of supposition. When I spoke with Roxanna she said she has a few educated guesses as to whom they might be. She still wonders why neither the former owners nor the real estate agent ever mentioned that they had either seen or heard anything out of the ordinary in all the years they had operated the hotel.

For starters, Roxanna said she knew there had been what she calls a "near murder" in the place back in the 1970s. The bizarre case concerned a local man who got wind of the fact his wife was carrying on a love affair behind his back. She and her paramour checked into the hotel for a lover's tryst. Her husband arrived at the hotel and demanded to know what room the two were occupying. He surprised the pair, and although he had gone up with the express purpose of confronting his rival, the other man got the best of him. In fact, the woman's husband was so severely beaten that there was blood splattered all over the room, and an ambulance had to be summoned to drive him to Lubbock to the nearest hospital. Unfortunately, he did not survive the severe beating.

Cummings told me that the wife's lover soon went to trial but got away scot-free because he managed to claim self-defense. The victim's widow soon married her lover. Both had children from their previous marriages, and they all settled cozily into a new his and hers family unit. But it wasn't long before both of them were killed in a tragic automobile accident, a grim ending to the whole sordid story!

Roxanna also told me that an elderly man who made his home at the hotel for a number of years passed away there. This was back when the place was still run by the Daily family. In those days, there weren't a lot of nursing homes, and often elderly people, especially old men, moved to a hotel or boardinghouse to live out their last days when their children or relatives did not step forth to look after them. This man, whose name was Mr. Cornelius, had been a local merchant at one time.

Whether the ghostly happenings at the hotel have anything to do with either of these deaths, no one knows. Roxanna believes there is both a male and a female spirit at the hotel. Recently a guest who spent the night there asked the two owners if they knew they had a spirit at the hotel. She told them, "She visited me last night. I felt her presence and smelled her perfume very distinctly." She went on to say that while she had not been particularly frightened, she did find it to be a rather strange and unsettling experience.

Cummings says there is often a cloyingly sweet fragrance that permeates the air, rather like magnolias blooming on a summer night. At other times they've caught a whiff of the unmistakable scent of Old Spice men's cologne.

Roxanna's mother, Evelyn Branch, used to say she absolutely did not believe in ghosts and there was a logical explanation for everything. Now, she's not so sure. Several times she has caught a glimpse of a man's feet and trouser-clad legs dashing up the stairs from her vantage point in the lobby. Usually this occurs after a large group has been there for a function. Once, the women ran upstairs to see if anyone was still there after having glimpsed the feet dashing up the stairs. A thorough check failed to turn up anything, or anybody, anywhere!

The Lamplighter as it appeared around 1920

Recently some missionaries came to speak at the local Baptist church. They checked into the Lamplighter and almost immediately checked out again. When they turned in their room key and asked for a refund, they were asked the reason for their hasty departure. They mumbled something about the room being too small. Cummings told them a larger room could be readied for them, but they said, no, they'd already called their Baptist hosts and arrangements had been made for them to stay at another hotel. Later, the mysterious exodus was explained when a local woman had lunch one day at the Inn. She was talking to Roxanna, who mentioned her resident ghosts. "Oh!" the woman said, "I know all about them. They scared the missionaries who visited our church." Roxanna pressed the woman to tell her what the pair had told her. She said they had just told her the room was haunted, and they wanted out of there fast!

Cummings and Branch used to have a dog that lived with them in their upstairs quarters. When they had to take him outside, he literally had to be dragged by the collar through the lobby. He didn't like to be in that part of the hotel at all.

Cummings revealed that sometimes the figure of a woman has been seen at an upstairs guest room window. She seems to be dressed in a style of the 1930s or '40s. The window shade, an accordion type that must be drawn, has been seen going up and down in the window when no one is occupying that room. At least one guest sensed the presence there, although she did not actually see the woman's figure.

Once, when Mrs. Branch was washing clothes in the downstairs utility room from which she had a clear view of the hotel dining room, she saw a woman clad in a purple dress walk into the empty dining room. She moved out of the laundry to see who the woman was and what she wanted, since the dining room was closed at that hour. The woman had literally disappeared, and neither Mrs. Branch nor her daughter has a clue as to whom she might have been.

In one of the guest rooms where new drapes had recently been hung on rods well secured into the wood frame surrounding the window, the owners were stunned one day when they walked into the unoccupied room and found the draperies laid out carefully on the floor, straightened out on their rods, not crumpled or wrinkled, but looking as if they had been most carefully removed and rearranged on the floor. When employees were questioned no one could explain the strange occurrence.

A letter I received from Roxanna dated October 24, 1994, revealed that a recent occurrence really has the owners puzzled. To quote from her correspondence:

"After our last large group left a couple of weeks ago... after everyone had left we cleaned up the hotel and straightened up. The next morning (this was when there were no guests at all!) we awoke to find a table set in the dining room, not for breakfast, but for lunch, complete with china, napkins, cups, glasses, and silverware. No explanation. By the way, it was set up for two."

Then Roxanna went on to say that she believes they have at least two resident spirits, one male and one female, and because of where they hang out, they've given them the names "Floyd" and "Ada." Roxanna says these names will just have to do until they can ferret out the real identity of their supernatural star boarders!

According to Roxanna, there are just lots of unexplained happenings at the hotel: sounds of footsteps, unusual noises, lights that switch on and off, doors that open and close all the time at all hours. The lady hoteliers often wonder if these haunting happenings are manifestations of the unfortunate husband still seeking out his two-timing wife and her lover, or could it be one, or both, of the star-crossed lovers themselves, slipping back to the place where their troubles began? And maybe Mr. Cornelius just misses his comfortable, friendly room at the Inn. No one knows.

Roxanna Cummings and her mother, Evelyn Branch, would welcome you for a visit, to spend the night, or just enjoy a good meal. All you need to do is pick up the phone and call them at (806) 983-3035. And just maybe you might smell the magnolias, too!

The Ghost of Alsate

Before the white men came, the land known today as the Big Bend area was the hunting grounds of the Apache; more specifically, the Mescaleros. Then the Texas Rangers came, and there were many altercations. Finally, the Indians moved over the Rio Bravo and made their camps in Mexico. Not wanted there either, things got uncomfortable for them and they once again moved over to the Texas side. There were also some renegade Mexicans who had fallen out of favor with the government and who had taken up with the Apaches. The Mexican government decided the whole lot should be exterminated, by whatever means available. For starters, they enlisted the aid of a turncoat named Lionecio Castillo who knew the Apache chieftains.

Now, for many years the greatest of the Apache chiefs was Alsate. So Castillo sent a message to the Apaches camped in the Chisos Mountains, to the effect that the Mexican government wanted to make a treaty with Alsate and his followers. They would be placed on a big reservation in Mexico and be well provided for there. Castillo told Alsate it was through his personal efforts that this was being accomplished, and he backed up the promises with fake papers, impressively signed, sealed, and beribboned to look official. The Apaches couldn't read the documents, but they looked legitimate to them and so they agreed to attend a meeting with the Mexican officials.

Alsate's chief lieutenant, who was named Colorado, went with a couple of other braves to San Carlos and met with the Mexican for a couple of days. Then they agreed upon a date where the whole tribe and their leaders would come for a big fiesta to celebrate the treaty, and there would be dancing, drinking, feasting, and gifts thrown in as a part of the bargain.

Well, it sounded good so far. Although doubtful about the whole thing, Alsate rounded up his followers and they duly arrived at San Carlos. Unknown to them, several companies of Mexican soldiers had encamped in a spot, under cover, away from the celebrations, and were ready to make their moves when ordered. After the Indians arrived, they were first showered with all manner of gifts, then much beef and mutton was barbecued over the open fires. Mescal, the fiery liquor, was passed out, and by nightfall nearly every Indian warrior was dead drunk. It had been quite a party! Even their lookouts had deserted their posts and had come to join in the celebrations.

During the night, while the Indians slept in drunken stupors, the Mexican soldiers sneaked into the town and captured and bound all the Indians. Before nightfall the next day, Alsate and his men had been shackled and marched to Chihuahua. When Alsate inquired where they were being taken, he was told they were being marched to Mexico City. Many of the group died along the way. Others died while in prison. Some few may have escaped. It was rumored Alsate was one of these. The rest were distributed to various wealthy Mexican families to serve as their slaves. All along the Rio Grande, and especially in the town of San Carlos where the ill-fated party had taken place, everyone rejoiced that the Apaches had been either captured, killed, or enslaved. The turncoat (they were called "rateros") Lionecio Castillo was especially pleased!

According to Virginia Madison, who wrote the book *The Big Bend Country*, this was not quite the last of Alsate. She wrote:

Many moons later, a dark rumor began to creep along the frontier. The story was more venomous than the deadly rattler, because it struck fear into the hearts of the border people. The pastores and the vaqueros had seen the ghost of Alsate! People in the vicinity became afraid to go out at night. Finally the Rurales were sent out to search the region to allay the fears of the people. They saw no ghost but they found a cave which showed signs of recent occupancy. After the search by the Rurales, the ghost appeared again and again, always in the vicinity of the cave.

Soon it became known as Alsate's Cave. Finally the ghost was accepted and seemed to worry no one except Leonecio Castillo, who became so nervous over the stories of the ghost that he left the country. After a long time he returned, and again there were reports of the ghostly appearances, and so Castillo disappeared again. Finally, the ghosts were seen no more, and the bravest and most curious decided to search the cave. There they found the remains of the great Chief Alsate near the ashes of a fire long dead. Alsate was the last of the Chisos Apaches.

NIGHT OF THE COMANCHE MOON

The Comanche moon is glowing;
The light shines o'er the land,
As warriors come once more to cross
The muddy Rio Grande.
As we stand upon the cliffs of stone
That overlook the stream
Sometimes we see them once again,
Caught in the moonlight's gleam.
We hear the eerie chanting
Of the warriors dancing 'round,
To the cadence of their war-drums
As they beat a hollow sound;
We see the fiery redness
Of their campfires glowing bright
And feel their lingering presence
In the stillness of the night.

Docia Williams

The Mystery Lights of Marfa

They bob like giant fireflies,
Glittering in the starlit nights,
A mystery still unanswered,
That they call the "Marfa Lights."

Any book delving into ghosts...spirits...and unknowns in West Texas would be incomplete without including the phenomena of the mysterious Marfa Lights. What they are and why they are there have been unsolved mysteries for well over a century. Where they are is more easily answered.

The lights, which frequently appear in the foothills of the Chinati Mountains, have been seen by literally thousands of people. In fact, they've become enough of an attraction that there is a special Marfa Lights viewing area about nine miles east of Marfa on U.S. 90. The site, near the old air base, is on the south side of the highway. There is a large turnout area on which stands a state historical marker, which reads:

MARFA LIGHTS

"The Marfa Lights, mysterious and unexplained lights that have been reported in the area for over one hundred years, have been the subject of many theories. The first recorded sighting of the lights was by rancher Robert Ellison in 1883. Variously explained as campfires, phosphorescent minerals, swamp gas, static electricity, St. Elmo's fire, and "ghost lights," the lights reportedly change colors, move about, and change in intensity. Scholars have reported over seventy-five local folk tales dealing with the unexplained phenomenon."

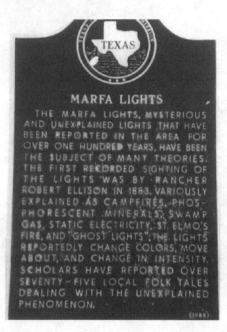

The town of Marfa, about 125 miles northwest of the Big Bend National Park headquarters, is Texas' highest incorporated city, at an elevation of 4,688 feet. The small city of around 3,000 population is the county seat of Presidio County. The locale boasts of being the location for the famous movie *Giant*, and of having the best conditions in the world for soaring. The television series *Unsolved Mysteries* filmed the lights in July of 1989. The producer, film personality Robert Stack, described them as "ghostly gold" in color.

The lights have become so famous that the city celebrates each Labor Day weekend with a Marfa Lights Festival, which includes a parade, arts and crafts, food booths, street dancing, a rodeo, a golf tournament, and a panel discussion about, what else? The Marfa Lights, of course!

Since Robert Ellison's discovery, the lights have appeared frequently, unlike many ghost lights about the state that appear infrequently, such as the famous lights of Bailey's Prairie that appear only every seven years. Marfa's bright orbs appear regularly, although not at any particular time or season. They generally appear to be about the size of a basketball and can be startlingly bright and very white, or they can be red or yellow or blue. Sometimes they are said to shine with the intensity of a locomotive's headlight! They often appear to dance about in a wild, weird, nocturnal ballet!

At first people said they were just the headlights of automobiles driving over on Highway 67. But then, there were reports by pioneer settlers who saw the lights more than a hundred years ago, and of course there were no such things as automobiles then.

Pilots have flown over the area trying to pinpoint the exact locations of the lights, but they have been unsuccessful. Hikers and campers have searched the foothills of the mountains for them, but the closer they come, the more the dancing points of brilliance seem to elude their trackers.

For years articles have appeared in magazines and newspapers around the state. Each story seems to expound a different theory. There was one legend I recall reading way back in the January 7, 1965 edition of the *Amarillo Globe News* that stated, "it is a campfire kindled by the restless soul of a wayward Apache brave condemned to roam the Chinati Mountains forever."

Ira Blanton, an English professor at Sul Ross University in Alpine, shared a similar story. A Chisos Apache chief, Alsate, is frequently credited as being the source of the Marfa Lights. He was betrayed and enslaved by the Mexican armies in San Carlos but later escaped to the Chinati Mountains near Marfa.

Alsate's spirit is said to be lighting his campfires every night in an attempt to summon his warriors back to assist him. Some people say that Alsate's wife is up in the mountains lighting her own fires as well!

The light, or lights, are visible on most nights. Then there will be nights when they make no appearance at all. Sometimes they will appear and go out and then reappear several hours later. Sometimes they will appear a few degrees to the left or right of previous sightings. Climatic conditions and temperatures, which vary greatly in summer and winter seasons, do not seem to affect the sightings at all.

Although some scientists say the lights are just reflections of the moonlight on a vein of mica, thorough searches of the Chinatis have revealed no veins of mica anywhere. And often the lights are seen on dark nights when there is no moonlight! Theories of "swamp gas" that might produce mysterious lights are pretty farfetched, as one would be hard pressed indeed to find a swamp in that part of West Texas! Some people have, fairly recently, latched onto the UFO theory. They think they are either spaceships or the landing lights put out (by whom?) to guide the extraterrestrial spaceships into their landing places. I don't think so!

Some people cling to the legends that the lights are the ghostly glow of Indian campfires where the spirits of long-dead braves dance in preparation for battle.

There was a good story about the lights, written by Rosemary Williams, which appeared in the August 1993 edition of *Texas Highways Magazine*. Also, you might like to read Wallace O. Chariton's detailed account titled, "The Best Mystery in Texas," included in the book *Unsolved Texas Mysteries*, by Wordware Publishing.

There was one story about the lights that might indicate they are actually "spirit" lights . . . of what, we know not. The late writer Ed Syers, in his fine book *Ghost Stories of Texas* (Texian Press), included a story called "The Mountain Light" in which he quotes Mrs. W.T. Giddens of Sundown. She told of an experience her late father had many years ago. Her dad was a rancher. He was up in the Chinati Mountains near Shafter rounding up some stray cattle when a blue norther blew in. He got caught in a howling, icy storm, with blasts of wind and snow that blew so hard his visibility was reduced to about zero. He tried to hurry so he could get to shelter before freezing to death. He soon found he was hopelessly lost in the blinding storm.

He came to an outcropping of rocks and tried to feel his way around them. Suddenly, from out of nowhere, a strong, mysterious light appeared. The man could never fully explain how they communicated, but somehow the light told him he was three miles south of Chinati Peak and was headed in the opposite direction from where he was supposed to be going. It also let him know he was very close to a dangerous precipice. The light advised him he'd better follow them to safety or he could die and led him to a small cave, where he was sheltered throughout the long night, and provided heat, light, and evidently some conversation as well! The light claimed it was a "spirit from elsewhere and long ago." It relayed to him that it meant no harm to him and wanted him to be safe from the storm. The next morning the man headed out, the storm having passed on through. He discovered he had indeed been off the trail and had been headed directly to the edge of a sheer cliff several hundred feet high. Had the light not headed him off, he most surely would have plunged to his death!

Mrs. Giddens said she believed her father. She recalls after that incident that lights often appeared in their pasture, and the family considered them friendly.

Having read and heard so much for so long about the strange lights, my husband, Roy, and I decided to go and see them for ourselves. On a clear spring night (April 11, 1995) we stopped at the Highway 90 drive-out, where a number of cars and campers were already situated. It was about 9:30 P.M. The moon was full, and the desert area was quite light. We got out of our car and for about an hour watched entranced as first one, then two, then finally as many as four lights danced and bobbed about, almost as if they were dancing in the moonlight, putting on a good show for their observers. The lights would dim and go out, then reappear, then brighten in intensity. Occasionally one light would separate into two or three segments. Mostly they appeared low, about at the foot of the far-off Chinati Mountains, but sometimes they would rise in elevation as they shifted positions. A couple of times all four went out and we thought it was all over for the night. Then, first one, then another, and yet another, would reappear. They are thoroughly fascinating, mystifying, and puzzling. We watched for over an hour, until the chill of the desert air drove us into our car and back to the warmth of our motel room in Alpine. When we retired, we believed in, but still wondered about, the Marfa Lights.

That the Marfa Lights exist, there's no doubt. Go see for yourself! But WHAT they are, and WHY they're there, remains a complete mystery, which is why they are still so fascinating!

The Ghost at the Reeves County Courthouse

Pecos is a real old-time Western town situated not far from the New Mexico border. It was established in 1881 as a stop on the Texas and Pacific Railroad and fast drew fame as a hangout for rowdy cowboys, gunslingers, and the lawmen who had to know how to draw fast, shoot first, and ask questions afterwards! One of the nation's oldest rodeo events began here in 1883 and is still staged annually.

And there's at least one ghost story attached to the old Reeves County Courthouse in Pecos. I had a long talk with Steve Balog, former Deputy U.S. Marshal. Now he has taken on a second career, that of the court security officer at the courthouse.

Back in the early 1970s ('72-'74 to be exact) Balog occupied an office on the second floor of the courthouse. The courtrooms and library were on the third floor of the old building, just above Balog's office. He said there was an accordion type metal gate that was used to close the staircase that led to the upper floors. This was secured with a padlock, and it was customary for anyone who planned to work late at night to unlock the gate, then lock it behind him as they left to go to their offices. This assured them that someone who didn't belong there would be unable to get access to the upper floors.

Balog said that they've always handled a lot of illegal alien cases there in Pecos, and often after he had been out in the district all day in his capacity as Deputy U.S. Marshal, it would be late, sometimes 8 or 9 P.M., when he finally got back to his office in Pecos. Then he would have a lot of paperwork to do, which was part of handling each alien's case. Sometimes he said they had as many as a hundred aliens a week to process, and the paperwork on each one ran anywhere from three to five pages. Often Balog would be at his desk at the courthouse until the wee hours of the morning, just trying to stay caught up with the workload.

Soon after going to work there, Balog began to hear the sound of footsteps up on the third floor, in the area right above his office.

He judged they were men's footsteps and said the person would have been a rather large man, at least 175 pounds in size. The sounds were clearly those of someone walking down the long hallway. Balog often went up the stairs, looking thoroughly all over the vacant third floor, calling out, "Who's there? Come on out, I hear you!" There was nothing ever; but by the time he could get downstairs and back to his second floor office, the steps above him would start up all over again.

Finally Balog asked a friend of his, J.E. Travland, who was then Superintendent of Mails, and later became the U.S. Postmaster, if he would come and spend a few late hours with him. He had told Travland about hearing the untraceable footsteps, as they had become quite annoying when Balog was trying to get his work done. Both of the men heard the footfalls during Travland's visits to Balog's office. The steps seemed to move from the east to the west corridor. Sometimes they seemed to come from the old library which was located directly over Balog's office.

On several nights Balog's wife came down to the courthouse to keep him company. She also heard the phantom footsteps. Finally, the couple brought a three-pound sack of flour to the building and went up to the third floor and sprinkled it all over the floor of the library, the courtrooms, and the corridor. About 1:30 or 2 A.M. the footsteps began. They were all over the place! After listening to them for some time, the Balogs went upstairs to check, and there was not a single footprint to be seen where they had sprinkled all that flour!

Finally, after months of hearing the disturbing footfalls, Balog said they suddenly began to be heard descending the stairs to the second floor. He said he believes now, looking back, the spirit, or ghost, was getting friendlier, and maybe it might have eventually materialized to him, as he had begun to see a shadowy form moving within his peripheral vision. About this time these occurrences were mentioned to a young woman clerk who worked in the courthouse and she said, "I knew it! I knew it!" She had also heard footsteps and had seen something passing her office when she worked there at night. After a couple of such disturbing evenings she elected not to work at all after regular hours.

Balog began to talk to the ghost so that it knew he recognized its presence. This seems to be what most ghosts want: to be heard or recognized. And often, in frustration, he would yell upstairs, "Knock it off, or else come down and help we with my work!"

Just as the ghost began to start coming downstairs, an extensive renovation and restoration project began at the courthouse, which was to last about eleven months. Now anyone who knows much about ghostly behavioral patterns knows they hate change, becoming very agitated and confused at times. This is just what happened to Balog's friendly ghost! The steps seemed to come from way in the back of the jury room, and there would be four or five steps in one direction, then they'd turn and come back, three or four steps, back and forth. They no longer came out in the corridor or to the library over Balog's office or down the stairs as previously. Now since Balog's job has changed he is seldom in the building at night, so he has not heard the footsteps lately.

Because he earnestly believes that someone from another time comes back as this walking spirit, Steve has done a bit of checking into the building's past. He said he heard that one of the construction workers who worked on the building when it was first built fell from the third floor or attic level to the ground and was killed. He also heard that back in the 1930s an illegal alien might have hanged himself in the building, but he isn't sure about this story, whether it was fact or fiction.

In speaking with Balog about "his" ghost, I ventured to offer my own theory. 1 believe the footfalls are those of the spirit of someone who spent a great deal of time in the old courthouse and was somehow locked there in time . . . not necessarily a person who had died there. It may have been a law officer, an attorney, a bailiff, a judge . . . someone whose working hours were spent on the third floor of the old Reeves County Courthouse. Maybe the man did not complete a job he had wanted to complete. Maybe he felt he had been derelict in his duties and had let somebody down. Maybe he was an attorney whose innocent client was adjudged guilty because he had not presented the case strongly enough. Maybe he was a judge who felt he had made a mistake in judgement. Who knows? The maybes are endless!

Balog is pretty sure the spirit is still there, just as it has been for a long, long time: caught in time, in space, in the dark of night, in the old Reeves County Courthouse, walking . . . walking . . . walking . . . .

WHEN DARKNESS FALLS

When darkness falls, the night-bird calls
And the moon glows full in the sky,
Out they creep, from where they sleep
They're the souls that will not die.
Silently they reappear
Lightly treading as they roam
Through time and space, back to the place
They consider their rightful home.
Sometimes you'll clearly see them;
Fleeting shadows on the walls
And sometimes, you'll only hear them
As they come, when darkness falls.

Docia Schultz Williams

The Sounds of Rushing Water

Maria and Cres Delagarza were married in 1966. They built their own house on a large lot in the small town of Mereta, which is about twenty miles east of San Angelo. A tiny little community today, it does not even appear on many Texas highway maps. Maria says there are a few houses, a cotton gin, a gas station, and a post office still remaining, but there are not even any grocery stores in the town. She estimated that around 125 people live in the community today.

Maria said the house, which was begun in 1966, was ready for occupancy in 1967. They built the dwelling of old wood, on the site of a former community schoolhouse. She said there was also a burial site on the grounds, somewhere between the Delagarza yard and the neighbors' backyard. She was told that a little boy died and was buried there sometime in the 1930s or '40s. The story she had heard was that the youngster was a son of a family of migrant farm laborers who were in the vicinity looking for work. The child, which the Delagarzas believe was named Manuel, took sick and died during a torrential rainstorm. The land was literally inundated with water, and the roads were impassable. The family had no means to take his remains to the cemetery for burial. Cres Delagarza, Maria's former husband, told me he understood the burial took place in the dirt floor of the tent in which the farm workers were camping. That is why the child was buried in an unconsecrated site in the back portion of Delagarza's lot. Whether or not a priest presided over the rites is apparently unknown to anyone in Mereta.

During the first several years that Maria and Cres lived in the house, nothing unusual seemed to happen. They were busy starting their family, and within about five years, Diana, Alma, and Norma had arrived to brighten their lives and keep them very busy!

Then, suddenly, about the time Norma was born, "strange things" started happening, and they continued to occur from time to time between 1972 and 1986.

For starters, the family often heard the gurgling, rushing sound of water flowing beneath the house as if there might have been a river or stream located there. It was the kind of sound one might hear while standing on a low bridge over a swiftly running stream. Frequent examinations under the house revealed no trace of any water at all.

Then the Delagarzas often heard scratching noises, like someone scratching on a screen window. Again, searches revealed nothing. They also sometimes heard noises up around the ceiling, like a raccoon or squirrel might have gotten up under the eaves between ceiling and roof. Careful searches revealed no animals or rodents of any kind, and yet the noises persisted for a long while.

In the room assigned to Diana and Alma, the Delagarzas had built a large, doorless, cupboard-like closet, which extended from one wall to the other. It had a lot of clothes-hanging space. For some unexplainable reason, the clothes would slide back and forth on their hangers from one end of the clothes rod to the other. This did not happen every day, but it happened often enough to be disturbing since there was no logical explanation for the movements.

Often little running footsteps were heard in the hallway of the house. They decided if they had a spirit, it was rather playful, like the ghost of a youngster, perhaps. Norma, who was the youngest daughter, felt someone, or something, sit down on the side of her bed, and once it even stroked her face.

One night in their room, Diana and Alma started to feel small objects pelting their heads. It felt like someone was throwing small pebbles, and some of the blows were quite painful. Diana firmly told Alma to stop it, and she added, "it hurts!" Alma replied that she hadn't thrown anything at all, and she had felt the rain of pebbles, too. In fact, she had thought Diana was throwing things at her! The two little girls became so frightened they huddled down in their bed and pulled the covers up over their heads, too terrified to venture out of their bed all night!

In view of the fact so many unusual things kept happening, the girls came to accept the presence of some other entity in the household. Diana even named their spirit Simon. Maria said there was really no reason for the name, but they all soon started referring to their "unknown" as Simon.

For fifteen years the family lived in their house. Then baby Menna Marie, whom they nicknamed Moe, arrived in 1983. Maria said things seemed to accelerate then, and the spirit or spirits started to get wilder and more frightening. Unexplained noises and feelings the family had long just accepted became more frequent and more upsetting. Maria said she often felt cold chills, especially after they remodeled the house and made some additions to it. She had sudden weird feelings as if something had grabbed at the back of her neck, and this always brought on a real feeling of fear, especially when she was in the master bedroom, near Cres' closet. She always tried to keep the closet door closed!

Then, suddenly, into the already slightly turbulent scene, entered one old-woman ghost. Maria first saw her when she decided to give the kitchen a complete cleanup after they had repainted the house. The kitchen stove had been moved out into the backyard for a thorough cleanup job. She said she recalled it was late in the afternoon, probably about five-thirty, and it was just starting to get dark. She recalled it was quite chilly, so she thinks it was probably in late October. Hastening to finish her task before darkness fell, she just happened to look up and out into the backyard for a moment. She was startled to see, at the far back of the yard, the figure of an old woman wearing a long skirt, with a shawl or rebozo pulled over her head. She was walking towards the garage. Maria called out to her, but she did not look up and acknowledge Maria's call. When the woman came to the far corner of the house she disappeared from sight, so Maria dashed over to see who she was and where she might be going. She said it only took seconds to reach the corner of the house, but when she got there, the woman was nowhere to be seen. She had literally disappeared!

Later on the family went to visit relatives in Mexico. A cousin of Cres', named Raymond, who also lived in Mereta, told Maria that while they were away he had seen "an old lady sitting in a chair under a tree," in their backyard. Raymond, who has since passed away, said he called out to the woman to see what she was doing in the Delagarza's yard, but the figure just stared straight ahead and did not acknowledge his greeting at all.

Once when little Marie was about three years old (her mother told me this was around 1986) the toddler was headed out of the kitchen into the hallway to the den where she wanted to watch TV. It was during the Christmas holiday season and they had promised the tot she could watch a special Disney production. Suddenly they heard a scream, and little Marie ran back into the kitchen, obviously terrified. She had seen "something" going into the bathroom and it scared her. Maria and Armando, her father, who was there visiting them, calmed the child down and took her on into the den to watch television. Maria checked the bathroom and found nothing unusual there. Then Maria's father confided to her that the child had not imagined things, because earlier he had seen a dark figure in a long skirt walk into the bathroom. She had gone right through the door. He had not told his daughter or the children for fear of frightening them.

That same evening Cres was working his shift as a deputy sheriff. He had been out near Eden, some forty-four miles east of San Angelo. About 1 or 2 A.M. he arrived home and dashed into the house. The first thing he asked was, "What happened? Has something happened to Marie?" This was the same evening, of course, that the toddler had been badly frightened by the dark figure in the hallway that her grandfather had also seen. Cres, some forty-four miles away, had such premonition of something frightening taking place at home, that he had asked to be relieved of duty and hastened home to see if anything had happened.

The family was so disturbed by all of this, they packed up their pillows and blankets and headed off in the cold night to Cres' family's house. Cres' father and Armando, Maria's dad, talked about the ghost situation for what few hours remained of the night.

The next day, which was a Monday, Maria drove into San Angelo to the Catholic church of St. Mary's, which she attended. After mass she asked the priest if he would spare her a moment. She told him about the events of the night before, and of some other things that had happened at the house, and pleaded with him to come and bless the house. The cleric told her that he would tell her something that she could do herself. If, after she had followed his instructions, things did not settle down, then he said he would try to prevail upon the Archbishop to give him permission to come out and take care of things. He did not use the word "exorcise," Maria said, but she presumed that is what he meant to do if necessary.

Armed with a vial of holy water the priest had given her, Maria sprinkled the water in each room of the house while reciting the rosary for five days. Then, on the fifth and final day, she did just what the priest had told her to do. When she came to the last room, after sprinkling the holy water and reciting the rosary, she firmly, forcefully, and loudly, told whatever it was to go away, right now!

Maria carried out the priest's instructions to the letter. And after that, for a period of about four or five months, things seemed to get better. Then, slowly and insidiously, little things began to start up again.

For one thing, the marriage that had produced four beautiful young daughters seemed to be crumbling. There were frequent disagreements and arguments. After one particularly bad argument, as Maria and Cres stood in their bedroom, a box suddenly came flying out of the closet for no reason! It could not have just fallen off the shelf, because it had been stacked in between two other boxes. And the box fell open to reveal a Ouija board! That certainly stopped that particular argument.

The Delagarzas had always managed to get by, but now there were serious financial problems as well. Finally, the couple separated, going their independent ways. The bank was forced to foreclose on their property and their home was put up for sale. Maria and the girls moved to San Antonio, and Cres stayed in West Texas where he now resides in San Angelo.

Maria recalls that the final days she spent in the house were very unsettling. She felt a frightening presence in it that, to her, was "evil and scary." She said it evidently affected the girls as well. One of the girls, Norma, who was about fifteen at the time, experienced something sitting down on her bed, and then she felt "it" lean over and press down against her body. Little Marie, still just a tot, started to have frequent conversations with "somebody." She also had frequent nightmares, where she said she saw ugly little faces flying at her! Of course, she was too little to tell her mother who it was she was speaking to, but she was definitely seeing something and talking to it as well. Looking back, Maria attributes many of the family problems to the presence of the spirit that seemed to permeate the house in Mereta. A friend of mine here in San Antonio has described this sort of manifestation as that of a "negative spirit." They are not as evil as a poltergeist, but they certainly are not among the desirables of ghostdom if one must live in a haunted house!

Maria learned that the people who purchased the house from the bank only stayed there about three months. They left because they said it was haunted. The next owners remodeled the place, spending quite a lot of money on the project. Yet they, too, left shortly thereafter. Maria was told they left because they constantly heard water running under the house. It was more than their nerves could stand, since they knew there was no water there. Maria hasn't heard lately what has happened to her former home. A conversation with Cres brought forth the information that the place changed hands a couple of times, and now it is used mostly for storage.

During our talk, Maria kept asking me if I could supply her with any explanation for all the things that happened in the house. I couldn't give her an answer then. Later on, I began to think. I do not pretend to possess psychic abilities. Neither am I a ghost-buster, nor have I made a thorough study of the supernatural. But having interviewed scores of people in the course of writing several books on the subject, and having read a number of works on the topic by other writers, I have sorted out several possible, fairly plausible explanations for the hauntings:

The youngster, whose name may have been Manuel, who died there on the property, passed away during a heavy rainy season. That is why he had to be buried there instead of in the consecrated ground of a cemetery. Could the sounds, so often heard, of running water under the house be connected to that time of flooding, when the child died? And the mischievous acts the Delagarza children experienced, such as the pebbles dropping on the girls' heads, the sounds of little running feet in the hallway, the scratching sounds—couldn't that be the little boy spirit reaching out to other children to come and play with him? And what about the figure of the old woman? Could she have been Manuel's mother, or even his *abuela*, or grandmother, who had returned to watch over the grave of her lost little one? Could she have been resentful that the Delagarza house was filled with healthy, happy children growing up normally, while her little one was denied that privilege and left to the confines of a dark, cold grave at the back of the property? Was this the reason her dark spirit took up residence with the Delagarzas?

Maria asked me if I thought a spirit would follow people after they moved from a haunted house. She went on to say one of her daughters, Norma, who is now a single parent living in San Antonio with her own two young daughters, has lately been troubled by water running from the faucets, which turn themselves on and off at will. And other strange things seem to happen at Norma's house. I tried to assure Maria that generally, spirits seem to attach themselves to places more than people, and if the spirits are still active in Mereta, they are still probably hanging around the Delagarza's former home. But the running water and various other strange things that are happening in Norma's San Antonio home might possibly be another spirit, completely different and apart from the Mereta ghost. I am afraid this is small consolation, indeed!

Charlie, the Friendly Ghost

Most ghosts are said to cling to places, not people. But here's a story that contradicts that common belief. Leona Billington of Petrolia, a small community near Wichita Falls, tells a story about a ghost who has been following her around from place to place for at least thirty-five years!

Leona first told the story to Gene Mathews, librarian at the Kemp Public Library in Wichita Falls. Gene relayed the information to me, and I then had a lengthy conversation with Leona in order to hear all the facts:

Thirty-five years ago Leona and her three children were living in Gladewater. She was separated from her first husband, and the little family rented a small frame house that was then about twenty or thirty years old.

At first, life was fairly calm in the household, but it wasn't long until strange things began to happen. For a while, Leona thought someone might be trying to break into the house. And then there were noises, like giant footsteps, on the roof over the master bedroom most evenings, around 10 P.M. Sometimes strange singing would be heard, and the piano would play a few notes all by itself, just a "plink, plunk" sound, no recognizable tune.

Leona and the youngsters, who were twelve, thirteen, and fourteen at the time, became so frightened they'd barricade themselves in the front room. Leona got a gun and sat up most nights to guard her little brood, and then she would try to catch some sleep during the daylight hours when the children were in school.

Leona said there were times when she knew she had turned the lights out, but upon returning to the house, they'd all be burning brilliantly in all the rooms! Several times when she'd be lying in bed, just about to go to sleep, the covers would rise up and fly off of her. Then she would smell gas and dash into the kitchen to discover the pilot light off and the gas turned up high. She could not figure out how this happened. She gradually began to realize the house really was haunted. At the time she moved in, there were rumors around town that the house was haunted. Now she believed there was something to the stories she had brushed aside as figments of someone's overly active imagination. She also began to sense there might be two entities in the house: a bad spirit and a good one. The bad spirit turned the gas on; the good spirit woke her up to warn her of the danger by pulling her covers off.

Leona told me she knew that a former resident of the house who had suffered from cancer had died there. The room where the woman had died always seemed to be cold and could never be heated properly. Leona was told the woman suffered great pain in her last months and may even have died of an overdose of pain medications, but she is not at all positive about this.

Billington is positive the good spirit is male and that he has permanently attached himself to her as her protector, sort of like a guardian angel. After she'd been in the Gladewater house awhile, the shadowy spirit appeared as a dark, tall, thin man in Western clothes. He looked misty and shadowy, but she could definitely make out it was a man. For some unexplainable reason, she started to call him "Charlie." She told me she would really like to know who he was in life and why he has attached himself to her and her family.

Today Leona doesn't live in Gladewater. First, she moved to California and lived for a time in both Los Angeles and Sacramento. Then the family moved back to Texas and settled in Petrolia, just outside of Wichita Falls. Charlie went along on all the moves! Unlike most ghosts, it wasn't the place but the people to whom he attached himself. Now that the children are all grown and gone and Leona has remarried, Charlie doesn't appear as often as he once did. But he still resides in her household. Tex, her husband, at first was dubious about the entity the family all referred to as Charlie. In fact, he outright scoffed at the idea! So one night, after they'd gone to bed, Leona said, "Charlie, Tex doesn't believe in you. Let him know you're really here." No sooner said, than done! Charlie began to pull on Tex's toes so hard the bed shook! And he did it the next night, too, just for good measure! Now Tex accepts Charlie's presence just as the rest of the family does.

Leona says sometimes she wonders if Charlie might be somebody she knew at some point in her life, or maybe in another life, if there is such a thing as reincarnation. Sometimes when she's about to fall asleep, she feels someone gently smoothing back her hair, or gently caressing or rubbing her face. This began in Gladewater and has continued for all these years. At first this frightened her, but she came to feel that these were gentle manifestations of a reassuring presence, and she felt as if she had a protector around her. It gave her a sense of security and she was never frightened.

Charlie is felt more than seen, but he has made a number of appearances. He has been seen sitting at the table, as well as in various rooms. He has even appeared in Leona's daughter's house in Oklahoma, and in her brother's home in Wichita Falls. Once her brother missed his pillow and then sighted it floating above his head! He reached up and snatched it, saying, "Alright, Charlie, quit hiding my pillow." It seems when there's a family reunion, wherever it is, Charlie comes right along. Sometimes he's very playful. Once, when Leona's daughter was about eighteen, they were having a party. The teenager bent over to get something out of a kitchen cabinet and there was a loud "whack!" as something, or someone, gave her a playful spank. Several people were present and heard the whack and saw Leona's daughter jump! But no one was anywhere near her when it happened (except Charlie, of course!).

While over the years Charlie has calmed down considerably, he is still there. His last appearance was in the spring of 1994. He still materializes as a tall, slim fellow in Western clothes. Sometimes he walks through walls, appears in the hallway, or sits down at the family dining table. When Leona is happy and things are running smoothly, he seems to stay dormant, making no appearances. But when she is sad, depressed, or disturbed, like she recently was when her young grandson died, Charlie appears to her, a caring and sympathetic presence, like a friend coming by to extend his sympathy.

Tex and Leona and the whole family accept Charlie. He is a part of their family now, and they all agree that life just wouldn't be the same without him!

Epilogue

Along the quiet thoroughfare, as darkness cloaks the city,
What is that we see?
A torn sheet of newspaper being hurled along the street,
Propelled along its way by gusts of wind?
As it tosses and tumbles along, do our eyes deceive us?
Are we seeing just an old discarded scrap of yesterday's news,
Or are we glimpsing something far more remarkable?
Could it be possible we are seeing into the mysterious realm of the
unknown,
As spirits, long slumbering in their dank and lonely graves
Return for a little while, to roam the quiet streets
And twisted little alleyways of a slumbering city,
Seeking out the places they once knew so well?
Their substance takes on a misty whiteness in the glow of moon
beams
Filtering down from a cloudless sky.
That wind-tossed wisp of white. Where did it go?
No newspaper that.
Only a soul intent on visiting a familiar place once more,
A respite from the grave. When darkness falls.

Docia Schultz Williams

Sources

Newspapers

Amarillo Globe News
    Jan. 7, 1965
Brownsville Herald
    Oct. 31, 1993
Dallas Morning News
    Oct. 31, 1982, Oct. 31, 1993, Oct. 31, 1994, Oct. 27, 1995,
    July 15, 1996, Oct. 29, 1995
Dallas Times Herald
    Oct. 29, 1987
Fort Worth Star Telegram
    Oct. 31, 1993
Houston Chronicle
    Oct. 29, 1993
Jasper Newsboy
    Oct. 1993
Port Arthur News
    Oct. 28, 1984
San Antonio Express News
    Feb. 5, 1894, Aug. 23, 1897, March 26, 1911, Feb. 10, 1965,
    Aug. 6, 1965, Oct. 30, 1983, July 3, 1988
San Antonio Light
    Nov. 21, 1909
Texas Express, Goliad
    Oct. 31, 1984
Tyler Courier Times Telegraph
    Oct. 30, 1988
Victoria Advocate
    Nov. 8, 1992

Magazines

Dallas Magazine
    Oct. 1987
San Antonio Express News Sunday Magazine
    Jan. 27, 1991
Texas Highways Magazine
    March 1985, Aug. 1993
Texas Homes Magazine
    Oct. 1980
Texas Parade Magazine
    Nov. 1971

Pamphlets

"Discover Historic Galveston Island" published by Galveston Historical
    Foundation
"Presidio La Bahia" Information Pamphlet, Goliad, Texas
"Ride the Texas Tropical Trail" published by the State Department of
    Highways and Public Transportation
"Silver King Restaurant Newsletter" Aransas Pass, year unknown

Stories

"Joe Lee Never Left Nederland" by Anne Malinowsky Blackwell

Books

Alamo City Guide by Stanley Gould, 1882
The Big Bend Country of Texas by Virginia Madison, Revised Edition, 1969
    October House Inc., New York.
Ghosts Along the Brazos by Catherine Munson Foster, published by Texian
    Press, Waco, Texas, 1977
*A Ghosthunter's Guide to Haunted Landmarks, Parks, Churches, and other
    Public Places* by Arthur Myers, Contemporary Books, Inc., Chicago,
    1993
Ghost Stories of Texas by Ed Syers, Texian Press, Waco, Texas 1981
*Guidebook to Some Out of the Way Historical Sights in the City of San
    Antonio* by David Bowser, published by the author
A Guide to Treasure in Texas by Thomas Penfield, published by Carson
    Enterprizes Inc., Deming, New Mexico

A History of Jefferson, Marion County, Texas by Mesdames Arch McKay
and H.A. Spellings, published by Women's Auxiliary, Christ Episcopal
Church, Jefferson, Texas, 1944
The Irish Texans by Dr. John Flannery, published by Institute of Texan
Cultures, 1995
Lafitte the Pirate by Lyle Saxon, Pelican Publishing Co., Gretna, La., 1989
The National Directory of Haunted Places by Dennis William Hauck,
published by Penguin Books, New York, 1996
Phantoms of the Plains by Docia Schultz Williams, published by Wordware
Publishing, Inc., 1996
1001 Texas Place Names by Fred Tarpley, published by University of Texas
Press, Austin, Texas, 1980
Unsolved Texas Mysteries by Wallace Chariton, C.F. Eckhardt, and Kevin R.
Young, published by Wordware Publishing, Inc., 1991
Weekend Escapes, Southeast Texas Edition edited by Mike Michaelson,
published by Rand McNally, 1986

Personal Interviews

I wish to especially thank the following individuals who shared their
information in the form of personal and telephone interviews or through
correspondence:

Paula Allen, feature writer, *San Antonio Express News Images Magazine*
Warren Andrews, bellman, Crowne Plaza St. Anthony Hotel
Nell Baeten, owner, Grey Moss Inn
Melissa and Tom Baker, owners, Catfish Plantation, Waxahachie
Sue Baker, former employee, Crowne Plaza St. Anthony Hotel
Steve Balog, former deputy U.S. Marshal, Pecos
Lorenzo Banda, Junior, night security guard, Cadillac Bar
Dr. Woodrow Behannon, president, Rusk County Heritage Association
Leona Billington, Petrolia resident
Kathleen Bittner, San Antonio psychic
Ann Malinowsky Blackwell, homeowner, Nederland
Ira Blanton, professor, Sul Ross University, Alpine
Paula and Steve Bonillas, owners, Blackbeard's Restaurant, Corpus Christi
David Bowser, San Antonio writer and historian
Kimberly Bradley, Fort Worth
Evelyn Branch, co-owner, Lamplighter Inn, Floydada
Jody Breckenridge, manager, Jefferson Hotel, Jefferson
Julio Caraker, manager, Beulah's Restaurant, Port Aransas

Frank Castillon, former homicide detective, San Antonio Police Dept.
Barbara Celitans, curator, Hertzberg Circus Museum
John Collins, former director, La Bahia Museum
Jackie Contreras, former employee, Camberley-Gunter Hotel
Georgia and Pete Cook, former residents, Fort Clark Springs
Brenda Cordoway, bartender, Cadillac Bar
Diane Cox, homeowner, newspaperwoman, Jasper
Mary Craig, vice president, Rusk County Heritage Association
Alma Cross, owner, Bullis House Bed and Breakfast Inn
Roxanna Cummings, co-owner, Lamplighter Inn, Floydada
Cres and Maria Delagarza, former homeowners, Mereta
Will Detering, owner, "Liendo" Plantation, Hempstead
Mark Eakin, bellman, Crowne Plaza St. Anthony Hotel
Manuela Espinosa, housekeeper, Crowne Plaza St. Anthony Hotel
Charlie Faupel, owner, Reeves Thicket Ranch
Mary Lou Polley Featherston, great-great granddaughter of Brit Bailey
Lydia Fischer, former employee, Camberley-Gunter Hotel
Clouis and Marilyn Fisher, owners, Bed and Breakfast Inn, Rockport
Billy Ford, contractor, Marshall
Catherine Munson Foster, deceased, author, owner Bailey's Prairie
Bonnie and Vaughn Franks, owners, Bonnie Nook Inn, Waxahachie
Linda Frazier, waitress, Cadillac Bar
Deborah Fresco, waitress, Cadillac Bar
Jet Garcia, former employee, Crowne Plaza St. Anthony Hotel
Jerry Gladys, partner, Marketing Relations, Inc, Fort Worth
Yolanda Gonzalez, librarian, Arnulfo L. Oliviero Memorial Library,
    Brownsville
Maria Good, story contributor, San Antonio
Dr. Joe Graham, professor, Texas A&M University, Kingsville
Casey Edward Greene, assistant archivist, Rosenberg Library, Galveston
Nancy Haley, former co-owner, Terrell Castle Bed and Breakfast Inn
Mark and Susan Hancock, owners, "Miss Molly's" Bed and Breakfast Inn,
    Ft. Worth
Patrick Hopkins, owner-chef, The Grove Restaurant, Jefferson
Mark Jean, "ghost stalker," Fort Worth
Linda Johnson, director, Witte Museum, San Antonio
Donna Kucholtz, former resident of Ennis
Ilona Langlinais, former employee, Wunsche Bros. Cafe and Saloon, Spring
Mario Lara, custodian, Hertzberg Circus Museum
Marcia Larsen, owner, Alamo Street Theatre and Restaurant
Alma Lemm, former employee, Wunsche Bros. Cafe and Saloon, Spring

Faye Leavitt, former owner, Mehren House, San Antonio
Vivis Lemmons, former employee, Institute of Texan Cultures
Al Longoria, former security guard, Southwest Craft Center
Gil Lopez, former general manager, Camberley-Gunter Hotel
Richard Lott, desk clerk, Gage Hotel, Marathon
Ernesto Malacara, assistant hotel manager, Menger Hotel
Dian Malouf, jewelry designer, Dallas
John Manguso, curator, Fort Sam Houston Museum
Karen Martin, former guest of Crowne Plaza St. Anthony Hotel
Gilda Martinez, desk clerk, Gage Hotel, Marathon
Gene Matthews, librarian, Kemp Public Library, Wichita Falls
Mildred May, assistant to executive secretary, San Antonio A&M Club
David McDonald, park ranger, Jose Antonio Navarro Historical Park
Jesse Medina, owner, Cadillac Bar
Ingeborg Mehren, former owner, Mehren House
Carol Meissner, owner, Jefferson Hotel
Rodney Miller, employee, Menger Hotel
Brenda Mitchell, owner, Wunsche Bros. Cafe and Saloon, Spring
Richard Moore, homeowner, Marshall
Marilyn Muldowney, president, San Antonio Aggie Wives' Club
Marjorie Mungia, docent, Mission San Jose y San Miguel de Aguayo
Gil Navarro, executive staff, Menger Hotel
Derek Neitzel, former assistant curator, USS *Lexington* Museum, Corpus
    Christi
Sam Nesmith, San Antonio historian and psychic
Barbara Niemann, former resident, Ft. Clark Springs
Dr. Robert O'Connor, museum administrator, Hertzberg Circus Museum
Catherine Polk, homeowner, LaMarque
Katherine Poulis, former co-owner, Terrell Castle Bed and Breakfast Inn
Michael Precker, Dallas newspaper columnist
Yvonne Ray, homeowner, Gilmer
Jessie Rico, custodian, Spanish Governor's Palace
Jo Ann Rivera, owner, Victoria's Black Swan Inn
Barbara Roberson, member, San Antonio Aggie Wives' Club
James Patrick Robinson III, grandson of Hall Park Street Junior
Colonel George Rodgers, former resident, Quarters No. One, Ft. Sam
    Houston
Franklin Roe, partner, Daisy Tours, San Antonio
Allen Russell, desk clerk, Gage Hotel, Marathon
Denis Russell, partner, Marketing Relations Inc., Fort Worth
Yvonne Saucedo, former employee, Menger Hotel

Bill Savio, historian, Jefferson
Sharon Shawn, owner, Rose of Sharon Bed and Breakfast Inn, Waxahachie
Kathleen Sheridan, executive secretary, San Antonio A&M Club
Cindy Shioleno, Kennedale, former guest, Menger Hotel
Rev. Ralph H. Shuffler, Episcopal priest, son of the late Henderson
    Shuffler
John Silva, story source, San Antonio
John Slate, curator, Hertzberg Circus Museum
Diane and Victor Smilgin, owners, Terrell Castle Bed and Breakfast Inn
Terry Smith, TV personality, "ghost stalker," Fort Worth
Wanda Sparks, former docent, Howard-Dickinson House, Henderson
Bill Stephens, general manager, Gage Hotel, Marathon
Mrs. Dorothy Stotser, former resident, Pershing House, Fort Sam
    Houston
George Stumberg III, former owner, Cadillac Bar
Michael Tease, manager, Bullis House Bed and Breakfast Inn
Jesus "Chuy" Tercero, maintenance man, Gage Hotel, Marathon
Robert Thiege, San Antonio historian, psychic
Marcia McCasland Thomas, owner, Living Room Theatre, Jefferson
Shari Thorn, executive secretary to geneneral manager, Crowne Plaza St.
    Anthony Hotel
Linda Turman, member, San Antonio Aggie Wives' Club
Bobette Vroon, Fort Worth resident
Newton Warzecha, director, La Bahia Museum
Cindy Waters, former employee, Crowne Plaza St. Anthony Hotel
Sue Watkins, Garland newspaperwoman
Jackie Weaverling, San Antonio story source
Dr. Donald Ray Whitaker, owner, Schluter Mansion, Jefferson
Mark Wilks, employee, Beulah's Restaurant, Port Aransas
Dr. Charles Wiseman, veterinarian, member San Antonio A&M Club
Dana Cody Wolf, former owner, Rafael House, Ennis
Kevin Young, former curator, La Bahia Museum
Linda Young, bookkeeper and secretary, Grey Moss Inn

Index

Other Books from Republic of Texas Press

100 Days in Texas: The Alamo Letters
by Wallace O. Chariton

Alamo Movies
by Frank Thompson

A Cowboy of the Pecos
by Patrick Dearen

A Treasury of Texas Trivia
by Bill Cannon

Alamo Movies
by Frank Thompson

At Least 1836 Things You Ought to Know About Texas but Probably Don't
by Doris L. Miller

Battlefields of Texas
by Bill Groneman

Best Tales of Texas Ghosts
by Docia Schultz Williams

Bubba Speak: A Texas Dictionary
by W.C. Jameson

Civil War Recollections of James Lemuel Clark and the Great Hanging at Gainesville, Texas in October 1862
by L.D. Clark

Cow Pasture Pool: Golf on the Muni-tour
by Joe D. Winter

Cripple Creek Bonanza
by Chet Cunningham

Daughter of Fortune: The Bettie Brown Story
by Sherrie S. McLeRoy

Defense of a Legend: Crockett and the de la Peña Diary
by Bill Groneman

Don't Throw Feathers at Chickens: A Collection of Texas Political Humor
by Charles Herring, Jr. and Walter Richter

Eight Bright Candles: Courageous Women of Mexico
by Doris E. Perlin

Other Books from Republic of Texas Press

Etta Place: Her Life and Times with Butch Cassidy and the Sundance Kid
by Gail Drago

Exiled: The Tigua Indians of Ysleta del Sur
by Randy Lee Eickhoff

Exploring Dallas with Children: A Guide for Family Activities (2nd Ed.)
by Kay McCasland Threadgill

Exploring San Antonio with Children: A Guide for Family Activities
by Docia Schultz Williams

Exploring the Alamo Legends
by Wallace O. Chariton

Eyewitness to the Alamo
by Bill Groneman

First in the Lone Star State
by Sherrie S. McLeRoy

The Funny Side of Texas
by Ellis Posey and John Johnson

Ghosts Along the Texas Coast
by Docia Schultz Williams

The Great Texas Airship Mystery
by Wallace O. Chariton

Henry Ossian Flipper: West Point's First Black Graduate
by Jane Eppinga

Horses and Horse Sense: The Practical Science of Horse Husbandry
by James "Doc" Blakely

How the Cimarron River Got Its Name and Other Stories About Coffee
by Ernestine Sewell Linck

The Last Great Days of Radio
by Lynn Woolley

The Last of the Old-Time Cowboys
by Patrick Dearen

Other Books from Republic of Texas Press

Letters Home: A Soldier's Legacy
by Roger L. Shaffer

More Wild Camp Tales
by Mike Blakely

Noble Brutes: Camels on the American Frontier
by Eva Jolene Boyd

Outlaws in Petticoats and Other Notorious Texas Women
by Gail Drago and Ann Ruff

Phantoms of the Plains: Tales of West Texas Ghosts
by Docia Schultz Williams

Rainy Days in Texas Funbook
by Wallace O. Chariton

Red River Women
by Sherrie S. McLeRoy

The Return of the Outlaw Billy the Kid
by W.C. Jameson and Fredric Bean

The Santa Fe Trail
by James A. Crutchfield

Slitherin' 'Round Texas
by Jim Dunlap

Spindletop Unwound
by Roger L. Shaffer

Spirits of San Antonio and South Texas
by Docia Schultz Williams and Reneta Byrne

The Star Film Ranch: Texas' First Picture Show
by Frank Thompson

Tales of the Guadalupe Mountains
by W.C. Jameson

The Texas Golf Guide
by Art Stricklan

Texas Highway Humor
by Wallace O. Chariton

Texas Politics in My Rearview Mirror
by Waggoner Carr and Byron Varner

Other Books from Republic of Texas Press

Texas Ranger Tales: Stories That Need Telling
by Mike Cox

Texas Tales Your Teacher Never Told You
by Charles F. Eckhardt

Texas Wit and Wisdom
by Wallace O. Chariton

That Cat Won't Flush
by Wallace O. Chariton

That Old Overland Stagecoaching
by Eva Jolene Boyd

This Dog'll Hunt
by Wallace O. Chariton

To the Tyrants Never Yield: A Texas Civil War Sampler
by Kevin R. Young

Tragedy at Taos: The Revolt of 1847
by James A. Crutchfield

A Trail Rider's Guide to Texas
by Mary Elizabeth Sue Goldman

A Treasury of Texas Trivia
by Bill Cannon

Unsolved Texas Mysteries
by Wallace O. Chariton

Western Horse Tales
Edited by Don Worcester

When Darkness Falls: Tales of San Antonio Ghosts and Hauntings
by Docia Schultz Williams

Wild Camp Tales
by Mike Blakely